Too *Blessed* to Stress

A Novel

ALLI HOFF KOSIK

GRAND CENTRAL

LARGE PRINT

This book is a work of fiction. Names, characters, places, and incidents are the product of the author's imagination or are used fictitiously. Any resemblance to actual events, locales, or persons, living or dead, is coincidental.

Copyright © 2026 by Alli Hoff Kosik

Cover design by Liz Connor. Cover illustration by Lila Selle.
Cover copyright © 2026 by Hachette Book Group, Inc.

Hachette Book Group supports the right to free expression and the value of copyright. The purpose of copyright is to encourage writers and artists to produce the creative works that enrich our culture.

The scanning, uploading, and distribution of this book without permission is a theft of the author's intellectual property. If you would like permission to use material from the book (other than for review purposes), please contact permissions@hbgusa.com. Thank you for your support of the author's rights.

Grand Central Publishing
Hachette Book Group
1290 Avenue of the Americas, New York, NY 10104
grandcentralpublishing.com
@grandcentralpub

First Edition: March 2026

Grand Central Publishing is a division of Hachette Book Group, Inc. The Grand Central Publishing name and logo is a registered trademark of Hachette Book Group, Inc.

The publisher is not responsible for websites (or their content) that are not owned by the publisher.

The Hachette Speakers Bureau provides a wide range of authors for speaking events. To find out more, go to hachettespeakersbureau.com or email HachetteSpeakers@hbgusa.com.

Grand Central Publishing books may be purchased in bulk for business, educational, or promotional use. For information, please contact your local bookseller or the Hachette Book Group Special Markets Department at special.markets@hbgusa.com.

All Scripture quotations, unless otherwise indicated, are taken from the Holy Bible, New International Version®, NIV®. Copyright © 1973, 1978, 1984, 2011 by Biblica, Inc.™ Used by permission of Zondervan. All rights reserved worldwide. www.zondervan.com. The "NIV" and "New International Version" are trademarks registered in the United States Patent and Trademark Office by Biblica, Inc.™

Print book interior design by Marie Mundaca

Library of Congress Cataloging-in-Publication Data

Names: Kosik, Alli Hoff author
Title: Too blessed to stress / Alli Hoff Kosik.
Description: New York : GCP, 2026.
Identifiers: LCCN 2025043998 | ISBN 9781538771969 trade paperback | ISBN 9781538771976 ebook
Subjects: LCGFT: Satirical fiction | Novels | Fiction
Classification: LCC PS3611.O749173 T66 2026
LC record available at https://lccn.loc.gov/2025043998

ISBNs: 9781538771969 (hardcover), 9781538771976 (ebook), 9781538783320 (large print)

For Nana:
You know, I know

"Our faith comes in moments; our vice is habitual."
—*Ralph Waldo Emerson*

"If I can hold God's attention, I can hold the world's."
—*Dolly Parton*

"You don't have to be dowdy to be a Christian."
—*Tammy Faye Bakker*

1

Kristin

Kristin had been the one to draw up the original event itinerary—and then to run it by the right people for notes, revise a few particulars, and finally have it approved—so she knew immediately that something was not going to plan. The run of show she'd written and rewritten called for a presentation of two minutes at the most—enough time to welcome the crowd and get them excited, but not so much that it would distract them from the dozens of carnival rides and food trucks that had been moved into the massive Moving Word parking lot. Kristin had arranged for those, too, happy to know that guests would have the chance to move directly from the sweetness of the speech to the sweetness of caramel apples, kettle corn, and other equally syrupy seasonal treats.

Earlier in the week, she'd also watched as Kyle and Cassidy practiced their remarks. *Thank you so much to our local sponsors for helping us get this special event organized! We are proud to be part of this community and to be the church home for so many of you. Let's eat, drink, ride some rides, and praise the Lord. It's fall, y'all!* Wedged into the corner of Kyle's office, Kristin had tracked their lines against the printout in front of her. The pastor was upbeat, as usual; his wife with an appropriately performative edge of treacle to her voice that left the building as soon as she'd run through the script a few times and entirely ignored Kristin's positive feedback.

Less than an hour before the couple was due onstage—undaunted by Cassidy's moods and committed as ever to her tasks as office assistant—Kristin had checked in with the Welshes while they tested their mics, proffering church-branded Stanleys of water and fresh printouts of the itinerary. While Kyle had graciously accepted Kristin's offerings, Cassidy had rolled her eyes and batted Kristin's carefully paginated and laminated schedule away.

According to the itinerary, the worship team—composed of musicians from their late teens to their early fifties, mostly misfits who had always been too cool for church and too square for real rock bands—would play a few songs after the Welshes walked off the outdoor stage, erected just for the day. Buoyed by the melody and the crisp autumn air, kids would enjoy the rides, adults would fellowship with other churchgoers, and everyone would have some good, wholesome fun. Kristin's first big feat of coordination since joining the team at Moving Word would be a success. Cassidy Welsh might even decide to like her.

But now, Kyle was lingering on the stage after the first round of applause from the large group of onlookers. Kristin and the rest of the congregation had grown used to the pastor improvising and making jokes, just as they'd grown used to—even grown to love—his fashionable sneakers and graphic tees printed with Christian wordplay (NOT TODAY, SATAN; NO OMGS; LIVING ON A PRAYER). His tone on the occasion of the fall carnival, however, seemed oddly serious, a marked departure for the usually easygoing pastor whose popularity was rooted not only in his sermons but also in his readiness to engage in a spontaneous dance-off with the youth group.

"We're not just here to ring in a new season, though," he said, putting his arm around Cassidy, who now looked surprisingly grim to attend an event with a ring toss, in spite of the work of a professional makeup artist. "As you know, human trafficking has become an increasingly urgent matter in recent years, especially with all the illegal immigration going on. My wife and I feel called to fight this with all of our God-given strength. You may remember that we've done a few smaller collections in the past for an anti-trafficking organization called ProtectUS."

Kristin was familiar with ProtectUS. Shortly after starting her job, she'd been tasked with designing flyers encouraging members of the church to attend a bake sale on behalf of the non-profit. In hopes of doing a little something extra to impress her bosses, she'd spent several hours poring over ProtectUS's educational resources so that she could really deliver in the language on the posters. Her parents railed frequently against the evils of human trafficking as it was depicted on cable news, and they'd been more than thrilled to purchase a few dozen cinnamon rolls in the name of fighting the good fight and in taking a philosophical stand against the politicians they suspected were perpetrators. Kristin was twenty-two years old, but it was like the Girl Scouts all over again, her capacity to make an impact distilled however temporarily into handily packaged bundles of sweets.

Kyle continued. "After a lot of prayer, Cassidy and I have decided to rally the power of our growing congregation to lift up this organization even more. Between now and Christmas, we will be mounting an epic fundraiser for ProtectUS to show what happens when people of faith come together for a meaningful cause! Are y'all ready to hear about our fundraising goal?"

The gathered crowd of Moving Word members and their guests applauded tentatively, then grew louder as Kyle leaned forward with a hand cupped over one ear. Shifting from grim to girlish fast enough to give Kristin whiplash, Cassidy threw her arms out toward the audience, her flouncy white blouse lifting to reveal a strip of toned abdomen. As the one responsible for managing the scheduling of sessions with Cassidy's personal Pilates instructor—a woman named Veronica who traveled to the pastor's home to conduct private classes on a Reformer machine she'd gifted them—Kristin knew how many hours had gone into that sliver of perfect physique. Many hours. Countless hours, probably.

"Over the next few weeks, our church family will be raising—are you sure you're ready for this?"

Kyle stirred up the air around him with the hand not holding the microphone. There were more cheers from the crowd, the kind of excitement that pulsed in the air like humidity that would inspire hairstyle-related hemming and hawing among the women in the group. As usual, Kyle's hair was holding perfectly under the pressure of his congregation and the friends and family they'd invited to enjoy the day.

"With God on our side, we're going to raise five hundred thousand dollars!" he bellowed.

Kristin resisted the instinct to cover her ears as the loudest cacophony yet rose up from the carnival-goers, entirely drowning out the tinkling melodies of the rented rides.

"We can't think of a better way to celebrate the start of this very special fundraiser than with a big party like this one," Cassidy added into her own microphone, beaming cherubically at her husband. In spite of the woman's resemblance to a Christmas angel in that moment, Kristin would hate to be in caroling distance of her should the newly announced goal not be met. "And we're going to celebrate the end of it with another one! The week before Christmas, Moving Word will be hosting its first major gala event, where we'll announce our fundraising total—which I'm sure will be the full five hundred thousand dollars, if not more—and praise the Lord for this opportunity to spread the Word during the season of Jesus's birthday. We're calling it the Gala for Goodness."

Kyle bobbed his head beside her like one of the sports figurines Kristin's dad kept on the dashboard of his car. "You'll find more details in your inboxes and in the Moving Word app as soon as things get wrapped up today, but you can get started by giving at the stations around the perimeter of the parking lot."

Kristin craned her neck to see the stations Kyle was referring to. Who had set those up? And when?

"Every cent counts, but don't get me wrong—we'll gladly take the big bucks!" Kyle paused for laughter—and got it. "Gala tickets will go on sale later this week, too, and we promise the event will be worth the price tag. But that's enough yakking from me. Let's ride some rides and eat some cotton candy and do some good!"

The worship team's band began playing so suddenly that it made Kristin jump. Kyle clapped his hands not quite on beat. The band had started too early! Or were they too late? Regardless of how right or wrong their timing was, the music—this song featuring bongo drums and maracas—was exciting the crowd even further. Between the spontaneous jam session, the Welshes' passionate praise hands onstage, and the news of another big party, everyone's energy had ratcheted up a few notches. More folks had abandoned the rides and the food trucks to congregate in the mass of people, a mass that had started jumping up and down to the beat of the drums. Others were streaming out to the giving stations, reaching into their purses and pockets for cash to shove into the Plexiglas boxes that had, as far as Kristin could tell, appeared there like manna from heaven.

The Gala for Goodness would be a lot of work for Kristin. Like, a *lot* of work.

More work than she'd known to expect when she'd accepted the gig at Moving Word—and more work than she felt qualified to do. The position had seemed fairly simple in the job description Kristin's mom had passed along right before graduation. She could manage schedules and coordinate meetings and play point person for church events, but she'd never been to a gala. She'd barely been to a fraternity party. Where, exactly, was the line between a gala and a party? What would it take to impress Cassidy at an event that obviously mattered so much to her? A sizable chunk of the work ahead of her, she worried, was in figuring out the answers to those questions.

But it would be a lot of work on behalf of something meaningful, she reasoned. A lot of work in support of a good cause, which was what made her still feel called to church. And a lot of work that would, hopefully, make her even more invaluable to the Welshes and the rest of the church. Left with only herself as an opponent after a lifetime of competing with others in the pool, Kristin wondered if there might be a raise or a promotion waiting for her should the fundraiser and the gala run successfully—and less than a year after she'd joined the team. The glimmer of those possibilities was enough to take the edge off the infinitely long to-do lists already writing themselves in her head.

* * *

The hard work would begin at the office, so Kristin did her best to enjoy the fair's festivities. The funnel cake stand was the last place she would have expected to run into Camryn Lee Cady—and yet, there she was, waiting to gossip as soon as Kristin stepped back from the folding table where shakers of powdered sugar had been set up alongside squeeze bottles of chocolate and caramel sauces, visibly melting in the Carolina heat. "Hey," she chirped, grabbing Kristin by the shoulder with a prettily manicured hand and guiding her to a nearby picnic table. As always, Cam looked perfect and perky, dressed for the evening in a pair of jeans and a floral top with puffy straps that draped artfully off her delicate shoulders. Kristin was relieved to find that she'd managed to sit down without spilling any of the toppings from her dessert on herself. Her chambray button-down and white shorts weren't anywhere near as fashionable as Camryn's outfit, but she'd prefer not to ruin them—or to draw unnecessary attention to herself with a mess. "Did you know anything about the gala?" Camryn asked. Her hushed tone seemed silly given that they were in open air and nowhere near any obvious eavesdroppers, to say nothing of the far from sinister nature of the subject at hand.

Kristin shook her head, dabbing the sugar off her fingers. "I didn't," she insisted. "I would have told you."

"Of course you would have," Cam said, nodding and staring into the distance. "That's why you're our insider." She winked, a move Kristin was familiar with just as much from real life as from Cam's videos.

"Right," Kristin agreed. She eyed her rapidly cooling funnel cake, mindful of staying focused on what Camryn had to say despite her hunger. Cam had, after all, trusted Kristin to join her personal pet project, the Moral Mavens Mainframe. Mavens legend had it that Camryn had come up with the name for the group's leadership team during an otherwise lackluster IT training for her day job when a joke about the company's computer systems had piqued her interest.

"Well, I haven't seen anyone else yet, which is weird since Savannah and Trishy both said they would be here," Cam said, looking around. "Anyway, I know the focus of the gala is ProtectUS—and it totally should be—but we should also talk to Cassidy about how we can get the Mavens involved. I know we're not *officially* affiliated with the church or anything, but everyone knows how valuable we can be."

"Alright," Kristin agreed. "Let me know how I can—"

"I definitely will," Cam said. "Can I have a bite of this?" She pointed at Kristin's funnel cake.

Unsure of what else to do, Kristin nodded, guiding the paper plate toward Cam.

"Wait, actually, do you mind if I just take the whole thing with me?" Camryn asked. "This is going to be so messy to carry around. I can pay you back for it later. I just have so many ideas to talk to people about. The gala's going to need a theme!" She gazed wistfully out at the parking lot, now lit by the soft colored bulbs of the rides and snack stands under the darkening sky.

Kristin smiled. "Take it," she said. "I'll get another one."

"You're the best," Cam replied, leaning forward to kiss Kristin on the cheek, where Kristin could feel the sticky ghost of lip gloss.

Cam was off and running into the crowd before Kristin could say goodbye, a yellow crossbody purse dancing off her shoulder as she went. The line for funnel cakes was longer now, but Kristin joined anyway. Even if her big night out of the house amounted to a work-mandated carnival, she should enjoy it. She should get the second funnel cake. She should pat herself on the back for the first evening in a long time spent on something besides indulging her mother's true crime documentary obsession. She was out! She was on the verge of helping people do big things with one of the coolest churches in town.

She also really wanted a bite of that funnel cake.

The only thing that would taste nearly as good as the single bite she'd had of her last helping would be her success with the Mavens.

2

Camryn

Zoodles had long been played out, and Camryn knew it. Her favorite food influencers—each of them a wealth of kitchen knowledge and high-end appliances in their custom kitchens—had portended their demise somewhere around 2019, when the art of turning zucchini into a sad substitute for pasta had gone from a weird underground movement isolated to the gluten-free crowd to a mainstream culinary technique championed by weight-loss experts and meat-eating foodies alike. As soon as the trend had saturated the Pinterest boards of suburban mommies wielding sleek discount zoodlers, it was over. Cam needed the recipe development team at 12th Pine to accept the fact that zoodles no longer merited top billing on their menu, and fast. It wasn't good for business—and Cam really, really needed business to be good.

"Are we absolutely sold on the zucchini noodle dish for the special seasonal menu? Is that nonnegotiable?" Cam asked Margo Toll, who, as head of the small but mighty marketing team for 12th Pine, was her boss and, in theory, equally invested in the company's success. Thanks to its fresh fare and smart, splashy direct-to-customer marketing—which Cam freely took full credit for—the farm-to-table fast casual restaurant had grown to five locations in the Charlotte metro area over the last few years.

Margo chewed on the long pinkie fingernail of one hand as she paged through the recipe development team's proposal with the other. The glossy pages were intended as a preliminary pitch of late winter offerings and were studded with high-resolution photos of potential new dishes as they'd been assembled in the drafty test kitchen downtown. Margo and Cam were sharing a table in 12th Pine's flagship location, a converted brewery in Dilworth.

"Those guys can be so temperamental," Margo replied, flicking her eyes up at Cam as she took a sip of kombucha from a hammered copper mug. She was referring to the recipe developers, a group of sour men with silver beards and full sleeves of tattoos under their aprons who did not appreciate feedback about how well—or not—their food would play to the social media savvy crowd who patronized 12th Pine.

"Could we talk them down to something at least a little more current? Carrots are boring, but still better than zoodles. Sweet potato or butternut squash, maybe? Good for the season? Or beets! Beets are still cool. Great color."

"And beets are current?" Margo asked.

Cam nodded. "Compared to zoodles? Absolutely," she said. She would have bet her next paycheck on it, but she was happy not to. "They're this decade's kale, but more photogenic. Better for the girlies with sensitive tummies, too."

Margo nodded slowly, still staring down at the pages resting on the reclaimed wood table in front of her. Her red hair was piled on top of her head in its usual messy bun, her V-neck accessorized with a seersucker blazer and a set of layered gold necklaces that Cam—who loved love—knew she'd received as a gift from her girlfriend in celebration of a recent anniversary. "Beets. Maybe," she said. "I need to think about it. Give me the weekend before I push back."

If Camryn were in charge, she would commit to courses of action much faster. She would also overhaul the chain's aesthetic, abandoning its industrial chic look in favor of neutral interiors, but that was neither here nor there. Cam loved Margo's creative vision, but she didn't have a lot of patience with her manager's indecisiveness. They'd planned to meet in Dilworth to have a late lunch and finalize their feedback on the proposed menu so it could be passed along to the test kitchen team with plenty of time for changes to be made. If the new items could be styled to look good on social media and had plenty of healthy ingredients—enough, even, to balance out a teeny white wine or Chick-fil-A habit—12th Pine's existing customer base would be ready to indulge. The restaurant was trying to maintain its aggressive growth track, a feat that would be a whole lot more feasible with a marketing team that felt empowered to comment on whether or not they'd actually be able to market its product to the target demographic.

Camryn knew her way around kind conversation, even if the subject at hand was contentious. Just that summer, she'd singlehandedly spearheaded a campaign at her apartment complex that had resulted in the installation of brand-new air conditioners in every unit. Was the management company excited about making that investment when the talks began? No. Had they even *technically* agreed to meet with her? No. But Cam had gone in there with statistics about heat stroke and a smile and worked it all out. Margo would have sweated her way through a miserable North Carolina August to avoid the discussion.

"Let me give it some thought. How's your lunch?" Margo nodded her chin in the direction of Cam's meal, an earthenware bowl overflowing with quinoa, chickpeas, kale, sweet potatoes, and a few other superfoods.

"It's good." Cam nodded, pushing the contents of the bowl around with her fork. Frequent free lunches were a perk of her job at 12th Pine. Manifesting gratitude for this fact—despite her misgivings about potential theological issues with manifestation—she resigned herself to a rain check for her crusade against zucchini noodles, at least until Monday. "Not as good as the grain bowl I had last time, but good. What kind of squash do we think this is? I was thinking maybe acorn but—"

"Camryn? Camryn Lee Cady?"

The voice came from behind Cam, who watched as Margo lost a chunk of salt-and-peppered avocado from the toast she stopped short halfway between the plate and her mouth. Margo's eyes were fixed on something above Cam's head: presumably the owner of the voice, whose outburst was no longer a novelty thanks to the increased visibility of the Mavens and the pastors who'd championed them at Moving Word. Camryn turned in her chair and found herself looking up at a trio of girls somewhere in their late teens, each one in some variation of the same matching loungewear set. One girl stood slightly in front of the other two, a big gray sweatshirt tied loosely around her waist, a brown paper bag stamped with the 12th Pine logo in her hand.

"That's me," Cam said, smiling up at the girls. With their bright eyes and sincere expressions and eager greeting, she could tell without asking that they were Moral Mavens. No matter their age, it wasn't hard to recognize a sister in Christ, particularly when, thanks to Instagram, that sister in Christ had a working knowledge of Cam's life and wasn't afraid to show it.

Anyone could call themselves one of the Moral Mavens, but there were only four women in the Mavens Mainframe: Savannah Truman, Trishy Collins, Kristin Rae Thatcher, and, of course, Cam herself. For the last year, the Mainframe girls had been stepping up their social media game to call in a sisterhood of believers and encourage even more people to read the Word, walk in faith, invest in themselves with the purchase of tummy-flattening teas and silk eye masks, and follow God's path for them. Cam thought it was pretty powerful—and it wasn't just because she'd started it, or because she was the unofficial leader. *Leader* wasn't the right word. She'd actually made the rule that no one mention hierarchy. They were all equal.

But Cam *had* started it.

There were Mavens girls all over Charlotte. Of Camryn's forty-nine thousand Instagram followers and the fifty thousand and change following the Moral Mavens official account, a sizable number were local. She had met them all over town—shopping for dresses for friends' weddings, pulsing their tiniest arm muscles in barre class, out on dates with clean-shaven boys, buying ingredients for Christmas cookies at the Whole Foods in Sharon Square. They'd even started showing up regularly at Moving Word, mostly excited to meet Camryn and her friends, but also willing to hear a sermon, add a little—or big—something to the offering plate, and consider membership. Those were the sweetest moments for Cam, of course, but adding the Dilworth 12th Pine location to the list of Mavens meeting places was exciting, a neat blending of her worlds.

"I thought from your hair that it might be you!" the girl said, her smile so big it looked in danger of jumping right off her cheeks. "That's probably so weird. Sorry. You just have really pretty hair." She covered her mouth with one hand, a blush creeping out around her eyes. But Cam was pleased. She tended her blond waves every day to ensure they'd be recognizable. "But then I heard your voice, and I totally recognized it. I had to say hi. My friends and I"—here, she gestured to the other girls—"we watch all of your videos and we read all of your posts. We've been following you since the beginning. We're obsessed. Seriously."

At this, one of the other girls nodded vigorously, her long caramel ponytail bouncing so it caught the light from the copper fixtures hanging above the bar. "Yes. We love you," she said. "We love your friends. We've told, like, everyone at school about you guys. We've probably gotten, like, at least two hundred people to follow you."

"That post you wrote about breakups at the beginning of the year helped me get through a really hard season right before prom," the third girl chimed in. "My boyfriend dumped me and then did a whole promposal a week later for this girl I'm pretty sure he'd never talked to before that. He made a whole TikTok about—"

The girl standing in front turned to look at her friend. Cam could only see one side of her highlighter-dappled profile, but she could imagine a venomous glare passing from one teenager to the other. Poor things. One day, they'd learn to lift each other up unconditionally, just like Cam and her friends and church family. It was what Cam tried to do with her followers, too, whether through sharing Scripture or offering helpful tips on the most flattering denim for every body type.

"—that's not important, though. We have to give everyone grace, right? I hope they're very happy together," the breakup survivor continued with a nervous laugh. All three of the girls were back to looking sweetly in Cam's direction. "I just really appreciate you."

"I'm glad the post helped," Camryn said. "And I appreciate you, too." She stood up from her chair and brushed off her midi skirt in case of crumbs from the grain bowl, which was now much less important to her than attending to the young Mavens. She could wrap it up and have the rest for dinner tonight, anyway. It might even stretch for another lunch. It would hardly be the first time she'd squeezed several meals out of a single comped 12th Pine lunch. "Can I give you girls a hug?"

The teenagers nodded up and down and wrapped their arms around Cam in a group embrace. They smelled like candy and perfume, like the more expensive aisles of a drugstore where things were shuttered behind locked sliding glass doors. Cam waited until each of them had pulled away from the hug before stepping back herself.

"Do you think your friend could take a picture of us?" the first girl asked, digging through her metallic fanny pack until her hand emerged holding a phone in a monogrammed case. "People are going to freak out when they see we actually met you. We're going on a service trip to Charleston this weekend, and everyone in youth group is going to think we're making it up."

Cam turned to Margo, who had finished the remaining bites of her avocado toast since being left alone at the table. Had she already been a little rude by failing to invite her boss into the conversation? "This is Margo. We work together," Cam said to the girls, who were so busy whispering among themselves that they seemed not to hear.

The girls snapped to attention. "Do you go to Moving Word, too?" one of them asked, her bright eyes trained on Margo.

"Do you help out with the Mavens?" another added, leaning forward so slightly it was almost imperceptible.

"I don't," Margo said through a tight smile. "But I can still take your picture."

The girls—who had momentarily looked disappointed at Margo's admission—nodded enthusiastically and fell quickly into a practiced pose, likely honed at church camps and semi-formals. Cam silently mouthed her apologies to Margo, who shrugged.

Still wearing a tense smile, Margo stood up, straightened her blazer, waved clumsily to the teenagers, and reached out to grab the phone from them. Cam motioned for the girls to huddle in closer and stepped into the middle of their formation, wrapping her arms around their shoulders and striking her go-to expression for photos, eyes bright, one side of her mouth pulled up in a grin that would display her dimples at their best. She knew from experience that the lighting at this particular 12th Pine location wasn't ideal for her, but the teens would know to edit the image before posting so they all looked beautiful. Margo held up the phone for a few moments, obviously snapping enough photos so they would have options.

"Thank you so much!" the second girl said. Her friends were already busy scrolling through the images on the phone Margo had returned to them, their heads pressed together over its tiny screen.

"We knew you worked for 12th Pine, but we did *not* think we'd ever see you here," the third girl told Cam breathily. "We come here all the time, though. It's basically our favorite place. Our bodies are a temple and all that! Do you come here a lot?"

"Well, I appreciate all of your support—for the restaurant and the Mavens. And I love to hear that you're stewarding your health," Cam replied. She gave the girl's shoulder a squeeze that she hoped communicated a big sisterly sort of care for the teen's recent heartbreak. "Be sure to tag me in that picture!" she added. "I'll share it."

"You will?"

"Obviously! Have fun in Charleston! And you girls should totally buy tickets to the big party we're having at Moving Word before Christmas." Would teenagers even be welcome at the gala? Cam actually wasn't sure—but she'd bring it up with the Welshes. It was good for the church to have more youth involved. "It's going to be *so* special—and for such an amazing cause. There's info at the link in my bio with all my discount codes, but you can DM me, too."

The girls squealed and thanked Cam repeatedly as they shuffled out of the restaurant. Their muffled, high-pitched chatter continued until they were out the door. Cam watched them pile into a minivan idling near the curb and returned to her chair. They looked like kids whose parents could afford the minimum $150 ticket price for the Gala for Goodness—if not for their teens, then for themselves. The girls were sweet. They would figure it out.

"Do you think they'll tag me as the photographer? Did I understand the assignment? One of these days, I'm not going to be able to take you anywhere," Margo teased, tapping her mug up and down against the tabletop.

Camryn shrugged. She didn't want to be presumptuous and agree with Margo, but to disagree would be dishonest, to bear false witness. "The whole thing has taken on a life of its own, I guess." If only it had been that easy. There had been so much strategy, so much time, so much love involved in cultivating the Mavens community.

"Your church must be pretty happy about it," Margo added.

"I haven't talked to them about it much." She had, though, and she knew they *were* happy about the additional PR her efforts were getting for their already impressive endeavors. Still, she didn't want to brag in front of Margo. *Humble yourselves before the Lord, and he will lift you up*—James 4:10. Cam's boss wouldn't understand the reference to Scripture, anyway.

"Well, it seems like that place is taking over town," Margo said in a way that made Camryn unsure if she was being sincere. Jokes aside, Camryn was proud.

"We're actually doing a big fundraiser for an anti-human-trafficking organization," Cam said. "Let me know if you want to donate. Or you could come to the party the week before Christmas! It should be a lot of fun."

"Okay. Not my number one cause, but great." Margo picked up the papers she'd been referring to earlier. "Anyway, let's get back to the zoodle issue. Maybe we can get this sorted out today so I'm not stressing about vegetables all weekend. What were you saying about sweet potatoes?"

* * *

Her meeting with Margo finished and the remains of the grain bowl wrapped up in a biodegradable container, Camryn stepped out of 12th Pine and began the walk to the corner where she'd parked. It was practically the weekend, the weather was gorgeous, and everything was moving in the right direction at work, online, and at church. There was room for growth in some aspects of her personal life, but that was no reason to be ungrateful on an other-wise beautiful day. She slid her Prada sunglasses over her eyes to protect them from the afternoon sun. The glasses had been a splurge, but they were worth it. One couldn't be too careful with their eyes or with crow's feet.

"Hey!" The voice wasn't familiar and could have been directed at anyone. Cam kept walking toward her car, searching her bag for her keys.

"Hey!" the voice called again, louder and colder this time.

Camryn turned to face whoever was calling out to her, further shading her face with her hand. A forty-something woman dressed in linen capris and a short-sleeved button-down printed with vertical pastel stripes appeared to be following her down the sidewalk, arms crossed over her chest and foam flip-flops slapping angrily against the cement.

"Can I help you?" Camryn asked.

"Yes," the woman huffed, coming to a stop a few feet away from Cam. She wore waxy pearl drop earrings and shiny lip gloss a shade or two too peach for her complexion. "You can help me by backing off what you're saying to my girls online."

"I'm sorry. What?"

"You're one of those who's been posting about church and prayer on Instagram and Facebook and whatever else, right?"

Cam nodded, her hand clammy around the strap of her purse. She could feel what was coming because the woman's tone wasn't altogether unfamiliar, though it was rare to experience it offline. While having this encounter in broad daylight felt incredibly invasive, perhaps it could offer an opportunity to create the sort of connection that felt so impossible to forge with angry commenters on social media. Face-to-face, at least, she knew she could make a better impression, calling on all of her charms and kindness as she plastered a smile on her face that keyboard warriors could never experience in-person.

"I get what y'all are trying to do," the woman said, her mouth settling into a firmer line, "but I'd appreciate it if you redirected your efforts. They're already so attached to their phones that I can't get them to pay attention in real church as it is."

Cam held her purse closer to her body. "I hear what you're saying," she said. "But we really are just trying to meet the girls where they are. And we think we can provide—"

"Look, you're a pretty girl," the woman said, leaning forward. "There's no question about that. You're all pretty girls. But this whole mission you've got going on is a little flashy. I can't have my kids growing up thinking vamping online is the most Christlike thing they can aspire to." She leaned in further, the smell of spearmint gum icy cold in Camryn's face. "Quit whoring yourself out in God's name and let us lead our own children to the Lord."

With that, she brushed past Cam, leaving no space for resolution or mutual understanding. Whoever this woman was, she was likely teaching her daughters far more about judgment—not to mention tacky footwear—than she was teaching them about God. This was exactly why the Mavens mattered.

And was it so wrong to be pretty?

* * *

When Camryn Lee Cady felt moved to share her heart, there was no time to waste.

Within ten minutes of arriving home from her meeting with Margo, Cam applied another layer of sheer Charlotte Tilbury gloss, misted a halo of hairspray around her head, refreshed her mascara, reenergized the soft waves around her face, and clipped her phone into the tabletop tripod her boyfriend had given her as a birthday gift a few months before. As always, she situated herself in the makeshift studio she'd put together when she moved into the apartment: seated on her bright yellow couch; legs crossed primly in front of her; her posture perky and perfect in front of the longest wall in the living room, which she'd personally wallpapered with a tasteful pattern of muted mauve bursts. Propped up on the entertainment center in front of the television, her phone in the tripod had the perfect shot. Thanks to the research she'd done on the apartment's precise orientation relative to the sun prior to signing the lease, even the natural lighting was of the highest possible quality. Since she put in so much work, she welcomed compliments about the way her videos looked—as well as the way she looked in them. The kind words were blessings she was glad to accept.

Camryn stretched her neck, fanned her hair out around her shoulders, and reached sneakily under a spangled throw pillow to tap the remote that would trigger her phone to start recording the video, which she'd preset to dispatch live to her Instagram followers. Her feed had experienced a 5 percent boost in traffic the week before, likely because of a giveaway she'd run in collaboration with Shepherd Lovely, the boutique publisher behind a line of bespoke Bibles and devotionals so beautiful they might be considered home decor. It was the first time Cam had worked with Shepherd Lovely, but with the engagement she'd seen on her posts, she was confident it wouldn't be the last.

When Camryn could see the red icon blinking at the top of the screen, indicating that the video was in progress, she paused for a few beats, smiling at her phone and her community. *One, two, three*, she counted to herself.

"Hi, y'all," she said. "I'm popping on here because something is on my heart, and I had to share it. When something sits heavy, God calls us to bring it into the light."

Camryn pictured her followers—first dozens of them, then hundreds, then thousands—tapping their way into her live video, pausing whatever they were doing to listen to what she had to say. Some only followed her because she was cute and wore cool clothes, but that could change. As long as they were listening. Plus, there would be more viewers later, people who couldn't watch live because of their work schedules and social plans, but who would still be sure to tune in. Her message would have eternal life on her feed.

She took a deep breath and went on. "This afternoon, I found myself face-to-face with a sister in Christ who does not approve of what I'm doing here," she said. "She accused me of distracting her daughters from the Lord. It was hurtful. For a minute, it even had me questioning if anything that I've built with you is worthwhile.

"I've heard plenty about the dangers of social media and how it can steal our attention from the most important thing in our lives." Cam extended one arm toward the sky, pointing a manicured finger up at the ceiling, which was, unfortunately, still covered in grimy gray popcorn that the property management company refused to address. "And while I think we could all use a good conviction every now and again, I must disagree with what this woman had to say. Respectfully, of course."

Cam paused meaningfully. From her spot on the couch, she couldn't see the small number in the top corner of her phone indicating how many eyes were tuning in. She also couldn't see the comments popping up in tiny text at the bottom of the screen. Insurance would probably cover an update to her contact lens prescription, and she was in dire need of one. At that very moment, important testimonies and prayer requests were coming through. She had to be able to read them without straining her eyes or straying from her seat. No matter how much prayerful thought and planning it required, everything needed to look effortless.

"I'm not saying that I use this platform perfectly," Cam continued. "But every day, I wake up and try to use my voice for good, to reflect the love of God to all of y'all, whether or not you believe the same way I do. Without social media, I don't think I ever would have felt bold enough to share about my heart for the church and for Jesus. It's thanks to social media that I've connected with all of you about my relationship with the Lord. It's so, so much fun."

Cam continued speaking to her followers. "And I'm not saying social media is all good. I don't have to tell you about the way it's led people astray! But social media can also help us connect with one another. It's been such a blessing to see a beautiful community building here on my page and on the Mavens feed. I'm humbled by this sisterhood, and I know we have more hearts to change. Why would anyone give that up just because this kind of fellowship is a little untraditional? People thought Jesus was radical in his time, too."

Camryn shrugged, lifting her shoulders so high that they tapped against her hoop earrings and made them swing back and forth. She loved the way it felt when the words flowing from her mouth were coming faster than she could track the thoughts in her brain. No wonder Kyle and Cassidy loved to preach.

"I guess what I'm trying to say is that I don't want any of you letting the judgments of others keep you from expressing your faith wherever you see fit. At Moving Word, we talk about being unshakeable and bold in our beliefs—and that inspires us here. Where are all of my Moral Mavens at?" Camryn squealed the last line, wiggling around on the couch and shaking her head from side to side. The Mavens loved her couch dancing. They'd told her so and shared videos of themselves doing the same thing.

Even across the width of the room, Cam could see an explosion of tiny heart icons burst from the bottom of her phone screen. People liked what she had to say. Many of them *loved* what she had to say. Even the nonbelievers among them—and Camryn knew from the considerable time she'd spent in her comments that there were many of those—appreciated her connection with God, whether or not they could precisely identify it as such. They saw her joy and wondered where it came from. They admired her positivity and the way she invited followers into it.

It had been a year and a half since she'd started posting with the #MoralMavens hashtag, and just about eleven months since she'd decided to channel the momentum she'd gained into a full-blown social media ministry. In that time, she'd highlighted Moving Word and recruited the others to help her run things, since there could be no impression that the ministry was all about her. It definitely wasn't! As a team, they were committed to sharing their love of God through Instagram, TikTok, and YouTube—and any other platform that might come their way. It was Camryn's calling to make it happen, no matter how strangers chose to twist their words or misrepresent their methods. She had her church's support and a determination that could only be God-given.

Cam grabbed for the remote in its hiding spot under the throw pillow and pressed the button to end the livestream, keeping her smile intact until it was clear she was no longer broadcasting. She took a deep breath, swept her hair into a ponytail with the scrunchie she kept in a convenient compartment under the coffee table, and stood up to grab her phone from its tripod. There was the matter of the comments to attend to before she could get on with the rest of her night.

> you melt my heart!
>
> cam, keep being you. beautiful inside and out.
>
> AMEN, sister. Don't let the enemy keep you from sharing your testimony!!!!!!
>
> u r a bright shining star and a warrior for the lord. MORAL MAVENS 4EVER.

> Where did you get your lip gloss?
> Gorgeous, girl!

> LOL to all of this. Come on, gf. Stop with the bullshit.

Even with plenty of positive comments to review, there was nothing like a public knock on her faith to keep Cam humble and remind her to take a break from her screen. She set the phone down. People really could be so hateful.

Whatever.

How heartbreaking for them.

The thousands of women who proudly called themselves Moral Mavens—who stuck stickers with the pastel MM logo to their laptop cases and posted TikToks about the Bible studies they were working through together—were kind and encouraging. They were striving to be the women God had created them to be. They were already coming together to celebrate Kyle and Cassidy's plans and to support ProtectUS. They would keep rising above the world's judgments about them. Matthew 5:14–16: *You are the light of the world. A town built on a hill cannot be hidden.*

Neither do people light a lamp and put it under a bowl. Instead they put it on its stand, and it gives light to everyone in the house. In the same way, let your light shine before others, that they may see your good deeds and glorify your Father in heaven.

Cam and her friends and the girls who followed them would remain a town built on a hill—a hill with a stunning view and year-round sun.

3

Savannah

The woman on the cover of the tabloid didn't look anything like Savannah's mother. Not really. Sure, there were certain similarities if you looked hard enough: the surprising sharpness of her jaw, hazel eyes somewhere between the color of jade and a turtle's shell, a shade of pink lip gloss that Savannah knew was only available through a now largely defunct Ohio-based mail order cosmetics company.

It couldn't be her mother, though, because the woman's skin was too unbothered. When Savannah's mom smiled, sunbeams of fine lines appeared around the outer edges of her eyes. She was proud of it. She didn't understand why other women in her position might spend any of their new money on chemicals that would, as she put it with a throaty laugh and a raised brow, "squeeze the memories out of their bodies." Savannah's mother would have thought the woman on the magazine looked like the kind of statue no one would care to admire in an art museum she'd never pay to visit in the first place.

In spite of all of this, her mother's name—Joanne Maxwell—was spelled out in screaming, bright purple capital letters below the oversized photo. And in spite of Savannah's best efforts to focus instead on the shiny pumpkin pie on the cooking magazine shelved nearby, she couldn't pull her own hazel eyes away from the rag. The jumbo bags of chips and pretzels in the basket hanging from her arm felt heavier. Her forehead itched from the baseball cap she'd taken to keeping in the glove compartment of her car, an old Carolina Panthers number from her husband Chad's closet.

"Just those, miss?" the cashier called down to Savannah. While she was lost in thought and cheap ink, the man ahead of her in line had, apparently, left with his groceries.

Savannah hurried to close the gap between herself and the cash register, then pulled the box of ovulation tests out of the armpit under which they'd been wedged. With whatever was happening in her uterus, it wasn't enough to hide her face. Even her purchases required a low profile. Aware, still, of their delicate nature, Savannah handed the box of tests directly to the cashier, along with the basket. "These too."

The woman smiled up at Savannah meaningfully as she scanned the box and set it gently into its own plastic bag, separate from the snack foods that would shortly be distributed to Savannah's students. A bejeweled cornucopia pin just below the collar of her store-issued T-shirt reflected the red light of the scanning gun. "Do we know each other?" the cashier said, fingers paused in mid-air inches above the cash register. "You look so familiar."

Prepared as always for precisely this scenario in a public setting, Savannah had already pulled out her debit card and was making every effort to hand it off. "I shop here every once in a while. I work nearby."

The cashier's fingers and gaze remained fixed. "It's not that. It's something else." She was still smiling as she turned back to the register. "You're like a secret agent or something with that hat on, too."

Grateful to have passed over her card to complete the transaction with only minimal interruption, Savannah looked up at the ceiling, tapped her foot against the store's tile floor, and tried to make out the lyrics of the song playing through the loudspeaker. Cam and Trishy were the best people to have around during close calls like this one or, worse, during full-on instances of *Oh! I know you! You were on TV, right? Didn't your dad do something terrible?* Her girlfriends were good at diversions, each one a slightly sloppy yet effective shelter for Savannah's shame that would later become part of the lore of their friendship. During one such incident at a restaurant, Camryn had deliberately spilled her glass of wine on the offending server. During another at a construction site where they were volunteering with a Moving Word service group, Trishy had batted her eyelashes and asked for help with a screwdriver to distract a man who was all too curious. In real time, these efforts were humiliating for

Savannah—perhaps even more than the comments that prompted them—but the girls could always laugh about them in the aftermath.

"Have a blessed afternoon," the woman manning the cash register cooed as Savannah accepted her receipt and bags. "I'm going to figure out how I know you the minute you walk away. I just know it. It always happens like that, doesn't it?"

Savannah nodded and smiled tightly once more. She'd spent so many years moving through the world comfortably as people recognized and greeted her family, called out their names, and testified about the way their show had impacted their lives. Back then, she'd loved talking with strangers and had been encouraged to do so. When fans shared their personal stories, her insides lit up like the sparklers her brothers kept hidden in the garage. They would let her talk to them about God for as long as she wanted. They would squeeze her hand with fervor. They would praise her and her family for helping them get their own lives on track. *Your show was the message I didn't know I needed. It inspired me to go to church. It's thanks to you that I'm right with God. It's thanks to you I'm saved.*

It had been less than a year since that familiarity had become a threat. Outside of going to work, most days, Savannah felt unequipped to do the things that normal people did the way that normal people did them. It was the anonymity that scared her—or at least the pressure to preserve the anonymity. Would it really be so much worse if she let people see her face, free from the itchy baseball cap's protection? It was hard to know for sure, but Savannah had heard through the grapevine enough stories about her siblings' public experiences of late to fear letting down her guard. The tight travel radius she'd constructed for herself between home and school and church and Dr. Clark's office, plus the occasional visit with Camryn or Trishy or Cassidy or her sister, was safe and controlled enough. Even casual errands out and about could be much harder to predict. The new stress of the Gala for Goodness—a big, flashy event that seemed to require her joyful attendance as part of not only the Moral Mavens Mainframe but also her friend group and church community—crossed her mind once again. She pushed it back as she hustled to the car.

For now, she'd secured the pretzels and chips,

which would hopefully make for a more pleasant play practice. The kids were always extra rowdy on Friday afternoons, and with the first performance of their *Footloose* production coming up, attention spans were more limited than ever.

As she pulled out of the parking lot, Savannah's phone rang. There would be just enough time to catch up with her little sister before rehearsal.

"Vance tried calling me again last night," Ruthie said as soon as Savannah answered, eschewing a standard greeting. "I didn't pick up, obviously, but he left a bunch of messages."

"What did he say?" Savannah asked.

"More of the same. Mom and Dad are heartbroken. Threatening to show up some Sunday at church to see us. They don't understand why I haven't spoken to them since I got engaged." To Savannah, it sounded like her sister was reading off a list of pesky weekend chores instead of recounting the fractured state of their family.

Ruthie and her boyfriend Wilder had gotten engaged at the end of the summer. Savannah was the only one of Ruthie's relatives who'd heard the news directly from the source. Better still, Wilder had invited her to be there in person when he popped the question—crouching behind a tree until her legs went numb, then running over to hug her sister as soon as she got the signal. Trishy had arranged a deal with her contacts in town to help him get a better ring than he could afford on his own. The other Maxwells had likely discovered that it had happened through a sloppy, desperate game of social media telephone.

"Did he really say they might show up at church?" Savannah asked.

"That's what he said, but who knows if they would ever do it. It's like herding cats."

Having any one of the Maxwells make a surprise appearance at the up-and-coming congregation would be embarrassing for Savannah—and for the church. Since getting a taste for television, they'd become prone to dramatics. Kyle, Cassidy, and the rest of Moving Word's pastors and staff would have every reason to get angry about a scene staged on their turf by recently shamed public figures. And while Cam was generous about supporting Savannah in the wake of everything that had happened, she'd be freaked out, too. For the health of the Mavens and their reputation—and even Moving Word's fundraising efforts—it was key to keep the drama associated with Savannah's family in the background. "Are you going to call him back?" she asked her sister.

"Nope," Ruthie said. "Are *you* going to try to call him?"

"No, no, I'm not going to call anyone," Savannah said—and she wouldn't. She wanted to, but she wouldn't. "Sorry. I still don't know what to say when we talk about this. I keep thinking we're getting space from it and then it comes back."

"Just tell me it sucks and let me complain." Ruthie paused, obviously frustrated. Complaining hadn't been tolerated in their home growing up. Their parents believed it demonstrated a lack of faith in God's loving command over one's life, not to mention an unattractive tendency toward negative thoughts that was bound to cause spiritual upset. "Anyway. What's up with you?"

"I'm headed to rehearsal," Savannah replied. "I saw Mom on the cover of some crummy magazine at the store while I was getting snacks for the kids."

"Lots of Photoshop, right?"

"You saw it?"

"At the gas station a few days ago."

"Why didn't you tell me?" Savannah asked.

"Probably because I knew you'd be weird about it," Ruthie said.

"Am I being weird about it?"

"I don't know. Everything's weird. You seem extra stressed lately."

"I'm sorry," Savannah said. She couldn't—and wouldn't—get into the other reasons for her stress with her sister, but any feelings she had about her family of origin were Ruthie's to bear, too. "I don't mean to be on edge. I'm almost at school, though. Can I call you later?"

"Sure," Ruthie replied. "Love you."

As Savannah pulled into the parking lot of Dolley Madison Middle School, she took mental stock of the particular weirdness to which her sister was referring. Just short of a year earlier, a local news station had received a tip that Carl Maxwell—devoted husband to Joanne, patriarch of Savannah and Ruthie's family, a self-deprecating man of God who so many people had grown up watching on television—was having an affair with his daughter-in-law: Vance's wife, Angela. The tip had come from a friend of Angela's who claimed in interviews to be "fed up with all this talking about God and sleeping with a married man." The friend had used a handful of other nasty words to describe Angela, but Savannah would never repeat those, not even in her head.

Throughout Savannah's childhood, her parents had preached to her and her nine siblings on- and off-screen about the beauty of being "in relationship" with folks of all kinds: one's friends, one's family members, one's parents, one's neighbors, and, of course, one's savior. They'd also preached the sanctity of the second most important relationship they'd ever be expected to nurture, this one with their spouse. Superseded only by a close connection with the Lord, one's marriage should be the most critical, meaningful relationship. It was the single relationship in which the kind of physical intimacy that was only whispered about in the Maxwell home was to be allowed. The fact that Carl Maxwell's so-called relationship with Angela included overnight hotel stays and Victoria's Secret receipts listing items Vance said he had never seen in the sacred privacy of their bedroom was a betrayal of practically infinite kinds.

Or it should have been. When the Maxwells' public relations team called Joanne to let her know that, even with ample attempts to keep the source and the media quiet, the news would be breaking the following morning, Savannah assumed the family would agree about what should happen next. She and Ruthie—who had been Savannah's first call after she heard from their mom—vowed never to speak to their father again. The eight other siblings would do the same. Everyone would rally around Vance, their brother's hurt and the years of memories they shared taking precedence over a father who'd failed to play by the rules he'd set for them. What else was there to do? Carl had broken his own wedding vows and encouraged his son's wife to do the same.

He had admitted to the whole thing, after all. Compelled to tell the truth by a higher power (or so he said), Carl released a statement confirming the rumors, explaining that he and Angela had struck up a "relationship"—again, that word—on a family trip to Scotland four years earlier. Four years earlier! On a trip that had been aired as a Thanksgiving special for their millions of fans to watch! The man had grandchildren… grandchildren born by the very woman he had now copped to sharing a bed with.

And yet, the other Maxwells remained steadfast.

Joanne was devastated, of course, but she'd forgiven her husband. In lieu of a full press statement of her own, she asked the Maxwell PR team to release her thanks for the public's support and a verse from Ecclesiastes: *Do not be quickly provoked in your spirit, for anger resides in the lap of fools.* White letters printed in a plain serif font on a black background and posted in all the places where fans would think to check. Even Vance had liked the post, presumably from the dim light of the one-bedroom apartment he'd been renting since the news broke.

For her mother's part, even the mild-mannered Savannah couldn't see how feeling mad about four years of a spouse's extramarital affair could be considered being *quickly* provoked, but her mother was unwilling to discuss it further. "God hates divorce," Joanne had told Savannah in one of their last conversations. "I can't control what he does. I can only control my reaction. I don't want to be angry. Do you? I would think your desire would be for all of us to come back together. That's what God wants."

It was hard to know exactly what to believe from the blogs and gossip forums, but from what Savannah could gather, Carl had moved out of the house shortly after that phone call—and not because his wife had seen the light and demanded better for herself. No, he and Angela had decided to double down, to try to make things work in a real, honest way. They were sorry to everyone they'd hurt, but they'd been praying about it, and they said it seemed to be God's will for them to be together. Joanne had been stuck with a divorce whether she liked it or not—and no matter how much God hated it. The situation had gone from bad to worse, and then from terrible to mind-boggling.

Somehow, after everything, that seemed to be the last straw for the people in control of the family's fate. The network that had made the Maxwell parents and their ten children famous for their show *MAXimum Family*—now syndicated nationally and available for streaming—announced they would produce no additional seasons of the series. *It has been a privilege to bring the Maxwell family into your homes for the last twenty years*, the statement read. *It is our sincere hope that they will take some much-needed time to regroup and rebuild away from the cameras. Our thoughts and prayers are with them as they navigate this difficult period. We hope their devoted audience will extend the Maxwells the same kindness as they remain connected to the family through previously aired episodes and via social media.*

And still, it seemed as though Joanne and the other Maxwell children refused to admit Carl's wrongdoing. Savannah's mother had even started a podcast about how to walk through painful periods of marriage using the Bible as a road map. Not that Savannah had ever listened to it—or ever planned to. There were rumblings that it frequently landed at the top of the charts.

The Maxwells didn't believe in luck, but it was lucky for Savannah that her parents had supported her becoming an educator—even though full-time mothering was the path they thought best for a woman. Teaching music had always felt like a calling, but Savannah had never felt as blessed by her chosen profession as she had in the months since the scandal. Preteens had no interest in *MAXimum Family*—and even on the off chance that one of her students was familiar with the show and recognized her, it was unlikely they were following the story of Carl's infidelity and everything it had caused. Plus, Savannah had picked up a new last name when she'd married Chad a few years earlier, giving her extra distance from the whole matter. If students or parents or other teachers were aware of the fallout, they had at least been kind enough to gossip about it behind her back. Savannah knew that people had been teasing her and her family for most of the previous decades. She was grateful to have been spared much of it—and grateful for friends like Camryn, Trishy, and Cassidy, who reminded her that there was life outside and beyond her family's past and present. Faith had always been so ever-present for Savannah that it was hard to be sure how much of it she'd lost, but she was glad to have Moving Word as a home base to help her rebuild.

For now, she could only handle the matters in front of her: namely, the hungry stars of *Footloose* and the sad box of ovulation tests that she'd shoved under the passenger seat before grabbing the other grocery bags and getting out of the car. First, *Footloose*. Later, everything else.

r/maximumfamilymaximumsnark

Savannah wedding ep????

nostalgianellie__9: Anyone know if the Savannah wedding episode is available to stream anywhere? Having a DAY and need a dose of my fave Maxwell.

_jesusjaded_xo: Pretty sure all the specials (weddings, graduations, etc.) never made it to streaming. Just the regular eps. All 5000 of them lol

victor1709: sucks because the specials are kind of the best ones. i would MUCH rather watch those tacky weddings all over again than have to see Poppa Pervy negotiate with another local dentist for orthodontia for one of the brood. Good thing Vance got his teeth fixed! /s

Ainttooproudtosnark47: good thing they're all still homely AF

missiontoopossible: they suck but they're not homely. that Maxwell bubble butt! ~god's work~

Ainttooproudtosnark47: they make braces for those????

nostalgianellie__9: (OP) ugh REALLY?

Ainttooproudtosnark47: no leg humping OP

Ainttooproudtosnark47: OP you know this is a *snark* page right. There are fan subs.

nostalgianellie__9 (OP): i know! i'm in those too:)

Ainttooproudtosnark47: sounds like you have a lot of time on your hands.

nostalgianellie__9 (OP): u r the one picking a fight with me:)

unsuspectingwaiters: mods are slacking again

missiontoopossible: that wedding was low-key kinda great

nostalgianellie__9 (OP): right??????? i cry every time. that dress was 14/10

wokepolicepolice: it's super messed up to get married on a plantation but i wouldn't expect anything less from the Messwells

_jesusjaded_xo: For sure. You'd think the Trumans would know how bad it would look, though. Are all southerners really that dumb?

foreignxxchangebarbie: all Republicans*

_jesusjaded_xo: rofl true true

foreignxxchangebarbie: didn't they have sponsors for it???

missiontoopossible: maybe? i feel like there was product placement…

DIANE2_: yessss it's all coming back to me now [celine dion voice] pretty sure they were shilling seltzer or something. Also gelato

foreignxxchangebarbie: 100%

missiontoopossible: that's NUTS. was the show really that popular? people weren't just hate watching back then???

> **Ainttooproudtosnark47:** weirdly ya
>
> **Ainttooproudtosnark47:** Poppa Pervy was making them deals
>
> **nostalgianellie__9 (OP):** i keep tellin y'all:)

victor1709: Can we get a wellness check on Savannah? She never posts on her social media...

> **missiontoopossible:** Sav was always the second-hottest after Ruthie
>
> **foreignxxchangebarbie:** ew Ruthie was a literal child on the show
>
>> **missiontoopossible:** yeah and I was a child when my parents made me watch. fundie kids need crushes too! /s
>
> **foreignxxchangebarbie:** 🙄

nostalgianellie__9 (OP): she seems good! she posts with Moral Mavens

> **DIANE2_:** my niece follows them
>
> **Ainttooproudtosnark47:** DON'T GIVE THEM ENGAGEMENT

DIANE2_: Dude my niece isn't in this sub

nostalgianellie__9 (OP): FUN! it's not MAXFAM but at least we get to see Savannah thriving. but I still want to see the WEDDING gah.

missiontoopossible: yeah but like probably better not to have them streaming. <u>THIS</u> article says they made millions off those specials in syndication. I'm not here to help them get richer.

nostalgianellie__9 (OP): ok but it's not Savannah's fault her dad sucks!!!!!!

nostalgianellie__9 (OP): i keep thinking maybe we'll get a pregnancy announcement soon. 🙏

missiontoopossible: Also why haven't we talked about the fact that all the Maxwells still in the cult deleted like ALL those pics from her wedding

nostalgianellie__9 (OP): wait really??? that's SO SAD

Ainttooproudtosnark47: for a leg humper, you're out of the loop

foreignxxchangebarbie: yup and Joanne did that whole podcast episode about knowing when to let your kids go. the pictures disappeared right after that. ALL the pics of Ruthie and Savannah

4

Kristin

The morning after the carnival, a printed note from Cassidy had been waiting on Kristin's desk, detailing the Gala for Goodness to-do list that had existed only in her imagination the day before. The only thing written in the pastor's wife's predictably beautiful handwriting was *ASAP*.

In the weeks since, Kristin had been moving as quickly as possible, acting as the main contact for everyone from a ballroom that had offered to discount their usual fee to the regional magazines the Welshes had invited to cover what promised to be decadent festivities. To that end, there were also dozens of emails about catering and decor and a live band. Cassidy had made a point of letting Kristin know that she would be personally responsible for all communication with the stylist and glam team that Cassidy had lined up for the event, as well as the florist, lighting designer, decorator, and the well-known high-end jeweler who would be donating several pieces to the gala's silent auction. "I've taken plenty off your plate already," she'd snapped at Kristin. "I'm incredibly busy, but I don't trust your taste."

Neither the urgency nor the pageantry made sense to Kristin, who couldn't fathom why any of these details were relevant to her job working for a church. Still, she hoped her proximity to the whole situation was giving her a much-needed opportunity to gain Cassidy's favor. Even with the work Cassidy took over for herself, there was plenty for Kristin to do, and there were weeks to go before the gala actually happened. Wouldn't it be easier for the Welshes to simply write the big check to ProtectUS—Kristin was fairly confident it would clear—and perhaps ask some of their fancy friends to do the same? It was a good thing her parents hadn't raised a quitter.

Friday afternoon, as Kristin reviewed her latest list of assignments—a list that had been deposited directly on her chair in the time it had taken her to grab lunch—Trishy swept into the office, leather bag swinging in time with the strains of worship team practice floating through the open door. Trishy always looked perky and put-together. They'd been working together on the Mavens for a few months, but Kristin still never felt quite worthy of sharing the same space. She knew it was silly—and it wasn't Trishy's fault! She, as Kristin's mom would say, just had *it*. Whatever *it* was.

"Hey, girl," Trishy said. Her teeth were distractingly white, which felt like a weird thing to notice. Kristin wondered if Trishy's dentist was taking new patients. "Is Cass in? I don't have an appointment, but she said I should stop by if I was in the neighborhood."

Kristin wouldn't expect Trishy to need an appointment. She and Cassidy were friends. Cassidy had so many friends! It was confusing. Camryn, Savannah, and Trishy, at least, were all polished and maybe even a little fancy, but they'd also been nothing but kind to Kristin. How could they be so happy to spend time with a woman who seemed hell-bent on maintaining a flat, unimpressed attitude at best and an inexplicable nastiness at worst? Her best guess was that Cassidy felt inclined to adopt a certain hardness around the office—a posture that might be unpopular among the wider congregation but that she would perceive as necessary in the world of Christian leadership, typically dominated by men. On her own time, she could easily be a gentler, more fun person. If the pastor's wife's behavior was about wanting to be taken seriously, Kristin could try reaching for empathy instead of what she felt naturally, which, no matter how hard she tried, was something like disdain.

"You just missed her," Kristin said. "She left a few minutes ago."

Trishy shoved her bottom lip out in a pout. "Bummer. I guess that just means I'll have to keep bugging you, then!"

"You're not bugging me at all," Kristin said.

"Oh, I know," Trishy said. "I was teasing."

Kristin's shame at her own obliviousness was buoyed by the admittedly juvenile joy of being on the receiving end of Trishy's joke. "Do you want me to take a message?" She wondered if

Trishy could smell the phantom of the everything bagel she'd eaten earlier.

"That's alright," Trishy said. She adjusted the trio of thin gold chains around her neck. "Cassidy wants to see if I can get my boss at Twist to sponsor the gala. Which I totally can. I'll talk to Claudia when I see her next. You're coming to our meeting tomorrow, right?"

Kristin nodded. As far as she knew, a Mainframe meeting wasn't optional.

"Perfect," Trishy replied. She gestured down at the mess spread out before Kristin. "Are you pretty swamped with party stuff?"

Kristin nodded again. "It's a lot of work." Looking at all of the papers and folders cluttered in front of her, she wished she'd cleaned up a bit. "But I'm having a lot of fun with it, obviously," she added, mindful not to sound whiny or ungrateful when the situation called for practiced and capable.

"For sure. Well, if Cam gets her way, the rest of us will be stepping in to take some of this off your hands any day now," Trishy said. Kristin thought back to the conversation she'd had with Camryn at the carnival, about her vision for the Gala for Goodness as some sort of outright collaboration between Moving Word and the Mavens.

"That could be fun. I don't know anything about these kinds of things, so I'm kind of nervous." It felt good to confide in someone, and Trishy's listening ear—dotted with an arrangement of complementary, delicate sparkly studs—was a pleasant surprise. "It's the biggest event we've had since I started working here, too, so I want to make sure it's perfect."

"I get it. First jobs are always stressful," Trishy said with a smile. "But I'm sure you're killing it. Plus, you have the Mainframe behind you! Is there anything I can do?"

Kristin wanted to answer that she had it all under control, but one thing did come to mind—and Trishy's open expression and casual lean toward the desk made Kristin feel okay about asking for a favor. "You know the Lamberts, right?" she asked.

Bo and Amber Lambert had only been coming to Moving Word for a short while, but their presence was a big deal—and their support for the gala and the fundraiser would be even bigger. After a successful career pitching for the Miami Marlins, Bo had been recruited to join the brand-new Charlotte Major League team. When the news of Bo's move had been made public, the Welshes had courted the Lamberts with multiple trips to Miami, treating them to lavish dinners out and organizing a beach picnic for the kids with the help of an event-planning company Kristin had found for them on Instagram. Given how quick the newly relocated Lamberts had been to start attending services, it was clear these efforts had hit the right note with them. It would be amazing for everyone if an invitation to get more involved with the ProtectUS event did, too. Cassidy had asked Kristin to reach out to them to set up a meeting, but all of her messages—and even the organic fruit basket Cassidy had insisted would be a home run with the health-conscious couple—had gone unacknowledged.

"We're not besties or anything, but Amber was following me before they moved here, and we've said hey a few times," Trishy said. "Why?"

"I've been trying to get them in to talk more with the Welshes about the party, and I haven't heard back." Amber Lambert was the kind of sweet and untouchably pretty woman who always seemed to be getting murdered in Kristin's favorite documentaries.

Trishy laughed and leaned in closer, dropping the volume of her voice. "Can you blame them? Wouldn't you be sick of people pumping you for money after you'd been in town for, like, five minutes? The Welshes should know how that feels."

"I'm not sure that's why—"

"Oh, that's *definitely* why," Trishy said. "It's fine, though. It's for a good cause. I'll tell Amber to call Cass. Maybe I can bribe her with some PR packages." She giggled to herself. "Not that she needs them. She probably gets way better ones than me. Maybe we bribe Cass instead and get her to cut you some slack? I have a whole box of La Mer that I haven't touched yet. She'd love it."

"It's totally fine. She doesn't need to cut me—"

"Teasing again!" Trishy replied. Kristin felt her shoulders fall as Trishy let out a breezy laugh. "Cass definitely doesn't need them."

It was true. Cassidy seemed endlessly supplied with whatever she wanted, fancy hair products—was La Mer hair products?—included. Over the years, there had been rumors that she came from a lot of family money, but Kristin's distant relationship with her had never exactly set them up for a heart-to-heart about their parents or childhoods. Kyle's origin story, on the other hand, had been described in one article as "rural rags to religious riches," but that didn't mean he was pulling in some massive salary as a pastor. He still worked for the church.

"When you talk to her," Trishy continued, "tell her I have things handled with the Twist sponsorship for the gala. Also, I'm not sure if she's already picked out her dress, but one of my stylist friends volunteered to help me find something, and I'm sure she would *love* to do the same for Cass."

"I think she already has a stylist booked."

"Figures. Someone big and pricey?"

Kristin shrugged. As far as she knew, working with any stylist was big and pricey. Until recently, she hadn't known that it was something people who weren't appearing in movies actually did.

"We'll have to find out," Trishy fake-whispered. "Do you know what you're wearing?"

"My mom kept all of my formal dresses from high school."

Trishy shook her head back and forth dramatically. "Absolutely not," she said. "I can't have this. You are part of the Moral Mavens *Mainframe* and are clearly a major part of this event.

Plus, you're representing the church. You're running this whole operation. We're getting you something new and great. Give me a little time, okay?"

Kristin nodded. She believed Trishy would come through. She believed that it might even be fun. People loved planning fancy parties, and there had to be a reason for it. She could feel herself smiling and she hoped it didn't look pathetic. Since most of her interactions with her Mavens Mainframe colleagues were in the context of the full foursome, she rarely enjoyed time with the other women individually—but this unexpected visit with Trishy had given her a needed boost.

"We'll talk more tomorrow," Trishy said with a decidedly non-pathetic grin. "I'll see you then. Thank you for everything!"

Kristin said goodbye and watched Trishy leave. It was hard to know exactly what she'd done in the last few minutes to earn Trishy's gratitude, but she would take it. She would take it all the way to the end of her afternoon to-do list and maybe—just maybe—all the way to an evening of feeling like she'd impressed Kyle and Cassidy at the gala.

5

Camryn

The Moral Mavens hashtag had been Cam's idea one morning after church. I love spending time with these sweet Godly women, she'd captioned a candid image of a few friends from Bible study laughing over their lattes. You won't find happier hearts or more moral mavens anywhere.

Cam had always loved a good wordplay—she did, after all, work in marketing—and the alliteration looked in an Instagram caption as good as it sounded rolling off her tongue as she repeated it to herself on the drive home that day. People began to take notice when she tested it out on other pictures. Friends told her it was cute and clever. When it eventually started gaining traction—with hundreds of girls she'd never met using it to tag their own photos from church events and summer camps—it was the branding experience she'd gained at 12th Pine that had inspired Cam to pull together the Mainframe and get organized with posting schedules and giveaways and collaborations that would bring even more eyes to their content—and, of course, to Jesus. Camryn's personal following grew right along with the Mavens community.

That part had been a happy accident.

Plenty of the Mainframe strategy came from Cam's days with Cru at UNC, too. After a challenging first year on campus, the organization—Campus Crusade for Christ—had become a cozy home for Camryn, much like Mamaw's kitchen back in Durham. It was a place so unlike the second-tier sorority that had humiliated her in the pledging process and then boxed her out of exec board on the grounds that she wasn't fulfilling her financial obligation to the house. That the small monthly payments she made instead of lump sum dues had been approved in writing by the organization's national body hardly seemed to matter to the girls inhabiting the grand, carefully manicured house partially shielded by lush red and purple flowers that had served as a hopeful backdrop on the day Camryn received her bid.

Shortly after that debacle but before she'd made her final decision to leave the sorority, Camryn had gone on her first dinner date with Jeff Bates, who she'd met in an American studies class. Dressed in a crisp blue button-down shirt and khakis, he'd picked her up in front of her dorm and taken her to Il Palio, a restaurant on Franklin Street that most students only visited when their parents were in town. They'd shared wood-grilled crostini with ricotta and wildflower honey, olives tapenade, and pappardelle pasta smothered with braised beef and hearty tomato sauce. Camryn was more accustomed to baskets of bland dinner rolls and plastic cups of sweet tea sweating through paper place mats, and to ignoring the appetizer section of a menu altogether. In between bites, Jeff told Cam about his childhood in Columbia, South Carolina, and how he'd come just short of his childhood dream: a walk-on spot on his beloved Tar Heels basketball team.

"If that was really your dream, I don't know that I can finish dinner with you," Cam had joked, hopeful it was coming off as flirtation. "My Mamaw's been working at Duke since my mom was a kid."

Jeff laughed. "I can forgive you if you can forgive me."

In the cozy light of Il Palio, Cam decided that she could forgive him for just about anything. When it was her turn to talk, she told Jeff about growing up with Mamaw, being without her parents from a young age, and the difficulty she was having finding her place at UNC. Jeff didn't flinch at any of it—not the story of the car accident that had made her an orphan or her admission that she didn't feel like she had the right clothes for the sorority whose favor she'd worked so hard to curry during the rush process.

"If you're from Duke country, what brings you to UNC?" he asked instead. "I mean, I'm glad you did come here, but you know what I mean. You're obviously smart enough to have your pick of schools."

"The scholarships were better here," she confessed. "My Mamaw wasn't happy about that after all those years working for Duke. Anyway,

I just don't think I've found my people here yet. The whole sorority thing hasn't been what I expected."

"I didn't even rush," Jeff replied, taking a bite of Bolognese. He waited until he'd chewed and swallowed before going on. "My older brother was the president of Beta when he was here and could have made a call to help me out, but I bailed. I met a bunch of guys on my floor. I started going to Cru, too."

Cam didn't know a lot of boys back home who would reject help from a cool big brother if it meant gaining easy popularity and recognition. She liked that about Jeff. She also liked his light blue eyes and reddish-blond hair. It was the color of Mamaw's caramel pudding.

"Cru's a church thing, right?"

Jeff nodded. "Yeah," he said. "I was into youth group in high school. The meetings are good, and they have parties that never get broken up by the cops. They do a lot of community service, too. Everyone's friendly, and it's kept me grounded since I got here."

It had sounded better to Cam, certainly, than the nightmare she was still living with the sorority. As Jeff graciously paid the bill for dinner, she'd asked if she might join him for the next Cru meeting. He smiled and said he'd be more than happy to bring her along, especially if she would be kind enough to join him for ice cream afterward. She didn't need to think too hard before she agreed.

"I *am* going to need you to get rid of your Duke sweatshirt first. I know you have one," he said as he held the door open for her so she could walk out of the restaurant.

"Never," Cam laughed. "And I have four." She dared to wink at him.

It had been that night at Il Palio that changed everything for Cam. Within a few weeks, she was calling Jeff her boyfriend and Cru her UNC safe haven. She'd bowed out of the sorority and realized before long that she didn't miss any of the girls she'd met there. Every weekend, she was going on service trips with her new friends from Cru, playing with kids from underprivileged schools, and selling frozen pizzas to benefit orphanages in Central America. She liked the people she met in Cru and the person she was when she was with them. Growing up, she'd sat in the pew of the local UCC with Mamaw most Sundays, but neither of them had ever gotten especially involved with the ministry. Going to church was just something they did, something almost everyone she knew did, like birthday parties or school dances.

With Cru, church became almost everything. She added quiet time with God to her daily morning routine, read every book she could find about pursuing a relationship with Christ, and was eventually elected president of UNC's Cru chapter. She liked knowing exactly what was expected of her and that, assuming she followed those rules accordingly, she'd be welcomed and loved exactly as she was, or just about. The Word made things so much easier, so much cleaner. It had all felt like a dream—exactly like what she'd hoped college would be—and she'd gotten to do it alongside Jeff, who she firmly believed had changed her life forever by inviting her to check out the organization after their first date.

It was only fitting, then, that, once they'd graduated, Cam would follow Jeff to Charlotte, where'd he been offered a well-paying job at a large bank. Shortly after sharing enthusiastically with the 12th Pine HR rep about the role wholesome Southern cooking had played in her childhood with Mamaw, she'd secured a job. She found her way to Moving Word within a few months of arriving to town, when she and Jeff had agreed that there was no time to waste in finding Christian fellowship in their new home. Two homes, technically. Camryn and Jeff didn't do sleepovers—and wouldn't until after they were married.

The Moving Word building was big and bright and beautiful and impossible to miss from the road, which was only the start of the church's impressive marketing strategy. Camryn couldn't get away from their gorgeous Instagram ads, which directed her to a tasteful website dotted with photos of attractive, smiling faces doing all manner of Christian things: worshipping onstage with their hands lifted in the air, emerging from baptismal pools, chatting in small groups, dishing out Thanksgiving dressing at a homeless shelter. Cam and Jeff quickly fell into a rhythm with Moving Word, meeting as a couple with a co-ed young adult Bible study on Tuesday evenings, separate young men's and women's groups on Wednesdays, and then, without fail, services every Sunday morning. And that was only the beginning! There were so many activities at Moving Word—all of which were available for nothing more than a highly encouraged but technically optional donation—that its congregants could be busy every night of the week if they wanted to be. Conceiving of the Moral Mavens just after her fourth anniversary as a Moving Word member was the icing on an already delicious cake for Cam.

Jeff had led her to her new life and to the Mavens. She could never repay him, but she hoped he'd give her a chance to show her appreciation somehow. The plan was to spend forever together, so at least there would be plenty of time. The ring was coming soon.

It was because Cam owed so much to Jeff—and because she looked so forward to their future as a couple—that she found herself walking into a Friday evening Financial Freedom class at Moving Word a few weeks after the carnival. For months, Jeff had been pointing out the flyers for the course, which were posted and growing wrinkly at the edges on bulletin boards throughout the building.

"That sounds kind of interesting," he said after his first sighting, fiddling with his collar. "You could pay a lot of money for something like this at other places, you know."

"Doesn't that kind of defeat the purpose?" Cam joked in reply.

"Exactly." Jeff tapped the sign with his thumb. "This is the way to do it. Could be a help for your shopping."

He'd been getting increasingly vocal recently about his concerns surrounding her spending. It had started with mostly lighthearted jokes each time he saw a new package on the welcome mat outside her apartment, but things had turned serious. For the first time, he was asking questions about what she'd spent after a shopping trip. *How many pairs of jeans do you* need? *You used up everything from that last Sephora order already?* When she daydreamed aloud about a future in which they were married, he always found a way to direct the conversation to finances, suggesting that it would be important for them to get their individual "business in order" before taking any big steps as a couple, or asking out of the blue if she'd ever considered reading one of Dave Ramsey's books. Most of the people she knew who sang Dave Ramsey's praises were dads wearing polo shirts. It wasn't her demographic.

Cam had done her best to ignore Jeff's hints for a while, but she could only play dumb for so long.

Money management wasn't her strong suit, but she wasn't dumb, and she didn't like pretending to be. Not even for Jeff or for the sake of her lifestyle.

Talking about money—especially with a boyfriend—was unbecoming, so Jeff didn't know much about her finances. Still, it was apparent that whatever little information he'd been able to piece together was enough to make him suspicious. Camryn dreaded what might happen if he somehow did learn about the forty thousand dollars in credit card debt—most of which she could barely account for now, with the exception of a couple dozen nice things hanging in her closet and a handful of months of rent when she'd found herself coming up short—she was barely making payments on. Or about the dozens of emails sitting in her inbox from robots who wanted to help her refinance the two personal loans she'd taken out since finishing at UNC, about the stack of late notices in her apartment that she wasn't sure what to do with. If Jeff discovered all of that, it would further delay a proposal—or worse.

So Cam had agreed to attend at least one session of the five-week class, which was—if nothing else—cooler than reading a Dave Ramsey book. In one of Moving Word's many event spaces, Camryn dropped her oversized leather tote in the middle seat at one of two long tables set up before a small lectern, behind which a middle-aged man in a pullover and glasses frantically tapped away at a laptop. Thanks to the confirmation emails she'd received about the class, Cam knew his name was Miles Mason and that he worked at a local accounting firm. She couldn't imagine anything more boring, but it was nice of him to offer his services.

"Camryn! I didn't expect to see you here." Cam turned on one heel and found herself face-to-face with Kyle Welsh.

Cam wasn't ashamed to pose for photos with a bunch of teenagers in front of her boss or even to endure a semi-public attack from a middle-aged mom accusing her of whoring herself out for Jesus, but being seen at this kind of class in the very place where she'd worked so hard to build her good reputation was another matter altogether. She couldn't bear to have people—certainly not Kyle—making assumptions about her or raising questions about her fitness to represent the church's teachings in such a forward-facing manner.

"Oh, actually, I'm just here to pick up some information for the Mavens," Cam said. "I deal with big budgets all the time at work." She smiled. "I've been getting a lot of requests from the girls for financial literacy resources. We have lots of new grads in the community, you know. They want to get started on the right foot."

"Of course they do," Kyle said. "And you're the girl to help them do it. You can never be too careful with your spending. I was just out making the rounds throughout the building. Stretching my legs, you know."

Cam nodded and turned toward the lectern. "Miles, do you happen to have those worksheets we talked about? You said you have worksheets, right?"

Miles didn't look up. His head was swiveling back and forth from the computer resting on the lectern to the sleek projector screen behind him, which remained black.

"I thought maybe I'd mentioned it to you before, but I may have forgotten," Cam said. She knocked gently on the side of her head with a closed fist. "There's always so much going on up here, you know? But, yeah, I'm pretty established, financially speaking. I don't know if you know this about me, Miles, but I don't work full-time in ministry."

She looked over at Kyle, who was nodding vigorously. Miles stared blankly at her, which Camryn thought was a little rude.

"I have a job with a big restaurant in town. I'm smart with my money. Financial freedom is really important to me." She took a deep breath. "Anyway, I think it's great you're teaching this class. Let me jog your memory. You know how a few other girls and I run the Moral Mavens, right? I think they'd really appreciate what you have to say. I'm sorry. I thought I emailed you about this. It probably went to your spam folder."

"Spam?" Miles asked.

"It's not just meat in a can!" Kyle joked.

Miles looked up at them briefly before digging into a pile of papers sitting on the table next to the lectern. "I don't know that I would call them worksheets, but you can take these if you'd like," he said. "I'm having some trouble with this computer stuff." He went back to wrestling with the laptop.

"Let me see if I can get someone down here from AV," Kyle said, pointing toward Miles. He shifted his finger to Camryn and began walking backward out of the room. "It was good to see you, Cam. I'm glad you're using all of these resources for the Mavens. Lots of synergy happening here. I know y'all have been helping lots with the fundraiser, too. Your reach is sick."

Camryn could almost feel a tiny spotlight warming her under Kyle's compliment. Nothing flashy. Just enough.

In the weeks since Cam and the other Mainframe members had started sharing about Moving Word's efforts for ProtectUS, she'd lost count of how many followers had messaged with screenshots confirming their donations, and of how many had continued to spread the details to their own networks. When she could finally get enough time with Cassidy to talk more about how she and the Mavens could pitch in to help with the gala, no one could accuse her of being anything less than overwhelmingly generous. What did it matter if she'd bailed on Jeff's class and stretched the truth to Miles?

Tucked into the comfort of her white Jetta in the parking lot, Cam already felt better. The rest of a Friday evening stretched before her. Normally, she'd check in with Jeff to meet up for dinner or a movie, but there was no need to get into the details of what had happened at the class and why she was available so early.

Instead, Cam pulled out her phone. Her ongoing text conversation with Cassidy Welsh wasn't hard to find. Just that morning, they'd been chatting about a new line of essential oils Cassidy had purchased. Cam was dying to find out if they were worth the hefty price tag. Her last text had been left unanswered, but she tapped out a new one, anyway. Cass could be flaky with her messages, something that Cam knew she should take just about as personally as Savannah's lack of personal social media activity and its accompanying liking power.

Hey gal! she wrote. Just ran into your hubs and thought of you! Can I stop by? I'll bring snacks!

6

Savannah

Chloe Featherton was red-faced and halfway through her rendition of "Holding Out for a Hero" when the text from Cam came through. The *Footloose* cast had done three full run-throughs that week, and everyone deserved a break. Chloe's voice, at least, had been pushed to its limit. Thankfully, it was almost the weekend, and Savannah and her co-director, Mr. Stiller, had agreed to give the kids some much-needed time off before dress rehearsals began. Mr. Stiller was the drama teacher and about thirty years Savannah's senior. In the three and a half years

Savannah had spent teaching music and directing musicals at Dolley Madison, she'd still never called him by his first name, nor had she heard any of her colleagues use it.

The phone buzzed against the interior of Savannah's purse, which she'd set as usual next to her notebook on the long table from which she and Mr. Stiller customarily observed rehearsals. Her students were prohibited from using all devices on campus, and while the rule didn't officially apply to teachers, she liked to play by the same rules whenever she could. Her single philosophy on educating preteens was this: If you showed them the same respect you wanted from them in return, they would exceed your expectations almost every time. It was a departure from the governing philosophy in her childhood home, where respect was only expected from child to parent, never in the opposite direction.

Chloe Featherton was most definitely exceeding expectations in that moment. After weeks of gentle vocal coaching from Savannah, the timid seventh grader was finally starting to project her voice out to the back of the auditorium. As suggested, she was making eye contact with imaginary audience members in almost every section of the theater and had even managed a few smiles throughout the song. The number still needed a little more attitude before it would be ready for opening night in a couple of weeks, but Savannah could hardly blame Chloe for that. The song was about adult feelings, and the girl standing onstage was a kid who still wore braces and glittery cat-eared headbands. Mr. Stiller would need to help her dig deep to channel her character. Chloe's voice, however, had never been the problem. Dozens of rehearsals into the process of staging *Footloose*, Savannah still found herself in awe of the girl's rich soprano, so removed from her normally hunched shoulders and reluctance to speak up in class. Seated in the first few rows of the auditorium, the cast erupted in cheers for Chloe as she sang the final notes. Chloe beamed. This was why Savannah did what she did—for that moment when a kid like Chloe gained her confidence through music. After spending much of her own childhood living out a contrived version of real life on-camera and publicly, teaching kids how to perform on *purpose* made Savannah feel like she had reclaimed some power, which she could then share with kids who wouldn't have to grow up in a cruel public eye that could giveth and taketh away.

This year's production was coming at an ideal time, too. When all of the news about her family had come to light months earlier, Savannah never could have anticipated that she'd still be receiving death threats in the fall. As she'd carried the snacks she'd purchased for the kids from the car and into school that day, she'd made the mistake of glancing at her phone, only to find a scathing message waiting for her on one of her long-dormant accounts:

> You and your family are the reason ppl in this country are turning away from God. You give us ALL a bad name. Your church should be ashamed to be associated with you. I hope the time you have left here on earth is short... and I don't have to tell you where you're heading next. It's a sign of His providence that you don't have children.

The hateful lines were accompanied by an empty gray circle meant to be filled with an actual photo of an actual person. There was never an actual photo of an actual person. Deleting the message, blocking the sender, and tossing her phone back in her bag didn't make Savannah feel any better. Praying for the person on the other end of the exchange or even turning to God—which would have been the recommendations of her parents—didn't, either. Being in a big room of young people clapping for each other did, if even a little bit.

Over the well-deserved applause, Savannah could hear her phone buzz twice more, then a third time. Long ago, she'd turned off notifications for all of her social media apps to minimize the attention she paid to messages like the one she'd stumbled on that afternoon with the random tap of a finger on the wrong spot on her screen. It had to be Cam. No one in Savannah's life texted like Camryn Lee Cady: first with the gentleness of the polite Southern woman her Mamaw had raised but growing insistent before too long. The phone buzzed again at the very moment that the whoops and applause from the front of the theater quieted. Savannah rushed to move her bag to her lap so she could dig through its contents and switch the phone to silent mode before it attracted the attention of Mr. Stiller. He couldn't stage the musicals without her help, but he was still technically above her in the school's hierarchy. She didn't need it getting back to their bosses—neither the chair of the art department nor the principal—that her phone was being disruptive, not when she was praying on a daily basis to remain under the radar at school. Should she be called in for any sort of special meeting, she feared she might also be asked to answer for her mother's face on the tabloids. A fat bead of sweat rolled down Savannah's back as she grabbed for the phone among the folders, lip balms, loose change, and pens in the bag. When her hand brushed against a tampon, she batted it away. It was a reflex. A game of hot potato.

"It's alright," Mr. Stiller muttered, obviously aware of the phone. He pushed himself up from his seat with a groan befitting a drama teacher and pulled at the end of his plaid tie. "I was going to give some notes to Ariel, Chuck, and the Reverend and then send 'em home for the weekend." During rehearsals, he insisted on addressing the students only by the names of their characters.

No longer captivated by Chloe's performance, the other kids were antsy for the weekend and growing rowdier by the minute, chatting among themselves and bouncing up and down in their theater seats so they clapped dully around their bottoms. A hush fell over the room as Savannah's colleague leaned against the stage and started speaking to the cast. Only a few brave students dared make a noise when Mr. Stiller was in front of the group.

In the meantime, there were five messages from Cam waiting for Savannah:

> Hi hi! I'm running to Cassidy's for a visit! You should come! I want to talk about the gala!

> I KNOW Chad does that thing with his brothers on Friday nights. You better not be sitting home alone.

> I'll be at Whole Foods in ten minutes. Do you have any snack requests?

> Oh sorry, you might be at rehearsal. I forgot. Oops! Enjoy the kiddies!

> But really, you should meet us there. Trishy's coming, too!

Savannah wasn't in the mood to be social. On top of the baseline stress of her family and the unwanted attention it brought her, the final stretch of putting together a production was exhausting, and she'd spent most of her days that week walking her classes through time signatures and meter, which tested her patience every year. Plus, there was still the matter of the news she and Chad received from Dr. Clark on Monday. She couldn't talk about that with her friends. To do so would require her to update them on months of similarly—but not quite as—disappointing appointments, and to apologize for failing to share with them earlier, which she'd done out of respect for the agreement she'd made with her husband. Beyond that agreement with Chad, Savannah was still trying to figure out how much of the shame she was feeling about the whole situation was rooted in her strained relationship with God, and how much of it she'd earned all on her own. Camryn in particular would be distressed to discover that such significant information had been withheld from her for any length of time.

Driving straight home from work sounded much more appealing than going to the Welshes' fortress-like house with a smile pasted to her face, but Savannah also knew that the reality of being alone was never as dreamy as her fantasy of it. Silence was only golden for so long when you'd grown up in a house bustling with siblings. Maybe that was why she'd chosen a profession that put her squarely in the center of boisterous young people every day.

Plus, Cam would be relentless, no matter what other excuses Savannah offered, and it would be nice to get some face time with Cassidy, who was growing increasingly tough to pin down as she took on more responsibilities as pastor's wife.

I'm just leaving school, she texted back. I should be there in 20.

I got three bags of those veggie chips you like, Cam replied. You can pay me back later!

It never occurred to Savannah to request reimbursement from a friend, but she shrugged off the text, reminding herself that Cam was well within her right to ask for payment. Personally, she saw no need to keep a record of transactions between them, but she also wanted to avoid resentment from her friends at all costs—literally.

As Savannah waved goodbye to the students and packed up her things to walk out to the parking lot, she figured she had two options when she met up with her friends. The first option was to lay bare the truth of her emotional state the moment she arrived at Cassidy's house—leaving out, of course, the things she and Chad had sworn would remain private, focusing instead on the pressures she was feeling at school and the latest in a long line of lingering aftershocks of her dad's actions. Cam, Trishy, and Cassidy would applaud her vulnerability, offer her sparkling water and tissues and shoulders to cry on, and pray with her.

But they would also ask questions. They would want to understand why a job—a job that Savannah claimed to love fiercely—was bringing her to such a low point. Savannah would not have a good answer for them, because it wasn't really about her job. And no one liked to talk about what had happened to the Maxwells. If forced to do so, the ladies would probably just get uncomfortable and dispense assurances that everything was going to be okay. Cassidy would probably find a reason to excuse herself briefly until the subject had run its course, returning with no less sympathy or care. Savannah had noticed this pattern in the past. Playing the role of the pastor's wife and serving as a public representative of the church forced some unofficial boundaries, even among friends.

There was also the second option, the one she knew, as she pulled out of the school parking lot in her comfortable old Volvo, was the better choice. She would go to Cassidy's house and be upbeat, or at least content. She would talk about the many ways in which her students blessed her life and how excited she and Chad were about his new wellness ministry at Moving Word. She would focus on middle school drama and bad pitch and botched choreography. She would eat the veggie chips and discuss glittery plans for the ProtectUS benefit, do whatever she could to benefit the Mavens and the church. She would be just fine. It was a part she had learned to play, just as Chloe Featherton had learned to play Ariel Moore. If Chloe could do it for *Footloose*, so could Savannah. They were both figuring out how to act the part of a grown-up.

Kids craved friendship and connection—gifts that the Maxwell children hadn't been granted outside of their brothers and sisters—and Savannah did, too. But growing up in a household where every trial was God's will and every anxiety simply the Devil whispering in your ear had left her unsure what she should be allowed to share, even as she knew her friends could be counted on.

Chad would already be on his way to meet his brothers for dinner, so Savannah called him from the car. She could picture him heading into the city in the Jeep he'd been driving since high school, flannel sleeves rolled up to just above his elbows. They'd known each other since they were seventeen-year-old seniors on a mission trip to Tanzania, the first of many similar trips they would take together over the years. Even their shared commitment to service had proven fair game for observers since Carl Maxwell's admission of guilt and Savannah's high-profile role within the Mavens. A photo that Savannah had posted to Instagram five years earlier—so long ago that it had since fallen into the deep abyss of the online world—had recently resurfaced, causing a brief but stressful stir. The culprit was an anonymous commenter on Camryn's most-hated forum ("There's a reason it rhymes with *forget it*," she'd said more than once), identifying him or herself only as bearwitness333. In the photo, both Chad and Savannah wore giant smiles and Sav's head was encircled by a brightly colored wrap, styled for her by one of the women at the orphanage. That was the day they'd presented the kids with a slew of musical instruments, all of which they'd purchased with the funds they'd spent the previous year raising from friends and family. Below the photo, bearwitness333 had added this commentary:

> I like to spend as little time as possible doom scrolling social media because we all know it's a giant dumpster fire, but I unearthed this little gem in the middle of the night while I was up with my sick kid. This is Savannah Truman... you know her from that weird christian family reality show with the pervy dad and now that creepy, culty Moral Mavens fundie thing. White savior much? I'm sure these Black kids gave their enthusiastic consent to be pictured here so that Savannah and her bootleg Kennedy could go home and gab about their good works, love for Jesus, etc. etc. /s how big of them to leave the cameras at home!!!! I always thought these Mavens chicks she hangs

> with now since her family blew up are shady af. Get over yourself.

For a couple of days that had felt like weeks, the post was shared and discussed enough to hit Camryn's radar and get her a little spooked about the way it reflected on the Mavens. The group was in its infancy at the time, and she'd chewed off her manicure each time they'd talked about the possibility of the discourse finding its way to Kyle and Cassidy. Luckily, the proverbial noise had quieted, but the stress lingered, and Savannah feared its aftershocks had at least something to do with the spiked cortisol levels Dr. Clark had flagged in her bloodwork. It was thanks to Chad that she'd been able to maintain perspective through the worst of it—and that she was able to keep that perspective in sight even now. Her husband was the one who'd encouraged her to make as clean a break as possible with social media, a position he doubled down on further each time she made the mistake of sneaking a peek, only to discover that dedicated acolytes of her family's show were now obsessively awaiting a redemption arc in the form of a pregnancy announcement.

Savannah liked that so much of Chad had remained consistent in all the years they'd known each other, even with the specific brand of fame she'd brought to the relationship, which had rubbed off on him. Would it really be so bad if things stayed the same? It had worked for them so far, with and without the cameras. With and without the rest of the Maxwells. Maybe her calling really was to enrich the lives of other people's children instead of her own.

"Camryn invited me to go to Cassidy's with her," Savannah explained when her husband picked up the phone, double-checking for oncoming cars before pulling out of the school parking lot.

"You sure you're up for that?"

He already knew the answer. Why make her say it out loud? Her response wouldn't change anything—not their circumstances, not the insistence of her friends, nor the fact that they'd need to forge ahead despite the hollow feeling that had become a third party in their relationship. Not for the first time that day, she thought of the verse from Romans she'd been praying over since leaving the doctor's office on Monday: *And we know that in all things God works for the good of those who love Him, who have been called according to His purpose.* Savannah had always believed that she had been called according to His purpose. She didn't know another way. Now she was just hoping God would make all things work for her good... and to make His purpose for her a little clearer.

"I'll be alright," Savannah told Chad. "I think some girl time will be good for me."

"Aren't you seeing them tomorrow?"

"We have a Mainframe meeting in the morning. Tonight's just fun. Plus, it will give me a chance to see Cassidy." Savannah eased to a stop at a crosswalk to let two little girls in blond pigtails cross the street with their bikes, faces locked in determined expressions that were more precious than tough. "I don't really want to be alone at the house all night."

"Whatever you think is best," Chad said. "Make sure you eat something, though. Is Cassidy having dinner?"

"Cam grabbed snacks."

Chad sighed. "I want you to have some *real* dinner. Like, a protein and a carb. Maybe a vegetable," he said, parroting the version of himself that offered dietary advice on Instagram on behalf of his health coaching business. "I'm sure

Camryn doesn't think she can save the world on veggie chips alone. Take a page from her book. We're still keeping everything between the two of us, right?"

Savannah nodded at her windshield as if her husband were in the seat beside her and could see. "Yes," she agreed. "You won't mention anything to your brothers?"

"No way," Chad said. "If the wrong person overhears, you could end up dealing with vultures online. There's an election year coming up. Plus, as soon as they get wind of anything like this, my parents will find out and start pushing it. Neither of us needs that kind of pressure. Trust me—I don't want to discuss grandchildren with my mother any more than you do."

Savannah wasn't sure about that, but she wouldn't argue.

If word *really* got out about their situation, her own family might be asked to comment on it by the press or random bloggers. She wasn't sure which part of that possibility she dreaded more: what they might say or the harsh reminder that the parents and siblings who had once been her universe now had only limited access to her life, mediated by meddling strangers.

"Alright, babe, let me know if you need anything," Chad said. "I'll give you a call when I'm on my way home. I love you."

Savannah returned Chad's love and refocused on driving, navigating the Volvo through another gorgeous North Carolina November evening. The leaves on the trees lining the road were beginning to light up like the flames in the woodburning fireplace at the Maxwell family cabin in Pine Mountain. For a moment, she wished she was back there, among the cabin's beautiful views and thick blankets, nearer to her loved ones. But she couldn't go back. Dr. Clark said extra stress would only exacerbate what they already had going on, and the comfort she imagined was a mirage more than it was anything else, a sun-bleached postcard from a trip that could never be re-created but still peeked out from layers of other mementos on a well-loved bulletin board.

While not quite as high-end as the landscaping in the exclusive neighborhood to which the Maxwells had moved a few years into the run of *MAXimum Family*, the yards in Kyle and Cassidy Welsh's brand-new development were nothing to sneeze at, with neat hedges and big sprays of flowers and hardly a branch out of place.

Construction on the homes had been completed less than a year before, but they were trying to look grandiose in a historic way, each one surrounded by what had to be nearly a half-acre of grass that appeared more turquoise than green, with oversized black lampposts looming like disciples of an allegedly simpler time. As Savannah turned into the development, she fought a momentary urge to feel ashamed of her car and its loud sputtering, like the click of a train making its way up the hill on a roller coaster.

Savannah had been invited to the Welshes' housewarming party along with Cam, Trishy, and a few hundred other members of the Moving Word congregation, plus a batch of local influencers and photographers. She'd been to Kyle and Cassidy's home many times since then but still felt unsure of herself pulling into its driveway. On her last visit, the back tires of Savannah's Volvo had made their mark on the front lawn during a shameful attempt at a five-point turn. Though Cassidy had refused to discuss Savannah's offer to cover the cost of a landscaper to hide the scar, Savannah hadn't missed her friend's grimace when they'd examined the damage outside. She still didn't feel right about it. There was a wide spot available next to Cam's Jetta in the driveway, but she parked at the curb. Just to be safe.

The Welshes' home was a two-story whitewashed brick structure that was trying very hard to be a farmhouse but was far too grand. Its shutters were painted a neat black to match the oversized double doors that welcomed guests in from the home's sizable wraparound porch. Black iron railings connected a series of dormer windows on the top floor, behind which Savannah knew there was a loft-style media room appointed with low-slung tan leather sofas sleek enough to conceal hardware that turned them into comfortable recliners. At the housewarming party, she'd overheard girls cooing over the "minimalist" aesthetic. Savannah hadn't bothered to correct them. By Pinterest's standards, their assessment of the space was perfectly accurate.

Savannah and Chad had a carefully monitored joint savings account and a financial safety net the size of the middle school auditorium thanks to the Truman family's old money and status, but Chad had read a book about minimalism in college, and their life had been built on only the most intentional of belongings ever since. In their home, minimalism was practiced in the literal sense. When it was possible to have and live on less, they chose to have and live on less. They didn't pretend to be saints—both of them had been raised with plenty and had to regularly tend to the muscle that reminded them to walk away from a gratuitous purchase or to donate an item that was no longer useful to them—but it was a discipline they'd committed to jointly after their admittedly over-the-top wedding at Alexander Homestead, an event over which their mothers had presided with little input from the bride or groom. Gathering her purse from the passenger seat and stepping out of the car, Savannah reminded herself that the Welshes hadn't committed to the same discipline, and that was okay. They were called to serve in other ways, and as far as Savannah could tell, they were rising to the occasion admirably in their roles at Moving Word. Their home was an extension of the church, and they stewarded it accordingly.

Even so, she was relieved not to have damaged their property this time. Savannah's brain was already packed with too many other concerns to make room for another set of tire tracks imprinted on the pastor's lawn, no matter how friendly she was with his wife.

nextdoor | The Retreat at Davidson Acres

Daniella Morrow: Just a friendly reminder that, per HOA rules, all outdoor events must conclude by 11:00 p.m. and be kept to a reasonable volume until then. If you'd like to host a larger gathering and anticipate lots of noise (i.e. a live band, concert-grade speakers), we ask that you clear it with the board first. Thank you!

Neil Robinson: The Welshes don't look at these messages. You can just call them out. They're the only ones staging concerts in their backyard. We can hear their "events" from the other end of RDA.

>**Bridget Corbin:** Can we make exceptions for the noise if it's a religious event? The worship bands can get loud, but it's for a GREAT cause.

Neil Robinson: I'm sure that's exactly the exception they'll claim if the HOA finally does something about it. "Religious persecution." Jesus loves a rager.

Bridget Corbin: There's no reason to be disrespectful.

Daniella Morrow: The HOA will review all complaints on a case by case basis, irrespective of their religious nature.

Skylar Hershey: is it true they have an indoor pool?

Daniella Morrow: Indoor swimming pools are not permitted, per HOA rules.

Skylar Hershey: ya but do they have one

Natalie Williams: Where does the HOA stand on film crews in the neighborhood?

Daniella Morrow: There's no written policy on this.

Natalie Williams: Cool cool cause I noticed like a FULL camera crew at the last loud outdoor event at the house I know you're talking about

Daniella Morrow: This is a general reminder for all residents.

Lillibet Raphael: Probably for Kyle's TikTok

Bridget Corbin: the videos are always very tasteful

Neil Robinson: See? It's getting out of control.

Daniella Morrow: The HOA has no jurisdiction over residents' social media.

Neil Robinson: I'm talking about our property, not TikTok. And what about that massive outdoor pizza oven I saw brought in there last month? Are those even safe for residential use?

Skylar Hershey: i want one of those pizza ovens so bad

Skylar Hershey: pretty sure they have a lot of teens there

Neil Robinson: weird

Bridget Corbin: YOUTH GROUP

Bridget Corbin: you're making it weird

Lillibet Raphael: Maybe y'all are just jealous. Those pizza ovens are really expensive.

Daniella Morrow: The HOA will evaluate your safety concerns on a case by case basis.

Neil Robinson: Just admit they invited the HOA to enjoy that new deck they built. It's gaudy as hell.

7

Trishy

Camryn had thrown open the front doors of Kyle and Cassidy's home before Trishy even made it halfway up the front walk, her friend's floral skirt still crisp after her day working at 12th Pine. The whole thing came off a little Stepford for Trishy's taste, but she had to love Cam for owning it so shamelessly. "What do you think of my new place?" Camryn said, lifting her arms out to either side like Moses parting the Red Sea. "I look great in here."

"You mean Kyle and Cassidy haven't handed over the keys yet?" Trishy teased back.

"It's weird, right?" Camryn wrapped Trishy in a hug. "I think it really suits me," she added quietly, a faint film of a whine stuck to the underbelly of her perky voice.

"I agree," Trishy said, stepping back from Cam. "It all looks good on you."

"They should just ask me to be their roommate," Cam whispered. "They wouldn't even know I was here."

"You don't need a roommate. You and Jeff are going to find something just as beautiful," Trishy said, stepping into the foyer as Cam closed the door behind her.

"Oh, Jeff couldn't afford something like this." Cam laughed. Trishy let the sound hang in the air for a few minutes. It felt weird talking about Jeff's finances. The man was a little dull but had only ever been kind and generous to Trishy, covering her tab at meals without making a production of it and asking thoughtful questions about her job. "Not yet, anyway. Maybe soon."

Of the four Mainframe girls, Trishy was the only one who was single and actively dating. Kristin was technically unattached as far as Trishy knew, but she'd shown no observable interest in finding a man. At twenty-two, she probably figured she had plenty of time left before she would really need to settle down. Trishy had made the same mistake (among many others) when she was younger. Now she could see she'd waited too long. In the last four years, most of Trishy's local friends—Cassidy and Savannah among them—had managed to get engaged and married. They'd had fabulous bridal showers (many of which were planned by Trishy and had, as a result, gone viral-adjacent as perfectly styled photos were shared from Charlotte influencer pages and beyond) and gorgeous lily-white weddings. Now they were living in light-filled homes and planning their futures. Some were already styling baby bumps in gorgeous wrap dresses, stocking closets in spare bedrooms with tiny gingham shorts and doll-sized turbans in shades of dusty rose and sage green. In the process, they'd hoarded away every appealing godly man in town.

Sometimes, it all felt so unfair.

A small (very small) part of Trishy took a sick pleasure in the fact that, while Camryn's serious relationship with Jeff put her well ahead of Trishy in the romance department, she had yet to tick off some of the other milestones that had become critical in Trishy's circles. For as long as

Cam was still waiting for a ring, she was available to Trishy as a fellow unmarried friend, and there was something reassuring about that—even if that fact also made her feel terrible. Old Trishy would find solace in Camryn's waiting game, but the Trishy of today—the Trishy of the church—should be past that. She should be trying harder.

"You'll have your turn," she told Cam. Trishy liked to think of herself as someone who knew the right thing to say in every situation, but she was unsure in these moments when marriage and joint bank accounts were on the line, even with a close friend like Camryn. Plus, as much as she wanted Cam to have all of the things she wanted—and as much as she adored Cassidy—she was confident that, with some patience, she'd find herself ensconced in marital bliss in a home that was perhaps more understated and less reminiscent of a West Elm catalog than what the Welshes had built for themselves. "You'll have your turn, and it will be amazing."

Just as Camryn began shaking her head and rolling her eyes, Cassidy Welsh floated into her entryway, long brunette waves falling past her shoulders and bouncing gently against the top of an olive-green waffle knit lounge set. Trishy had the same one in four different colors. "Did I hear engagement talk out here?" Cassidy said. "I don't want to miss anything." She reached out both arms to hug Trishy, who wondered about the woodsy vanilla smell of Cassidy's perfume and where she could get it for herself. "Savannah's inside. Totally exhausted from the day with the kids. Come on in."

Cassidy gestured to follow her out of the foyer and into the kitchen. As she had every time she'd been in the Welshes' home, Trishy noticed at least a dozen new photos to admire on the walls. Whether on a glamping safari in South Africa or attending a formal event, Kyle and Cassidy were a gorgeous couple. Everyone already knew that, but the gallery wall visible behind the wrought-iron railings of the foyer's staircase was an unmistakable reminder. Trishy made a sizable chunk of her living by posting photos of herself online, and she still would have been uncomfortable with a home wallpapered in her own face, a vain game of Where's Waldo. Good for the Welshes for maintaining that level of self-esteem. They were created in God's image, et cetera.

"So *is* there any tea to spill about Jeff?" Cassidy asked as they turned into her kitchen.

"Ring tea?" Camryn asked.

Cassidy nodded.

"Sadly, nothing to report," Cam sighed. "When there's news, you'll hear right away."

Cassidy raised her eyebrows at Trishy behind Camryn's back as they walked farther into the house. It was common knowledge among the twenty- and thirtysomething women of Moving Word that Camryn was long past losing patience with Jeff's as yet unrealized proposal. No one was a more enthusiastic bridesmaid than Cam—Trishy had seen it firsthand—but no one used florals and floor-length gowns and dance floor renditions of "Proud Mary" to cover their own sadness better than she did, either. Trishy had never heard someone speak aloud about the fact that Camryn seemed to have kicked her plans for the Moral Mavens into high gear at precisely the same time that a half dozen of her closest girlfriends were planning their weddings, but she imagined others had noticed and wondered about it, too. If the ministry had started as a consolation prize for the new last name she craved, it had become much more than that since, but the hurt was still there. And Camryn's time *would* come. It couldn't be far off. Her wedding and her marriage would be nearly perfect. Camryn would accept nothing less.

"News about what?" Savannah asked from her perch beside the marble-topped island that occupied an impressive amount of space in Cassidy's kitchen. "Trishy!" She leaned against Trishy without standing up. In the crook of her shoulder, Trishy worried that Savannah felt thin enough to break. The Trumans were always trying out a new diet regimen or fitness plan, but on this particular Friday afternoon, Trishy squeezed her friend's frame a little tighter, checking to be sure of something she couldn't quite name.

"Wedding stuff," Trishy said, kissing the top of Savannah's head.

"Jeff," Camryn replied at the same time. "Not that there's any news."

"Here's the real question, though," Cassidy said. She pointed to the barstools lined up on the other side of the island, and Trishy and Camryn took their seats. "Will we hear from you first, or will you make us find out with all the Mavens?" She put her hand up in front of her to pause Camryn's reply. "Before we get talking and I forget, can I get you girls something to drink?" All three women waved off their hostess's offer, but

Cassidy grabbed a pitcher of iced tea and a set of cut-glass tumblers from the cabinet and presented them, anyway. "Okay. You've got the ring. Who gets the first call?" she said as she poured four glasses.

"Easy. Mamaw," Cam said. "Not sure she'd show up to the wedding if she didn't."

"That's petty and I like it," Trishy said. She'd never met Cam's Mamaw, but she felt like she had. Finally coming face-to-face with the woman who had raised Cam was one more reason to look forward to Camryn and Jeff's eventual wedding. Based on the stories she'd heard, Trishy imagined a ladylike first impression masking a no-nonsense core, someone warm enough to spoil an orphaned granddaughter but too disciplined to allow indulgences.

"Anyway. Enough of that." Camryn brushed the statement away with a wiggle of her hand in front of her face and took a sip of tea. "Let go and let God, right? I'm glad we can all be together. It feels like we haven't seen each other outside of church in ages." She grabbed a veggie chip from an oddly formal gold metallic serving bowl and took an emphatic bite. "Also, Savannah, you can pay me back for these whenever it's convenient, by the way. I think it was five dollars. Maybe six. Whole Foods is so overpriced. Seriously, though—no rush."

Trishy hated when people talked about money, and Camryn's way of working it into conversation made her especially uncomfortable. The problem wasn't that she had a tendency to nickel-and-dime even her close friends or even the frankness with which she approached the subject. No—it was that she somehow managed to be charming while doing it.

Still gracious as ever, Savannah nodded at Cam and helped herself to a chip. Trishy was glad to see it. The girl needed to eat if she was going to keep up with her husband's latest HIIT circuits. Trishy had seen Chad previewing a new routine online just a few days before, and given how frail she looked, Savannah was in no state to try it.

"I agree," Cassidy said. "It's been way too long since we were all together."

"I saw Kristin at the office today," Trishy said. Kristin wasn't exactly a friend, but she felt uneasy that the new girl hadn't even been mentioned yet in the context of their gathering. While Kristin wasn't technically part of their *social* group, she'd been asked to help lead the Mavens, and that should earn her some respect. Plus, Trishy liked Kristin. She appreciated her earnestness and her commitment to doing well in her first job. The way she presented herself could use some work, but that was no big deal. It had taken Trishy time to shed her formerly unremarkable Northern California aesthetic after landing in Charlotte, too.

"You were at the office?" Cassidy asked.

"Yes! I was looking for you," Trishy said. "To talk about the Twist sponsorship thing. It's all good, though. I ended up chatting with Kristin about getting Amber Lambert involved with the gala. It was a productive conversation. She's so sweet."

Sweet (along with *precious* and adjacent phrases like *sweet boy* and *precious moments* and other phrases like *hard season* and *blessed beyond measure*) had all been added to Trishy's vocabulary since she'd moved to North Carolina. Sometimes, they felt a little insincere coming out of her mouth—but not now. Kristin was sweet. *Sweet as pie*, in fact.

"Sweet but incompetent," Cassidy groaned. "Well, actually, maybe she's competent. I don't know. Something about her just bugs me. Maybe she's a little rough around the edges? I wish Kyle had been able to find anyone else for the job. Literally, anyone else. I know it's terrible to say that, but this is a safe space, right? Dealing with her is a real challenge for me."

"Should we head into the family room?" Camryn pointed toward the vague transition from kitchen into vaulted ceilinged space, the room where Cassidy and her husband had been known to host game nights and Bible studies. Trishy loved the attempt to distract their hostess from the gossip about Kristin. She knew Camryn felt blindsided by the strained relationship between the pastor's wife and the latest recruit to the Mainframe team. Kristin had been invited to join the group so quickly after being hired at Moving Word that there hadn't been time to ensure everything was copasetic. It would be hard for Camryn to admit that it had been a strategic move, but Trishy imagined that this was the bottom line. Now the situation was awkward for everyone. To her credit, Cam seemed to be doing her best to minimize it. "Didn't you redo some things in here? I want to see." Camryn grabbed the bowl of veggie chips and started to make her way out of the kitchen before Savannah and Trishy could stand up from their rattan stools.

Trishy followed Cam into the family room, which had been repainted since her last visit. Once a pale gray, the walls were now covered in a deep navy blue that made the pale, crisp furniture decorating the space stand out even more.

"It looks great in here," Cam squealed. "Is this Pottery Barn?"

"It's actually custom," Cassidy said as Camryn ran her hand over an armchair across from the couch. That was new to the room, as well. "You just get to a point where you want to spend the money for quality, you know?"

"Absolutely," Cam replied. "That's been my philosophy lately, too." This was the first Trishy was hearing about it, which was weird, given the number of shopping trips they'd taken together in recent weeks.

"I think that one girl from *The Bachelor* has that coffee table," Trishy added, pointing at the fluted, asymmetrical piece in the center of the room.

"Are you sure you didn't see it in *Architectural Digest*?" Cassidy replied.

Trishy shrugged. She knew the pastor's wife had indulged in her fair share of reality television over the years. It was how she'd known to go out of her way to engage with Savannah and Chad when they'd started attending services at Moving Word two years before. Trishy knew now that the Trumans had made the decision at the recommendation of the Maxwell family's PR team, who had suggested it as a church home for them shortly after their wedding, noting that the up-and-coming congregation would be a "better fit" than the more traditional Baptist church where the extended Truman line had been worshipping locally for several generations. It had been a good call, especially in light of what had happened since. It didn't hurt that it meant she'd get to worship alongside Trishy and Cam, who she'd met a couple of years earlier through mutual friends around town.

Anyway, Trishy was pretty sure Cassidy didn't even read *Architectural Digest*.

"What else has been going on with you girls?" Cassidy asked, lighting a trio of stump-sized candles on the mantel. She tucked the matchbox behind a large black-and-white photo of her and her husband printed on canvas—the two of them backed up against what Trishy figured was an abandoned barn somewhere, Kyle looking somewhere off into the distance while Cassidy wrapped her entire body around his arm—and settled herself cross-legged on the rug. Cam mirrored her movements and found a spot for herself on the other side of the coffee table. Savannah sat between them. Trishy claimed a bulbous burnt orange armchair.

"Well, y'all know I'm spread pretty thin. It's been so nonstop with ministry stuff lately that we've barely been home. The house feels like such a mess! I'll have to talk to the cleaners. We have them coming twice a week now."

Where had the cleaners gone wrong? The errant throw pillow on the couch? The quarter-sized burst of chandelier-illuminated dust on the mirror? Trishy's apartment—*that* was a mess of abandoned seltzer cans and loose chargers sticky with hairspray.

"It seems like the travel has been going well, though!" Cam said. "I've been watching all the sermons online. Kyle's doing great."

"I also saw that speech you made to the women's group in...was it Kentucky?" Trishy added.

"Arkansas, actually," Cassidy said gently.

"You should totally do more speaking," Cam said.

"Maybe," Cassidy said. "But I'm tired of talking about me. I was keeping a close eye on what y'all have been doing with the Mavens while I was away. That post about sexual discipleship was so, so good."

"Savannah wrote that one," Cam said, pointing to Savannah. "I loved it, too."

Savannah nodded.

Trishy knew the post the other women were talking about. Don't count on movies or your friends or even your own instincts to help you prepare for your first night alone with your husband, it read. One of the best things I ever did was seek out an older married woman I trusted for advice on what to expect and how to prepare. I felt so much more confident heading into the honeymoon after having coffee with her a few times. I would never speak for my husband, but I think he feels the same way about the biblical counseling he got, too. Not that I'm going to spill any of the details of our wedding night!

Trishy had offered Savannah moral support while she was writing the post, which was well outside the typically shy woman's comfort zone and (annoyingly) required a few signoffs from Chad. Her own thoughts about sex had changed since she'd made her way to the church, but she still didn't quite understand why it was okay to talk openly about bedroom activities in the context of "biblical counseling" yet shameful to bring it up anywhere else. Given her marital status, she rarely let things get that far with a guy these days—and when she did, she didn't chat about it with anyone, least of all the older wives at church. Keeping those details to herself was one way she could hang on to the sexual agency she'd been raised to fight for.

It was posts like Savannah's that served as the starkest reminder of how different the world she'd started in was from the one where she'd landed. Trishy had been surprised by how many views and shares the post had garnered since it went live on the Moral Mavens page. Apparently, there were plenty of other women in their community who'd grown up in a world similar to Savannah's and who aspired to a similar path with respect to sex. At the end of the article, an affiliate link prompting readers to browse an online lingerie and toy shop founded by a Christian couple had yielded a surprising conversion rate. Trishy wondered if the owners would be interested in partnering with an unmarried gal for future campaigns. The answer was probably no.

"I'm happy it's been useful for people," Savannah said. She was always so sweet. So humble.

"I'm sure it has been," Cassidy said.

"I *know* it has been," Cam said. "All you have to do is read the comments!"

Trishy watched Savannah sip on her tea and looked down at Cassidy's rug, a blue and green design that had to be another new addition.

"Another thing, Savannah," Cassidy said. "I've been hearing such good things about that group you and Chad are running. It's so cool that you've been writing the meal plans for it."

"Thanks." Savannah nodded. Trishy was relieved to see her brighten a bit. "Chad said he'll run it again in the winter if people want to sign up."

"I think he should," Cassidy said. "We'll really need it in the winter. You know how it goes, everyone letting themselves go with all that Christmas food. No one wants to go to the chubby church! Have y'all had a chance to try the workouts?"

Trishy shook her head. "I know I should," she replied. "That's why he needs to do it again."

Blessed with a quick metabolism and her dad's lean build, Trishy had never had to work especially hard to keep her figure. Someday, she knew she'd have to come to terms with the fact that health was more important than any number on a scale, but for the time being, she was content simply to feel comfortable in her clothes.

"People are going to want to look snatched for the gala, too," Cam said. "Did you know Chad finally taught me how to do a burpee? If he can manage that, everyone is going to look fire for the ProtectUS party. Cassidy, do you know what you're wearing yet?"

"I have a few options," Cassidy said. "I just want the whole night to be perfect. ProtectUS means so much to us, you know? I hope people keep donating."

"Oh, they definitely will," Cam said confidently. "The Mavens are so into it, and we've been linking to it everywhere. Speaking of, I still want to help. We'll literally do anything you need. Does the gala have a theme yet? I was trying to think of other G words that sound expensive. I got *gem, garnet, glamorous,* and *generational*. What do you think? I can draw up some logos."

"If you could keep sharing about the event and

the fundraiser, that's huge. More than enough," Cassidy said. "We're handling most of the details in the office."

"It looked like Kristin has a pretty serious to-do list," Trishy said, recalling her conversation from hours earlier.

"You should delegate, then! Are you sure there's nothing I can do?" Cam asked, disappointed, perhaps, to miss the first round of assigned chores. "You know I love a task!"

"Well, we need your followers, so we really do appreciate all the promotion. Sex trafficking is *such* an issue. Raising more money for the cause is what's most important," Cassidy said, scratching her temple. "I'll let you know when other things come up, but we have to stick to certain vendors. You understand."

"What do you think about incorporating one of those words into the name of the gala? *Garnet Gala for Goodness?*" Cam asked, seemingly ignoring Cassidy. "Like you said, the night needs to be perfect."

Trishy didn't like Cam's suggestion, but she would never say so. She could tell from Cassidy's face that she wasn't fond of it, either. Trishy shifted uncomfortably and tried to catch

Savannah's eye, knowing neither of them wanted to play negotiator.

When Cassidy spoke again, her voice was clipped. "I love your enthusiasm, but honestly, the best thing the Mavens can do is help us raise more money. It's that simple."

From the crestfallen look on Camryn's face, it clearly wasn't what she had been hoping to hear. Trishy knew that her friend had been dreaming of the glory of a more active, creative role. Some version of a movie montage in which she and Cassidy were frolicking through evening gowns and flatware samples had surely been flashing in her brain for weeks. Asking followers for money wasn't nearly as fun. Even Trishy could admit it, and she had no problem asking her followers for money by shopping her affiliate links and using promo codes (usually TRISHY20 or something similar).

"Well, we would love to do more," Camryn said.

"Just let us know," Trishy said, hoping to force a pivot and cut the tension. What was the point of gatekeeping party planning? Cam could take things too far, but Cassidy was the one making it weird. "We're all on the same team."

Cassidy's expression turned serious. "Same team or not, the party isn't about any of us. It's about ProtectUS. And for the good of the church as a whole."

Trishy crossed her arms over her stomach. In high school, she would have taken Cassidy's tone as an invitation to escalate the argument. Now she had to be above that—and she didn't have anything nice to say.

"That's what I mean," Camryn said, her voice stumbling a bit. "It's synergy, you know? We just want the Mavens to be able to highlight Moving Word. That's always one of our biggest goals, but especially now. And the fundraising. Anything I can do to help, I'm here."

"And we know how big the cause is," Savannah said.

"We will absolutely keep that in mind," Cassidy said. "Let's talk about something more interesting."

"The gala is *super* interesting," Camryn said.

"I have some other news," Cassidy said without so much as a nod toward Cam's sworn interest in the gala. "I can't believe I'm saying this, but Kyle and I are kind of—a little bit—starting to talk about trying for a family."

Cam immediately began squealing and reaching out for a hug, the gala and any related frustrations forgotten. Savannah was quiet but smiling, clapping her hands quickly in front of her chest as her friends unraveled from each other.

"I shouldn't say anything more because it's all so new," Cassidy continued, still blushing. "Kyle wouldn't want me blabbing. We've been praying about it, though, so we'll see!"

"We can be praying for you, too," Cam said.

"Definitely," Savannah said.

Trishy helped herself to another veggie chip.

The women stayed for another hour, snacking and chatting about upcoming church events, the still-to-be-finalized winter menu at 12th Pine, and a Nordstrom sale that promised to be the best of the year. Trishy was glad to have moved past conversation about the gala, to see her friends ease back into their usual dynamic. Camaraderie with other women, she'd learned, knew no religion.

8

Kristin

It was humiliating enough that Kristin was home again, living not only with her parents but also among her mother's collection of wooden signs bearing various verbs, maxims, and instructions—COZY UP AND SETTLE DOWN; AS FOR ME AND MY HOUSE, WE WILL SERVE THE LORD; EAT; LAUNDRY—and what had to be a higher-than-average number of her own high school graduation photos hanging throughout the house's wallpapered rooms.

On top of that, she was still employed in the administrative office at Moving Word, the church her parents had discovered while she was away at school after they'd grown bored of the more conventional congregation they'd attended throughout her childhood. Kristin could still remember the gleeful phone calls she'd gotten from her mom after those first few "hip" Sundays. *Just wait until you hear the music! It's like a rock concert. There's this one pastor named Kyle Welsh, and the way he preaches, he might as well be a young Bruce Springsteen.* It wasn't that Kristin had walked across the stage at graduation with a specific professional plan in mind, but she realized now that she'd made those steps with the confidence of a person whose hard work had always, historically, resulted more or less naturally in something impressive. She'd worked hard in college to earn her business degree and had assumed that would mean something important. She'd trained hard for races and had countless medals and trophies to prove it.

Despite her best attempts at an ongoing winner's attitude, life as the office assistant was far from thrilling. Kristin felt especially ashamed to be caught in what felt like an ever-simmering conflict with the pastor's wife, a woman who was universally adored by everyone in the community, including Kristin's own parents.

But now her mom had arranged a playdate for her on a Friday night, and it really couldn't get more embarrassing. She really hoped it wouldn't get back to Cam and the other Mainframe girls. As if she wasn't already self-conscious enough about being new on the job and newly part of their circle.

"It's not a playdate," Rae laughed as she arranged snicker-doodles on a platter on the kitchen island. "I wish you'd stop calling it that."

"You're organizing cookies on a plate for us," Kristin said. She wasn't trying to sound unkind. It was just that she'd never been given a manual for how to handle it when one's mother invites a couple of strangers who she promises are "about your age"—one's age being twenty-two—over for the evening.

"Do you think I'd leave you with nothing to eat?" Rae said. "Now, I really think you're going to love these kids. Charlie and Cara are twins and seniors at UNC. Home for the weekend, I guess. And I think Rory graduated this past May like you."

Charlie, Cara, and Rory were the children of two of Rae's friends from Moving Word's Craft Cafe, an organization of women who met on the first Friday of every month for a few hours of "creativity and Christly chatter," according to the note Kristin typed up in each week's member newsletter. Crafters could bring their own projects or sit in on a tutorial led by a congregant who specialized in a particular skill. Tonight's Craft Cafe featured Patti Sherman's lecture on crocheted Bible satchels—this time for a ten-dollar admission fee that, like everything else at church lately, would benefit ProtectUS—and Rae and her pals had evidently decided that it was about time they rally their grown children for the sort of parent-imposed bonding that Kristin had dreaded even as a preteen. The playdates arranged by Rae had disappointing results back then, and Kristin's hopes were no higher now. She'd always found her people on swim teams. It was one more reason she felt lost without the sport.

"I don't want them to feel like they have to come over here," Kristin told her mom, picking at a stain on the hem of her sweater. She'd have to be sure not to wear it in front of Cassidy or the Mavens. "They probably have better things to do."

"Better than hang out with you? I doubt that. Are any of *them* helping to plan one of Charlotte's biggest parties of the year?" Rae stood back to admire her cookie arrangement. "Anyway, they're all in the same boat as you. I really do think y'all are going to get along."

Having spent the majority of her childhood and adolescence strapped into her mother's minivan sucking mindlessly at the chlorine-soaked end of her ponytail, Kristin had never been one to argue with her mom. The ample time they spent together in close quarters without anyone else to turn to would not have allowed for walking on eggshells or for the squabbling Kristin had so often observed between mothers and daughters in movies and on television. Plus, it hurt her to see her mom hurt. She wanted to be a good daughter almost as badly as she wanted to be a champion swimmer. She'd achieved both, and where had it landed her? Back home, with no prospects for a long-term swimming career, longing as much for her days back in the pool at Queens University as she did for friends who hadn't been selected for her by the church craft club.

Shortly after Kristin's mom finished setting out a tray of fruit between the cookies and a bowl filled with glitter-dusted pinecones fragrant with acrid evergreen spray, there was a knock at the door. Rae traded places with the three young strangers who'd been waiting with their mothers—they did, to be fair, look to be about Kristin's age, which was at least a baby step in the right direction—and before long, Charlie, Cara, and Rory were leaning around the kitchen island, devouring the snacks that had been laid out for them.

"You're friends with Camryn and Savannah and Trishy, right?" Cara asked, one hand over her mouth as she finished a bite of a cookie. She was wearing a T-shirt with Greek letters that Kristin couldn't identify. "Those girls are so cool."

"I'm getting to be friends with them," Kristin said. "They asked me to help them run everything with the Mavens."

Cara nodded thoughtfully but remained silent as she chewed the remainder of the cookie, her mother's lessons about the importance of basic manners apparently more important than getting the inside scoop about Camryn Lee Cady and the rest of Kristin's alleged girlfriends. Only a subtle glint in her eye betrayed that she might actually be impressed.

"That's the TikTok thing, right?" Charlie asked. He'd been playing the edge of the counter like a drum set with his two pointer fingers since he'd arrived.

Kristin nodded.

"You're not on their feed much," Rory chimed in. She'd made a point of refusing a cookie and was poking at a strawberry wedge with the tines of a plastic fork.

"The social media part isn't really my thing," Kristin told her, aware for the first time that her conscious choice to let the others take the spotlight might put her proximity to them in question. She helped herself to a scoop of the fruit salad and popped a piece of watermelon into her mouth with her fingers, immediately regretting that she hadn't reached for a fork or a napkin first. Rory seemed like the kind of girl who would assume that Kristin was only pretending not to care that she didn't feature in the Mainframe's carefully curated content.

"Is that your full-time gig or what?" Charlie's fingers were still moving.

"For now," Kristin told him. "Well, working at the church is. I was pretty busy with swimming in school, and I missed out on a lot of networking and interning. I'm an assistant in the Moving Word office. It's okay, though. I'm saving money."

"So you're like *really* into church," Charlie said.

Kristin shrugged.

"I had an internship at Wells Fargo this summer, but it was unpaid," Cara said. "Our dad says it will look good on my resume, but I mostly got coffee."

While Kristin was only occasionally responsible for *getting* coffee for Kyle, Cassidy, and the rest of the church staff, she did spend an inordinate amount of time staging coffee stations and buffet lines for various meetings and events. Each time Kristin had been tasked with fetching coffee for the pastors, she'd been reprimanded by Cassidy in some way, whether for her lack of speed or her sloppiness. Still, she'd made herself an expert in what Camryn might call "the space," collecting enough firsthand research to write a thesis on serving caffeinated beverages. Oversized urns should never be placed within eight inches of a table or counter ledge, because even if you *think* they won't be disturbed by a curious child or a clumsy man during fellowship hour, they will be. Dessert- or appetizer-sized paper plates—while cuter than their full-sized counterparts—are never to be offered as the only available serving vehicle for flaky pastries, particularly not in any proximity to carpeting or other fabrics that do not take kindly to crumbs. Even women who *say* they only drink skim or oat milk with their coffee will, eventually, inquire quietly about the availability of "just a teensy bit" of half-and-half because "you know, it's the weekend and all."

But there was no need to share any of that with the rest of the playdate attendees. If she knocked it out of the ballpark with the gala, her coffee days could be numbered, anyway.

"I teach seventh-grade science," Rory said.

"Do you know Savannah? She teaches music at Dolley Madison."

"I know her, but not from work." Rory finally ate the strawberry. No one added anything while she chewed it. Kristin didn't know how to act when the Maxwell family drama came up in conversation, and she didn't feel right gossiping about Savannah. "I teach in another district."

"She seems really nice, though," Cara said. "And isn't her husband the one who runs that fitness class that all the old people go to? He's hot. They're basically the perfect couple."

"You know who else seems cool?" Rory said. "Cassidy Welsh." Here, she turned her attention to Kristin. "Like, cool and nice but mysterious.

Have you been to their house? I've heard it's sick. Is it true they have an indoor pool? I almost wish I qualified for youth group still so I could go to a meeting there."

"I haven't been yet." Kristin hadn't been invited.

"I was hoping they'd have that big party at their place," Rory said. "But I guess they're having it at that lame ballroom instead."

Was the ballroom really lame? Had Kristin missed the moment when she was supposed to protest the selection and suggest a cooler alternative? Had Cassidy laid out a trap to prove that they'd hired the least cool recent college graduate in the greater Charlotte area?

Now she was just being paranoid.

"At least you get to go," Cara said, sighing. "The tickets are so expensive. Plus, our parents say the whole human-trafficking thing is 'a racket.'" She used air quotes on the last two words. "They like the other pastors better."

Charlie nodded. "I get it. Kyle kind of creeps me out. I don't think I've ever seen him blink. His shirts remind me of, like, adults playing kids on TV. And Cassidy seems like she should be on one of those shows about housewives."

"Last time I went to church, I talked to Cassidy about how hard it is to meet nice guys around here," Rory said. "She's super sweet. I asked her if Kyle had any single friends."

"What did she say?" Cara asked, looking hopeful.

"She said no. Well, she said they're too old for me."

Kristin couldn't imagine confiding in Cassidy about her love life. Most of their conversations revolved around the logistics of youth group events and whether copies should be printed double- or single-sided. While Kristin had a laundry list of small incidents with Cassidy she could dwell on, their most memorable exchange to date had taken place in July, when Kristin had stayed at the office until two o'clock in the morning to help the pastors organize donations that had come in at a charity barbecue. Cassidy had looked surprised to find Kristin set up in a conference room with stacks of cash, all of it collected from the oversized cardboard boxes assigned to each of the four hired pit masters. "We're a little overeager with that money, aren't we?" she'd said, popping her head in on her way to Kyle's office with their travel coffee mugs. "Don't let those fingers get sticky." If Cassidy was actually suspicious of Kristin, it didn't seem to bother her husband, but it had soured the already distant relationship between the women.

"I've seen plenty of cute girls around church lately," Charlie said. "Just saying."

Rory rolled her eyes.

"Well, that doesn't help *her*," Cara said, pointing at Rory. "Obviously."

"I mean, love is love or whatever," Rory added tepidly.

"Right," Cara laughed.

Rory nodded enthusiastically. "Speaking of which, did you guys hear that we finally have a gay guy at Moving Word?" Her eyes widened. "My parents are so mad. I told them to get over themselves."

Cara gestured to her brother. "We don't really pay attention to any of that."

Charlie chuckled and crossed his arms across his chest. "Just don't make any moves on me, and we'll be good."

There were plenty of people at Moving Word who *were* paying more attention than Rory and Charlie's family. In the three months since Brandon had started coming to services, there'd been plenty of gossip, even among Kristin's colleagues in the office. Apparently, a series of anonymous emails had landed in the inbox the pastors shared, each message increasingly insistent about how disgusted its sender was by the church's new member and the apparent lack of concern from its leaders about his "choices."

Kristin hadn't had the chance to meet Brandon yet.

"Do you guys want to watch a movie or something?" Kristin asked. She and her teammates back at school had fallen asleep on the couch in front of a lot of documentaries after tough practices. Her best friend, Dana, was legendary for her ability to conk out—snoring and all—in practically any location and in front of accounts of even the most heinous of cults, home invasions, kidnappings, and murders. Kristin probably owed Dana a call.

Charlie shrugged. "A movie's fine," he said. "We could go out, too. If you guys wanted."

Kristin hated that she had failed to consider leaving the house. Just because the moms had left them there didn't mean they had to stay. They were all adults, each of legal age to both drive and drink. Maybe a casual beer at a bar in town wouldn't be so bad. After so many years of limiting her drinking due to swim team rules and her own fitness concerns, her relationship with this sort of booze-eased socializing was mostly brand-new.

"It's fine," Rory said, grabbing the bowl of fruit. "We should just stay here." Maybe she didn't want to be seen out with Kristin and the twins.

"Yeah, let's just chill," Kristin said, leading the way to the TV room. "I have to be up early for a meeting with the Mavens girls."

Cara groaned. "That's awesome. They're so cool."

Kristin may have been stuck at home with Cara while their mothers made crafts together, but she did have something going for her, if only by association. In the morning, she would get to be cool.

9

Trishy

As was too often the case (as far as Trishy was concerned, anyway), the pickings were slim on the dating apps the morning after she met with her friends at Cassidy's house.

For the last few years, she'd been monitoring her profiles in good faith—in every sense of the word. Trishy had a presence on every Christian dating app there was, even the unremarkable ones without promising fairy-tale testimonials and well-designed user interfaces. She'd gone on her fair share of dates. She'd made it her responsibility to the Mavens community to continue doing so, even when she didn't feel like it. Followers loyally tuned into her date recaps, cheering her on in her search for love from what felt like all corners of the world. She'd even helped plan a few mixers at Moving Word, all of which offered exclusive Moral Mavens swag to participants. Dating was the niche she'd created for herself within the Mainframe, and she was glad to have it.

She just wished she could get more excited about her prospects.

It was hard for Trishy to imagine having a weeknight dinner or going for a walk in the park (a popular proposition in her circles) with most of the men whose faces appeared on her phone screen that Saturday morning. Forget marrying them. There were so many pale blue button-down shirts. An astounding number of references to Matthew 6:33: *But seek first His kingdom and His righteousness, and all these things will be given to you as well.* (What exactly, Trishy wondered, were "all these things"? And what was all the fuss about righteousness?) It also seemed to Trishy that every marriageable Christian man in the greater Charlotte area was the owner of an Australian shepherd—sometimes of the miniature variety—who'd earned a spot in his profile photo, which could be a deal-breaker. Far more judgmental than her owner, Trishy's King Cavalier spaniel, Layla—who was at that moment curled up against her arm on a silk pillowcase—wouldn't stand for it.

Trishy had to keep trying, anyway. Her followers counted on her for advice about how to date with purpose, how to show up as their best selves for a date, how to (charmingly) create and enforce healthy boundaries, and how to find the kind of man who would love and lead in equal measure. *For the husband is the head of the wife as Christ is the head of the church, his body, of which he is the Savior. Now as the church submits to Christ, so also wives should submit to their husbands in everything. Husbands, love your wives, just as Christ loved the church and gave himself up for her.* That was Ephesians 5:23–25. It was old school, but there was obviously something to it. Even if it did creep Trishy out. And she wasn't just doing it for the Mavens! Trishy would really like a boyfriend. A person who could order her favorite dessert at a restaurant without consulting her. A person to compliment her equally on her outfits and her content strategy. A person who would share his jacket when she got cold, even if she didn't complain about it.

"We missed our shot," Trishy muttered to Layla as she continued scrolling. "That's what we get for dating all those randos."

Layla didn't so much as twitch an ear.

Trishy checked the time on her phone. Seven thirty. The Mainframe girls were set to arrive at Twist at nine o'clock. Trishy's boss, Claudia, had agreed to open the store to shoppers at half past ten—thirty minutes later than their usual Saturday opening time—to accommodate the meeting. She'd gratefully accepted Trishy's promises that the girls would post photos and videos from the boutique while they were gathered there. Claudia knew the Mavens' reach, and it was more than she could get for the shop even with Trishy's help. Twist was already one of the most popular shops in town, but an exclusive breakfast visit from the upwardly mobile Mainframe ladies could only add to its allure. Suburban teens would see Cam, Savannah, Trishy, and Kristin sharing pastries and prayer, surrounded by the store's winter dresses and wide-legged jeans. They would insist their parents drive them in from Davidson, Cornelius, Huntersville, and

Fort Mill to take them shopping. The Mainframe would have a pretty (Trishy-designed) backdrop for their monthly meeting. Trishy was good at helping everyone get what they wanted.

But she had to get moving. It would look bad to arrive late to her own workplace, the one that was doing her and her friends a generous favor—and, hopefully, making a donation to ProtectUS and the upcoming gala. Also, practically speaking, she was the one with the key.

Layla was in no rush to go outside, and Trishy could tell from the way her shoulder-length brown hair was falling against her cheeks that it was going to be a good hair day. It wouldn't take her long to get ready. She brought her phone up to her face again, this time for a quick look at the other dating apps, the ones she kept in a designated folder that she couldn't access without swiping through the home screen five times. It wasn't like she was going to *do* anything with them. It was only a quick look. For research, really. If Trishy had to bear the unwieldy responsibility of advising the broader Mavens community about how to navigate dating and singleness (which was perhaps an unfair responsibility), she had to know what they were up against in the secular world, too.

It was a relief not to be immediately impressed by any of these men. They were lighter on talk of righteousness, but still just as unexciting in their button-downs; toasting cameras with cans of beer; lifting dead fish in the air; their arms slung around friends, the better-looking of whom were almost certainly already happily married or soon to be. Single nonbelievers were no more enticing to Trishy than their God-fearing counterparts. Things were grim, but at least she didn't feel tempted away from the path on which God had set her since meeting Him at Moving Word. The mediocrity of what she saw helped Trishy keep the faith.

She exited the apps, ensured that they were tucked away and visible only in their hidden folder, and got out of bed.

Trishy wasn't so desperate for approval and likes that she went live to her sixty-one (almost sixty-two) thousand followers while getting ready for the day *every* morning. If she could remember to do it (and if she wasn't rushing around too much), she tried to bring them along two or three times a week—four if she was going somewhere interesting and had a cool outfit to go with it. She applied a thin layer of primer to her face, popped her phone into its tripod, and started recording.

"Hey, y'all!" Trishy said to her own reflection, leaning into the camera. She'd worked hard on cultivating *y'all* in a way that sounded natural. The viewer count at the top of the screen ticked up immediately. "It's so good to have you here on this beautiful Saturday. I was getting ready for a meeting with the rest of the Mainframe gals this morning"—a satisfying stream of heart icons exploded from the bottom of the screen—"so I thought I'd say hey. Let me grab some options from the closet, and we'll go from there."

Dressed in the ribbed pajama set that she'd changed into from the oversized UNC T-shirt she wore to bed, Trishy waved her fingers at her phone and retreated to her walk-in closet. She pulled a few items from the racks and hung them on the row of hooks she'd installed on the back of the door expressly for this purpose. The lighting in the bathroom was pretty good, and it was nice for her followers to be able to see pieces of Trishy's wardrobe hanging like they were merchandised in a store. Just because you wanted to spread a meaningful message didn't mean you couldn't look good doing it.

"I picked up this top at the boutique the other day, and I just think it's precious," she said, adjusting the hem of the rust-colored wrap sweater she'd settled on after holding up a few other options and letting the viewers weigh in. "It's a great color for the holidays, and just the right amount of skin." She pointed to the sweater's neckline, which dipped barely below her collarbone. "There are so many cute options out there right now that aren't giving it all away, you know what I mean?" She struck a few goofy poses. "Now, I know for a fact that both this top and these jeans are available on the Twist online shop, so you can grab them for yourself even if you don't live in the Queen City. There's a discount code for you in my bio! And if you *do* live in the area"—here, she pointed at her phone and screwed her mouth into a pout—"you better come visit me at the store!"

There was time to answer a few questions from followers while she put her makeup on, so she settled into the chair that lived tucked under her bathroom counter and waited to see what folks wanted to know. There were more than seven thousand people tuning in. Trishy scrolled through the comments with one hand and applied bronzer with the other.

> **adelaide_mcguire4:** Any tips for going thru a bad breakup? Love you and your spirit!

"Oh, girl, first of all, I am so sorry," Trishy said, blending her bronzer. "There's nothing worse than a bad breakup. Before you do anything else, I hope you've watched a few rom-coms and eaten some ice cream and cried to your girlfriends." Cam and Savannah had showed up to do this with her a time or two in the years since they'd been friends. "If you're watching this, actually, why don't you lift up Adelaide for a moment? Let's all love on her." Trishy paused to give her community some time to send heart emojis and supportive messages to Adelaide. In the meantime, she found the concealer she was looking for at the bottom of her makeup case.

"But the thing you have to remember is that

you can't chase what God sent," Trishy continued, invoking one of Camryn's favorite bits of wisdom. "If things didn't work out between you and this boy, it just means that He has someone better set aside for you. My advice would be that you spend some time getting right with yourself so that when the perfect guy comes along, you'll be ready. Your husband is already out there. It's only a matter of time before you find him." She tested the concealer under her eyes. "And there's no use being angry, either. If this boy hurt your feelings, he's not worth it, and the best thing you can do is to be praying for him, anyway."

Trishy still struggled with anger sometimes, but she'd had to learn to tame it, both for the camera and for a post-secular (for her) world. Here, people expected her to be a certain kind of woman. She blew a kiss into her phone and finished contouring her face.

> **made_for_joy11765:** You + the other MMM girls seem like such good friends. I just moved to a new city + am still trying to meet people. HOW???

MMM was the acronym that the larger Mavens community had come up with for the Mainframe girls—and many of them seemed to aspire to the friendships they saw among Trishy, Kristin, Savannah, and Camryn. To the outside world, all four of them were a big, happy family—and it was nice that Kristin was included in that picture, even if it wasn't entirely true.

"It's so sweet of you to notice our friendship," Trishy said. She opened her favorite Dior eyeshadow palette (gifted in a PR package) and selected a brush. Gold shimmer bloomed above her eye. "Friendship is something I don't talk about enough. It's easy to get wrapped up in finding a man, but surrounding yourself with people who love and challenge you is important."

Camryn had asked Trishy to join her for breakfast one-on-one after her second Sunday service at Moving Word, during which they'd immediately connected over their years in Chapel Hill. In college, they'd run in different circles and had never crossed paths, but adulthood changed things, and they started going to church events together. It was a good thing, too, because as much as Trishy liked the way she *felt* at Moving Word right from the start, she'd been a little insecure about how new she was to the faith. Regardless of all of her questions and the way she'd fumbled attempts to locate the indicated Scripture passages during the first few months of services she'd attended, Camryn had made Trishy feel comfortable. Like she belonged to a cool girl gang of a different sort than the ones Trishy had idolized back in high school, when a fleece-lined denim jacket perfumed with the earthy smell of weed had been the quickest way to popularity.

"I like to think that God put us in each other's lives for a big reason and at the right season," she explained to her followers, perfecting her other eye. "But you do have to put yourself in community if you want to find people to do life with. When I started going to church with the other Mainframe ladies, it was a big shift for me, and when I made that choice, I was bound to meet people who would encourage me in this direction."

Only a few months after first connecting, Trishy and Camryn had been introduced to Savannah at a mutual friend's game night. Since Trishy's crunchy Northern California parents had limited her access to TV when she was growing up, it wasn't until months later that she learned about her new friend's low-key television celebrity. This only made Savannah more likable.

"It's all about being intentional and authentic. You have to be unafraid to show your true self." Trishy looked her followers right in the eye, simultaneously deciding that she was pleased with the overall effect of her makeup. "Find a place where you can be in community with other believers. Be on fire for friendship. The right people will come your way as long as you show up as who you really are. I'm telling you. I know because it happened for me."

All that Trishy needed was a little eyeliner. She checked the time. There was just enough time to take Layla out for a quick walk before heading to Twist. "I can answer one more," she told her phone, scrolling through the comments as they rolled in.

> **xxheartofgracexx:** i'm on a budget saving money for my wedding but i want to come to the christmas party you've been talking about!!

xxheartofgracexx (whose real name was simply Grace) was a loyal fan. She was a junior at Wheaton College and had gotten engaged to her boyfriend on the first day of classes not too long ago. Trishy knew this because Grace had described the proposal to her in detail during several recent livestreams.

"I'm super excited about the gala, and I'm sorry that money is tight right now," Trishy said, careful not to explicitly encourage followers to shell out for tickets if they couldn't afford them. Bad financial advice was not meant to be on offer to her following—but she recognized that she showed them a lot of aspirational items with price tags attached. "But do you know what I'm even more excited about? That the party is for ProtectUS, which is an *incredible* anti-trafficking organization. It's actually so much more than a Christmas party. As a reminder, our church has a goal to raise—I know this is going to sound crazy, but we know with God all things are possible—five hundred thousand dollars for them before Christmas." More applause and prayer hand emojis. "I'm going to drop the Moving Word donation link in my bio so y'all can contribute.

So many of you tell me all the time that you wish you could come see us on Sundays, and this is a great way for you to join us in spirit. The other Mainframe ladies and I really believe in what this organization is doing and in the power of your dollars. If you can't buy a gala ticket, you can still participate in our efforts with whatever you can spare! I wish we could all meet on the dance floor IRL, but I promise to do some thinking about how else you can get involved, too." And she would. She would take that back to the rest of the group that very morning.

"I'm going to say goodbye because I've gotta get to Twist. I love you!"

She waved goodbye and ended the livestream.

She really did love all sixty-one thousand of them. Almost sixty-two thousand. By the end of the day, there would be sixty-two thousand. Thanks to her strategic tag, ProtectUS would absolutely share the video.

10

Kristin

Kristin had already been at Twist for twelve minutes by the time Trishy arrived with the key. Faking a phone call wasn't a cool thing to do, but it was cooler than leaning uneasily against the store's brick facade with nothing else to occupy her. When Trishy did appear, she was kind enough to play along, giving Kristin a few beats to say goodbye to the nonexistent person on the other end of the phone before approaching the entrance to say hello.

"Yep. She just got here, so I have to go. I'll call you later. Bye, Dana," she said into her phone, hoping the pretend call might serve as a reminder to actually touch base with her friend later that afternoon. It wasn't totally Kristin's fault that they were in dire need of a catch-up. After graduation, Dana had accepted a job on the coaching staff at the University of Tampa, so she was busy. Kristin couldn't be worried about that right now, anyway. Twist and the Mavens needed her focus.

Technically, it was Trishy who was right on schedule. Kristin just liked to be early. As the only late add to the Mainframe team, she still wanted to prove to Camryn—the rest of the girls, too, but mostly Camryn, who probably had the most influence with the Welshes—that inviting her to join their ranks had been a wise choice. Many a swim coach had drilled into Kristin's silicone-capped brain the importance of punctuality. Swimmers who were late for a race could ruin everything for their team, so swimmers who were tardy to practice spent an extra thirty minutes in the pool doing sprints.

It was a good thing all those coaches had been so tough, because Trishy looked like she needed an extra pair of hands. "How long have you been waiting? You didn't need to be here so early," she told Kristin as she leaned against the shop's glass door and riffled through her purse, presumably looking for the key.

Kristin grabbed one gold-chain strap of Trishy's bag and used it to pull the purse away from her body so it would be easier to search, balancing the bakery box of doughnuts she'd grabbed on the way on the fingertips of her other hand. It was possible she'd miscalculated and made things weird by beating Trishy there altogether. Nothing could be done about that now. All she could do was try to keep the good vibes going from their conversation at the office the day before, to help make their relationship feel a little more lived-in. "It's no problem," she replied. "I watched your live and saw you were leaving your apartment. I figured I'd pop over."

Trishy retrieved a tastefully bejeweled keychain from the depths of her bag and unlocked the door. "There's not much to set up," she said. Her eyes flashed to the bakery box. "You stopped for doughnuts and you're still early?"

"It's really no problem."

The shop flooded with light as Trishy flicked a series of switches hidden behind a rolling rack of clothes against the wall. "See? It always looks nice." She led the way inside. "Someone's a bigger overachiever than I realized."

"I only live about five minutes away," Kristin said, pointing vaguely out the window, unsure if she was actually indicating the correct direction. "And the bakery is basically on the way. I stop there to grab stuff for events and for the office all the time." Her eyes landed on a trio of white tufted benches and a floor-to-ceiling mirror positioned in the back of the store. Trishy had used them as the set for many fashion videos for the Mavens YouTube channel. "Maybe we can move those closer to the desk? We can put the coffee and snacks right on that counter and keep it away from all the clothes." You could never be too careful to prevent stains at a Mavens event, during which hands had a tendency to fly everywhere in praise and clapping and hugging.

"We could try that," Trishy said. "I'm just going to grab something in the back." She retreated behind a lush pale pink curtain hanging from the ceiling. Now alone in the front of the shop, Kristin could feel the weight of the stylish clothes around her. She'd come dressed in jeans and her favorite striped turtleneck, but she was suddenly sure she'd done something terribly wrong when choosing her outfit in the shelter of her bedroom that morning. Ever since inviting Kristin to join the team, Camryn and Trishy had been guiding her fashion choices, sending her links when they saw a great sale online and complimenting her when she showed up to church wearing something other than the fleece zip-ups that had composed ninety-nine percent of her wardrobe back at school.

"We only get one body to show up and praise the Lord with," Camryn had told her once. "There's no shame in making that body look its best."

At first, comments like this had made Kristin uncomfortable, but after getting to know the girls better, she realized it was all well-intentioned. Her old clothes were comfortable and designed to reinforce membership on a team, and she supposed her new wardrobe did the same thing. Kristin was making decent money in the Moving Word office and saving most of it by living with her parents, anyway, so she had some extra cash to spend on better-fitting jeans and tops that didn't sport the name of her alma mater or a cartoon rendering of its mascot. Sartorially and otherwise, the Moral Mavens meant a fresh start for Kristin.

Busying herself with the logistics of Twist's space and how it could work best for the meeting was a good distraction from the pressure of faux leather, linen, and synthetic wool—each fabric magicked together into pieces that now seemed like almost necessary alternatives to what Kristin had selected for herself at home.

She got to work. Work, she knew. Work, she could do.

Formal Mainframe meetings like the one set to happen that Saturday weren't a frequent occurrence—and Kristin knew they were really just glorified hangouts to which she merited an invitation. In the months since she'd become the official fourth member, there had only been one other such gathering. Most of the time, the girls lingered after church or met up for brunch to discuss Mavens business as it was necessary. Usually, casual discussions of that sort were more than enough to power the engine of the Mavens Mainframe.

Then again, Camryn could be full of surprises. I think we should get together for an official meeting! she'd texted the Mainframe group earlier that week. Lots of opportunities coming up for ministry and to connect with our girls this holiday season. The gala is going to be HUGE. We'll go live while we're all in the same place. We could use some new photos, too. EXCITING!

Kristin hated her current headshot, an image that had, since it started appearing on the Mavens' channels, markedly increased the amount of time she spent closely examining her face in the mirror. Had her cheeks always sat so low on her face? Did she always look so tired when she smiled? Perhaps it was *her* headshot that needed updating. Camryn didn't want to single her out, so fresh photos were in order for everyone.

Trishy had secured Twist as the venue, and Camryn had asked the other three girls to show up ready for the camera, preferably in winter styles that would look appropriate in Moral Mavens content in the coming months. Marin Bradley, a sophomore at Hickory Grove who'd recently been named the associate editor of the school yearbook, was set to arrive with her camera later. She'd been getting school community outreach credits for all of the hours she'd spent taking pictures for the Mavens.

"Good morning, ladies!" Cam called, breezing into the shop in a pair of camel faux-leather pants and a dark brown coat. Kristin would look silly wearing the same items. "I don't come bearing coffee, but Savannah can't be far behind with it."

"Good morning!" Kristin said. "I brought doughnuts."

"Of course you did. Our competent queen!" Camryn said. She squeezed Kristin into a hug as she made her way into the store, then shrugged out of her coat and tossed it carelessly onto the chair behind the cashier's desk. "With the vanilla cream?" It was well known that Camryn Lee Cady—yes, *that* Camryn Lee Cady—could not get enough cream-filled doughnuts.

"I got four cream-filled," Kristin said. "The rest are a mix. But no powdered sugar and no jelly because of—"

Camryn pointed at Kristin and smiled. "Because of the mess. That's perfect. You're always thinking." It would be nice if Cam would be willing to subtly communicate that sentiment back to Cassidy.

Trishy came through the curtain separating the back of the store from the front, a pile of long cardigans draped across her arms. "It's true. If we get jelly everywhere, Claudia will never let this happen again. Here." She handed the rose-colored sweater to Camryn, who shook it out to give it a quick glance before setting it down on a chair. "Speaking of Claudia, she said to give these to y'all." She tossed a navy blue one to Kristin. "She was getting ready to put them on clearance, but I told her we'd wear them for some pictures. We want to keep her happy so she comes through with the sponsorship."

Cam nodded. "Of course." Her brow furrowed as she took a closer look at the sweater. "I wish these were cuter. But Cassidy seemed really excited about the sponsorship last night."

Obviously, Kristin had missed something last night. "Will this work?" she asked Cam, gesturing to the store and doing her best to ignore the familiar sensation of having earned an invitation to one thing while being unceremoniously excluded from several others. She knew the other girls were close friends, but it still didn't feel good.

"This is a great setup," Camryn replied. "I never would have thought to move it all around like this."

"Kristin came up with the whole thing," Trishy said over her shoulder as she straightened a rack of flouncy tops near the door.

Cam whirled around on a camel-booted heel to face Kristin, a perfumed weather system all her own.

"I thought it made more sense like that," Kristin told her.

"It does. Nice job," Camryn said. "I love all of it." She moved her hands around in the air in the general direction of the newly created seating area. "Would you mind taking notes?"

Kristin nodded. She had a notebook in her bag. It would come off better, she thought, than using her phone.

"Great," Camryn said. "Maybe when you get home, you can type them up and distribute them to everyone? Whenever you have a sec, obviously. I'm sure you'll be better at it than our assistant at work. She is so *not* thorough."

"No problem," Kristin said. She told herself that Cam mentioning her assistant at 12th Pine wasn't meant to imply that Kristin was the assistant for the Mainframe.

"We can get started without Sav," Cam said, looking down at her phone. "I'm sure she'll be here in just a sec. She wouldn't want us to waste time."

"I agree," Trishy said. "Where do you want

to start?" The three of them were seated on the cluster of white benches and ready to begin; Camryn with a cream-filled doughnut in hand, Trishy empty-handed and looking as comfortable in her surroundings as anyone could hope to be, and Kristin ready with a pen poised over her notebook.

"I don't need to be the one to start," Camryn said, brushing crumbs off her pants. Kristin made a mental note to find a vacuum before they left. "Does anyone else have anything to say?"

No one said anything.

"I really would love to hear from you girls first," Cam said.

A few more moments of silence.

"I can go," Trishy said. "I was thinking maybe we could put something together about budgeting. Budgeting sounds like a drag, but we can make it cooler—money management, that kind of thing. I had a question on my live this morning about saving up for a wedding, and I feel like that's something everyone could benefit from."

"I think you're right about it sounding lame," Cam said. "We're going for maximum engagement here, you know? People aren't going to click on anything about a budget. It would bum them out. Maybe it would be helpful, but it's not a priority right now. We can come back to it later."

"It's time-sensitive because of the gala, though. The girl said that she can't afford to buy a ticket because she's saving," Trishy said. "That made me sad."

Cam looked unaffected.

"What if we made it holiday-themed?" Kristin ventured, making a note. If not for her association with the church's inner circle and the free seat it earned her, she wouldn't be shelling out the money for a gala ticket. It wasn't the kind of thing her parents had taught her to spend on, so she felt for the girl who'd asked the question—and everyone like her. "You know, like, saving up for gifts and stuff. College girls and new grads would love that." The rest of the Mainframe members weren't *so* much older than Kristin. Still, by bringing in the perspective of the college-aged Mavens from whom she didn't have all that much distance, she hoped she'd make herself indispensable to the group beyond grunt work.

The bell on the door rang out again and Savannah hurried in, balancing a tray of coffees in the crook of one arm and already apologizing for her lateness. "We got a slow start this morning and the line took absolutely forever," she said, divvying up the beverages to each of the other girls. Savannah's eyes looked a little swollen, her hair a few days past the good wash even Kristin could see it needed. There was a baseball cap on her head. She took her seat without taking off her jacket. "What did I miss?"

"Nothing," Camryn said, sipping the coffee Savannah had handed her. "Thanks for the coffee. Did I not tell you we were taking photos today? I thought I reminded you last night."

Another mention of some gathering the night before, when Kristin had been stuck at a playdate organized by her mother. Charlie, Rory, and Cara had been picked up by their own moms by nine o'clock, leaving the women of the Thatcher home to cozy up in their usual spots on the couch and hunker down for whatever true crime documentary popped up to stream first. Before leaving the den for bed, Kristin's mom had insisted on their usual ritual of praying for the victims *and* perpetrators, staring in earnest at the iron cross on the wall as she did.

"We were just talking about budgeting content," Trishy said. "Kristin thought maybe we could make it holiday-themed, which is so smart."

Smart! She was smart. Kristin made a few more notes:

- Holiday-themed budget guide
- Gift expense tracker
- Holiday charitable giving how-to... connect to ProtectUS!?!?!?

Savannah nodded as she sipped her own drink. "I've been reading through Proverbs over the last few weeks. So many verses about stewardship there. I could pull those out and write something about minimalism, too, if you want."

"What about that guy who teaches the financial freedom class?" Trishy asked.

"Miles Mason," Kristin said. She was responsible for maintaining the facilities calendar at church and was used to seeing his name listed there every Friday night. He also held the record—by a wide margin—for requests for IT assistance, all of which she forwarded directly to Moving Word's tech director. "He and my dad are friends."

"Anyway," Cam said, moving right along, "Sav, Trishy, and I can report back from an informal meeting with Cassidy last night. Cass said she's loving everything we've been posting lately."

"Is Cassidy getting more involved with Mainframe now?" Kristin asked. She'd often wondered why the pastor's wife had yet to take a more active role in their ministry.

"I wish she would," Trishy said.

"They're overextended right now," Cam replied quickly. "I talked to Cass about it a few times. I bet she'll want to get involved when their schedule opens up."

"Should I just ask her? Wouldn't it be good for us to add someone high-profile to the mix?" Trishy asked.

Out of the corner of her eye, Kristin saw that Savannah was looking down at her lap. Technically, the group already had someone high-profile.

"You don't need to ask her if I already asked her," Cam said, smiling but firm.

"If you're looking for high-profile, we could also maybe reach out to Amber Lambert," Kristin suggested. Perhaps dropping the name of the baseball player's wife would distract the group from Savannah's embarrassment, and from the awkward business of Cassidy Welsh altogether.

"True!" Cam squealed. "I've been meaning to talk to her about helping out with the gala, anyway. I wouldn't be opposed to having her join the Mainframe if she was interested."

"I owe her a text," Trishy said, pulling out her phone again. "Thanks for the reminder. Cassidy wants to get her involved with the gala, right, Kristin?"

Kristin nodded, worried that, in doing so, she was somehow slighting Cam. She kept her eyes down on her page of notes.

"I can also reach out to Amber," Camryn said. "I wish Cassidy had mentioned this when we were at her house. I specifically asked how I could help."

Savannah either shared Kristin's acute discomfort with the line of conversation or was completely ignorant. "Remind me of the date of the gala?" she said, pulling a giant paper planner from the tote resting against her feet.

"December 18," Kristin told her.

Camryn put a finger in the air as if to check the direction of the wind. "I still want to talk more about that. The Mavens should be more involved. Cass doesn't want to look needy. That's all. She hates asking for help."

That hadn't been Kristin's experience, but, whatever.

"Let's just not overstep," Savannah said, obviously skeptical.

"She asked me to help with sponsorships," Trishy said.

"I never said anything about overstepping," Cam snapped, the phantom of a whine dangling from her words. "And fine, sure—you're doing sponsorships, Trishy. I just think we should be *ready* with some good ideas. What do you all think of calling it the Garnet Gala for Goodness?"

"That's literally not the theme, though. Cassidy wasn't into it last night," Trishy sighed. "You know what we *could* look into, though? Do you think the Welshes would mind if we came up with a virtual conference or event to go with the gala? Like, followers could buy special tickets or something and everything they spend would go straight to ProtectUS? Cheaper than the real thing, but still." She'd started tapping her toe against the carpet. "It would be totally our thing, so we could make it whatever we want it to be, but I can't see why the Welshes wouldn't be excited about it. We could still link everything back to them and the church. What do you think, Kristin?"

It felt good to be considered, even better to be asked. She clearly hadn't merited friend status with the rest of the group, but she did spend more time with the Welshes than anyone else sitting at the boutique. "I think it sounds cool," she said. Kristin wasn't sure how cool her fellow recent graduates would find it, but she wanted to be a team player. "I don't see how it would take away from anything they're trying to do with the gala. It would just be an add-on."

"Exactly," Trishy said, nodding. "By the way, Cam, did you get the metrics back about that collab you did with Shepherd Lovely?" The question seemed sudden. "Maybe we could get them involved if we move forward with this. They could spread the word and amplify, donate some things for a swag bag at the gala. All of your posts looked really good, by the way."

"Aren't those devotionals just the most gorgeous?" Cam replied.

Shepherd Lovely's products *were* gorgeous—and expensive. Even with the discount code Camryn had secured through her collaboration with the trendy publisher, the price point was steep. Kristin hoped that Cam might gift them to the Mainframe team for Christmas. She had, after all, written an entire blog post and shot a series of TikToks about how the devotionals would make perfect presents for every occasion. Their products had always seemed overpriced, but Kristin coveted the Bible journal her mother had gifted her for her last birthday. When taking notes on its embossed pages, she was careful to use only her smallest penmanship to save space so it would last longer.

"Yeah, but did they get back to you about how the campaign went?" Trishy pressed. "They'd be such good partners. Cassidy loves them, too. She already ordered their planner for next year. I think she said she upgraded to the deluxe package with the custom cover and the special stickers."

"I don't think I've heard anything yet," Cam said, tapping at her phone screen.

"I usually get metrics back from brands within a few days," Trishy said. "You should ask."

"Interesting," Cam said. "I'll keep my eyes peeled. It was fun, though."

The Shepherd Lovely deal had been Cam's biggest partnership to date. Kristin had overheard her telling Savannah as much a few weeks earlier at church.

From there, the conversation spiraled into idle

brainstorming and chatter. Based on the glowing feedback from its participants, Savannah and Chad were starting another round of the wellness program, and she was happy to create some posts about it, with easy steps to a few exercises. Trishy was almost finished sourcing items for her modest winter fashion video. Cam had some ideas about preserving your purity during the holiday season that she wanted to get out there in a fun way. Kristin nodded along through all of it, making notes as she went and offering her assistance to each of the other women as she could. Once Kyle and Cassidy had approved the idea for the virtual event to coincide with the Gala for Goodness—if they even *had* to, which, in itself, the group was debating—there would be even more for her to do.

"Everyone feeling good?" Camryn asked. "Should we go live for a bit, then? Marin will be here in a little while to do pictures."

She didn't wait for a response. Instead, she immediately began fiddling with the gadgets, getting the phone properly locked into her tripod.

Even with the boost from her new clothes, Kristin still got a funny feeling in her stomach knowing they were moments away from a livestream—and a photo shoot after that. What would people think of her? She wished she'd spent a few extra minutes shaping her hair instead of getting the doughnuts. She wished she was allowed to wear it in the kind of ponytail that didn't require styling, too.

"Y'all ready?" Camryn said, fluffing her hair. "I have hairspray and lip gloss in my bag if you need them."

Kristin did her best to mimic what Camryn was doing to her scalp and took a deep breath. Along with the rest of the girls, she squeezed onto the bench only Trishy had been sitting on for the rest of the meeting, trying not to think about the fact that her All-American college swimmer's figure meant that she took up more space than any of the rest of them did. Camryn counted down and squeezed the Start button on the remote linked to her phone's camera. "Hey, Mavens sisters! Your Mainframe gals are comin' atcha on this gorgeous Saturday morning," she squealed. "We love you...and we have big—I mean, *big*—things coming for you! Have you heard about the gala?"

11

Savannah

Marin Bradley's younger sister Addison was in eighth grade and had been an enthusiastic member of Select Choir since starting middle school, so Marin hadn't been a complete stranger to Savannah when she started photographing the Mavens a few months before. Savannah had actually been the one to facilitate the whole arrangement. Mrs. Bradley—her first name was either Lauren or Audrey; it was hard to remember which—had offered up her older daughter's services at chorus practice pickup one afternoon in the spring.

"You know my oldest, right? Marin?" she'd asked, one hand on Addison's thin shoulder while the rest of the students filtered out of the music room, tripping awkwardly around the mother and daughter pair that had rooted themselves in the doorway.

It wasn't typically a good sign when the grown-up frame of a mom or dad filled the threshold of the music room at rehearsal, but Savannah had never experienced a problem with this particular family. "You must know all about the graduation projects they have the students working on up at the high school. Marin's only finishing up ninth grade now, but they're already pushing them to get started. I don't remember feeling all this pressure. Do you?"

Savannah could have told her that she'd been no stranger to adult pressures as a teenager—even if hers had centered more on upholding standards of modesty than they did on academic performance—but she didn't. The district's mandatory graduation project was detailed during the August all-faculty kick-off meeting for every new school year. In order to be eligible for their high school diplomas, students were required to mount a community service or creative project of their own design and present the fruits of their labor midway through their junior year. It was common knowledge that the project was fairly easy to outsmart with a signature from a generous Scout leader and a well-crafted five-minute speech.

"Well, Marin's been really involved with the yearbook this semester and—I might be a little biased—but she's gotten pretty good with a camera," Mrs. Bradley went on. "Isn't that right, Addison?"

Addison's head bobbed up and down, the ribbons in her hair bouncing.

"Anyway, I was thinking maybe Marin could volunteer with the Mavens." Mrs. Bradley tucked a lock of curly hair behind one ear. "I just think what y'all are doing is so important. These girls need good role models. Marin would be happy to help out with pictures. It would be amazing for her to see behind the scenes of what you've got going on—a bunch of women just a few years older than she is using social media for good, getting something started and making it happen."

The rest of the Mainframe—especially Cam—only needed to hear that Marin's services would be free and that her mother was already a fan of theirs. Before Addison had even performed her solo at the spring concert, her big sister had shown up to shoot a Mavens event: a wine and paint party at a local gallery that yielded precious images of members smudging acrylic landscapes onto canvas and pressing their paint-kissed cheeks together as they hugged. Savannah had been glad to have Marin on board; the photos would be useful, and she always liked to support a family from school—but she was also glad to have further proof that her students' parents weren't judging her harshly based on the headlines about her formerly famous family.

"Claudia's going to be here in twenty minutes," Trishy was saying through gritted, smiling teeth as Marin's camera flashed before them after the Saturday Mainframe meeting. "Cam, are we almost done?"

Marin lowered her camera and the four Mainframe members relaxed. They'd been pushed together on the white bench in the Twist try-on area, playing with various group arrangements.

"Is there anything we missed?" Cam asked the room. Kristin had stood up from the bench and was swinging her arms and pacing in front of the store windows. Trishy's eyes were down on her phone. "I want to make the most of the time we have together, you know?"

"Right, but I feel like we got a lot," Trishy said, her eyes still downcast. "Right, Marin?"

"I think so," Marin replied, looking down at the preview screen on her camera. As always, she'd shown up to photograph them in what Savannah assumed was one of her best outfits. This time, it was a pink baby doll dress—better suited for summer, really—and chunky brown mules. "These are all really pretty. You look really good."

"Did we get enough of that setup with Kristin sitting on the counter?" Cam asked. At her request, Marin had shot a series of the newest Mainframe member astride the Twist cashier's desk, looking serious. "People need to know that Kristin is the one running things at the office! She means business," Cam had explained when she'd suggested it. Kristin had been busying herself with doughnut crumbs, but Savannah could see her beaming.

"Definitely," Marin told her. "Kristin, you look really good in these."

Kristin nodded with a tight smile, a tacit

acknowledgment, it seemed, that what Marin saw in her camera was pretty. It was nice to see Kristin accept the compliment. Savannah was still getting to know her, but she'd always been kind and helpful. Whatever was going on between her and Cassidy around the office was silly, a big waste of time, the sort of thing that made Savannah grateful to spend more of her workdays with preteens than she did with adult colleagues.

Under the right circumstances, Cassidy could be sensitive. She'd get over it.

"Okay, okay." Cam's eyes flashed up to the ceiling. "I know we got Trishy and me. Sav, do you feel like we got enough of you?"

Savannah nodded and hoped Camryn would buy it. She'd come to the end of her increasingly limited attention span. After the years she'd spent in the show's spotlight and the countless publicity shots that went along with it, she would be more than happy to never pose for another picture again. While some of the other Mainframe girls seemed taken with the flashier aspects of being part of the team, Savannah would have been thrilled to give them up. The only good part about the photo shoots for *MAXimum Family* had been the time they afforded her with her siblings, especially as each one married, moved out, and started a family of their own. When the network asked for updated imagery, it meant a reunion for the Maxwells—an afternoon of posing, laughter, and silliness that was funded and endorsed by the very company already putting food on their table.

In her lowest moments, Savannah prayed to have all of her brothers and sisters back—her whole family back. For more than twenty years, they'd done everything together. Joanne homeschooled all ten children, which meant the Maxwells had not only lived and played together but also had spent in the same orbit the many hours that most children spent apart. Vance was more than Savannah's big brother, because he'd also taught her about fractions and dried her tears when kids at the co-op teased her for her glasses. Ruthie was more than Savannah's little sister and playmate, because they'd worked through their homeschool curriculum at the same pace and graduated in a ceremony at home on the same day. Together, all ten children had experienced a strange fame that almost no one else in the world could understand. This made it all the more frustrating that they couldn't reach an understanding now.

Now, being in front of the camera felt like something Savannah had to do to stay connected to her convictions and a new community, something she could do to prove to the outside world—even if she didn't quite believe it—that she felt no shame on behalf of her family. But she could only take so much of the pageantry. She craved a relationship with her religion that didn't require quite as many bells and whistles... but since she'd landed herself in a place where more was always more, Savannah could only pray that God was still leading her where she was meant to go.

Mrs. Bradley had installed herself at a nearby coffee shop while her daughter attended to the photo shoot, which meant that, within minutes of Camryn's dismissal, Marin had excused herself to meet her mother, reassuring the group as she exited that she'd have pictures edited and sent over in the next few days. Savannah had already decided that she would ask Mrs. Bradley if she would allow Marin to attend the Gala for Goodness as Savannah and Chad's guest. After all of her volunteering, she deserved it. Plus, if the Trumans purchased another ticket, it would be an additional drop in the fundraising bucket. Watching Moving Word galvanize around a cause had so far proven itself a boost to her faith.

"You know, I've been thinking," Savannah said as they restored the shop to its immaculate pre-meeting state. "We should make a big donation to the ProtectUS drive. Like, as the Mavens." She and Chad had already written a generous check from their personal account, but she didn't see why the Mainframe couldn't—or shouldn't, really—do the same. "I think it's an important gesture, especially if we're encouraging followers to contribute."

"For sure," Trishy said. "I have the donation link in my bio, but we should put our money where our mouth is, especially if I'm asking someone like Claudia to be a big sponsor."

"Kyle and Cassidy would love that," Kristin added earnestly. "I'm sure they're making a big contribution, too, right?"

"That's not really our business," Cam replied, her eyes pointed at the ceiling.

"I wouldn't be surprised if Shepherd Lovely wanted to match donations or give a percentage of whatever you brought in with your campaign or something. Did you tell them about the fundraiser?" Trishy added, ignoring Kristin and facing Camryn. "That's totally their thing. I can ask some of my brands, but if we get these other partners involved, the Mavens could bring in tons of money. It would be cool to leverage a collaboration like that and show our solidarity with the church."

"Do we think that's really our role, though?" Camryn asked. "Like, do we really want it to come off like the only way you can contribute is financially? It might set a bad precedent. I would hate for any of the Mavens to think that they should be ashamed if they can't donate."

"I don't think anyone would see it that way," Kristin said.

"That's the beauty of it," Savannah said. So much of the social media–centric work they did as a group felt squishy and nebulous to her. Making a donation, on the other hand, was a tangible way to make a difference. One of the things Savannah had struggled to process most in distancing herself from her family was their lack of real generosity. The years they'd spent on television had earned them plenty of money, and yet, they hadn't given any of it to the less fortunate or used it to support some other meaningful cause. "The girls that follow us who aren't in a position to give anything themselves will still get to feel like they're part of it because they're in our community. I think it would be great."

"How much money are we talking about?" Camryn asked.

"We must have some put away from the brand deals we've done," Kristin suggested. While Savannah hadn't personally been involved in most of the branded content produced by the Mainframe, she knew that there had been an uptick in those kinds of offers recently, and that her friends had collaborated on photos and videos in partnership with a local juice bar, a woman in Costa Rica who made leather jewelry, and a handful of various subscription services selling everything from sugared nuts to medical-grade skin care.

"I can give a portion of my affiliate income from the last couple of months, too," Trishy said. "And then Cam's new Shepherd Lovely gig."

"Let me check in with them first," Cam said. "You're so obsessed with that collab!"

"I'm empowering you," Trishy said. "You're in a *business* relationship with these people. You have a right to know what's going on."

Cam cocked her head and raised her eyebrows at Trishy but said nothing.

"I don't have any affiliate income," Kristin said, laughing. "But I'd be happy to give some of my own money. I was going to do that, anyway, but I think Savannah's right. It would be more impactful if it came from the Mavens."

"I'd give a little extra, too," Savannah said. "Cam, how much do we have banked for the Mavens?"

"I'd have to check," Camryn said. She was the hub for all of the group's collective efforts. "It's not as much as y'all seem to think, though."

"Moving Word is doing the kind of work that more churches should be doing." Savannah felt more energized than she had in weeks. It was a relief to see that she could still be so determined. "We should show our girls that we're behind it. And it might get Amber and Cassidy more excited to jump in with the Mavens, too. We can show Kyle and Cass that we're taking it seriously and committing as much as we can, that we're making ProtectUS and the fundraiser look cool and appealing to our followers."

When the bombshell about Carl and Angela came out, Savannah had seriously considered silently disappearing from Moving Word altogether and backing out of her commitment to the Mainframe. Was it fair to subject their church community to the nightmare of her family's downfall? Was it appropriate to impose her personal dramas on people who were just trying to have a good time while obeying God's word? For a while, she wasn't sure. But then, a hefty flower arrangement had arrived at their house with a card signed from "Your MW family," and Camryn had shown up with a plate of chocolate chip cookies from a bakery whose online price list Savannah had perused and scoffed at on more than one occasion. The Trumans were still welcome there. Plus, it would have done Savannah no good to lose her connection to the Lord at the very moment when she needed it most. Maybe spearheading this small part of the big donation that would be awarded at the gala was exactly what God had waiting for her as His still-loyal daughter. Maybe investing further in what was in front of her could help restore the faith she could feel herself losing with every month of negative pregnancy tests.

When they weren't airing assumptions that Savannah and Chad had grown their family in secret, bloggers loved speculating that she and Ruthie—who followers knew had stopped speaking to their relatives—would break away from God entirely as a result of the scandal. LOL to "Christian" values! they'd write. No doubt the bb Maxwell girls are about to find their freedom. Maybe Jesus isn't cutting it anymore. But that was ridiculous. Savannah's father's actions hadn't soured her on the fundamental beliefs on which she built her life. Savannah had always believed that God works in mysterious ways, and this was perhaps the most bizarre game of mischief He'd ever played. Still, He had not forsaken Savannah, and she would not forsake Him, nor would she miss an opportunity to redeem herself or her family in His eyes. One of those opportunities was right in front of her.

"I'm not making any promises, but let me look into it," Cam said.

"Kyle and Cassidy would really be thrilled," Kristin said.

"I hear you," Camryn sighed. "Trishy, you're going to talk to Claudia about the sponsorship and see what you can work out for dresses. Plus the Amber thing, I guess. Kristin, you'll keep us looped in on what you're working on at the office.

I'll start brainstorming about the virtual event, and Savannah, once I look into our finances, I'll let you know if you can take the lead there. Does that sound good to everyone?"

Marching orders received, all three women nodded.

Savannah gathered her bag and her jacket, then said polite goodbyes to Trishy and Kristin. As she attempted to manage a similarly quick moment with Camryn, her friend caught her in a hug and held her there for a few seconds longer than Savannah would have expected. "I'm so glad we're doing this together," she said. "You have the most generous heart. We're lucky to have you. I'll see you tomorrow morning."

She would.

Medical issues and family scandals and middle school musicals aside, Sunday services were a constant—even when Savannah wasn't sure she wanted them to be.

12

Camryn

"Are we making any progress in there?" Jeff called.

From her post in front of the bedroom mirror, Camryn could picture him sitting on the couch, his neat gingham button-down made a tad austere by the sunny yellow upholstery surrounding him. He didn't sprawl across sofas like other men, legs flung wide open, arms draped sloppily across any available surface. No, Jeff sat like a gentleman, his limbs tidy and his posture as respectful as the distance—not to mention the solid wall—he was keeping between the two of them without complaint as she prepared for church.

"Two minutes!" she called back.

Really, she was just about ready. She'd had her outfit picked out since Tuesday, when she'd arrived home to find a box of clothes from a new online boutique waiting at her apartment door. The shop was running a sale, so it had been the perfect time to place her first order, especially since there had been a coupon sitting in her inbox since April. Missing out on a good coupon was almost always financially irresponsible. Plus, she was planning to post a few photos and tag the boutique, which would likely lead to some freebies and maybe even a business opportunity. She could teach Miles Mason a thing or two about money management! If the other girls were going to insist on budgeting content for the Moral Mavens, it would have to be her responsibility to make it fun and not boring. She was up to the task.

Jeff's voice came back through her bedroom door. "Do you mean *real* two minutes or the kind of two minutes you tell me because you don't want me to get nervous that we're running late?"

Cam smirked at her reflection in the mirror,

charmed, as usual, by her man. "Real two minutes, sweets. Three, maximum."

She was dressed in a Peter Pan–collared floral sleeveless blouse tucked neatly into the waistband of a pair of wide-legged pale pink corduroy trousers. It was a different look for her—a bit funky, really—and she couldn't wait to see what the girls at church thought of it. More brands would partner with her if they saw her demonstrating some range, a flexibility beyond her classic standbys.

She applied one more layer of hairspray, gave herself a final up and down in the mirror, and presented herself to Jeff, who was not sitting on the couch at all and was instead lingering in a spot where he didn't usually: beside the chest of drawers where she kept her keys and mail. With all of the running around she'd been doing recently, the mail had stacked up more than usual. Jeff hated clutter.

"What's all this?" he asked, eyes still down. Frozen in her bedroom doorway, Cam didn't answer. Jeff picked up a few envelopes and flashed them so she could see. His expression was an unfamiliar one. An unhappy one. "These all say 'final notice.'"

Cam allowed only one hiccup in her throat before she took a step forward. "I have to call these companies," she said. She grabbed the envelopes back, fanning through them as if she hadn't before. "Somebody has their wires crossed somewhere. You know how poorly some of these companies are managed. There's absolutely no focus on customer service."

"I thought you said that class at church was—"

"Helpful. It was totally helpful," she said. "I just get a little behind now and then. But this is definitely an admin issue on *their* part." She tapped the envelopes with one finger.

"You know how I feel about this. I want us to be able to move forward—"

"I'll call them this week. I promise."

"We can't operate with secrets. This would be a big secret."

Camryn felt sick to her stomach. Jeff looked serious. "There's no secret. I'm actually just embarrassed you had to see them," she said, fearful she might be coming off more flustered than she ever had in his presence. "I didn't want you to worry about it, because I know how much it means to you."

"I didn't mean to embarrass you," Jeff said, sliding back into the same polite tone he used with his mother and grandmother back home, regaining the gentleness of the boy who'd chosen not to rush a frat in college in spite of the social capital it would have given him. His jaw softened, but the edge in his eyes remained. "I just want to make sure we're very clear about all of this."

"We are." Cam lifted up on her toes and kissed him on the cheek. "It's taken care of. Now, can you please look at what I'm wearing and tell me how pretty I am?"

"I really didn't mean to make you feel bad." Jeff rubbed the back of his neck. "I got nervous and—"

Cam tugged at her boyfriend's hand. "Can you please look at me?" she said.

Finally, Jeff's face lost its harshness, brightening as he took in the final product of her work in the bedroom, decidedly different from the sweat-suited version of her that had greeted him at the door an hour before. Just like every other Sunday, he'd arrived with coffee from one of her favorite local spots. Each week, he surprised her with a different beverage, which she'd sip at her kitchen table while he enjoyed his Americano and they talked about the week ahead. She could tell he was in an especially good mood when he picked something from the seasonal menu, since he was always going on about how all the extra syrups and flavors were unhealthy at best and a scam at worst. This morning, he'd presented her with a caramel pecan latte, which was a good sign. The conversation about the bills had only derailed them momentarily.

After coffee, they'd prayed together for a few minutes before she kissed him on the forehead and excused herself to prepare for church. Their Sunday routine was sweet, something Cam looked forward to every week. The only way she could think to improve it was to eliminate the part where they woke up in separate apartments. It would be that much better when they started their Sundays—and every day—in the same apartment. Maybe the same house, if they found the right place. Certainly in the same bed.

Of course, they couldn't make that adjustment until they were married.

"You look pretty. Let's get out of here," Jeff said. He pecked her on the lips, expertly preserving her gloss, then opened the door and stepped back to indicate that Camryn should go ahead.

"Don't let me forget that I need to grab Cass after the service," Cam said while they inched toward Moving Word. The church traffic was to be expected. Cam loved knowing that she was sharing the road with so many others who had opted to rise from bed on a day otherwise intended for rest—and for the sole purpose of being in fellowship with their brothers and sisters in faith.

"Mavens stuff?" Jeff asked.

"Yeah. We didn't quite get to everything I wanted to talk about on Friday."

"Friday? Was she at the class with Miles?"

Cam had forgotten the exact sequence of events that had taken place two evenings before, along with which of those events she'd shared with Jeff and which she hadn't. Not a single lie had been told, though, and she intended to keep it that way.

"You know we never run out of things to talk about, no matter how many times we see each other," she replied. "There's always more work to do. More ideas flowing." She'd looped her left arm into the crook of Jeff's right elbow so he could keep both hands on the wheel of his prized Tesla as she looked out the window.

Outside, there were lush green lawns, wide-porched farmhouses, and perfectly symmetrical subdivisions rife with big white SUVs and waterslides, now covered for the colder weather. "We talked a lot about the gala at our meeting yesterday, and I have all of these ideas for getting us more involved. By the way, did you ask anyone at work about making a donation?" Jeff's company was huge, with more money than Cam could begin to wrap her head around. All the late nights and weekends he'd been putting in had to have improved his standing enough to merit a sizable contribution to ProtectUS. She'd suggested that he encourage them to purchase a table—or two—at the gala, which would have the added benefit of serving as an opportunity for her to be seen among his coworkers on such a special night. By then, she might even have a ring to show off, an emerald-cut diamond on a thin yellow gold band to match the photos she'd sent him earlier in the year.

"Not yet," Jeff said. "It's hard to get time on Cliff's schedule."

"Well, you spend enough time with him." She wondered if she sounded bratty. Or sad. She felt sad—sad for the nakedness of her left ring finger, sad for the still unknowable number of wedding celebrations she might have to attend for others while still unsure about the status of her own relationship, sad for the door that had separated her from Jeff earlier that morning and that would continue to do so until they said their vows before God and their families. But only girls without faith openly sought the sympathies of their boyfriends by whining. Girls like Camryn knew that feelings were only temporary, that the Lord would always work all things together for good in His divine timing. That was the kind of example she wanted to set for the Mavens and anyone else who experienced her in real life or through a screen. Philippians 4:6: *Do not be anxious about anything, but in every situation, by prayer and petition, with thanksgiving, present your requests to God.* Cam thought she'd prayed and petitioned and presented enough.

Still, she wouldn't give up.

Camryn tried for a happier tone. "And this is for *such* a good cause."

"I know. I'll get to it," Jeff said. "We never talked about that class you took the other night. How was it? Miles Mason seems like a smart guy."

"Well, it was a lot of information," Cam said.

"Useful, though, right?"

"Oh, yeah. Like I said, I just haven't had a lot of time lately. And those final notices are a mistake. A big waste of paper."

"Global warming, right?" Jeff laughed to himself. "But if I can help you get anything sorted out, let me know." He turned the car into the Moving Word parking lot and approached an available spot. Even twenty-five minutes before the official start of the first service of the day, the crisp black macadam teemed with vehicles and well-dressed believers. "I'd be happy to go over it with you."

"You're the best," Cam said, glad that she'd already dismissed even a hint of frustration toward the handsome man in the driver's seat so that she could celebrate his kindness now. Plus, she could hear the things he'd left unsaid: *I want us to be on the same page so we can really start our life together. I want to make a family together.* "We can talk about it another time."

By the grace of God, he'd forget about the whole thing before the offering plate was sent around inside.

Episode 74: CAN TWO THINGS BE TRUE? with Influencer Trishy Collins | *Handling the Haters* Podcast

Daphne Webster: Welcome back to *Handling the Haters*, where I interview people who've taken hate from the public and who keep on keeping on. I've got something a little different for you this week, haters! Today's guest is Trishy Collins, a fashion and beauty influencer who has found a new niche for herself over the last couple of years. Buckle up, because I'm talking about the *Christian* side of social media. You all know I don't fuck with organized religion, but it turns out that Trishy is a regular listener, and when she sent me a DM introducing herself last month, I had a feeling this could be a juicy convo. Welcome, Trishy! Thanks for being with us.

Trishy Collins: Thanks for having me. I love your neon sign!

Daphne: Flattery won't get you anywhere here, Trishy. JK. But let's jump in. Tell me a little about how you found your way from fashion and beauty influencing to... Christian influencing? Is that what you would call it?

Trishy: I still consider myself a creator in the fashion and beauty space. Most of what I create these days just comes through a Christian lens. I still do a lot of my own stuff, but I'm also part of a group called the Moral Mavens, which is a little more focused on believers.

Daphne: Believers. Is that code for Christians?

Trishy: [laughs] "Code" sounds so sneaky!

Daphne: We get it. You speak a different language now. We don't need a story about getting saved or anything, but TLDR: How did you land here?

Trishy: I can tell you're not going to like this answer, Daphne, but I was led here.

Daphne: You're right. I didn't like it.

Trishy: [laughs] I warned you! Anyway, I was born in the Bay Area and found my way to North Carolina, then to church. It's just been, like, one sign after another. Life got easier when I stopped trying to ignore the signs. I'd met these amazing women who showed me what it's like to live in faith. Those are the same girls I work with on the Mavens now. We get to work closely with our church, which is awesome. It's all been super God-led.

Daphne: Can't relate to any of that but appreciate the transparency. When we were DMing, you said you get a lot of hate online. Tell me more about that.

Trishy: Well, it's kind of hilarious because—as you know, I'm a fan, so I've heard from a lot of your other guests and this feels like a very specific experience—when I was just sharing about fashion and beauty without being open about my testimony, people critiqued me for being superficial and vapid and stupid. But when my content started shifting to reflect my spiritual life, I started getting feedback from two different groups. Religious people still thought I was being superficial, but also said I was using God as a shield to be slutty online. And *non*religious people—especially everyone who followed me before I was going to church regularly—started accusing me of being homophobic and MAGA and basically, like, a terrible person.

Daphne: Are you homophobic and MAGA and basically a terrible person?

Trishy: [laughs] I don't think so. I just think people make a lot of assumptions.

Daphne: Can you blame them, though? I would think someone born and raised in the Bay Area would appreciate those concerns. I scrolled through your feed before we jumped on, and I gotta tell you: I have a visceral reaction to someone dressed like you talking about modesty.

Trishy: What do you mean?

Daphne: It's not like you're some nun.

Trishy: Daphne, I have lots of videos about modest dressing on *all* of my platforms. The Bible is actually surprisingly unspecific about what it looks like to dress modestly. I believe you can look cute and still honor yourself and the Lord by embracing your body and your femininity. That's one of the—

Daphne: But it's confusing. I'm just saying. I might be siding with the haters on this one a *little* bit. And you know I hate to say that. What do you think, haters? You better sound off in the comments.

Trishy: Do you want me to tell you how I handle the haters or not?

Daphne: Whoa. Chill. What would Jesus do, am I right?

Trishy: I think Jesus would be a hell of a lot more open-minded than you're being right now. Let me just say: Two things can be true. I was raised by feminists. *Raging* feminists. I lost my virginity when I was fifteen, and that wasn't the last or the only time I had sex. The clothes I post about might not fit everyone's modesty standards. But if you were paying literally any attention to my content, you would know that I'm not hiding any of that. I work through *all* of it in real time with my followers, because I think women should know that they can have self-respect and agency and *fun* and also a church community. Maybe it's messy for some believers—and I work through it with my friends and the Mavens all the time. That's exactly what I tell my haters, too.

Daphne: And how do they respond to that?

Trishy: Usually with a lot more grace than you're giving me right now. And when they don't, I block them and pray.

Daphne: Fine. Any final words for the listeners?

Trishy: Definitely. Support the big fundraiser our church is doing for ProtectUS! There's a link to it in my bio, or you can go straight to the Moving Word website. Haters like to do good, too, right?

Daphne: Sure. Just so you know, we got messages from a handful of listeners asking to remain anonymous who think that this fundraiser is bad news. People think the Walshes are sus.

Trishy: Do you mean the Welshes?

Daphne: Okay. Anyway, they think it might be a bad look for your friends to be associated with them.

Trishy: Well, I—

Daphne: We're out of time!

13

Trishy

It was inconvenient for Trishy that meetings of the Charlotte Creativity Collective were occasionally scheduled on Sunday mornings, but the good food and conversation almost always made the stressful rush to church worthwhile. This week, the women attending had the opportunity to participate in something cheekily described in the invitation as "Sunrise Speed Dating." *Rise and shine and get up and at 'em with some energizing conversation to fuel your creative process!* it read. *We'll bring the croissants and the coffee... you bring the great ideas and an open heart!*

Trishy would have felt better about her membership in the Charlotte Creativity Collective if she felt that the email copy was a little less exclamatory. She also wondered if people were still calling things "speed dating" when there wasn't any romantic intent involved. These were not concerns that she was prepared to raise with the collective's founders—Macy and Bryleigh, both lifelong residents of the Charlotte area who had only achieved *real* influencer notoriety when they started building communities of other influencers about influencing.

"You know all those times you've wanted to message one of your favorite creators to ask if you could pick their brain?" Bryleigh asked the hotel conference room full of gathered women through a microphone. "Well, now is your chance! And you don't even have to stress about treating them to matcha!"

This was true, but also a convenient time for Bryleigh to forget that Trishy and her fellow creatives were required to pay a not insignificant annual fee in order to be included in these networking events. Additionally, they received a curated package of products from local, women-owned businesses every month, but Trishy could have scored most of those items on her own. She didn't like feeling that she might be too cool for the Collective, so she considered her continued participation as an exercise in staying humble. Plus, the girls were sweet—and as much as she loved all things Moving Word and Mavens, it was nice to keep one foot partially grounded in the somewhat secular world.

Macy and Bryleigh had organized today's event so that each pair of women had five minutes to chat before they cued a Taylor Swift clip indicating it was time to rotate. If everything proceeded as scheduled, attendees would get twelve different pairings by the time the hour was up, but Trishy knew they should have added buffer time for everyone to dance and make small talk while passing from one arranged one-on-one to the next. If speed dating ran late, she'd have to make an apologetic, ladylike exit to get to church on time—and she knew she wasn't the only one. Charlotte was full of devoted Christians with all kinds of social media followings.

Trishy's first few matchups were women she'd met at previous Collective events: a girl named Kendra, who'd recently racked up a big following on CleanTok thanks to a new line of fragrance-free products she'd been formulating; a mom of four who'd been posting family vlogs on YouTube for the better part of a decade; and a dance teacher from the suburbs who'd learned to edit video during pandemic lockdown in order to offer step-by-step instructions on the hottest tween choreography. They were all kind enough, but Trishy didn't have much to learn from them.

Finally, after the fourth Taylor Swift clip blasted through the conference room, Trishy found herself sitting across the table from an unfamiliar face. The young woman (clearly younger than Trishy, which was upsetting, but whatever) wore a nametag that said DYLANN in friendly all-caps and an oversized green button-down that looked like it could have come from her dad's closet. "I'm Dylann," she said, sticking out her hand and standing up from her seat. Her unexpected formality put Trishy on edge. "I'm *pumped* to talk to you. I've been following you forever."

"Is this your first event?" Trishy asked. She'd already been squatting into a seated position when Dylann stuck out her hand, and she now let her bottom find its way to the chair. "I don't remember seeing you before."

"Second." Dylann took a sip from a pink travel mug with the Charlotte Creativity Collective logo. The founders had handed them to attendees at the door as they entered, each one stuffed with an index card reminding the women to tag the organization on social media if—when—they posted a photo of their new drinkware. Trishy had slid hers directly into her purse. Dylann's still had a sticker from the manufacturer on the bottom. "I'm new. Obviously," she clarified. "I actually work for my dad's insurance office, but a video I posted of myself singing went viral last year, so I figured I should see if there's anything else I should do with that."

"That's awesome," Trishy told her, genuinely impressed. The last time she'd attempted to sing karaoke, her girlfriends had gently grabbed her by the shoulders and walked her off the stage. This was years ago, before she'd gotten involved with church. Her Moving Word friends might be a little softer with her feelings, but that didn't make her a good singer. "How did you hear about the Collective?"

"My mom and Bryleigh's mom were sorority sisters."

"Cool." Trishy nodded, her eye catching the

clock above the door. If Dylann had questions for her, she better go ahead and ask them now.

"Actually, I know someone you know," Dylann said. "Kristin Thatcher."

Trishy understood that her role in this particular pairing was likely to offer advice to an influencer earlier on her path, but chatting about folks she and her speed date had in common would be way more fun.

"Really?" she said. "I love Kristin!"

Dylann nodded. "We went to high school together. I'm not sure she would say that we were friends, exactly, but we always had a few of the same classes. We were on the same soccer teams until middle school. She had to quit to focus on swimming. I always thought she was cool."

"For sure." Trishy nodded. She considered what she could say about Kristin that would ring true to someone who'd known her for years. Something both complimentary and honest. "She's a very hard worker. And very real."

"Absolutely. People were so shitty to her in school." Dylann's face reddened. "Sorry. I didn't mean to swear." She paused. "People were just really sucky."

Trishy—once the owner of a more colorful

vocabulary than she dared use now—ignored Dylann's apology. "What do you mean?"

"You know how it is," Dylann said, fiddling with the handle of the travel mug. "A girl who's really into sports, who never seems to have a boyfriend, who isn't around at a lot of parties. You'd think we'd be over all that by now, but I guess not. People are the worst. There was this really gross thing that happened in a locker room one time. The other kids got suspended. Anyway, I was so glad when she got that scholarship—and then when I saw that she's in some big-shot influencer thing now. Those girls who were such bitches to her must be so mad." She reddened again. "Sorry."

Macy or Bryleigh—Trishy wasn't necessarily sure who was who when they were dressed in similar outfits, as they were for speed dating and almost always—rang the bell indicating that Taylor Swift was a mere thirty seconds away from pushing the women to their next pairing. Around them, Collective members were exchanging social media handles and phone numbers, snapping selfies, and squealing over invitations to collaborate. Trishy wasn't doing any of those things. Instead, she was deciding how she might be able to squeeze more information out of Dylann without coming off as a creep.

"Tell her I said hi," Dylann said, recovered from her second cuss word of the conversation and beaming across the table. "Also, do you know Avery Adams-Wallace? She's my favorite tradwife. Well, like, favorite *fancy* tradwife. It's such a weird aesthetic, but I dig it."

Trishy shook her head. She and Avery had exchanged a few messages but nothing more. Trishy had no ambitions to be in the tradwife space—she'd have to be a wife first, anyway—but Avery Adams-Wallace was still one of the few influencers online who made her feel small. Given the chance to have coffee with her, she (unlike Dylann) would use the time wisely and ask for advice. Dylann had missed the point of speed dating, but Trishy was still glad they'd been matched up, and that the girl had shared what she did. For the first time she could remember—during the networking event or otherwise—she hated that Taylor Swift was playing.

As she pulled out of the hotel's parking lot, Trishy regretted skipping the breakfast buffet inside. After the poorly executed speed-dating event, there was no time to waste if she was going to make it to church on time, but she was hungrier than she wanted to be ahead of sitting in Sunday service for an hour or more. There would be plenty to eat at fellowship hour afterward, but Trishy preferred using that time to mingle. It was awkward to juggle a plate alongside conversations with other members of the congregation—and the food (not that she was judging) tended to be on the greasy side. It was Kristin's job to make arrangements for weekly catering, and Trishy had never dared mention it to her. In light of her conversation with Dylann, that certainly wasn't going to change going forward.

Trishy made a mental note to give Kristin an extra hug when they saw each other. As much as she would have loved to tell her that she'd met one of her high school classmates at the morning's event, she'd bite her tongue. It would be terrible to accidentally open up a conversation about the bullying Dylann had mentioned—or worse still, to risk someone else at Moving Word overhearing it. Trishy's life before Moving Word made her the perfect person to keep whatever version of a secret might have been floating in the air between her and Dylann in the conference room of the Hyatt. Kristin had no idea how lucky she was to have Trishy in her corner. The versions of both women that had come before were safe with her, tucked into a cozy nook of her brain, somehow managing to simultaneously indulge in pastries and chat about the many ways Moving Word had transformed her for the better.

14

Kristin

Kristin had always been a strong competitor. Her dad had signed her up for the local swim league when she was just four years old because he'd been worried that, as an only child, she wasn't making enough friends. A former high school swimmer himself, he'd told a white lie on Kristin's registration forms so that she would be able to compete against kindergarteners before she was technically eligible. It was a lie that Rae had uncovered the first time she'd observed a practice, seeing that her daughter's new teammates were showing off vocabulary and social skills that Kristin had yet to master. For months, she'd been mortified about her husband's deception—until it became clear that it was their swimmer, in fact, who posed a challenge to her older counterparts. From then on, Kristin had encountered few competitive challenges she couldn't face. Rivals knew that Kristin Rae Thatcher had speed, strength, and tenacity on almost anyone.

What she'd never had, however, was smack talk. While her teammates had learned the basics of friendly but fierce jabs somewhere around middle school, insults—no matter how good-natured—had never come naturally to Kristin. Maybe it was her lack of siblings to rehearse with at home. Whatever the reason, she'd realized early on that it could only hurt her credibility among the competition for her to reveal just how incapable she would be of snapping back should she attempt the sort of banter she'd seen other swimmers test out in locker rooms and natatorium lobbies.

Now, at twenty-two, sitting in her childhood bedroom dressed and ready to go to church on a Sunday morning with her phone in her hands, she wondered if she'd missed out on some critical practice.

> I know the one on the far left is some washed-up D2 college swimmer, but would it hurt her to hit the treadmill now that she's with our queens? Cam's gotta keep an eye out for her, i bet... homosexuality is SEXUAL IMMORALITY and A SIN. Moving Word should DO SOMETHING ABOUT THIS

First, Kristin felt the instant shame of her body. She'd known that she was taking up more than her allotted space on the bench in Twist. If her official retirement from collegiate swimming had shown her one thing, it was, unfortunately, that a strong frame—with curves and muscles visible to the naked eye, some genetic but most cultivated with great effort and determination—was much less desirable out in the real world. Now it was a liability, and it made her want to curl in on herself like a baby bunny who needed to be carried from place to place. Kristin had never had a shot at being the kind of girl who could be or cared about being dainty and delicate. But seeing it spelled out in the minute monochromatic digital handwriting of some anonymous Moral Maven felt like a hand wrapped around her windpipe. With anticipation for the gala ramping up and the inevitable expectation to look perfect that came with it, it all seemed to matter more. If she looked good, the Mavens and Moving Word would look good, which would make the Welshes—especially Cassidy—happy, in turn. When had taking a job as an office assistant necessitated this level of physical perfection? Was Cassidy's apparent disgust with Kristin's mere presence ultimately just a repulsion with her *body*?

This was why she had avoided reading comments on the Mavens feed. This was why it was dangerous to be ready for church with minutes to spare, to have idle time in one's schedule to obsess over a stranger's nasty feedback from beneath the empty gaze of a faded Katie Ledecky poster. Maybe she should start spending more time on making herself look pretty. She'd look better and have less margin for time-wasting activities that made her feel worse in every possible way. It was embarrassing that her phone could make her feel so unsure of herself. Kristin had seen the headlines about the negative effects of social media on people in her age group. She'd read about the science—and she was still falling prey to the kind of discourse she knew would be described in church jargon as directly from the Devil.

It wasn't just vanity, either. It was the all-caps supposed sexual immorality of it all. The feeling of emotional waterlogging sharpened at the thought of Dana, whose firmly platonic friendship was easily one of the most meaningful fruits of Kristin's college experience. Dana and her girlfriend, Shauna—a record-setting butterfly specialist who'd been a year ahead of Kristin and Dana at Queens—were the only couple that Kristin had ever met who seemed happier together than her parents. Their four-year relationship was imperfect and still highly functional, the kind she aspired to have at whatever point in the future she felt ready to let someone into her life.

Kristin had met other gay people before becoming friends with Dana. She knew how the churches she'd grown up in felt about their "lifestyle," but her exposure to nonbelievers through swimming had stretched her way of thinking in multiple ways, including this one. It was a subject about which she and her parents had never talked. After inviting Dana to spend several holidays with her family in Charlotte when a busy swimming calendar didn't allow the time she'd need to go home to Austin, Rae had even started referring to her as "the fourth Thatcher." If they cared that their surrogate child was intimate in every possible way with another woman, the senior Thatchers never mentioned it. They preferred to stay out of the business of what happened in *everyone*'s bedrooms—not just those belonging to gay people.

It was because of this that, in spite of her awareness that many members of her faith would not be so welcoming to Dana and Shauna, Kristin frequently forgot that people could be so cruel toward the queer community. She ached less for the insinuation that she herself belonged to that community—really, she'd never had any romantic interests at all—and more for the way the comment might make her friends feel, especially when piled atop the countless similar comments that had come before it. Dana and Shauna weren't exactly the target audience for the content being produced by and for the Mavens, but it wasn't terribly hard to find, either, and it wasn't an impossibility that her friends might stumble upon this particular brand of commentary and clock that Kristin was adjacent to it. A quick search would uncover a video of Kyle explaining his reticence to perform weddings for people of the same gender. *I'll just have to wait for God's wisdom to change my heart on that one*, he'd said, his usual charm winning out over the scary fire-and-brimstone quality of other preachers. *Have you seen the incredible work we're doing in Liberia?* Kristin wished she'd never seen it.

Now her finger hovered over the mean comment. She didn't have to accept what this person had to say. But there were also so many people who agreed with it—ninety-three, to be precise, according to the number next to the heart icon. If she tapped another link, she could see more replies to the original poster. Sure, people might be piling on, but there had to be someone defending her.

Defending her for what? For her body? For an unfounded assumption about her love life that she knew required no such thing?

There was nothing to defend and no good to come from reading more, except a worsening of the ache brewing deep in her gut. And if she were to engage, there was almost no upside—she would just piss people off and generate more ugliness. If her attempts at getting down and dirty with the insults turned out to be as lame as she expected, it could prompt teasing and humiliation. Either way, she sensed the potential for more drama—exactly the opposite of what she wanted the other girls to see her bringing to the table when she herself was working so hard to be a champion of authentic giving and kindness as a representation of the church.

Plus, if anyone could do anything about the bullying, it would be one of the other Mainframe members, someone who hadn't been appointed purely because of their convenient proximity to Kyle and Cassidy Welsh and their colleagues in the office. A statement from someone else might actually be taken seriously. A sharp comeback from Kristin would do nothing but fire the commenters up, which would embarrass the Mavens and Moving Word more broadly. No leader at the church or in the Mavens ministry would be happy if their credibility was compromised simply because Kristin's feelings had been hurt. Cassidy, like Camryn, was proud. A sensitive, chubby—no, muscular—girl could detract from their image. Just because Kristin couldn't figure out her beef with Cassidy and didn't know where the money for the supposed indoor pool and fancy closet came from didn't give her the right to cheapen the impression the Welshes made on other people. If the broader world was going to judge them for their extravagance—and Kristin was growing increasingly hopeful that, as their platform and profile grew, they might—let them. Perhaps Cassidy would even reveal herself to be less kind than everyone assumed her to be. Let her do it all on her own. But let Kristin keep her job, too.

Kristin would stay above reproach.

She wouldn't react, or leave a record of doing so.

She would keep doing the right things.

She swiped out of the app, then closed her eyes to clear her head the way she'd trained herself to do before a big race. It was time to go to church, anyway.

15

Camryn

Moving Word welcomed members and visitors into a three-story atrium built entirely out of glass on one side, the remaining walls made from some sort of bright white natural stone. Lush jasmine vines spilled upward with such vibrant abundance that when she saw them, Cam couldn't help thinking of the old story of Jack and the giant beanstalk. She pictured herself climbing up the vines—just like Jack had done in the fable—reaching and grabbing and reaching and grabbing in pursuit of the higher power waiting for her at the apex.

The atrium that morning looked much the way it did any other Sunday. The palpable energy from the parking lot carried inside, thanks largely to the room's acoustics, collecting the joyful noise of congregants greeting one another and recycling it back out at ten times the volume. As always, Cam and Jeff held hands while they navigated the crowded atrium to get to the sanctuary. She was on at least a first-name basis with most of the people in the room.

"Hey, girl!" Lacey Bergey called out to Cam, her adorable identical twins in tow, blue eyes shining below oversized pink hair bows.

"Morning, Cam," Melanie Tartwell said as she crossed the atrium. A forty-something soccer mom who'd sworn that she would never join social media, Melanie had recently secured Facebook, Instagram, and TikTok accounts just so she could participate in the Mavens community along with her friends from the school drop-off line.

"I *loved* your posts this week," Maddie Turner said. Cam didn't actually know very much about Maddie, but it was nice to know she was keeping up with the Mavens ministry. Their content that week had been focused on identifying green flags in a church's culture, calling out many of her own favorite things about Moving Word. It was good stuff.

Cam returned the greetings from other churchgoers and doled out the occasional hug, taking in the rest of the scene as she did. Little ones dragged each other down the Sunday school hallway, waving goodbye to their parents and giggling among themselves. The soft beat of the worship team's warmup songs made its way into the mix, too, like the soundtrack to a movie. Folks serving as volunteers for the week—there was a rotating schedule—stood just outside the doors that led to the main sanctuary, holding stacks of programs. All of the materials were available online and through the Moving Word app—with bonus video content and links to other pastor-recommended books and other resources—but there were still a handful of traditionalists in the flock who wanted physical copies.

Camryn waved politely at Brandon Goddard, a still recent addition to Moving Word. She'd overheard whispers about the tiny rainbow flag he wore on his lapel every Sunday, which made her hesitate to offer her usual friendly welcome.

Brandon, she'd learned while chatting with him during a charity walk several weeks after he'd started attending services, had moved to Charlotte from San Diego for work—something to do with graphic design. From beneath the slick shimmer of a light sweat, he'd even offered up his services to the Mavens for free after hearing more about the ministry, which was very sweet. Camryn hadn't gotten back to him yet.

Bo Lambert and his family shuffled quickly through the corner of Cam's field of vision. The outrageously tall man had his gorgeous wife on one arm and three gangly boys just behind them, all with their focus on the sanctuary doors. The Lamberts still kept mostly to themselves, but Cam knew they'd open up before too long. Getting them involved with the gala—even if it *was* Trishy taking the lead on making it happen—was bound to help. As her husband got more tied up with baseball, Amber would need girlfriends to lean on. Cam had already confirmed that she was following the Mavens across social media platforms, which was a flattering gesture. Kristin had been correct at the meeting—it would be huge to have a public figure like her involved with the event, and with more Mavens plans in the future. Plus, she could be a nice connection for Camryn to have for all manner of reasons going forward. Someone whose image hadn't been compromised, by circumstances outside of their control or otherwise.

"Camryn!" a voice echoed from the other side of the atrium. It was Kristin, emerging from the corridor leading to the church office, her eyes looking a little watery. She wore the cardigan she'd picked up at Twist the day before, layered over a plain black sack dress and paired with simple black ballet flats. There was something not quite right about the overall effect, but still—a vast improvement for Kristin. In any event, the outfit must have been comfortable, conducive as it was to its wearer hustling her way across the atrium's marble floors to get to Camryn. The girl was in good shape—better shape, even, than Cam, despite Cam's (nearly) religious commitment to Pilates. "I grabbed the Welshes before they went in," Kristin continued, nodding her head toward the sanctuary. "I told Cassidy you needed to chat with her. I hope that's okay."

"It's fine," Camryn said, startled. "Are you okay?" Kristin was always a little high-strung, but she was even edgier than usual. With Cass's tendency to snap at Kristin, the office assistant was perhaps a less ideal addition to the team than Camryn had originally hoped.

"I'm fine," Kristin said. "Actually, can I talk to you? I had a question about something I saw on the feed this morning."

"What?"

"A comment on that photo we posted from Twist the other day."

Everyone knew you weren't supposed to read the comments.

Well, Camryn read the comments. But Kristin hadn't struck her as the type to try. "Don't let it get to you," she said. "Matthew 6:33, okay?" *But first seek the kingdom of God and his righteousness, and all these things will be added to you.* "You know how people can be. Don't read the comments. I should have told you that earlier. Did I not?"

"No, for sure, but I accidentally looked this morning, and I wanted to ask you about it."

"What were the comments?"

"I don't think I want to say right—"

"I can't help you if you don't tell me." Cam really did want to help, but she could only be bothered with so much drama.

Kristin looked over each shoulder and lowered her voice before speaking. "It was sort of... homophobic."

"What do you mean?" Camryn thought she might know what was coming, but she wanted an extra second to consider how best to handle things.

"People were saying stuff about *me*."

Camryn had seen the brand of comments Kristin was describing. They made her uneasy, but she understood that such commentary had to come with the territory. There was no point in further engaging with it, even if she did regret Kristin's role as the burden's unwilling bearer. She put a hand on the girl's shoulder. "Come find me after the service, okay? You're making a big accusation, but we can talk more then." Maybe Kristin would forget.

"You're talking to Cassidy after the service, though."

"Exactly. So you know where I'll be. But I'm going to head in and sit down now, alright?"

Kristin stepped away as Cam reached for Jeff's arm. It was almost time for the service to start, and everyone had their own ritual. Savannah and Chad would be setting up their Sunday school classrooms by now. Kristin sat with her parents in one of the church's six tiered balconies so she could sneak out as the service neared its end to help situate catering for the weekly fellowship celebration. Trishy would probably show up after the worship team had started in on their first big song and slide in wherever she could find a spot. She'd been attending an influencer get-together before the service, and who organized an event like that on a Sunday morning? The price tag for membership in the Charlotte Creativity Collective was also absurd.

Camryn and Jeff had their customary seats in the fifth row from the front, where the view was so good there was no need to constantly look back and forth from the stage to the giant screens. She settled into her seat next to Jeff, pulling her well-loved Bible and an embossed Shepherd Lovely notebook from her purse and resting them both on her lap. She wrote the date in the top corner of a fresh journal page.

Lit from above by a sparkling whirlpool of blue and purple spotlights and surrounded by the subtle output of a fog machine, the worship team kicked things off with a moving performance of "Build Your Church," leading straight into a series of announcements from members about upcoming events and church news. The youth group was raising money for a mission trip to a Guatemalan orphanage in the spring. Auditions would be held the following week for the Nativity play, for which, at that very moment, new wardrobe was being designed by a Tony Award–winning costumer. Prayers were requested for several congregants, some of whom were sick, others of whom were walking through difficult times that were described in only the vaguest of terms.

Everyone listened intently enough through the announcements, but the entire congregation burst into cheers when Kyle Welsh stepped onto the stage. He took the short flight of carpeted stairs linking the floor of the sanctuary to the stage quickly, making it to the top in two steps when most people would have needed six. His left hand already gripped a microphone, his right fist bounced up and down in the air to the rhythm of the band's rendition of "Waymaker." Thanks to the intense glow of the stage lights, he was dwarfed by his own giant silhouettes. The size of the stage amid the proportions of the room added to the optical illusion: a preacher the size of an action figure. LED lightbulbs the likes of which Cam had otherwise only seen around the scoreboard at college football games sparkled on either side of the projector screens.

"How is everyone feeling this morning?" Kyle said into the mic, still half-dancing as the worship team gradually quieted their instruments and the light show faded out. A healthy cheer rolled in from all corners of the cavernous room, but it wasn't enough for Kyle. He held his hand to one ear and leaned out to the crowd. "No, no, no... How is everyone feeling this morning about having eternal life in Jesus?"

Cam felt a chill make its way up from the soles of her feet to the base of her neck. She shouted at the top of her lungs in harmony with the several thousand other bodies sharing the sanctuary air with her. The space vibrated on all sides.

"That's what I call an *amen*!" Kyle said, beaming. Whenever he was onstage preaching a message, Cam thought he looked like a mischievous little boy. He wasn't particularly handsome—at least not the way Jeff was—but his slightly crooked nose and uneven smile managed to work together in such a way that the whole was greater than the sum of its parts. When he preached, it lit up his face with a smile that was no doubt one of the reasons he'd become an icon for young Christians, especially unmarried girls. Not that Camryn thought about him that way.

"Today, I want to talk to you about a little something you've heard about before. It's called honesty," Kyle said. He paused to hold his microphone out toward the crowd, allowing time and space for a few dozen whoops. Kyle wore jeans, a quilted gray cashmere bomber jacket, and a black T-shirt screen-printed with the words HONK IF YOU LOVE YOUR NEIGHBOR in neon green. His sneakers—one of the sixty-two pairs that Camryn happened to know lived in the master closet in the Welshes' home—were impossibly white. His hair was styled into his signature perfect peak. "Alright, alright. Y'all are making honesty sound like a party, and I am here for it," Kyle said. The tip of his tongue escaped between his rows of teeth as he smiled.

"Let's get things rolling with some Scripture, alright? I've got two nuggets of truth to share with y'all today," he went on. When he preached, Kyle managed to harness the power and toughness of an old-school minister with the unbridled energy of a DJ, sprinkling his sentences with emphases on words and even syllables that might otherwise seem unremarkable. "In John 14, we read 'The Spirit of truth. The world can*not* accept him, because it neither sees him nor knows him. But you know him, for he lives with *you* and will be in *you*.' And while we're quoting the apostle John, I'll also turn your attention to First John 4, which tells us, 'We are *from* God, and whoever knows God listens to us; but whoever is *not* from God does not listen to us. *This* is how we recognize the Spirit of truth and the spirit of falsehood.'

"Now, as so many of my best messages do, this one starts with my wife. Does everyone here know Cassidy?" Kyle pointed at Cassidy in the front row. A purple spotlight found her, the worship band's drummer improvising a quick beat. "Of course you know her." Camryn cheered for her friend, knowing it would embarrass her. The wave of whoops and applause was richer this time. The pastor had started making his way slowly from the center of the stage to its left side. By the time he got really into the sermon, he'd be walking purposefully back and forth, covering as much ground as possible while keeping his eyes down on his sneakers. Kyle held up his left hand so his chunky black wedding band could be more easily visible to the whole congregation. One member of the trio of church photographers circled the perimeter of the stage to capture him. "I know, I know. I'm not deserving. Have I ever told you about our first date?"

Camryn knew the Welshes had met through mutual friends while Kyle was in seminary. But she didn't know anything about their actual first date. Had she really never gotten around to asking? Had Cassidy never felt called to share the details?

"Since we're being honest today, I've gotta tell you the truth. I would have gladly gone to Taco Bell for that first date." The photography team's candid close-ups of laughing congregants would be great this week. "Granted, it was about all I could afford, but it should also tell you a lot about the kind of guy I was back then." Cam laughed, too. The version of the Welshes he described was hard for her to visualize. "But it's a good thing I overcame my baser instincts! God knows I may not have won my beautiful bride over all those years ago had I taken down a Chalupa Supreme right in front of her." He paused for as long as it took him to complete another pass of the stage. "I'll have you know I took Cass to Baja Fresh instead," Kyle stage-whispered.

"So we're sitting at Baja Fresh, right, and I'm all nervous because I've never been alone with a girl this pretty before, and I'm like"—here, Kyle shook both of his arms as they hung loose against his sides and bounced up and down on the balls of his feet—"'I don't think I've got this, man. I don't think I've got this.' And she's telling me about her family and her friends and all the ways the Lord is moving in her life, and now I'm just sitting there eating tortilla chips and the crumbs are all over me, and I realized that I better start praying for guidance in this moment or else I'm going to lose my shot."

Expanded to larger-than-life proportions on the eight enormous screens on either side of the stage, Kyle's top row of teeth grabbed at his bottom lip. He'd stopped walking, something he only did when he was about to launch into a new, important part of a sermon. "So finally, this gorgeous female takes a breath and a bite of her taco. By the way, I don't know if y'all have seen how my wife looks at Mexican food, but let's just say it's about a half step away from adultery, which means that she's about to be pretty occupied for the next I-don't-know-how-long and I'm going to have to start putting in a little more work at this Baja Fresh." He punctuated the last few words by slapping the side of his leg with the hand not holding the microphone. "And so I start talking about seminary and my family and a few mission trips and the little routine I had with my buddies who I liked to watch basketball with back then, and it's all going pretty well." A few misplaced baritone cheers emerged from the congregation. "And then, I'm just not sure what happened.

"Y'all already know I was nervous in front of this beautiful young lady, but the message I preached to her right there at Baja Fresh that day would make what you're seeing up here today look downright bashful. I launched into a whole sermon—that's right, a sermon—about what *I* was doing to get out God's Word, what *I* was doing to speak truth, what *I* was doing to spread the power of prayer all over the dang place." Kyle caught his breath and shrugged out of his jacket, dropping it on the ground. Camryn hollered encouragingly and clapped her hands in the air. Jeff kept his applause at chest-level. It would have been fun to see him be a little more effusive, but

Cam respected his restraint. "And every word I said—and I mean *every* word I said—was technically true, but hear me when I tell you that it was told in a spirit of dishonesty that somehow came through me that day straight from the enemy himself.

"Because here's the thing: Honesty is not about what's fact and what's fiction. It's not about arguing the particulars. It's about your heart." Kyle pounded on his chest and looked thoughtfully out at the congregation, their whoops rising up around him. The dancing lights framing the projector screens flashed to life again. "It's about recognizing your place in God's plan and staying humble and keeping it real. I am lucky that Cassidy nodded along with me as I spewed a whole bunch of nonsense that I devised for my own image, rather than the glory of the Kingdom. I am lucky that she forgave me these sins. I am lucky that she saw through the veneer and straight to my heart, that she has since then been guiding me to become the kind of man that is truthful not only in word, but in spirit and in intent. I pray that every single man here today finds that in a wife."

Loud cheers rang through the sanctuary even

as Kyle continued speaking. Cam glanced at Jeff again, wondering if he had taken the pastor's words to heart, if he'd clocked the fact that exactly such a wife was already standing beside him.

"And so I ask you as you head out into the world this week to work hard and love your families, to think about the real meaning of honesty. Brothers and sisters, it is not sufficient to simply tell the truth. Facts are of the world. An honest spirit? An honest spirit is bigger than the world. An honest spirit is of the Lord."

Kyle pointed up at the soaring ceilings of the sanctuary and took several laps around the stage. The worship team played quietly. "We as a body in Christ must rise to the occasion with an honest spirit, with good intentions, whether we're on a first date at Baja Fresh or leading our families or running companies or governing nations. That's why we're challenging you to help us meet our goal to raise five hundred thousand dollars in support of ProtectUS between now and December 18. That gives us just about a month." A chorus of *Amen*s came up to meet him. "Because if we *really* believe that none of us are free until *all* of us are free, if we *really* believe that with God's help we have the power to liberate people from suffering, then it's high time we properly steward the gifts that He has given us. If you're listening to this message and you're ready to commit to real, abiding honesty, I want you to lift your hands with me and shout to the Lord!"

Before she knew it, Camryn was standing, arms thrown up above her; joyful scream lost in the voices of those around her, swallowed by wispy fabricated smoke and the colorful lights dancing from the ceiling.

After more worship and a few final announcements, the service began to wind down. Camryn hurried out of the sanctuary as offering plates and laminated flyers with a tithing QR code—along with a dedicated code for the ProtectUS drive—circulated up and down the pews. She wasn't ashamed that she'd forgotten her contribution that day. Jeff was content and able to give a gift to the church on behalf of both of them—and she was doing so many other things to benefit the congregation and ProtectUS, anyway.

Ever the perfect pastor's wife, Cassidy always joined Kyle to exit the room when he was finished preaching through a door behind the stage. Camryn would wait for her there so she could report back on what the Mainframe had come up with the day before. Busying herself by double-tapping on a few dozen Instagram posts and checking the response to a few of her own recent photos, she could hear the rest of the congregation filtering into the atrium, where four long lines of chafing dishes would be ready to offer sausage links and French toast fingers in the buttery sunlight of the late morning.

When Cassidy emerged into the dimly lit hallway on her husband's arm, she didn't look as excited to see Cam as Cam expected. Kyle greeted her first. "Camryn Lee Cady, hasn't anyone ever told you that you've got to stay in your seat for the *whole* service, or it doesn't count?" he teased. He pulled her in for a one-armed hug, connecting only the sides of their bodies. His jacket was back on and he smelled sweaty. "What are you doing back here?"

Cassidy tugged at the hem of her navy-blue dress and shook out her hair, revealing the gigantic princess-cut diamond earrings she'd received from her husband for their last anniversary. "Can we help you with something, doll?" she said.

"First of all, I wanted to compliment you on that message," Camryn said. She stepped back on one foot and opened her mouth soundlessly.

"I mean, you had me at a loss for words there for a few minutes. And we know that doesn't happen often."

Kyle held a hand to his chest and bowed his head. "I appreciate that."

"While I have you here, Cass, I have a question—and I'm so sorry if Kristin bothered you with this earlier. I know how enthusiastic she can be."

"Oh, we do appreciate her enthusiasm," Kyle interrupted. He took a big slug from an oversized Yeti water bottle.

"Okay. Great. Well, anyway, Kyle, you might actually be able to help me out, too," Cam said. "I was talking to the girls yesterday, and we were thinking about the gala—you know, brainstorming ways to get the word out about the event and spread a little extra love before Christmas. I know you said you had it mostly covered, but since we're so connected as it is, anyway, I was wondering what you would think about us building things out a little more for the Mavens on social media and—"

Cassidy pulled on Kyle's arms. "Actually—speaking of the gala—babe, didn't you say you wanted to talk to the Lamberts right after the service? Cam, I'm so sorry."

Camryn watched as the Welshes looked at each other, only their profiles visible as they appeared to have a full conversation using their eyes and the tiniest muscles in their jaws.

"You know what, you're right," Kyle said, pointing at his wife. He turned back to Camryn. "I'm so sorry to run. I'm sure Cassidy can fill you—"

"Cam, how about you shoot me an email?" Cassidy said. "I'm feeling—and I know Kyle will agree with me—a little nervous about y'all undermining what we're trying to do here. We'd rather focus on donations than more programming."

Kyle clasped his fingers together in front of his face, squeezing them tight. "Like you said, Cam, the church and the Mavens have a tight connection. But we need to be on the same page at every step here. And we appreciate you letting us take the lead."

Cassidy nodded. It was strange, seeing Cassidy like this. In the time they'd known each other, Camryn couldn't remember her ever looking so uncomfortable or in such a hurry to rush off to something else. She always made time for people, and she certainly always made time for Camryn. Then again, whatever the Welshes were masterminding for the gala and the fundraiser was bigger than what Cam had to say, which could wait.

Still, the word *undermining* stung. It made her cheeks feel hot and red, like they'd been slapped. She wished there were more people around, a crowd into which the awkwardness she now felt lingering between her and her friend could disappear. "Totally get it," Camryn said, desperate to smooth out the icky contours of the conversation. "I didn't mean to seem like we were taking over—"

"We've got it," Cassidy said quickly, her face tight.

"No apologies necessary," Kyle said. "You know we love what you're doing. We'll catch up with you later on, okay?"

The Welshes walked away, leaving Camryn alone in the hallway with extra time to kill before meeting up with Trishy, Savannah, and a few others for brunch downtown. She texted her friends to let them know she would meet them in the parking lot. If Kristin really needed to talk to her—if some prayer and time alone didn't make her feel better—she'd track her down eventually.

* * *

By the time she'd gone to brunch and met up with Jeff for a run, Cam had nearly forgotten how strange she'd felt after her conversation with Kyle and Cassidy. After all, they were only human, and they deserved grace. She'd check in again with Cassidy in a few days. By then, she would have even more ideas to share. Better ideas.

As she did most evenings, Cam sat down on the couch with her laptop to see if there was anything pressing in the Moral Mavens inbox and—since it was Sunday—to plan out her social media schedule for the week. If they were going to run with the budgeting idea they'd discussed at Twist—as much as she didn't want to—she would need to start breaking down the financial information from Miles Mason into digestible bites for the girls, and since the Mainframe team had responded so positively to her idea for a "maintain your purity during the holiday season" series at the meeting, she should probably get going with that, as well. Maybe she'd focus on the holiday content first and hold off on the money business for a few more months. It was better as New Year's resolution material, anyway. New year, new you. At least with a little extra time, she might be able to round up discount codes from a couple of stores to help followers save some cash right away.

Anyway, that could wait.

For now, the Mavens inbox was filled with the usual combination of prayer requests, glowing testimonies, and junk mail, along with a few hateful messages that Camryn immediately deleted. In her personal inbox, Cam found something more interesting: a note from her point of contact at Shepherd Lovely. Truthfully, she'd received the results from the campaign a few days earlier. The Mainframe meeting hadn't felt like the appropriate place to talk about how successful it had been. The Shepherd Lovely team's metrics had revealed that their partnership with Camryn had been one of their top three most lucrative to date. They'd seen a major uptick in visits to their site and an increase in sales. She was flattered, but not surprised. Shepherd Lovely was wise to recognize what she had to offer.

What was surprising, however, were the details of the message in her inbox that Sunday night.

Camryn Lee,

I hope you're having a fantastic weekend! I don't usually email on Sundays, but I'm getting ready to head OOO for a wedding-planning trip (so many details, so little time!) and want to make sure you have this info before I go!

As I mentioned in my email the other day, we are extremely pleased with the results of our collaboration. You've clearly cultivated a great deal of trust and goodwill with your followers.

We're trying something new this holiday season: a Shepherd Lovely Advent Ambassador Program!!!! We've cooked up an amazing new product line for Christmas, and we want intentional influencers like you to help us spread the word. Advent Ambassadors will get early access to all of the products to share exclusively with their followers. Here's the exciting part: YOU are one of only FIVE gals around the country we're offering this to!

In addition to free product and lots of special content, we are able to offer you $2,000 per promotional post. Candidly, this is more than we would typically be able to manage for someone with a platform of your size, but I have a good feeling about you and your relationship with Moving Word and the Welshes (what an exciting time for them!), so I made it happen. Plus, it's Christmas!!!!

Practically speaking, we'd expect you to post at least three times a week, and if it goes well, we'd be more than willing to talk with you about continuing our partnership into the new year.

I know Christmas is coming up SUPER quickly and we're not giving you a lot of time to consider. The idea for the program came up in a meeting recently, and we didn't want to wait another minute to get started. The Ambassadors we've picked (like YOU) are dynamic enough to pull it off! Please let me know ASAP if you're interested! I have our partnerships coordinator copied. She can answer any urgent questions while I'm off being bridal! Fingers crossed we can get some paperwork signed with you when I get back.

So excited to work with you!
Lara Irving
Director of Partnerships, Shepherd Lovely

Camryn read the email four times. Money like that wasn't enough to erase her debt completely, but it could bring her some peace, make her feel as though she might actually be able to catch up to it someday. It was better than barely making the minimum payments on her credit cards every month, better than deleting voicemails from debt collectors whose power to punish Camryn was a scary indefinite. It was better than hiding from Jeff. And it could mean strong momentum for future big partnerships, too. If she could prove to other companies that she could be successful in a trailblazing program like Advent Ambassadors, there was nothing stopping them from offering her similar terms. One deal like this stacked on top of another stacked on top of another—her financial worries could disappear and she could leave 12th Pine to give her full attention to her ministry.

She could talk to Lara and her colleagues about contributing to ProtectUS and the gala later. Once the papers were signed.

A less optimistic person might think it was all too good to be true, but why shouldn't it happen to her? In her faith and prayer and diligence, she'd grown deserving. Perhaps the time for worry was almost finished.

Collaborative Doc: Moral Mavens Budget Content Brainstorm

Kristin:

<u>IDEAS FROM MTG:</u>

    Holiday-themed budget guide
    Gift expense tracker
    Holiday charitable giving how-to…connect to ProtectUS?!?!?

Savannah:

Proverbs 10:22: *The blessing of the Lord brings wealth, without painful toil for it.*

Proverbs 10:4: *Lazy hands make for poverty, but diligent hands bring wealth.*

Proverbs 22: *The generous will themselves be blessed, for they share their food with the poor* (***especially perfect for holiday, giving season, etc.).

Kristin: YES! @Savannah totally agree

Trishy: we could make shirts?????

Trishy:

Holiday sale round-up

Guide to companies that give back

For holiday-themed budget guide…

- DIY holiday party hacks

Kristin: I can ask my mom for her tips!

- Best rewards programs

Kristin: I'll also ask my mom lol

- Regifting dos and don'ts
- Q&A: "We just started dating. Do I have to buy his sister a gift?" etc.
- Budget-friendly gift guide

Savannah: Love this. @Camryn should we try for lower price points on all existing gift guides?

Camryn: I think we should keep the old ones and add a budget one if we have extra time to work on it.

Kristin: @Camryn can we donate affiliate income from all of our gift guides?

Trishy: @Camryn ^^^

Camryn: tbh I'm not sure how that would work

Kristin:

[DOCUMENT: gift expense tracker.pdf]

Just threw this together! You can totally change it if you want. Maybe the graphics are too much...

Trishy: omg how did we not know you were this good at graphic design? slay!

Kristin: aw thanks! 😊

Savannah: The graphics are perfect! I like all the categories

Trishy:

[DOCUMENT: Mavens posting schedule.pdf]

Thoughts on swapping out some of my dating Q&A stuff and moving the budget series up to early December? @Camryn????

> **Camryn:** Super love all these ideas girls but also still kind of think this could be better for New Year, New Me!
>
>> **Trishy:** @Camryn that defeats the purpose of all the holiday stuff
>>
>> **Savannah:** Also the philanthropy angle…
>>
>> **Kristin:** @Camryn Just tell me how to adjust the schedule!
>>
>> **Camryn:** Will do:) working on my purity blogs now! more to come on money…

16

Savannah

If the diagrams hanging in Dr. Clark's waiting room were meant to make patients feel better about their upcoming appointments, they were failing. Miserably. At least, they were failing Savannah miserably. Each one was printed in a tight range of shades, all in the general ballpark of blood red. The cartoonish diagrams were silly and embarrassing, but looking at their more clinical counterparts made Savannah's stomach churn. Could all of that really be packed inside of her, all of those mechanisms and tubes and the pinkness surrounding them? Probably not, since something of hers was broken. If under normal circumstances a woman's innards were meant to match what she was seeing on the wall, what could possibly be happening in her own body? Savannah didn't want to find out, and yet it was all she could think about as she and Chad entered minute twenty-three of waiting for a nurse to call them back to an exam room.

"Remember what I told you about looking at the diagrams," Chad said quietly, nudging her leg with his knee. "Don't." His calf hadn't stopped bouncing since they'd taken their seats in a set of vinyl chairs lining the perimeter of the waiting room.

Both Trumans had grown up in families that didn't discuss the subjects illustrated by the charts on the wall, a fact that was probably at least partially to blame for Savannah's distaste for them now. She wondered what might have been different for her if she'd had the kind of mother who sat her down for a conversation about the birds and the bees, a mother who made herself readily available for even the most uncomfortable of questions. If that sort of thing happened on the show, it probably would have been televised as a primer for Christian parents who wanted to discuss sensitive matters of the flesh with their kids in a virtuous, delicate fashion. As a follow-up, dedicated viewers might have been offered the chance to unpack their questions with Joanne using the hashtag #MAXFamBirdsnBees.

Savannah had claimed the first available appointment that Monday morning—bright and early at seven o'clock—and the waiting room was empty. Conveniently, she hadn't been assigned a homeroom or first period class to teach that semester, so when she could secure that slot, there was always plenty of buffer time between wrapping up with Dr. Clark and collecting herself before second period with her seventh graders.

The door separating the waiting room from the hallway along which the practice's dozen exam rooms were located clicked open, and Clara emerged. Clara was Savannah's favorite nurse. They were about the same age, which was enough to make her feel a little more normal during the otherwise excruciating visits. It was almost like seeing a friend, like having Trishy or Cam waiting for her in the doorway. Almost.

"Hey, girl," Clara said from the threshold. "Want to come on back?"

Savannah stood up from her seat, clutching her bag between her arm and her side to steady herself. "I'm not sure I *want* to," she said. She smiled at Clara as she passed her in the doorway. "But it's always good to see you."

Chad followed Savannah and Clara down the hall, repeatedly clearing his throat. It was a nervous tic he'd had for as long as they'd been together. His dad and brothers did it, too, so on the rare occasions when they took place, difficult conversations with his side of the family quickly devolved into guttural symphonies that pained her ears.

"Anything new I should add to the chart for this week?" Clara asked as Savannah perched on the edge of the examination table, moving the plastic-bagged, spearmint green gown to rest on her lap. When Clara excused herself to get Dr. Clark, it would be time for Savannah to change out of her work clothes and into the scratchy, flimsy tent of fabric. She knew the drill. In the meantime, Clara flipped through her clipboard. It had to be a formality—a kindness, really. Savannah had been at the office exactly seven days earlier, and exactly seven days before that. It went on and on for about three months, not to mention all the routine, less-frequent visits that had come before, when they were just a regular couple trying to have a baby in the regular way.

"Nothing new." Savannah paused. "Last week, Dr. Clark mentioned something about 'unexplained infertility.'" She played with the crinkly plastic in her lap. Chad cleared his throat.

Clara flipped through a few more sheets of paper on the clipboard. The first time they'd met, Clara had admitted that she'd grown up watching the Maxwells on television—and she'd been kind enough never to mention it again. It was the closest thing Savannah could hope for in the way of assurance that Clara wouldn't spread her personal information outside the office. "He's run you through the full battery of tests, then," she sighed.

"I guess so," Savannah told her.

"I think you're about to get some tough love," Clara said, crossing one chunky white sneaker over the other as she leaned back against the countertop on which the doctor set his exam tools. The hand holding the clipboard hung at her side.

"What does that mean?" Chad said, shifting with a squeak in the second vinyl chair he'd claimed that morning.

Clara looked back and forth from Savannah to her husband. There was a different feeling in the room when Chad was the one asking questions. It didn't seem right to Savannah that the awkwardness should be more pronounced with her husband in the room, like he'd invaded a top-secret clubhouse in which only women who understood firsthand the pain of giving—or, in some cases, not giving—birth were allowed.

"This is about the time when Dr. Clark usually suggests that patients start seeing someone else," Clara said. She looked down at the chart again. "Yep. You're past the year mark now, too."

The fertility forums had given Savannah plenty of warning that this moment was coming. She was glad to have it confirmed by Clara's friendly face before she had to hear it from her doctor, whose habit of biting into breath mints in the back corner of his mouth sent a shudder through a low part of her spine. There were stories all over the internet of women being passed off from their regular ob-gyns to fertility specialists once they'd been trying and failing to conceive for a full twelve months. In this club to which Savannah had never sought admission, the one-year mark was an important milestone.

"He's breaking up with us?" Chad said.

The nurse smiled. Chad Truman couldn't have been the first husband to show up to this exam room with pockets full of misplaced levity. "Sort of," she said. "*When* you get pregnant"—here, she looked at Savannah—"you can continue seeing Dr. Clark and have him deliver your baby if you'd like. In the meantime, since y'all have been at this for a little while now and he hasn't been able to get you answers, he's probably going to say that you've moved out of his zone of expertise. He's your standard-issue ob-gyn, so if you're wanting more information to help you move things along faster, he'll recommend a physician whose focus is higher-touch fertility treatments. I've heard the nicest things about the specialists he refers out to. People love them. You can be more aggressive about next steps, if that's what you want."

Aggressive was not a word Savannah had predicted anyone would use to describe her journey to motherhood. *Tender* was what she would have hoped for. *Private* was what she'd assumed she was entitled to. For a woman who'd never been introduced to so much as the basic birds and bees, the notion of inviting additional parties into this already claustrophobic conversation between her and her husband presented a real challenge. Sure, the forums had helped her see this coming—and Dr. Clark's dismal update the previous week had reinforced the inevitable—but it didn't soften the blow.

Chad was silent as Clara took Savannah's vitals, resting her fingers on the inside of her wrist to clock her pulse, then wrapping the cold blood pressure cuff near the top of her arm and pumping it with air until it pinched. The tightness of the cuff no longer fazed her. Clara made notes on the clipboard and chatted idly about how beautiful the weather had been lately and the trip she'd taken to a holiday market over the weekend. Savannah knew that Clara had three children, two redheaded boys and a toothless girl who she'd described during one of their first meetings. She'd stopped talking about them after a while, another act of generosity.

"Vitals look good. No surprise there," Clara said. Savannah's consistently good health was perhaps the single most infuriating part of these Monday mornings. "Any questions for me before I go get the doctor?"

Savannah shook her head. Chad said nothing.

"Y'all hang in there. I'll see you back here soon for one reason or another. It'll be a good reason, though. I can feel it," the nurse said, squeezing Savannah's knee before exiting the room.

"Sounds like we have a lot to talk about," Chad said. His knees were spread wide, one elbow leaning on each one, wrists supporting his chin as he looked down at the mottled yellow tiled floor.

"I guess so," Savannah said. She held the plastic-wrapped gown in her lap, unsure why she should have to change into it if Dr. Clark had already done everything he could. If there was nothing else to be done, there should be no need for any further examinations, for the humiliation of the open-backed paper monstrosity and laying bare the parts of her that were clearly not working—the parts of her she'd been taught to keep private—to be tinkered with.

Over the last few months, Savannah and Chad had discussed the possibility of seeing a specialist here and there, but every conversation had been left unfinished, hanging in the space where they'd started it, usually in the car. Knowing they were likely coming to the end of the road with Dr. Clark, Savannah had done a bit of research into the standard treatments that might come next, things like Clomid and IUI and IVF. She'd mentioned them now and then to her husband, but nothing had ever been decided or even explored—and she was happy not to push. The whole matter made her worry she might be interfering with God's plan for her life, or that God didn't care if she even liked the plan He'd drawn up for her—a scary notion.

Other paths to parenthood existed. Savannah knew that. Together, she and Chad had met and fallen in love with dozens of motherless, fatherless, love-hungry children on mission trips all over the world. Once, she would have said that welcoming one of them into her home would be enough. Now, adopting a child would be a specific kind of unfinished business, a loving yet desperate attempt to somehow make things right. It wouldn't be fair for an innocent little boy or girl to carry that burden for Savannah, even if they might fill some of the gaps in her heart and find him- or herself happy, too.

"If you don't think it's a good idea, we can leave. Fertility treatments, I mean." Savannah's voice sounded shaky to her own ears. "We can leave if you don't think fertility treatments are a good idea." In the refrigerator-like conditions of the exam room, hers wasn't the voice that helped Chloe Featherton project her once-shy soprano to the back of the auditorium.

"I don't know what I think."

Savannah wasn't sure what she thought anymore, either. Thousands of women had smiling children thanks to the treatments she'd dared look up online and that she knew Dr. Clark would recommend to them shortly. Savannah had seen IVF and IUI babies all over Instagram and YouTube, even though she'd promised Chad that she'd stop following the mommy bloggers and so-called fertility warriors who sent her spiraling. She had a responsibility to her students at school and at church—not to mention Camryn, who was putting more pressure than ever on herself and the other Mainframe members to present the best possible image of the church to their followers. She couldn't do that if she was a constant blubbering mess, whether it was her hormones or the mommy bloggers to blame.

Maybe what Camryn had given her when she'd asked her to be part of the Mainframe was a meaningful distraction from the difficulties she was having conceiving. Throwing herself fully into the Mavens ministry might be exactly what she needed to cede control of the things that had never really been up to her to decide, a reminder that it was only a commitment to faith that could pull her through. If there was any truth to what people on the forums were saying, that kind of distraction might even lead to successful babymaking of the more traditional variety.

There was also, then, the matter of how all of this would play to the Mavens community—not to mention the larger following that still kept tabs on her from her *MAXimum Family* days. The Mavens, in particular, wanted to know that their faith in the Lord would earn just rewards, including a happy family. So many of them wrote in their comments and messages that they were saving themselves for marriage, trusting that the intimacy they'd reserved for their husbands would one day result in a child born from love—naturally and in due time, but not *so* far in the distant future. Savannah didn't want to lie to them.

But making the decision to forge ahead with building a family in what could be considered an unnatural, ungodly way would not sit well with many followers. Introducing scientific intervention to what was meant to be a Creator-ordained process would be controversial. It wasn't something that the quiet folks who still gathered multiple generations to watch syndicated episodes of *MAXimum Family* after family Bible time would understand or like. If those folks were still making a game of guessing how long it might take Savannah—the compassionate sister from the family they'd followed for years who'd centered her life around working with children—it could only be a matter of time before they started accusing her of abandoning her beliefs in pursuit of the little one she desired. Christian women online had plenty to say about the growing overlap between science and conception.

> IVF and IUI are sinful. We've made idols of modern medicine.

> Job 33:4: "The Spirit of God has made me; the breath of the Almighty gives me life." Test tube babies + aborted fetuses are NOT of the Almighty.

> THERE ARE MILLIONS OF BABIES WHO NEED HOMES STOP PLAYING

GOD AND ADOPT I'M PRAYING FOR YOU

life begins at conception and does not deserve to be treated like a science experiment!!!

"I don't know what I think, either," Savannah said.

Chad stood up from his seat and wrapped his arms around her. The plastic-bagged gown crinkled between them. She rested her head on his shoulder. Right here in this very spot, she could almost pretend that none of this was happening, that nothing bad had ever happened, or ever would. They were still in college, hugging each other after a few weeks apart. Back then, they had yet to get anywhere close to doing the kinds of things that would have put them in spitting distance of parenthood. They'd both taken and stuck to purity pledges when they were younger, Savannah when she was eight and Chad when he was ten. While Savannah had been shocked by how handsome she found Chad in the early days of their relationship, physical intimacy had been a nonissue between them from the start. They'd both committed to saving sex—and practically all of the steps along the way—for their wedding night, so there had been little need to discuss it. Most of their friends were similarly committed to their purity. When Savannah found herself feeling curious or for the briefest of moments questioning her own willpower, she could turn to the girls from youth group, the ones she shared bunk beds with on mission trips and with whom she'd made friendship bracelets at church camp. They'd encouraged each other all the way to their respective wedding nights, when each of them had allowed their perfect match to admire and then remove the white lingerie they'd been gifted at their bridal showers.

Then, one after another, they'd all announced their pregnancies. Savannah figured it would be the same for her. At first, she and Chad had been so busy enjoying their newfound freedom with each other that "trying" for babies seemed unnecessary. With all of the time they were spending in the bedroom, it was bound to happen.

It didn't, though, so as the Trumans' friends began celebrating the first and second birthdays of their offspring, they'd decided to be more deliberate. Chad was a health coach. He believed the human body was a mechanism to be learned and mastered. Savannah had gained weight from all the extra full-fat dairy she was consuming, and she hadn't eaten a turkey sandwich since the Fourth of July. Their grocery bills had skyrocketed for a two-month period during which Savannah tried seed cycling, an all-natural fertility booster that required her to choke down various combinations of flax, sesame, pumpkin, and sunflower seeds, depending on how close she was to her period. They monitored and tracked and tested and scheduled and did everything one could do to ensure conception, everything Savannah would be far too bashful to discuss with her mother, or even her friends. After all, she was still so young! She still had so much time! Everyone said so.

But still—with flaxseeds and whole milk and enough meticulously timed sex to make up for their years of abstinence—nothing.

"We can listen to what the doctor has to say, but I feel a little funny about it," Chad said, bending his knees so that he could look directly in her eyes. "Maybe I just need some time."

All that Savannah had wanted was for her

husband to have a stronger conviction than her own. Now that he had shared one—that what might be the only way for them to have a biological child made him feel funny—she wanted to be sick. Why should he get to decide?

But they weren't going to sort it out right there in the office. And she knew his instincts were fair, if frustrating.

"People online have a lot of bad things to say about IVF," Savannah conceded.

"Okay, well, I don't generally put a lot of stock in what people online say, but that's good to know."

"The people who used to watch the show will hate it. Also the Mavens. And people at church, too, maybe."

Chad sighed and rubbed his chin. "I'd hate to see you dealing with all that. You've already been through so much."

"Cam's going to think this is too complicated. It's going to make her nervous."

"Camryn is a big girl. I mean this with a lot of love and respect for what you all are doing, but it's not like you're the Kardashians. Anyway, this still is a private decision."

Savannah heard her phone vibrate in her

purse, which she'd set on the ground near Chad's feet.

"Can you hand that to me?" she asked, nodding at her bag.

"Are you sure?" Chad said, even as he riffled through the purse. "Right now?"

Savannah nodded and held out her hand. Nothing waiting for her on the phone could possibly make her feel any worse than she did already.

Except, perhaps, the appearance of a phone number that was no longer paired with a name or contact profile, for the express purpose of trying to separate—in as kind a way as possible—its owner from the living, breathing humanity that had once felt so real to her, as a presence at family holidays and moments of crisis and, most annoyingly, in Savannah's wedding photos. While it was only a series of meaningless numbers that popped up at the top of the screen, the inane stream of emojis that accompanied the message below meant that it could only have come from one person: Angela Maxwell, the woman who—along with the Maxwell patriarch himself—was responsible for the humiliating undoing of everything Savannah had once trusted.

GOOD NEWS!!!!! Just bought tix for the family to that party your friends are throwing next month. Pricey! CANNOT WAIT to see you. Reunion is long overdue and figured there was no better occasion. We will see you THEN!

The family?

Any combination of the family showing up at the Gala for Goodness would end in a disaster. For Savannah, it was bound to be a disaster of the emotional variety—but if Angela or any other Maxwell opted to make a scene in such a high-profile moment, it could be something far more theatrical, a performance that would make the Mavens and the church and even the entire ProtectUS mission look stupid. The Welshes would be devastated.

"We need to go," Savannah said to Chad, grabbing her things. If there had been any food in her stomach, she most certainly would have thrown it up before they made it to the elevator of the medical complex.

Savannah rarely wasted time hustling out of Dr. Clark's office and into a world that didn't care about her inability to conceive, but she'd never moved faster. With her husband close at her heels, heart pounding as she settled into the car, she looked down to find that she was still clutching the wrapped hospital gown to her chest.

17

Kristin

"I really think we need to consider upping our game with the AV," Kyle said. He was on the phone in his office, just a short walk down the hall from Kristin's cubicle. She knew eavesdropping was wrong and unprofessional, but this was the latest in a series of expensive-sounding calls Kyle had made that morning alone. "Have you seen the videos from that event at Hillsong? They had this insane backdrop in the space, like…" His voice tapered off for a few seconds, then returned a bit louder and aimed more in Kristin's direction. "This needs to be big. Hey, Kristin? Can you come in here for a second?"

She double-checked that she'd saved the document on her screen: the latest version of an itemized budget of what the Welshes had decided was absolutely necessary for the Gala for Goodness. Silver rentals, a live band, a local TV host to serve as emcee, a wall of fresh poinsettias in lieu of a traditional step and repeat. While some vendors were offering discounts because the gala was for charity, the price was still becoming astronomical by any measure. Over the course of the party-planning process, it had become increasingly clear to Kristin that Cassidy and Kyle's taste was even more inexplicably expensive than she'd thought. Assuming there was truth to the conventional wisdom about *making* money requiring *spending*, the gala would far exceed all fundraising expectations as a result of the church's financial output. Wouldn't it be easier to donate all of that money directly to ProtectUS? Was there so much more to be collected in exchange for an evening of dinner and dancing personally styled by Kyle and Cassidy Welsh? Kristin wondered what additional expenses the pastor might be taking on in his office at that very moment.

Technically, it was Kyle's office, but since Cassidy had started taking a more active role in his ministry, she'd adopted it, as well. A few months before, Kristin had been asked to arrange the delivery of a sleek new desk for the pastor's wife, along with a crew of volunteers to help reappoint the space so they both could work there comfortably. They'd surprised Cassidy with the final results as if they were on an HGTV design show, Camryn and Trishy hosting the reveal in a pair of complementary pink blazers. The Mavens had shared the video from the church's feeds and invited followers to vote on whether they'd prefer to work in Kyle's space or Cassidy's. Unsurprisingly, the overwhelming majority had opted for the shinier, more feminine corner of the room, where a slim white computer monitor that Cassidy almost never touched was shaded by an oversized artificial philodendron tree in a blush pot.

As Kristin crossed the room to Kyle's desk, he tapped a knuckle against a photo on his computer screen, presumably from an event at Hillsong, a massive congregation founded in Australia.

"What would you call this?" Kyle asked, glancing up at her with the phone still tucked under his ear. "Yeah, I'm just asking my assistant what she thinks," he said into the receiver.

There was a lot going on in the photo. Too much. "Of what?" Kristin asked, stalling.

"This lighting," Kyle said, tapping with his knuckle again. "How would you describe that? I'm on the phone with one of the guys at Reid." Reid Enterprises was a local production company that Moving Word relied on for the technical aspects of most of their events.

"It just looks kind of like a night sky to me," Kristin said. Before her was a velvet-draped, expensive-looking space illuminated from floor to ceiling with glimmers of bright white lights sparkling at what appeared to be random intervals. Beautiful people mingled among the gleaming backdrop as if floating in the stars. "I mean, I think that's what they had in mind."

Kyle nodded thoughtfully and pulled on his bottom lip. "Did you get that, Devon? Kristin is saying it looks like they have a giant night sky behind them. I can send this to you so you can see it." Kristin started walking out of the room. "You know what, though? Kristin, do you think this is what we should be going for? Does it feel like Moving Word to you?"

She paused and turned back around on her heel. "I mean, I guess it depends on the vision. Like, if you want to keep it Christmassy, go for snowflakes or something instead."

Kyle pointed his finger at Kristin and smiled. "You're right. We'll bring some Christmas snow to Charlotte," he said. "Actually, Devon, do you know anything about artificial snow? Nothing tacky, of course. My wife will lose her mind." Kristin had never seen artificial snow in-person, but the concept alone did seem at least a tad tacky, by virtue of being fake.

As Kyle listened to the voice on the other end of the phone, he pulled at his bottom lip again. "I'm not worried about the budget on this. We're going for a major celebration of Jesus's birth here. We have some partners working with us, anyway." Right. The partners. Kristin still wasn't sure exactly what that meant. Despite being responsible for tracking the costs, she hadn't talked to any partners yet. Kyle paused, still playing with his lip. "Alright, then. Sounds good. Have a blessed day." He blew out a stream of air as he hung up. "Thanks for that, Kristin. Why don't you take a seat, actually?" Kyle gestured at the armchairs in front of his desk. "We haven't touched base in a little while."

Kristin followed his directions. When she'd first been hired, she'd had check-in meetings with a different pastor each week, depending on who was available. Now that she was accustomed to the job, those meetings had tapered off. Kristin had a good working relationship with all of the pastors—especially Micah Rivers, who was almost as young and new to Moving Word as she was—but because Kyle was so proactive about launching new projects and events, he required more administrative support.

"Is everything still going good for you?" Kyle asked. Instead of a play on words, his hoodie of the day featured the neon outline of a Jesus fish. "I know we keep you busy."

"Still good," Kristin said, shifting in her seat. There was no need to bring up the several hours she'd spent the evening before discovering that Mavens followers had posted a few hundred other rude comments about her body and what they assumed was her sexuality. If Kyle's evasive behavior in response to the interview question about gay marriage that still loomed large in her memory was any indication, he would likely ignore it altogether. "I'm happy to take on more if you need it." Working at her parents' church wasn't her dream job, but if she was going to do it, she wanted to do it well. A guy like Kyle was connected around town—plus, the scale of the Gala for Goodness suggested there was more money to be made *somewhere* at Moving Word. She couldn't help but want it. It would be nice to be able to help her parents out someday when a need inevitably arose. The Thatchers had been faithful with their tithing for as long as Kristin had known what it meant to contribute 10 percent of your income to the offering plate, and probably longer than that. There was beautiful symmetry, she thought, in using her earnings from the church to make sure they wouldn't have to worry as they got older.

"I know you've jumped into things with Cam and the Mavens, too."

Kristin nodded.

"That's a great opportunity for you," Kyle said. "Camryn knows what she's doing. We're lucky to have her in the church, and to have y'all as ambassadors."

"For sure," Kristin replied. "I've been learning a lot."

"Not to mention all the spiritual growth," Kyle added, tenting his fingers.

"It's nice that there's been some overlap with the work I'm doing for the office, too," Kristin said. "With the gala and the online event for the Mavens."

It had been a week since the Mainframe had met at Twist and brainstormed ideas for ProtectUS. Via a rambling voice memo in the interim, Camryn had reported to the rest of the group that she'd met with Cassidy and Kyle about what she'd decided to brand "Garnet Gals for Goodness." The idea was to mount a splashy virtual counterpart to the gala that would support the cause, while also offering registrants special Mavens swag and exclusive holiday content. The concept was a little murky for Kristin, but Camryn had sounded thrilled about the prospect of getting it off the ground with the Welshes' blessing.

Then again, as she sat across from Kyle in his office, Kristin suspected that the blessing had been withheld—or, at least, granted less eagerly than Cam may have suggested. Kyle suddenly looked angry, and the expression didn't match his features. It made him look uncomfortable, like he was on the verge of getting sick.

"Online event?" he asked, fingers already grabbing for his phone on the other side of the desk. "Was that what Camryn was talking about?"

"Yeah. Garnet Gals. Trishy's been working on the website so we can launch sales this week."

"Sales?" Kyle's face looked more bizarre the angrier it got.

"Sales. For tickets and VIP packages and everything else you talked about with her."

Kyle was busy tapping at his phone.

"I'm sorry. I thought you knew about this. Cam said you spoke about it."

The pastor seemed to regain his composure, a calm settling over his body. "Right," he said. "I'm sure I knew. I just need to connect some dots here. Apologies for the confusion. Thank you for your time. You can get back to work."

Abruptly dismissed, Kristin scrambled out of her chair and out of the office. Her cubicle had never felt like a safer space. As she hustled back to it, she heard Kyle's voice whisper words like *interfere*, *distract*, *profit*, and *undermine*. If this was how friends talked about each other in the real world, maybe she didn't want them. Maybe everyone was better off with partners like the ones helping the Welshes throw a seemingly budget-free event, whoever they might be.

Kristin tried to forget about it, diving back into work on informational literature set to be distributed to gala attendees. She wasn't convinced that human trafficking was the only evil worth mobilizing against as a church, but the ProtectUS website was persuasive. *According to estimates, over seventeen thousand Americans were victims of trafficking last year alone… and thousands of other cases go unreported.* Kristin wondered how the Welshes—apparently so concerned about the issue—could justify being so choosy about where donations originated.

What else might be going unreported?

18

Trishy

There hadn't been any references to Scripture in Brady's dating app profile, but now, sitting across from him at the sports bar he'd suggested for their meeting, Trishy made a game of guessing the verses he might have chosen to put there, had he been a different kind of man.

He could be a 1 Corinthians 16:13 guy. *Be on your guard; stand firm in the faith; be courageous; be strong.* Up and down his forearms, there were enough tattooed renderings of various knives and guns to suggest that standing firm might be a priority for him.

Or maybe he would prefer that verse from Job that Trishy could never understand: *Now gird up your loins like a man; And I will ask you, and you instruct Me* (NASB). *Loins* was a terrible word. No matter how many times it appeared in the Bible, it would always be a terrible word.

"You gotta remember that I'd bet the guy a foosball table," he was saying. "Like, a real foosball table. Do you know how much one of those costs? We're talkin', like, eighty-five bucks *minimum* on Craigslist." Trishy sipped her cocktail from a tall, cloudy plastic cup. "So this kid's not going to go down without a fight. I'm tellin' you, he went hard in the paint. Literally."

Maybe she was just making him nervous. Maybe he was putting on the whole macho act because he was uncomfortable. (There was no way to explain the gun tattoos away, really, but those could have been mistakes. Everyone made mistakes. Trishy still had the scars to prove she'd once had her belly button pierced.)

Brady pantomimed a motion that Trishy assumed was something akin to the loading, aiming, and firing of a paintball gun. "This course is crazy, though," he said, shaking his head, fake paintball gun still cocked and ready to go. "Have you ever played paintball?"

"I haven't," Trishy replied.

"You would love it." Brady cleared his throat and forged ahead with his story. "Anyway, my buddy was *not* ready to deal with some of these obstacles. I was *on* his ass." He set down the imaginary gun to take a drink of his Pabst Blue Ribbon. "So anyway, that's how I ended up with the foosball table in the basement. We got a nice one, too. You gotta be careful on Craigslist. Lots of stuff on there is covered in cat piss. Are you into foosball?"

"Never played."

"Seriously? No paintball and no foosball?" he asked, looking genuinely shocked. "You should come over."

Brady was, at least, as good-looking as he'd appeared in his profile picture, the one in which he was holding a toddler in pigtails atop a four-wheeler. According to the caption, the girl was his niece. That made him a real family guy—a green flag.

"Maybe," she said, clearing her throat. "How

long have you been single?" There was still time to get things back on track with her typical first-date questions. That spring, she'd collected her favorites and printed them on bright pink playing cards. *What's your ideal date night? Tell me about the best day you ever had. Tell me about the five people you spend most of your time with. Describe your perfect Sunday. Who is your most important spiritual teacher? How often do you plan on praying with your wife? How do you see yourself setting a Christlike example for your future children?* Several thousand of her followers—most of them Mavens—had purchased Q&A decks for $24.99 (including tax and shipping). She was considering another print run, maybe even an expansion pack.

"Around two years," Brady replied, leaning back. "I dated this girl for about three months back in March, but I don't count that as a relationship."

"Why not?"

Brady shrugged. "She was a nice girl and all, but I didn't even know we were dating until after we broke up," he said.

"How does that work?" she asked him.

"I sort of thought we were just hanging out,"

Brady said. "When she got all pissed off and told me she wanted to stop seeing each other, I thought she was over me. But then she said that all of her friends were on me about being a 'bad boyfriend'"—here, he made quotation marks with his fingers on either side of his face, the gesture big enough to be a dance move—"and I was like, well, damn, I didn't even know I was supposed to be trying to be a good boyfriend."

This was why Trishy was always encouraging her followers to *over*communicate with the men they were seeing. Even the Christian dudes she'd dated seemed hell-bent on misunderstanding anything that presented even the smallest inconvenience to them. It was never too early to define a relationship. She'd written and designed a downloadable DTR guide, also available for purchase in her shop (priced at $9.99 and ready to be printed in the buyer's home office or local UPS store). Claudia hadn't agreed to stock them at Twist yet ("too religious," she'd said), but Trishy expected she'd change her mind eventually.

"But yeah, other than that, I've pretty much been single," Brady continued. "I've met a couple cool girls on the apps, but nothing that's stuck, you know?"

Trishy gestured down at the plasticky menu in front of her. "Are you getting dinner?"

"That was the plan, right?" Brady said, opening his own copy. "I think they do half-price burgers on Monday nights. Have you ever had sweet potato fries?"

"I'm good with just the nachos," Trishy said, lifting a single chip from the pile and taking an enthusiastic bite to prove her point.

"Really? That's all you're going to eat?"

Still chewing, Trishy pointed at the plate. "They gave us a lot, don't you think?"

Brady shook his head, resisting eye contact with her as he squinted at the menu. "I like a girl that can eat," he said.

Trishy wanted to get away from this guy. She slurped the rest of her drink through the cheap plastic straw, then grabbed her phone out of her pocket. Unfortunately, she hadn't received any messages that required her legitimate, urgent attention. Just a handful of notifications about new entries to a denim giveaway she'd posted earlier. Why wasn't there anyone around to blow up her phone when she really needed it?

"You know what?" she said, hopeful that her tone was that of a concerned friend mentally preparing to deal with a serious but not quite emergent situation. "I actually think I have to go help my friend. She just texted me."

"For real?" Brady asked.

"For real," she confirmed. "Can I give you some money for the nachos?" She stood up from the table and began to gather herself, grabbing her bag from the floor and checking her jeans for crumbs of stale tortilla chips. The heels of her boots crunched the leftovers into a dull beige powder on the floor.

"That's alright," Brady said. He was tapping at his own phone screen now. "Nachos and a drink. You're a cheap date. I've got you. I hope your friend's okay."

"Cool. Thanks." As much as his comment about her being a cheap date made her want to withhold final pleasantries, Trishy stuck out her hand for a handshake. Now that she was standing over him, Brady looked so small. Even the guns inked on his arms were less intimidating, though no less ugly. "It was nice meeting you."

"For sure." Brady grabbed Trishy's fingers and shook at them weakly. "Would you want to go out again?"

"Maybe," Trishy said. She wouldn't. "I'm

pretty busy. I'm always at Moving Word on Sunday mornings, though. It's a pretty cool church. You should come, if you want."

There. She'd done the good work, just like it said in Mark 16:15. *He said to them, "Go into all the world and preach the gospel to all creation."* Trishy hadn't quite made it into all the world yet, and she hadn't exactly preached the gospel, but she *had* found a way to invite a nonbeliever to church in the most unlikely of places: a seedy sports bar. It was enough to make her feel almost okay about meeting a man from one of the secular dating apps that the rest of the Mainframe girls—not to mention the thousands of Mavens who trusted her—were under the impression she'd given up long ago.

"I could maybe come to church," Brady said, to her surprise. It was the sweetest he'd been all evening. "I think I've seen billboards and Instagrams and stuff for Moving Word. It looks chill. Y'all have the minister with the hot wife, right?"

* * *

Back at her apartment, Trishy did what she could to erase the memory of the evening. It was weird to come home from a night out with a boy and skip her usual routine of laying out a full play-by-play for her followers. They liked hearing about her impressions of the guy, the conversation she'd had with him, the hints she'd picked up about his relationship with his family and the Lord (or lack thereof—equally important).

Tonight, there could be no livestream, no post-date question-and-answer session. The date had been bad, but since she'd made the match via an app from her secret folder, she shouldn't have been surprised. Tonight, it was just Trishy, Layla, a sugar-free Popsicle, and a bunch of people on the internet who couldn't know the truth about how she'd spent her evening.

Anxious for something—anything—that might make her feel better, Trishy applied her favorite sheet mask (gifted!) and leaned against her pillows. She snapped a selfie, the gummy pink paper of the mask sparkling in her go-to filter. Working hard tonight on something to share with y'all very soon. Can't wait for you to see what's coming to my shop! she typed beside the image before posting it. She *had* been brainstorming new products and downloadable goodies for her followers. A girl could only be dependent on other brands for so long. Just because she'd been out with Brady instead of actively working on those to-be-determined projects on this *particular* night didn't mean they weren't in motion.

As Trishy pondered the possibility of another Popsicle, a beaming headshot of Cam filled her phone screen. "I'm going to need your help," Camryn answered in lieu of her usual chirpy greeting after Trishy picked up. "Damage control."

"What do you mean?" Trishy asked, picking Layla's sleeping form up from a pillow and setting her down on top of her chest. Cam had a flair for the dramatic (and that was coming from Trishy, who had often been accused of the same).

"Savannah called. The Maxwells are threatening to show up to the gala. They all bought tickets," Cam said. "It's going to be an absolute disaster. I'm so mad right now."

"Is it really that big of a deal?" Trishy asked, making her way to the freezer for a second Popsicle. She didn't want to get involved with Savannah's family and whatever drama—or trauma—they were inflicting on her friend. Not unless Savannah asked. "It's more money for the fundraiser, right? We can keep Savannah away from them. She can handle herself."

"I don't think you understand how crazy these people are," Camryn said. She sounded practically out of breath. "I know that's not nice to say, but it's true. They are *so* tacky and they're going to draw so much attention and Kyle and Cassidy are going to be *so* angry. It will be a terrible look for Moving Word and also the Mavens, especially with all the press the event is getting. They're going to make us look awful and ruin everything. Plus, Cassidy's all mad at me already about the Garnet Gals thing."

"Wait. You said she was excited about that," Trishy said, recalling the late nights she had already spent building a landing page for the virtual event.

"There was a misunderstanding," Cam sighed. "It seemed like she was cool with it, but now she's freaking out, saying we're turning the fundraiser into a joke and distracting from the church's efforts. I've been trying to get back in touch with her since she called me a little while ago but it's going right to voicemail."

"Is it possible you're overreacting? Maybe she's

just taking time to cool off. There's no way she's actually mad at you for coming up with ways to raise more money."

"I've never heard her like that. And that's before she even knows about this thing with the Maxwells. Like I said, these people are going to ruin everything, I'm telling you—and she knows it, too. Jesus Christ—and you know I don't say that lightly. What should we do?"

From the start of the Mavens, it had been clear that Cam was a little weird about the size of Trishy's following. Since the massive dip in followers for all of the Maxwells and Savannah's subsequent retreat from social media, Trishy was the only one with a larger reach than Camryn herself. For Camryn to come to the expert for help, things must have really been bad. Trishy would never say it out loud, but it felt good to be needed—and better still to be just a little superior to Cam in a moment of crisis. While she didn't entirely understand the nature of the chaos that had apparently descended on the Mavens, Moving Word, the ProtectUS fundraiser, and the Gala for Goodness, she was more than prepared to be the one to fix it somehow. Trishy was savvy and sparkly enough to pull it off. And she knew just who to call.

* * *

It was convenient that the date with Brady had been so terrible, ending early enough that Trishy could reach out to Amber Lambert after her call with Cam without seeming like a total creep. They'd been casually texting in the weeks since Kristin had asked for Trishy's help securing the Lamberts' support for the gala, but the time had arrived for her to come in with a harder sell. After hanging up with Cam, Trishy drafted a note to Amber, letting her know that she was in the Lamberts' neighborhood—everyone knew where the superstar athlete and his family had decided to put down roots after their big move to Charlotte, and it wasn't *that* far away from Trishy's apartment—and would love to drop by to show her some sneak peeks of jewelry that was coming to Twist in the spring. Amber replied that her kids had recently gone to bed and that Bo was having a meeting, but that she'd be more than happy to take a look.

Trishy didn't have any jewelry to share, and she wasn't sure exactly what she would do when she arrived at Amber's house. She'd have to improvise when she got there. That broadcast journalism degree she'd busted her butt for at UNC was still good for something every once in a while. For the right cause, she knew how to make things up as she went along.

19

Savannah

Savannah tended to avoid trendy coffee shops like the one smack dab in the middle of South End where she'd agreed to meet Cam for a catch-up that afternoon after school. Middle school music teachers who were not only married to the progeny of local politicians but also had families that had recently turned from Christian role models to walking advertisements for hypocrisy had nothing to gain from being in public gathering places, especially when they were nearly always on the verge of tears because of their difficulties creating a fresh start in the form of a family of their own.

"Hey, girl!" Cam chirped as Savannah made her way to her friend's table and stepped into a hug. As usual, Cam's hair smelled good, like cloves and apricots, but also a little like the nicest parts of the beach. "Do you want to grab something to drink?" Cam asked, motioning to the series of menu blackboards posted above the checkout counter. "This macchiato is heaven in a cup. I think it's maple? Maybe pumpkin. Something fall. It's a good splurge." Whether a splurge of the financial or caloric variety, Savannah couldn't be sure. Either way, ladylike as always, Camryn pulled her skirt tightly against the back of her legs and sat down again. "Take your time ordering, though. I'll sit tight."

"Do you want anything else?" Savannah asked her.

Cam shook her head. "That's alright," she said. "You go ahead. I should probably take it easy on the caffeine for a bit, anyway. You know how I can get!" She mimed jumping up and down in her chair, then went back to typing away on her laptop.

Savannah walked to the cash register, where a man who looked to be in his early thirties was waiting to take her order. She smiled at him for a moment before looking up at the blackboards. "Just a green tea, please," she told the cashier, digging into her purse for her wallet.

"What size?" he asked. Seconds after he looked up, Savannah could pinpoint the moment when he recognized her, when he connected the real-life woman standing in front of him with the many hours of footage of her younger self that were available online—and, unfortunately, with the ample headlines related to her family. His eyes got a little bigger; his jaw shifted just a touch.

"Small is fine," Savannah replied, handing over a ten-dollar bill.

"Sucks about your dad," the cashier said, extracting her change from the register drawer. "He seems like a creep. There was always something about him I didn't like."

"Thanks," Savannah said, already holding out her hand for the bills and coins she was owed. Maybe having something in her hand would hold off the tightness around her eyes and the humiliation that might come with it.

"For what it's worth, I don't think Angela's even that good-looking." He was fishing the individual coins from their respective compartments far too slowly. "Your mom is much prettier. I know she's your mom, so I don't mean to make it weird. I'm just saying."

"Right." It was the only reply that came to mind as she collected her change and beverage. Before the man could say anything else, she walked away from the counter and to the table Camryn had claimed against the opposite wall.

"Everything okay?" Cam asked, closing her laptop.

"The guy at the cash register knew my family," Savannah said, exhaling. "It's fine."

Cam glanced back at the counter. "Do you want me to go say something to him?"

"Like what?"

"I don't know. You can't just walk around telling people you know stuff about their family. I don't care if they *are* on TV. It's stuff like this that's keeping the drama going when it's so unnecessary. Why can't people just move *on*?" Cam was growing flustered, her neck turning a shade of coral she would have been upset to see clashed with her lip color. "I guess that brings us to why I thought we should get together," she continued, her eyes back on Savannah. "I wanted to make sure you were okay after the text from Angela. I know they make things so complicated for you."

"I'm okay," Savannah lied. "I just feel bad that it's interfering with the work everyone's doing on the fundraiser. Drama or bad publicity is the last thing the church needs."

"Don't be silly. Anything is fixable. I mean, I'd be lying if I said I wasn't a little nervous that they would embarrass us and the church, but that's not your fault. Actually," Cam said, putting a finger up and glancing at the glass pastry case near the cash register. Everything inside was covered with big chunks of sugar visible even from their table. "Are you hungry? Would you want a cookie or something? I'll split one with you. I went to Pilates four times last week."

"I would have a few bites," Savannah said.

"Perfect. You know what? Would you actually mind grabbing one? Maybe oatmeal chocolate chip? One of the big ones? I'm just going to run to the ladies' room." Camryn stood up from her chair, patting the wrinkles out of her dress, this one printed with a pattern of sunflowers. "We can talk more when I get back." As she walked toward the back of the building, her hips swung just enough to make her skirt look like a church bell.

As happy as she was that Camryn hadn't followed through on her empty threats to engage the cashier, Savannah wondered why her friend couldn't have given the man a piece of her mind wrapped in a cookie order. She steeled herself and approached the offending barista, this time handing the cash to him at the same moment she placed her order. He worked faster and didn't say anything as he walked to the display case and handed her the treat on a plain white ceramic plate.

"Okay," Cam said a few minutes later, plopping back down in her chair. "Sorry about that. I was bursting after that coffee. Thank you for this." She pulled the plate closer and broke off half of the baseball-sized cookie. "It looks delicious." Savannah watched Camryn take her first bite of the cookie, amazed at how her friend still managed to look like the picture of a perfect Southern belle as she did—at least until her expression turned to one of such surprise that a waterfall of crumbs poured onto her lap.

Savannah turned in her seat to follow Cam's eyeline to the coffee shop's door. Three women had made their way inside. First, Savannah spotted Trishy; then the slightly less familiar Amber Lambert, dressed down, predictably, from her usual church attire in dark jeans and a tailored black sweater—plain, but obviously expensive. Beside Amber was a woman who Savannah registered as someone she'd seen before—but just barely. It was this woman who was the first to speak, her vowels long and flat and nasally.

"I'm sorry I'm such a mess," she said. "I just got off a plane." She may have been dressed in a sweatsuit, but even Savannah could tell it was the kind that had been sold as a complete, expensive set—and with her pristine hair and makeup, she couldn't have looked less like a mess. Or less like Savannah did after a flight. The newcomer's thick copper hair descended in a beautiful curtain over one shoulder as she trotted toward Savannah and Camryn's table. "Camryn Lee Cady! I can't believe we finally get to meet IRL! This is a total God thing."

From the corner of her eye, Savannah could see that Camryn's face remained ashen, even as she stood to give the woman an unusually cold hug. Amber and Trishy fell in line behind the women as they embraced. "You know Avery Adams-Wallace, right, Savannah?" Trishy asked, nodding her head in their direction.

Avery Adams-Wallace. No wonder Savannah had recognized the redhead. Avery's face had been a staple of Savannah's social media feeds back in the days when she spent more time scrolling them, pre-scandal. A full-time influencer who managed to make sourdough five times a week and run a combination cattle farm and artisan flea market with her husband somewhere in rural Illinois, Avery Adams-Wallace was also one of Camryn's online nemeses. Trishy joked with Cam about it all the time. Cam insisted that her comments about "hate following" other women occupying a similar space to the Mavens—like Avery—were all in jest, but sometimes, it was hard to be sure. In her old life, Savannah had enjoyed following Avery, who wrote lovely meditations about the overlap between her faith and the real world. Plus, she always looked like she was having genuine fun in her photos, whether she was folding her husband's laundry, making her own preserves, or hosting a dinner party with friends. And her kids were precious. Looking at her page gave Savannah permission to think that she might one day have those things, too.

"Of course," Savannah said, rising from her chair to extend a hug. Not a single trace of airplane smell lingered around Avery. Impossible.

"Avery and I are friends from college," Amber said, nodding.

"We sure are," Avery confirmed, stepping back. "We pledged KG together."

"Small world, right?" Trishy said, clearly making every effort to avoid eye contact with Camryn. Avery had been one of the first major players in the Christian influencing world, and her follower count had been well ahead of anyone in their circle for a long time. If there was one thing Camryn hated, it was feeling like she'd been beat. "I stopped over at Amber's to talk shop last night and she told me Avery was flying in this morning. I couldn't wait to meet her and introduce everyone."

Avery smiled broadly and surveyed the scene before her. "That's right," she said, nodding. "My in-laws are going on a cruise for Christmas—I don't know why anyone would go on a cruise over Christmas—and wanted to spend some quality time with the littles before they left, so I figured

I'd do a mommy getaway while the grandparents and my hubby handle things on the farm. I've been hearing about this big benefit, and now I'm wondering if I should stick around for a few weeks to help get ready."

"Isn't that fun?" Trishy asked, her eyelashes batting strangely in Camryn's direction.

"*I* think so," Amber said, nodding. "I know I've been a little shy since we moved here, girls. I'm sorry I've been making it hard on you to get in touch with me to help with the fundraiser. But between Trishy and Avery, I'm ready to get involved."

"We're getting her out of her shell. I told her God's calling her in on this!" Avery said a little too loudly. "By the way," she added, turning directly to Camryn and dropping her volume, "I heard that you're also working on this whole Advent Ambassador thing with Shepherd Lovely. How great is that? And don't you just love working with Lara?"

Savannah had no idea what Avery was talking about, and it was hard to predict if the woman's acknowledgment that she and Camryn had landed in any common league would make things more or less icy. Camryn had been uncharacteristically quiet since the others walked in. Finally, she spoke. "Yes!" she said. "It was such a generous offer."

"Let's save business for later," Trishy said. "I managed to get us some private shopping time at a fancy new shop Claudia's friend just opened down the street. While we have Avery and Amber, I figured we could go see if they have anything we like for the gala. Cam, you posted that you were here meeting Savannah, so we decided to swoop in and surprise you on our way. Surprise!"

"It's still working hours for me," Camryn said, gesturing to her laptop. Savannah thought she looked a little smug.

Trishy rolled her eyes. "Come on," she groaned. "You and I both know you can be tempted away from 12th Pine for a little shopping, especially for Moving Word business and the Mavens."

Savannah never would have been the one to say so out loud, but Cam did routinely bend the bounds of her theoretical nine-to-five working for the restaurant in favor of the Mavens and church matters—and even the occasional social event. She finished her green tea and sat back.

Avery stuck out her bottom lip. "Yeah! Come

on!" she said. "I can't possibly go on a big Charlotte shopping trip without Camryn Lee Cady."

Avery had said exactly the right thing. Now Camryn's 12th Pine schedule would surely clear up for what was left of the afternoon. No one had bothered to ask Savannah if she was free, but school was out for the day and *Footloose* had opened and closed—to multiple standing ovations—the week before. While she wouldn't have opted to spend her limited free time trying on—or even looking at—expensive evening gowns, Cam would be grateful to have another friendly face. Given the kindness she'd exercised by inviting Savannah for coffee just to check in after the drama with Angela, Cam was owed that. Plus, anything that could be done to turn the tides in a more positive direction for the gala, the Mavens, and the church as a whole was a win. Savannah would keep her mouth shut and follow the rest of the girls.

"Aren't you sweet?" Camryn said. "I can probably move things around."

The smile on Avery Adams-Wallace's face proved that Midwesterners, unlike Southerners, were prone to assuming that a phrase like "Aren't you sweet?" could only ever be used in earnest.

Or maybe the woman was just *that* pure of heart.

Savannah followed the other women out of Bean Bar and decided she would look forward to finding out.

r/AveryAdamsWallacefans

North Carolina??????

BunnyLove0624: Why is Avery in Charlotte rn? So random and so unlike her to be away from the kids so close to Christmas. I know her in-laws are there but STILL. Thoughts?

firstfarmerswife: Did you see she posted with the Mavens girls?

dandelioness567: Yes! I'm kind of obsessed. Mavens are the cutest. And who knew she was besties with Bo Lambert's wife? My hubby loves him. GO SPORTS lol #friendgoals

keylimehi: so so so bummed for the kiddos. they don't want their mom to leave during the holiday season! i'm disappointed...

> **BunnyLove0624 (OP):** SAME! why do we care so much lol

dandelioness567: Looks like she's maybe helping with the big benefit the Mavens have been posting about at Moving Word. Cute!

> **firstfarmerswife:** I don't know how to feel about it. My cousin used to go to Moving Word but she left because she said Kyle Welsh made her uncomfortable.
>
> > **FamilyFirst45__:** that's the pastor the Mavens love, right?
> >
> > > **dandelioness567:** Yeah. And he's kind of running the benefit...

> **dandelioness567:** Made your cousin uncomfortable how?
>
> > **firstfarmerswife:** Just always pushing people to come to events at his house and wearing flashy outfits. Nothing terrible, but no one

wants to feel unsure about their spiritual leaders, you know?

> **keylimehi:** for sure. all the more reason i'm sad for Avery's kids. missing Christmas for a flashy pastor? SAD!

FamilyFirst45__: Dress shopping looked fun! She's so beautiful and genuine!

loveispatientloveiskind: Seems like she's there for a good cause. I'm going to donate to ProtectUS. It *is* Christmas!

> **BunnyLove0624 (OP):** That's a nice way to think about it!

> **dandelioness567:** same

20

Trishy

Avery Adams-Wallace's face was beautiful in real life, but it might as well have been sparkling with fairy dust in the photos on her Instagram.

Avery Adams-Wallace flipping pancakes as a group of tiny blond heads stared lovingly at her from the other side of a laughably oversized kitchen island.

Avery Adams-Wallace cuddled up in the corner of a sectional larger than Trishy's living room, a Shepherd Lovely devotional in one hand and a steaming mug printed with Scripture in the other.

Avery Adams-Wallace leaning up against a dapple-gray horse while showing a Shepherd Lovely journal to the camera.

Avery Adams-Wallace celebrating an anniversary with a throwback photo of her and her husband smiling over a wedding cake in a dress Trishy would not have been caught dead in, fifteen years ago or not. How was it possible that Avery looked younger *now* than she did then?

Absolutely nothing about Avery's lifestyle appealed to Trishy, but as she scrolled through her feed, the pictures made it seem pretty good. She almost couldn't blame Camryn for her animosity toward Avery.

Almost. The whole thing was overblown. Trishy didn't like to brag about the relative size of her social media personality compared with Cam's, but the difference was substantial—and even with her larger reach and less righteous background before Moving Word, she didn't have internet enemies.

"Are you kidding me right now?" Cam had seethed at Trishy as they walked from the coffee shop to the store. "Avery Adams-Wallace?"

"I didn't invite her to come here. Or to the gala. I would never do that to you," Trishy said.

"When I went to Amber's last night, their history and the visit came up and everything just happened. I love you, but you're being a little intense about this. No one's betraying you. I just met her a little while before you did."

"Is she horrible?" Camryn asked, her tone only slightly less fiery. "I read somewhere that she doesn't tip her waiters." Trishy couldn't remember the last time Cam had tipped more than 10 percent, but now wasn't the time to bring it up.

"She seems fine. A little trad for me, but fine," Trishy said. "You're missing the point, though. This is a great way to get Cassidy back on our side with the gala. Avery Adams-Wallace is a trustworthy brand. As long as she's here, we might be able to help get her to Moving Word!"

"*I'm* a trustworthy brand!" Cam said. "*We're* a trustworthy brand."

"Right, but Kyle and Cassidy are a little ticked off at you, so we might not be for them right now," Trishy said. Camryn had been the one to call Trishy in need of "damage control," begging for her help to set things right with the Welshes to keep attention away from the Maxwells and keep Moving Word's reputation intact. The opportunity to bring Avery Adams-Wallace into the fold had fallen into Trishy's lap when she'd arrived at the Lamberts' to find Amber preparing for her friend's imminent arrival. As a newer believer, Trishy didn't yet have many testimonies of God working things out in perfect, unexpected ways. This would be added to the list, a boon to her still nascent faith. Cassidy would be thrilled to have the beloved Avery Adams-Wallace associated with Moving Word, ProtectUS, and the Gala for Goodness—especially if she could be convinced to hang around town or return for the party itself. "If you make nice, maybe she'll support the online thing and you'll be able to run with that, too," Trishy added.

"Garnet Gals?" Cam asked, a sweet squeal betraying her steel-faced annoyance. She glanced up the street. Amber, Avery, and Savannah were half a block ahead of them on the way to the shop that, according to Claudia, promised excellent dress options for the party.

"Yes," Trishy said. "Can you imagine what would happen if she promoted it? Kyle and Cassidy couldn't be mad anymore. They would probably get behind it, too. Avery could bring in a whole new group of people. And lots of money. That's how it works. You know that."

Perhaps she wasn't happy about it, but Cam had apparently decided to swallow the grudge she'd been nursing against Avery. At least for the time being. She'd deigned to enter the store.

Trishy had already committed to working with a stylist friend for the gala and was acting as an observer for their try-on session, watching as the other women donned different looks. Initially, Avery had done the same. "I'm just here for moral support," she'd said. "I still don't know if I can make it to the gala. You know how busy things are around the holidays. Especially with littles at home."

"There's no harm in playing dress-up!" Trishy replied. She knew from experience that having a dreamy outfit was often what someone needed to be convinced to attend an event, "littles" notwithstanding.

Thankfully, Avery had obliged and was, at that moment, showing off a mermaid-style emerald gown that looked flawless on her body. Trishy thought it was a little expected for a redhead to gravitate toward green, but she couldn't fault anyone for doing what worked for them.

"I love that on you," Amber said, looking her friend up and down. She turned to her own appearance in the mirror and evaluated the simple black column she'd selected. The armful of gowns Amber had summoned to the dressing room all looked the same: dark and muted. "Is this boring?"

Avery turned to her friend. "No," she assured her. She grabbed Amber's shoulders and forced her to shimmy a bit. "You've been going for classic since formal freshman year. And look at that body! Can you believe this woman gave birth to those three handsome boys? Cam, what do you think?"

By inviting her into the conversation, Avery was breaking Cam down without knowing she needed to. Thawing Cam's iciness toward the newcomer would be good for the Mavens and the church, but it would also make Camryn happier. Trishy wanted to see her friend relax into the special shopping trip, which was the kind of activity that—under other circumstances—would have her absolutely giddy.

"She looks amazing," Cam replied. "I wish I looked like that, and I don't even have any kids."

Savannah—who'd been hanging on the periphery in a navy dress that did absolutely nothing for her figure—retreated to her dressing room. Good. Trishy hoped she would put something else on. Even in the unflattering silhouette, she was obviously thin enough that Trishy thought it might not be a good thing.

"See?" Avery said to Amber. She turned to Camryn. "And that red is stunning on you."

"Would you call it garnet?" Camryn said into the mirror as she played with the shimmering skirt of the dress.

That's my girl, Trishy thought.

"I'd say so," Avery said. Standing next to each other in their red and green gowns, the women looked like an over-the-top tribute to the Christmas season, like they should be holding old-fashioned microphones and headlining a December concert that promised to turn classic carols into hip new staples. The overall effect wouldn't have been Trishy's top choice.

"Perfect," Cam said. "I'm planning this online event to go with the gala called Garnet Gals for Goodness, so I want to be sure I'm dressing on theme. It's to get more followers involved with ProtectUS."

"And to raise more money for the fundraiser!" Savannah's shout was muffled through the dressing room door.

"That goes without saying," Cam said.

"Well, that sounds fantastic," Avery said. Looking at her in the gown, Trishy could (almost) understand the chip on Camryn's delicate shoulder. No one had the right to look so beautiful hours after getting off a flight—let alone mucking stalls or scrubbing the kitchen floor with organic cleaner as she often demonstrated online. "You really have done such great work with the Mavens. Is there anything I can do to help with Garnet Girls?"

"Garnet *Gals*," Cam corrected politely. "And that would be amazing! I'd love to tell you more. You are so sweet."

This time, at least, Trishy knew that Camryn meant it when she called Avery sweet. Her damage control job looked like it was about done. It was a good thing Cam kept her around.

21

Kristin

Trishy had been kind enough to extend an invitation to the impromptu dress shopping trip to Kristin—and, despite the fact that she knew it would be miles from her comfort zone, Kristin almost wanted to go. Almost. In the preceding weeks—between all the excitement about the gala and the fundraiser and the growing holiday cheer and the conversations with Trishy, especially—she'd felt increasingly close with the rest of the Mainframe team. Maybe they didn't just need her. Maybe they wanted her. Maybe they *liked* her.

Matters with Cassidy, however, hadn't changed. The pastor's wife didn't appear to like Kristin any better than she had before, but still very much needed her. In the meantime, the pastors at church who *weren't* Kyle seemed to be growing increasingly irritated with her limited availability, and Kristin wasn't always sure if their annoyance was directed at her or at their semi-famous colleague. As a result, the office felt uncomfortable even in Kyle and Cassidy's absence. The Welshes were out on church business that afternoon and had left yet another extensive to-do list for their assistant to complete, all in service of the gala. Kristin had heard through the Mainframe grapevine—and then from an irritated Cassidy, who blamed Kristin— that Camryn's plans for the online event had caused friction between the Mavens and the Welshes, and she wanted to do what she could to smooth things over. If she could forge ahead with her tasks for the party, it would be good for her reputation at work. A gorgeous gala would make the Welshes happy and offer photo ops for the girls, who would *ooh* and *aah* over her involvement. Maybe if she kept her head down in the details, everyone in her orbit would put aside their weird behavior and get along, if only for long enough to snap some pictures and toast to the holidays. Kristin just wanted to *work*. Work yielded results.

Plus, did she really want to prance (or attempt to prance) around a store dressed in fancy dresses for Camryn, Trishy, Amber Lambert, *and* Avery Adams-Wallace? Kristin was evolving... but maybe not that much. Not quite yet. No, thank you.

She hummed to herself as she collected the linen samples that had been dropped off earlier that day from various local rental companies. She'd already attached a label to each one identifying the type of fabric and the price per unit, adding an asterisk for the options that would be discounted thanks to the generosity of a business owner with a heart for the Lord and/or victims of human trafficking. The plan was to lay all of the shiny fabrics out in a rainbow of festive colors on Kyle's desk so that he and Cassidy could approve their favorite when they returned.

It was rare for the office to be this quiet. Kristin helped herself to a cup of coffee from the machine and took her time treading the gray-carpeted floors to Kyle's office. It was a relief to feel free from observation, released from a microscope she hadn't anticipated would be her fate. The coffee had a welcome sting on her palate—she was drinking it hot, which was unusual. Was this how normal people felt at their workplaces, having already proven their worth and made themselves comfortable?

With the exception of Cassidy's corner, the Welshes' office was a pretty standard workspace: shoddy bookshelves stacked with textbooks, a few framed posters bearing messages and signatures from people who'd been involved in programs Kyle had led in the past. Kristin had never before had the time to read what they had to say, but she took it now, grateful for a well-deserved break from her uncomfortable chair. *You are God's love!* one note read. *Thank you for your generosity of spirit!*

While Kristin had never been much for snooping, the influence of her mother's interest in true crime had taken hold—and a weird itch somewhere in the back of her throat or behind her ear told her to perk up as she stepped away from the posters and brought the swatches to her boss's desk. Too many things had felt off lately. Kristin couldn't begin to account for all of them, or for the fact that she was letting her eyes linger a little longer than was normal on everything they touched. If God had put it on her heart, there had to be a reason for her suspicions, so she allowed herself to look closely at the photo of Cassidy from their wedding day, a pocket-sized book of Proverbs, and the sermon in progress open on Kyle's computer monitor. She didn't quite have the nerve to grab the mouse and see if she could find anything interesting tucked away in email inboxes or project folders. But a stack of papers on top of Kyle's keyboard caught her eye as she began arranging the samples, so thick it was hard to miss. When something looked awry, you were supposed to trust your gut. It was a clear takeaway from all the murder and kidnapping podcasts she'd listened to.

The top sheet was covered in the pastor's sloppy handwriting in bright red ink; a long list of dollar amounts next to last names—many of which Kristin recognized as belonging to church members—or vague phrases that appeared to be tied to fundraising events. *PTA breakfast. VFW picnic. FOP chili cook-off.* Printed in a smaller, tidier version of the same handwriting at the bottom of the sheet was a single figure: $423,736.42.

Suddenly sick to her stomach, Kristin didn't want to linger in the office for much longer. A quick thumb-through of the papers below what she had to assume was some extremely shoddy accounting revealed what looked like bank printouts, each one confirming an individual transaction of a random balance, each related to a different financial institution, most of which she'd never heard of. She grabbed her phone from her back pocket, snapped photos of a few pages, and hurried back to her cubicle.

Maybe it was too soon to make assumptions. Maybe all it would take to restore her peace of mind that Kyle and Cassidy—certainly Kyle— were above reproach in their stewardship of the ProtectUS fundraiser and church cash, in general, was a few days and some time to review the pictures she'd taken more closely. But maybe not.

I don't put much stock in any of it, Kristin's mom had said of the rumors about Kyle and Cassidy's finances. *It's not right to count other people's money, especially not your pastor's. We should just pray for 'em. Gossips can poison just about anything.*

Kristin had obeyed the instructions and included the nameless busybodies on her prayer list. She prayed that God would heal whatever it was inside of them that was making them accuse the Welshes of using church funds to build their new house. She prayed that they might find another spiritual home if Moving Word wasn't the right place for them. She prayed that Kyle and Cassidy's reputations would survive all of the chatter making its way through the community. Gossip like that could ruin a church family. It could ruin the Mavens and everything the other women had done to build it into something meaningful.

But prayers could be misplaced, and even Kristin's mom—who had, in recent years, given hundreds and hundreds of dollars of her own money to the church—could be wrong sometimes.

More and more, as she tapped through the newest photos on her phone, Kristin thought she might be.

22

Camryn

**Blog Post: Peppermint & Purity:
Protecting God's Plan for Intimacy
This Holiday Season
by Camryn Lee Cady**

Christmas is almost here...and there's so much to look forward to.

First and foremost, of course, you're reflecting on the real meaning of the season: the birth of our Savior! Personally, I can't think of a better excuse to throw a month-long party, so I'm all for the trappings of the Christmas holiday. Just don't lose sight of what's most important! Look for opportunities to serve in your community, to give back just like Jesus would (you can donate to our church's ProtectUS fundraiser <u>HERE</u> to fight human trafficking). How fun is it to spend this time honoring Him? Remember to take advantage of your home church's offerings this Advent season. (If you're in the Charlotte area, make sure to join us at the Gala for Goodness on behalf of ProtectUS! You might just see some familiar faces! You can also make a donation or RSVP to our online event Garnet Gals for Goodness at the link in my bio. VIP tickets are limited, but so worth the extra spend.)

You have family traditions to get to. You and your girls are probably planning all kinds of festive events, too! There are sparkly red tops to be worn and you need a place to wear them. Holiday happy hours, Secret Santa exchanges...any celebration is the right moment to break out your best outfits and celebrate the fruit of this joyous time of year. Candy cane martini, anyone?

But Christmas is about so much more than all that. As Christians, we're called to be generous throughout the year, but there's no time like the present (pun intended LOL!) to love on your people. I hope you're having the best time coming up with special things to wrap in pretty paper and leave under the tree for your friends and family members. If you need gift ideas, don't forget to check out our Mavens gift guides! (Fun fact: 5% of all of our affiliate fees will go straight to ProtectUS because generosity never sleeps.)

If you're in a season of dating or engagement as we begin the Christmas celebrations, you and your man have your share of exciting things planned amid the magic of twinkling lights and holiday cards. But Mavens, I'm here to challenge you, because the temptations are also plentiful. Don't be so distracted by all the glitter that you let the enemy creep in! Safeguarding your purity can be a challenge no matter the time of year, but the joy and romance of the holiday season make it that much more difficult. Remember: Your purity is the ultimate gift, even if you can't put it under the tree!

As always, I want to support you in your walk with the Lord, so over the next few weeks, I'll be offering advice to give you the extra help you need to stay pure and have lots of fun in the dreamy weeks between Thanksgiving and New Year's Eve.

Exhaling, Camryn leaned back against the cushions of the yellow couch, already satisfied with what she'd written. A second draft probably wouldn't be required. Cam hit Save. It felt good to pour energy into the post after the last few days of making nice to Avery Adams-Wallace. They'd hung out several times since shopping for dresses—at lunch, then a tour of Moving Word, then dinner before Bible study at Cassidy's house the night before. It had been a treat to have extra face time with Amber—who was lovely—and the tension with Cassidy seemed to have fallen away, which felt to Cam like implicit permission to forge ahead with publicizing Garnet Gals. It was too late to cancel, anyway—there was no choice but to go all in! She'd announced the event to the Mavens before things had gone left with the pastor's wife. Her intentions had always been good, anyway.

In any case, she was exhausted from the drama of being on her best behavior and glad to be doing what she knew she did best: counseling her followers.

> Let's get one thing out of the way, girls: God built us for desire! With all the celebratory

trappings of the holidays, it's no wonder that some of the usual protections for your purity are falling like snow on Christmas morning. We're only human! Luckily for you, your Mavens sisters and I are here to help you stay true to yourself and to God and to give you some helpful tools so you don't look back on this Christmas season with regret.

Cam wished that someone had cared to give her a few helpful tools, ideally back in high school. Maybe then she would have been ready for a boy like Bryce Peters, who'd invited her to homecoming when she was a sophomore in high school and asked her to officially be his girlfriend during the final notes of the dance's first slow song. For more than two years after that, he'd been so polite, so quick to take the extra time to visit with Mamaw after dropping Camryn off well before curfew, to carry her backpack out to the parking lot when it was packed heavy with textbooks during final exams, to always know exactly what to order for her when they went out for ice cream and how to order it with such good manners that the person working behind the counter seemed genuinely interested in his friendship. But being polite wasn't necessarily the same as having good character, and it didn't make Bryce immune to the temptations and sins that boys far less gentlemanly than he had fallen prey to long before. Camryn had learned this for herself just a few weeks before Christmas break during her senior year of high school.

> Gather up your inner strength, throw on your favorite sparkly top, and swipe on another coat of that red lipstick. The armor of God looks a little different for everyone, and I can testify firsthand to the power of a bold lip when it comes to doubling down on your conviction to just about anything, including 1 Corinthians 6:18: *Flee from sexual immorality. All other sins a person commits are outside the body, but whoever sins sexually, sins against their own body.* ☺︎♡

That evening at her friend Shay's holiday party, it had all happened so fast after Cam and Bryce had excused themselves to the guest bedroom to exchange Christmas gifts away from the curious eyes of the two dozen or so attendees. Mamaw had helped Cam pick out a watch for Bryce at Dillard's, and he'd presented her with a dainty heart charm dangling from a thin silver chain, which he clasped gently around her neck. She caught a glimpse of the way it hung perfectly above the neckline of her black party dress in the full-length mirror on the back of the door. Shay's family wasn't expecting guests, but her mom had still decorated the spare room with plenty of twinkling white lights and real, fragrant garland. Reflected back to Cam, everything looked miraculous.

"I think you're really special," Bryce had told her.

"I think you're special, too," she'd replied, holding the silver heart around her neck between two fingers. "I love you."

"I promise I love you more," he'd said. It wasn't the first time they'd said they loved each other, but something about it felt different. Better.

One minute, she and Bryce had been staring into each other's eyes, talking more about how much they loved each other and all of the plans they wanted to make during the upcoming break, and the next they'd been kissing just a little more than they usually did. She started feeling the pressure of his body against her in unfamiliar ways and then there was the crinkle of foil unwrapping and her underwear was gone and her lipstick was a red confetti all over Bryce's face.

He'd been so kind to her after it happened, so concerned that she was comfortable and not in pain. She had been comfortable, and she wasn't in pain. Before that night, they'd done their fair share of making out and wrestling with the loose fabric of each other's clothes, and while Cam knew that having sex with Bryce at seventeen wasn't exactly right, it didn't feel exactly wrong, either. He promised that he loved her *more*. Back then, that was all the sense she could make of things. Aside from a few awkward lectures from her school health teacher, Cam couldn't remember ever communicating with anyone about sex. No one had been there to make her feel regret.

Years later, Cam wanted to be for the Mavens what she'd needed then: a trustworthy friend to help them catch their mistakes sooner and to guide them through their regrettable behavior. If she could show them how to avoid the mistakes in the first place, all the better.

She hadn't regretted the night at Shay's house until long after it happened, when Bryce was accepted to college out of state and suggested that they break up right then so they wouldn't risk more inevitable heartbreak by "dragging out the relationship." Only then—and after several weeks of nursing her pain with doughnuts and clutching bags of frozen peas to her eyes to dull the swelling from her tears—did she find, in the deep recesses of her brain, vague memories of Sunday school lessons that had warned against the dangers of getting intimate with someone before marriage. She hadn't heeded these warnings, and that was surely why she was hurting so much. It was why she now owed her obedience to the church. It was why she'd worked hard to reclaim her purity in the years since.

When Cam got involved with Cru in college the following year, her shame became less confusing. There, she learned, she'd deviated from God's plan for her at Shay's party, which broke her heart more than Bryce Peters and his move to Missouri ever had. And as much as she hated that any of it had happened—as much as she avoided bringing it up with anyone—Jeff and her friends included—she wondered if the Moral Mavens would have been possible without her feeling so convicted, without the personal experience she'd had with sins of the flesh and God's forgiveness. Without that testimony, what kind of difference would she be able to make? Maybe she'd had to go through that to know the power of His design.

Everything had been better since she'd dedicated herself more fully to her faith, including the memory of that long-ago Christmas.

> I hope you'll check back for practical tips every week of this blessed holiday season! We're in this together. xoxo, Cam ♡
>
> P.S. There's more to come on this subject for the Garnet Gals! Don't forget to grab your ticket ASAP. Upgrade to the VIP package for a cozy Q&A with me and some other special friends, plus lots of other surprises.

As Cam reviewed what she'd written, a selfie she'd snapped of herself and Mamaw lit up the screen of her now vibrating phone. In the picture, they were posing together on the front porch of Mamaw's house during a trip Camryn had taken home to Durham earlier that year, her grandmother's lips coated in her signature red lipstick.

"Hi, Mamaw," she said into the phone, saving her document again and closing the laptop.

"You're a hard lady to pin down these days," Mamaw said.

Cam laughed. "Sorry. Do I owe you a call?"

"I'm not over here keeping tally," Mamaw told her. "What's been going on down there?"

"It's just been so busy," Cam sighed, rising from the couch to make herself some tea. "The pastor and his wife asked me to help plan this huge Christmas party. It's a benefit for charity. There are all of these famous people involved. And that's on top of work."

"I'm sure you can handle it," Mamaw said. "We don't do anything halfway in our family." She was probably already in bed, her feet elevated on a stack of cushions after spending the day trapped in a pair of ladylike heels. "Do y'all need help?"

Cam set the full kettle—a pretty cast-iron thing gifted to her by the very woman on the other end of the phone—on the stove. Mamaw was always reminding her that she was only a phone call away. As if Camryn could ever forget. Beneath those reminders always lingered a silent apology about the missing generation between them, the gaping absence, perhaps, of a more approachable mother figure to whom Cam might go in a tough situation. Mamaw couldn't know that Cam rarely considered what life would have been like had her parents survived the accident—the intoxicated party the other driver, not Cam's mom or dad—that had killed them when she was only three years old. Camryn allowed her to operate under the assumption that her own daughter had not been forgotten and was still grieved on a daily basis by the little girl she'd barely gotten to know. Mamaw had almost always been enough for Cam.

She paused for a few more seconds. "How are things with Jeff?"

Grateful for the change in subject, Cam located her favorite mug and a tea bag. The lapsed bills Jeff had found a few Sundays before were now shoved in with her tea collection, a stack thick enough that it threatened to jam up the hardware in the drawer and spill into whatever was hidden behind. If only making them disappear permanently was as easy as making the phone calls she'd promised. "Oh, he's great," she said, ignoring the envelopes and closing the drawer. Mamaw had never seemed quite impressed with Jeff, no matter how hard Cam worked to help her see his best qualities. "I barely see him because he's working so much. He's up for a promotion. Once he gets it, I'm hoping I'll have big news for you."

"That will be nice," Mamaw said.

"Nice? That's all?"

"Well, it *will* be nice," Mamaw went on. "Everyone loves a wedding."

"Especially mine."

"I'm sure your day will be very special, Camryn Lee. You've always loved a little sparkle."

Cam tried not to be offended, distracting herself instead with the whistle of the kettle and busying her hands with the task of removing it from the stove. If Cam's love for the so-called finer things was worthy of shame—and it wasn't, really, because she hardly lived extravagantly, and she worked hard for everything that was hers—it was only because her grandmother had brought her up to admire them. The wedding that Camryn had been planning in her head for as long as she could remember was not only a reflection of her own preferences, but also of Mamaw's. Extra funds would need to be spent on larger floral centerpieces, because that's what Mamaw always noticed as a wedding guest. The cake would need to come from a top-tier bakery because Mamaw was quick to comment on a lackluster dessert. Those things cost more money, but that wasn't Camryn's fault. She and Jeff would figure it out together, and it would all be well worth it—the expense, and even the wait.

Everything would be better when they were married.

"Anything else happening up there?" Cam asked, making her way back to the couch.

"Not really," Mamaw said. "I'm having that same old trouble with my knee again, but I went back to the doctor, and I'm not sure there's much more to do about it. Everything they're recommending would need to be out of pocket. I guess we'll just keep playing the lottery, won't we?"

Cam had not adopted her grandmother's ritual of buying lottery tickets each time she visited a convenience store. Anyway, she had a few surer things in mind—things that felt less biblically questionable than the gamble of a scratch-off.

"We'll see what we can do," she said into the receiver. "I love you, Mamaw."

"I love you, too, sweet girl," Mamaw said.

With the call disconnected, Cam was reminded—as she always was when she finished chatting with her grandmother—that she should make a point to call home more. She owed Mamaw more than just the occasional check-in—more, even, than a generous check to help with medical expenses. Mamaw couldn't work forever. Cam wanted to give her all the things she deserved, especially the opportunity to age gracefully and without worry.

It had been many years since she'd lived back home in Durham full-time, and yet she still couldn't wrap her head around what Mamaw's life was like with her gone. Camryn's own time in the house nearly overlapped with the years her mother had spent there, so the family's matriarch had long been accustomed to serving in the role of caretaker. Having lost her young husband to a stroke when she was pregnant with their first and only child, Mamaw had very little time for anything outside of work and fulfilling her daughter's needs, then her granddaughter's, for the vast majority of her adult existence. How much time could one spend playing bridge? Mamaw acted like she was as happy as ever, but with all the long quiet evenings and weekends she must spend home alone, Cam wasn't so sure. Eventually, she'd have to retire from her job, and what would she do then?

By Mamaw's inevitable retirement, hopefully, the Mavens ministry would be large enough to justify Cam running it full-time. Good exposure from the gala should help get them there faster. With Jeff doing well at work, permanently leaving Charlotte for Durham probably wouldn't be a feasible option, but the trip only took a few hours. Cam could pack their toddlers into the car and sing along to kiddie hymns with them until they pulled into Mamaw's driveway. Things would get complicated later on, when the children were in school all day—though Cam would love to homeschool if she could—and running to various activities in the afternoons, but with enough time, Mamaw might consider selling the house and moving to be closer to the family, maybe even settling into a mother-in-law suite or guest house in whatever home Cam and Jeff decided to buy before their wedding.

But Camryn was getting ahead of herself. She retrieved her laptop from the coffee table, woke up the screen, and navigated to her bank's website. She'd deleted the app on her phone. Inhaling sharply, Cam clicked around until she was invited to view her account balance, something she generally avoided. It had been months since she'd last checked it. Now she saw the numbers plainly in front of her—a figure for her checking account that was much lower than it should have been; another one for her savings that wasn't even worth considering; and a third, much larger one the bearer of the bad news that she already knew: that her debt on this one credit card alone was a load heavier than she could bear. There was no question of what should happen next.

It had been a few weeks since she'd accepted Lara Irving's invitation to the Advent Ambassador program, and Shepherd Lovely seemed thrilled with the content she'd been producing as part of the partnership. The money the brand had promised wouldn't come in until the new year, and while it would be wonderful when it did, there had to be more to get—and faster.

Cam looked at her accounts again. They were still ugly.

Cam didn't like anything ugly.

Hi Lara, she typed into a new email window,

I'm having the absolute BEST TIME working with you and the team! Thank you THANK YOU for having me as an Advent Ambassador.

I hate to be presumptuous, but I would also hate for you to miss out on anything meaningful God has working in my life... so I wanted to let you know about this big online event I'm leading. It's called Garnet Gals for Goodness, and it's meant to support the gala we're hosting in partnership with our church for ProtectUS the week before Christmas. I'm spearheading it with the Mavens, and everyone is so excited!

I was wondering if Shepherd Lovely would be open to making a contribution to Garnet Gals? As you can imagine, it's been quite the undertaking... and I'm covering most of it on my own. We're doing what we can to bless ProtectUS with the proceeds, but if y'all would be open to sponsoring us, it would be such a gift.

Thank you for considering! I appreciate you!

                                          Camryn Lee Cady

Camryn had run proposed pricing for Garnet Gals by the rest of the Mainframe team before the sales page went live. Only Kristin had voiced concerns that it might be a little steep, but that was typical for her. She was always trying to speak on behalf of the "younger Mavens" who she said were "just starting out," as if she represented everyone under the age of twenty-five. Maybe Kristin didn't understand philanthropy, but there would be plenty of women who saw things clearly. And while Camryn had truthfully not had the time to craft the prices for Garnet Gals based on any sort of spreadsheet or formula, everything was bound to shake out in the end. She knew enough about and had attended enough other online programs to trust that she wasn't asking for anything ridiculous. Kyle and Cassidy would get their money to share with ProtectUS, and it would be a coup for the Mavens, too.

And why shouldn't Cam get a little something for her time? Shepherd Lovely could afford it, and sponsoring Garnet Gals—whatever that meant—would be good for their brand. Camryn worked in marketing. She knew this. Was that really any different than the company making the big donation to ProtectUS that she had never gotten around to inquiring about? She could ask about that later on, too. Would God really care what accounts the donations were coming out of and into when they were all for the good of His people?

Camryn Lee Cady sincerely doubted it.

23

Savannah

Of all of the spaces in Savannah and Chad's house, the home gym was the most extravagant—the least minimal—furnished as it was with the best exercise equipment that money could buy thanks to the many hours Chad had spent researching. It had started as a never-used guest bedroom with the kind of ample natural light that inspired Savannah's private daydreams of pastel mobiles and teddy bear wallpaper and made her want to use the word *dappled*. Neither of them had ever said out loud that it was meant to be the nursery, but this long-term plan for it had been obvious to Savannah when they'd purchased the house. Its full potential still unrealized, the room had been converted into a gym using funds gifted to the Trumans by Chad's parents, who had a habit of sending each of their sons a hefty check every few years for no apparent reason. After a months-long conversation about the possibility of using all of the money to make a donation to a missionary organization, they'd decided to use a large chunk of it to assemble the home gym—which would also be an investment in Chad's growing, newly profitable health coaching business—and donate whatever was left to a local shelter for victims of domestic abuse.

"You're going to be happy you did this today, babe. I promise," Chad told her as they stretched on the rubber tiled floor. "I saw about ten new studies this week about exercise and stress."

Savannah's focus remained on reaching for her toes.

"I also saw another article this week about exercise and fertility," he added.

Chad had apparently forgotten that they'd been working out together at least three times a week for the entire year they'd been trying so hard to get pregnant, plus the many years that had come before. Savannah had even run a couple of marathons shortly after graduating from college. Plenty of articles also linked having sex with getting pregnant—and God knew the Trumans had been putting their best foot forward to prove the truth of that research, as well.

Savannah crossed to the rack that held her husband's collection of free weights, each set its own bright shade. "Should I start with these?" she asked, gesturing to the orange five-pound dumbbells.

"You barely stretched," Chad said, reaching further into the space between his extended legs, beaming up at her. He tapped the empty space next to him on the floor. "Come on back. Do you have somewhere to be? Hot date? How was school?" he asked, walking his hands over to the side to pull on his left toes.

Savannah had only been home from work for twenty minutes. "Fine. The kids are getting antsy for break."

"And remind me what we have this weekend?"

"We still need to plan our Sunday school lesson," Savannah said. "I'm getting together with some of the girls to get things ready for the gala. Other than that, we can lay low."

"I'm glad you have time planned with your friends," Chad said, walking in small circles and thrusting his arms back and forth to loosen them up. "I know you've got a lot going on with the doctor stuff."

"*We've* got a lot going on."

"You know that's what I meant."

"Okay."

"I was trying to be respectful of the fact that I know it's weighing heavier on you."

Savannah really did want to trust that this was where Chad was coming from. But it was hard to hear what he was saying, and even harder to always be the one to assume the best about every step of their impossible walk to parenthood. As far as Savannah knew, her own mother had been solely responsible within her marriage for the ladylike beginnings of each new member of their family, just like her mother before her and her mother before that. It wasn't fair. None of it was fair. In choosing Chad as a partner, she'd hoped there would never be any doubt that burdens and heartbreak would all be shared equally between them.

"You really think that if I keep coming up here and moving weights around, we're suddenly just going to get pregnant the way everyone else does, don't you?" she said.

"Well, I'm not making the studies up. Also, maybe some fun would be good for you. People say that sometimes when you stop trying so hard, it just happens. Like a miracle."

Savannah laughed. Continuing to believe in miracles felt as futile as approaching the heaviest weights in the room with earnest confidence in her ability to pick them up one-handed. Job 5:8–9: *But if I were you, I would appeal to God; I would lay my cause before Him. He performs wonders that cannot be fathomed, miracles that cannot be counted.* Perhaps she'd laid her causes at His feet too much or for too long.

"Like a miracle," she scoffed. "Okay."

"It would be better than IVF. I read up on it a little more, and it's not sitting right. Morally, I mean. Plus, my parents would lose their minds if they found out."

This was the first they'd talked about it since the day they'd run out of Dr. Clark's office. Dodging near-constant calls from Angela—and the occasional other Maxwell family member—about the

Gala for Goodness had been about all Savannah could handle on top of her daily responsibilities.

"Why? Because it makes the Truman lineage a little less perfect?" she asked.

"I never said that."

"Of course you didn't. You didn't have to. It wouldn't exactly line up with their politics, either."

"Does it line up with ours?"

"Let's not even go down that road." As a rule, Savannah and Chad avoided the subject.

"I'm not trying to ruin our night here," Chad said. "I think it's nice for you to spend time with your friends."

Savannah wanted so badly to be angry, but she didn't feel like fighting with Chad. "I agree," she told him. "I'm sorry. I'm tired of talking about this. That's all."

"I know you think I don't understand, but I do."

Savannah nodded. She had no choice but to believe—in her husband, if nothing else.

"So what's the plan with the girls?" Chad pulled heavier weights from the rack.

"We're having brunch together after we meet up for the gala planning."

"You love brunch," Chad said. His smile looked relieved. "While you're there, can you let Camryn know I'm low on protein powder? Maybe she can get me some free product." Chad could only hold back his laughter for a few seconds before letting it loose from his throat. He dropped the weights on the floor with a muffled thud.

Savannah tossed her damp workout towel at him and went back to exercising. If they couldn't get pregnant, at least they could laugh.

* * *

Since the ballroom where the Welshes had decided to host the Gala for Goodness was booked and busy every night of the week year-round—not to mention throughout the holiday season when they also, Savannah had discovered, accommodated late morning and early afternoon events—Cassidy had asked the volunteers to meet her in one of the church's larger gathering spaces to work on party details. That Saturday morning, Savannah found herself at Moving Word with Camryn, Trishy, Kristin, Amber Lambert, Avery Adams-Wallace, and some teenaged volunteers from the youth group. Brandon Goddard had also showed up to help, dressed in yellow joggers and armed with impressive conviction about ProtectUS.

"LGBTQIA+ teens are at a higher risk of being trafficked than any other group," he shared with the women in the room after Avery asked about his interest in lending a hand. "Most people don't know that."

Savannah watched as the others—all except one, anyway—smiled politely at Brandon. She could feel a pit form in her stomach. Her students were on the verge of becoming teens. They were babies, nowhere near old enough to fear the world's evils or how they might be targeted for identifying with the acronym Brandon had recited.

"Thanks for sharing, Brandon," Cassidy said, her smile tight, weight distributed awkwardly as she shifted from one foot to the next. "All groups impacted by human trafficking are equally valuable, though. Let's remember that the ones you just mentioned don't matter *more*."

Brandon cocked his head and furrowed his brow. "I wasn't—"

"This really isn't a topic we prioritize discussing," Cassidy added tightly.

"Cassidy kept saying I should fly back for the party," Avery explained, taking her turn to greet the others before the exchange between Cassidy and Brandon could continue. Savannah had been surprised to see Avery present, smiling right along with the rest of the volunteers through the youth group's litany of names and Brandon's introduction. "I figured why not come in a few days early to help? I'm invested now!"

She sure was. Savannah had heard from Trishy that the Adams-Wallaces had donated ten thousand dollars to Moving Word's fund for ProtectUS. Avery had also been talking up the drive to her following of nearly nine hundred thousand, even surprising everyone by matching their collective contributions a few days before. It was no wonder Cassidy wanted her there in person.

If Camryn was still salty about the situation, she was barely letting it show. Savannah was proud of her friend for putting her feelings aside for the good of the larger goal. While Cassidy had been celebrating Avery's contributions, Camryn had resumed work on Garnet Gals, delegating tasks to the Mainframe and building out a full schedule of online programming that included giveaways, a remote worship music dance party, a series of virtual "How's Your Heart?" sharing sessions, and several presentations that were all connected in one way or another to the idea of preserving one's purity during the holiday season.

For now, though, Camryn seemed to have shown up ready to focus solely on the event. Dressed in baggy jeans that were somehow still flattering, she fell into step behind Savannah as they received their assignments from Cassidy.

"Trishy, Avery, and Kristin, I'm going to have you with me on decor duty," she said, indicating a long table stocked with high-end craft supplies. "Amber, Savannah, and Camryn, I'm going to have you work on stuffing our swag bags. All of the materials are over there by the door." Cassidy pointed to a mountainous pile of cardboard boxes and tote bags. Stuffed into one of them, Savannah knew, was a stack of cards outlining directions to a landing page where attendees could redeem a free membership to Chad's newest two-week online training program. As frustrated as she was by the stalled nature of their conversation around IVF, she loved him a little extra in that moment, remembering how excited he'd been to contribute something of his own for the occasion.

"Everyone else, would you mind cross-checking the place cards with the list on that clipboard over there on the table? Let's get to it!" Cassidy finished. She tapped the screen on her phone and the room filled with the sound of a popular new worship song as she gestured for the women helping with decor to join her at the nearest table.

Camryn, unsurprisingly, was quick to take the lead on the swag bags. She directed Amber and Savannah to begin unpacking the donations and sorting them into assembly line-style stations. "Then we can just stuff the bags like one, two, three!" she said animatedly. Savannah was relieved to see her back in her usual good spirits. Camryn was at her best when there were things to be done and made lovely.

Amber and Savannah chatted as they unloaded the riches with which the church had been gifted for the event: Christmas tree ornaments, coupons for local businesses, travel mugs printed with Matthew 6:19–21 (*Do not store up for yourselves treasures on earth, where moths and vermin destroy...*), glittery bags of peppermint tea, samples of essential oils, and more. Savannah was pleasantly surprised by how easy it was to make conversation with Amber. Perhaps she'd allowed Amber's status as a professional baseball wife—not to mention her friendship with the conspicuous Avery Adams-Wallace—to cloud her expectations of the newcomer.

"You know, Bo feels pretty strongly about having the boys in private school for security reasons because of crazy fans and all that, but if it were up to me, we'd just send them to the public schools in your district," Amber said after they'd giggled about a crate of particularly gaudy crystal keychains donated by a car dealership down the road. "And really I know that homeschooling would be great for them, too, but I'll be honest with you—I couldn't do it." She laughed and covered her eyes in mock shame. "I just don't have the patience."

"Homeschooling isn't all it's cracked up to be," Savannah said. "My parents bit off way more than they could chew trying to handle that."

"I feel better hearing you say that. I really do. I was worried I was being a quitter."

"Not at all. My parents were in no way qualified." Savannah forced a laugh before she realized that she may have offended Amber. "Not that you and your husband are like them. You know what I mean."

It was the perfect time for a voice from the past, which was precisely what emerged in a current of echoes down the long hallway outside the room Cassidy had claimed as their makeshift workshop. "Savannah Maxwell!" the voice called over and over again. "Savannah!"

Before Savannah could figure out how she knew the voice—because she did—its owner was in the room, winded and bending over herself; hands clutching knees; a long, pale, straight blond braid nearly brushing against the ground. There was only one person with hair like that who knew Savannah by name.

"Really, Angela? Are you kidding me?" Savannah snapped, suddenly aware of a sick feeling in her stomach and a tightness somewhere around her windpipe. Immediately mortified at the prospect of seeing which of the other volunteers had already clocked the uninvited guest, she refused to look at anyone but her former sister-in-law, regardless of how disgusted she was by the sight.

Angela rose slowly, inhaling deeply. She looked much like she always had, her face free of makeup and only subtly touched by the signs of aging she'd always attributed to angels. Smiling, she patted her hands up and down her long houndstooth coat. After a few strange moments, she managed to pull her phone out of a pocket. "I saw that you were here," she said, still winded. "I was in town already, shopping for a dress for the gala."

"What do you mean you saw I was here?" Savannah asked.

"Here," Angela said, keeping her phone at arm's length with the screen out as she moved closer. There, Savannah saw a selfie Camryn had posted of herself, Amber, Avery, and Cassidy, dressed in the outfits they were wearing that morning, with the decor table in the background. While Savannah was not centered in the photo—thankfully, too, because even she could see that her choice of outfit left much to be desired—it was impossible to miss her presence in the corner of the image, mouth open, one hand reaching for a swag bag. *So blessed to be with these ladies at Moving Word today!* was written in pink, curlicued text atop the smiling faces of Cam and the others, a clip from Cyndi Lauper's "Girls Just Want to Have Fun" playing on loop.

Over her shoulder, Savannah could see that Cam had retreated to a far corner of the room.

"You're tracking me through my friends' Instagram?" Savannah said. "You see me in the corner of a picture, and you're down here in twenty minutes? That's creepy."

"Creepy? Come on. You've been impossible to get in touch with. What else was I supposed to do?" Angela said, pleading. "We thought you'd want to make up once we bought those tickets. When did you get so stubborn? Your daddy misses you. He hates that y'all aren't speaking. He knows he was wrong."

"Just *he* was wrong, Angela?" Savannah said, all of the anger and frustration of the previous year leaking out of her body in five words.

Angela sighed and walked toward Savannah, arms outstretched. Savannah ducked away from her, coming dangerously close to tripping on the pile of cardboard boxes still stacked beside the door. "Come on, Sav," Angela said, refusing to budge. "You really can't find it in your heart to forgive? It's almost the holidays. Vance has forgiven us. Your mom, too. The kids are happy. Vance and I are co-parenting. We're all spending Christmas together."

"That's their business, and they should be embarrassed. Please leave."

"What do you want me to tell your daddy?"

"Nothing," Savannah said. "I'd prefer you not tell him you saw me at all."

"We have a total honesty policy," Angela said smugly. "Plus, you're going to see him at the party. Won't it be nice for all of us to have some peace?"

"I don't care if he never has peace."

"When did you start talking like that? It's ugly."

Savannah could feel another body step up next to hers. She hardly cared who it belonged to. She was just glad to no longer be alone. "Angela, I really do think it would be best for you to step out." It was Cassidy. "We can agree that God's house is no place for this kind of spectacle. My husband is a pastor here, and I'm asking you kindly to leave."

"Oh, I know who you are," Angela said, narrowed eyes flashing from Savannah to Cassidy. "I've heard plenty about you around town."

"You have quite a reputation yourself, and—with all due respect—I don't think that's a conversation you want to get into," Cassidy replied, impressively calm.

"Do you have any idea how humiliating this

is?" Savannah hissed at Angela. Her face was on fire. "First buying the tickets to the gala, and now showing up here? You're making a mockery of my church."

"Don't be silly. A church can only make a mockery of itself."

"Are you trying to stir up drama for the tabloids? Do they pay you for this?"

"You know how we feel about the tabloids," Angela said.

"You didn't answer my question. You don't think I've seen the magazines?"

"What your mother does is her business. I think that picture of her on the cover of that magazine is beautiful, by the way. She was just over to the house for family dinner the other night, and I told her so. I made chicken pot pie."

"I need for you to leave," Cassidy said. Savannah had never been more grateful for her, or to belong to Moving Word. The Welshes had sworn they'd protect her after the scandal with her father. In spite of the weirdness of the weeks that had come before, Cassidy was making good on her promise

"I won't argue with a pastor's wife," Angela said, sniffing and straightening up. "And I won't cause problems in God's house. But you've chosen to host this event elsewhere, haven't you?"

Cassidy nodded.

Angela turned to Savannah and smiled. "We'll see you there, Sav. Your sister, too. Hopefully, we'll be allowed to talk then."

As Angela exited the room, Savannah prayed to disappear. There were too many eyes in the room, each one boring an acidic path into her body. She'd already been forced to watch as her family's traumas played out in front of the faceless public. Now she'd had to be in close proximity as it became theater for a small group of the most fabulous women she'd ever met and an assembly of fresh-faced teens. Finally releasing the breath she hadn't known she was holding, Savannah turned to Cassidy, her gratitude for her friend's support practically coming to the surface in tears. Before she could say a word, Cassidy had started marching toward the other side of the room, her shoulders up near her ears and her hands on her hips.

"How would we feel about taking a quick break and getting an earlier bite to eat? I just realized how hungry I am," Avery said brightly. "All of this decorating cuteness will still be here when we get back. Brunch on me?"

24

Kristin

All week long, the documents Kristin had discovered on Kyle's desk nagged at the back of her brain. In the rush of preparations for the Gala for Goodness—and now Garnet Gals—there hadn't been time to address her concerns with anyone else from the Mainframe in person, and it didn't seem like the kind of thing she'd want to be caught texting about. A person needed to watch only so many documentaries to understand how dangerous it could be to have evidence of one's meddling—however well-intentioned—in writing. Then again, an upscale brunch spearheaded by Avery Adams-Wallace wasn't the right venue to bring up what she'd found, either. She wasn't going to tell.

For someone from out of town, Avery seemed wildly well-connected in Charlotte. Less than fifteen minutes after Angela Maxwell's exit from Moving Word, Avery had confirmed a reservation for the group at a restaurant with a brunch so notoriously tough to crack that Kristin would have never even made the attempt—and on a Saturday, no less. When the women arrived, they were promptly informed that "the events nook was ready and waiting for Mrs. Adams-Wallace," then escorted to an oversized banquette with a tablescape so pretty that Kristin had to wonder if everything already planned for the Gala for Goodness should be reconsidered and redesigned from scratch. No one had mentioned Brandon or the youth group volunteers, all of whom—Kristin imagined—had remained at church to gossip about Angela Maxwell while they continued checking place cards. Hopefully, the Maxwell drama had distracted Brandon from the uncomfortable tension with Cassidy during introductions.

As Cassidy and Avery directed seating

arrangements for everyone who *had* made the cut for brunch, Kristin was grateful that Savannah was there, if hanging toward the back of the group. Understandably, she'd been withdrawn since the run-in with her sister-in-law.

"If it makes you feel any better," Kristin told Savannah quietly as they waited for direction from their impromptu hosts, "I made the mistake of reading comments on Instagram this week. It sucked."

"Why would that make me feel better?" Savannah asked, her eyes mostly blank.

"I don't know," Kristin admitted, feeling stupid. They were quickly ushered to opposite ends of the banquette.

Since she'd been under the impression that she'd be spending the day on manual labor and the prompt fulfillment of Cassidy's requests, Kristin had dressed that morning in an old pair of jeans and a swimming sweatshirt—an outfit that was now on full, unflattering display to the trendy dining room milling outside the apparently VIP events nook. If Camryn had been in charge of seating, she would never have allowed Kristin to be seated at the end.

For the moment, Cam didn't seem bothered

by the statement Kristin's appearance might be making on other, less-VIP restaurant-goers. Her leather jacket was still draped carefully over her shoulders, but she'd already taken out her phone and started snapping photos of their sophisticated surroundings. Avery—seated directly beside her—reached out a hand to cover Cam's, pushing the phone down to the table. "How about we keep this outing device-free?" she said. How did she manage it without any passive-aggression? "I do that with my girlfriends back home sometimes. It's so good for the soul." She tapped on her chest. It was her heart, really, but everyone—except Camryn, who looked like she'd rather be anywhere but on the receiving end of these instructions—seemed taken with the gesture. Phones were quickly stowed in purses under the table. Kristin was glad to be freed of hers.

"Fantastic," Avery said. "Savannah, I bet that makes you more comfortable, huh? Does that feel good?"

Savannah nodded through a strained smile.

A server approached the table, and Avery took the lead on an order for the group. As far as Kristin was concerned, it was just as well. Left to her own devices, she would have asked for a basic stack of pancakes, and she knew there were plenty of other, more interesting things on the menu: buckwheat waffles; smoked salmon benedict; drunken French toast, whatever that was. Everyone looked unsettled without their phones to anchor them, but they managed a few minutes of small talk while waiting for a round of mimosas to arrive.

"I didn't get to see the place cards up close," Cam said. "Were those poinsettias around the border?"

Cassidy nodded, then looked to Avery, more deferential than Kristin had ever seen her be, even to Kyle. "Did you think the poinsettias were too much? I was worried."

"Not at all," Avery said. "Very tasteful. 'Tis the season, anyway."

"The swag bags are coming together beautifully," Camryn bragged. "We're almost done. I can add Moral Mavens laptop stickers later." This was the first Kristin had heard about gifting Mavens laptop stickers to gala guests.

"I don't think we need those," Cassidy said.

"It's really our pleasure," Cam said. "We have plenty to go around."

"We're not including free pens from a bank or anything like that, are we?" Trishy said quickly.

Kristin was glad to be able to speak on behalf of both the Moving Word office and the swag bag team. "Definitely not," she said. "No bank pens." Not that Kyle and Cassidy didn't have plenty of banks to choose from. Maybe.

"Did I miss a bank sponsorship?" Cam laughed nervously. "Pens aren't aesthetic or anything, but, I mean, if they want to throw some cash in the swag bags, I don't think anyone would complain!" Most of the group joined in on the giggling as the server approached with a tray of mimosas. Kristin couldn't bring herself to laugh along with the rest. "For charity, obviously."

Avery beamed at the server and accepted her drink. "Did I see this is fresh-squeezed?"

The server nodded.

"What a delight!" Avery said.

As the server retreated to the kitchen, Avery raised her glass toward the middle of the table. Everyone followed suit. Kristin moved the flute at what she feared was an awkward pace, paranoid that she might spill her drink and ruin the moment if she went too fast. Thankfully, her glass managed to find the others without incident.

"I'd like to make a toast to the women of Moving Word," Avery said, resting the hand not holding the glass on the collar of her still-crisp white Oxford shirt. "I can't tell you how blessed I feel that all of this has worked out so well and that I can be part of this incredible event you're putting on. It's been so special getting to know all of you. Thank you for being so warm and inclusive."

"And I'd like to make a toast to Savannah," Camryn added. The other women had already started pulling back their beverages after lifting them to acknowledge Avery. "I don't want you to worry one bit about what happened with Angela today. We all have your back. We're sisters."

"Cheers to that!" Trishy sang—a little too loudly, perhaps.

Savannah looked mortified as the other ladies finished toasting and sipped the top layer of orange bubbles from their champagne flutes. Trishy shot her a knowing look as she dabbed her mouth with a linen napkin.

"Now, I don't mean to ruin the mood or anything," Cassidy said, immediately ruining Kristin's mood. At least the mimosa was giving her something to do with her hands. "I do think we should chat about what you think we can expect from your family at the event, Savannah. We do have your back, but it's also very important that the gala goes off without a hitch. Is there nothing that can be done to discourage them from coming? I feel awful even saying that, but you know what I mean. You said yourself that this could make a mockery of the church."

"That's right," Camryn said. Keeping up with her contributions to the conversation felt to Kristin like watching a tennis match, or perhaps playing spectator to someone bouncing a ball off an immovable wall. "We're here to support you. How can we help? The church's and the Mavens' reputations are on the line."

Savannah's face went nearly as pale as it had in front of Angela Maxwell.

Amber jumped in quickly, perhaps sensing Savannah's discomfort. "We were planning to have at least one of the guys from our security team with us for the night, anyway. Bo wouldn't mind asking him to keep an eye out for the Maxwells. Savannah, would you be comfortable with that?"

Again, Savannah's attempt to respond was foiled—this time by Cassidy. "That's very sweet of you to offer, Amber," she said with a smile. "But security or no, if there's any possibility of some big meltdown, we need to do something more drastic. There's a lot of money on the line here. Plus, Kyle's reputation. And the church's."

"Exactly," Camryn said, nodding. "The Mavens have a reputation to uphold, as well. We're mindful of that."

Kristin took a big swig of her mimosa. Shouldn't a restaurant of this caliber offer a pastry basket or something—especially for their finest table? Even a slice of warm bread would pair nicely with the fizzy sensation of the bright cocktail in the back of her throat. Kristin's experience with nice restaurants was fairly limited, but she guessed there would always be slices of warm bread around.

"Do you want me to stay home?" Savannah asked. "I can."

"Is that necessary?" Amber said, looking to Cassidy.

"That would be a bummer," Trishy added.

"And it's not fair," Kristin said. It sounded childish, but it was true. Savannah should be there. She and Chad had been generous with the fundraiser, and it had been her idea to make the large donation on behalf of the Mavens. As confusing as Kyle's documentation had looked, it seemed only right that people who'd been legitimately philanthropic should be in attendance. Plus, Kristin liked Savannah and Chad. Feeling the eyes of the table on her, she sipped heartily from her mimosa. She was almost ready for a refill.

"I'm just going to pop out to the ladies' room before the food gets here," Avery said, looking apologetically at the women who would need to slide out of the banquette to allow her to pass them. "Four kids later, you know?"

"I'll join you," Cassidy said.

Both Cassidy and Avery looked more graceful scooting out of a vinyl booth than anyone had a right to. Kristin felt angry about it, and it surprised her. She was used to being frustrated with Cassidy, but something about the pastor's wife's reaction to Savannah's plight—especially in front of Avery and Amber, not to mention her treatment of Brandon—accelerated the impact of the champagne on her empty stomach. Every lesson Kristin's mother had ever taught her about keeping things to herself and acting like a lady disappeared from her brain in fireworks of fresh-squeezed orange juice, resentment toward Cassidy Welsh, and her need to protect the underdog—in this case, Savannah. "I think Kyle and Cassidy are stealing from Moving Word."

For the first time in her life, Kristin heard someone actually gasp. Probably Cam.

She couldn't believe she'd actually *said* it. After sitting on what she'd seen in Kyle's office and all the suspicions she'd heard around the church about the pastor's finances, the only thing she could think of to keep attention away from Savannah was to prove it—and fast, before Cassidy could come back to the table. Recalling the no-phone rule, she paused briefly in reaching into her bag before realizing that its enforcer was also in the restroom.

Bigger rules were already being broken, anyway.

Kristin opened her photos and found the one she was looking for. "I didn't know what else to do," she said. "I didn't know what I was looking at. Here." She thrust the phone at Savannah.

Savannah held up her hands. "I don't know that I want to look," she said.

"It seems bad," Kristin said. "I didn't want it to cause any more trouble for us if it got out somehow. Especially since we've been hyping up the fundraiser so much and we're now doing the Garnet Gals thing."

"Keep your voice down," Camryn hissed. "You're acting insane." She glanced over her shoulder to make sure there was no sign of Cassidy and Avery's return. "Amber, I'm sorry you have to be here to see this. I'm so embarrassed. This is so unlike us."

Amber Lambert looked concerned, not angry or uncomfortable. "I'd like to hear the rest," she said. She reached out for Kristin's phone. "We need to protect ourselves, too. If this is true, it's fraud. Bo would want to know."

Surprised to have found an ally in Amber, Kristin handed over the phone. "It looks like a record of big pledges from important organizations and people at church," she explained. She glanced toward the bathroom. Avery and Cassidy weren't on their way back, but she started talking faster, anyway. It was what any informant would do. "I'm pretty sure the other papers are records of deposits into different accounts at different banks. I know that none of them are associated with the church. The money came in and it must have gone somewhere, but Moving Word doesn't have it, and it hasn't gone to ProtectUS. That means we don't really know what's going on with all the money we've asked Mavens followers for, either. It's going to look like we helped the Welshes steal their money."

"Can we call this serious evidence, though?" Savannah asked. "Maybe they're trying to keep some of the money hidden so that the big announcement at the gala will be a surprise."

"I dug around in our internal systems to make sure I wasn't missing some more official record of the donations or communication with the bank. I can't find anything."

Trishy had leaned over Amber's shoulder to look at the phone, too. "This is sloppy," she said quietly. "I don't like it." One prettily manicured nail crept its way between her veneers.

"Is it possible you're being paranoid?" Camryn asked. "I love you, but paranoia is real." Did Camryn really love her, though?

"Don't call her paranoid, Cam," Trishy said. "You should look at this. Amber's right. This could be major fraud. For real. If it's not, Kyle sucks at accounting, and there's no excuse for that."

"Why should the pastor have to be good at accounting?" Cam asked. "There are *accountants* for that. It's not like everyone knows how to balance a checkbook."

Amber was still scrolling through Kristin's phone, her mouth screwed up thoughtfully.

"This isn't how things are usually done around the office. Or with Kyle. I was also thinking about all those rumors about their house," Kristin continued. How had she sobered up so much in a matter of a few minutes?

"Rumors about their house?" Amber asked, eyes still down on the phone. She'd probably missed all that chatter from the summer in the rush of moving her family from Miami to Charlotte.

"People say they have an indoor pool," Kristin said. "A spa bathroom in the basement with a cold plunge. Heated floors everywhere. A full professional-grade outdoor kitchen with a pizza oven." At last, she could share the claims she'd seen made on the online discussion boards for the Welshes' neighborhood.

"That's all just gossip," Camryn said. "I've been there."

"They have very expensive taste," Trishy said.

"Is it so wrong to have a beautiful home?" Cam said.

"Quiet," Trishy—who had the clearest view of the path from the bathroom—said.

"We're done talking about this," Cam said through gritted teeth. She made a big show of fixing her hair. Kristin wished she would look in her direction.

"Done talking about what?" Cassidy said, sliding back into the booth.

At the same time, Avery made a *tsk* sound with her mouth and pointed to Amber. "I see a phone," she scolded. "Even my bestie has to follow the rules."

Amber brought Kristin's phone down to her lap and locked eyes with her across the table. Kristin had a feeling she wasn't finished talking about what she'd seen in the photos—and she hoped she was right. Thankfully, the server—with several reinforcements behind her—had arrived with trays of gorgeously garnished breakfast dishes. Kristin spotted several leaning towers of whipped cream.

"What did we miss?" Cassidy asked as she settled back into her seat. "Did I see whispering?"

"We weren't whispering about anything," Camryn said, smiling. She raised her glass to

Cassidy. "Just getting excited about the gala. Cheers to that."

Cassidy raised a single eyebrow, a trick Kristin hadn't yet seen. "Come on. Tell me."

"I was actually hoping to order something else to eat," Cam said, looking around the restaurant, her eyes wide. "Would anyone share more bacon with me?"

"You guys are being weird," Cassidy said. "What's going on?"

No one said anything.

"Tell me what you talked about while we were in the bathroom."

More silence. Kristin prayed for the server's speedy arrival.

It didn't happen. It was terrible. And Kristin was hungry.

Cassidy's eyes continued to narrow.

"I've been trying to get pregnant for a long time and I can't and we've been seeing a doctor about it and I'm scared everyone will hate me if I do IVF," Savannah said suddenly. She remained still, her admission settling around the table as platters of omelets and French toast were deposited in every empty space. The color drained from her face. Her complexion had taken on the look of the whipped cream dollops that had looked so appetizing mere moments before. "Sorry," she added frantically. "I was asking the girls if they had any advice."

Unfazed by the shift in tone at the table, the server lingered—finally—near the banquette. "Can I get anyone anything else?" she asked. She looked so proud. Kristin wondered if it was her first time catering to the special events nook. She had no idea what was happening right in front of her.

25

Camryn

"Seriously, Sav?" Cam snapped through a mimosa-infused hiccup. "IVF? Really? Are you okay?"

"I'm fine," Savannah said.

"You're not fine if you're talking about IVF and acting like a crazy person," Cam replied.

"I think we have bigger things to worry about," Kristin said. Camryn wished she was close enough to kick the girl under the table. If she thought that returning to the subject of Kyle and Cassidy's alleged dishonesty—with Cassidy right there at the table—was a good idea, then *she* was the crazy one. Transparency could only be taken so far.

"Should we talk more about the gala?" Trishy said.

Trishy could be so insensitive—or worse, she was deliberately working against Savannah's diversion and approaching the subject of church finances to put Cassidy in the hot seat. "I'm sorry, but my bigger concern right now is for my friend's health," Cam told her. "Savannah, what can we do? Other than pray for you, obviously, because I don't like where this is going for you spiritually."

"I don't want to get into it," Savannah replied, covering her face with one hand.

Camryn didn't like the idea of Savannah hiding this secret. Infertility was not the same as a bad credit score. And while Kristin's accusations of the Welshes had no proof, Savannah was here *owning* her confession. "How long have you been keeping this to yourself?"

"It really doesn't matter how long," Savannah said. "We've been hoping to have a baby for a while, and it wasn't happening. I asked my doctor about it, and he can't figure out what's wrong, so he's referring us to a specialist."

Cassidy was shaking her head back and forth. "You don't want to go down that road with a specialist. Why don't you look at adoption? Kyle's been in touch with this incredible orphanage in Kenya. So many beautiful babies there need homes. He can put you in contact with them."

"I don't know that that's a fair solution," Savannah replied.

Camryn couldn't see how it wouldn't be. Then again, there had been the whole incident with the photos of the Trumans at the African orphanage and the commenters accusing Savannah of being a "white savior." Was Savannah still hung up on that? And since when had being called a savior become such an insult? Cam took a sip of her mimosa. She wished she liked the taste of orange juice better.

"Our friends from church back home adopted their kiddos from Kenya. Beautiful children," Avery said, reaching across the table to grab Savannah's hand.

Camryn reached for Savannah's other hand. "That sounds like something to think about."

"Actually, maybe the Philippines," Avery added. "They're all so happy with how it's worked out."

The plates of food piled on the table had been all but forgotten. They smelled delicious, but there were important conversations to be had. It was a relief to have moved past Kristin's drama. Why did she have to make so many things so hard?

"Come on now," Cassidy said. "Next thing you know, you'll be trying to convince me abortion's okay, too. You and I both know you don't want to do science experiments on little babies. That's what IVF is. Anyway, my doctor told me it can take a few months to get pregnant. I thought that was encouraging."

"We've been trying for a year. Like, *really* trying," Savannah said. Her face looked almost guilty.

Camryn was at a loss for words and didn't like the way it felt. She was grateful when Amber Lambert slid a platter of waffles in Savannah's direction. "Why don't you have a few bites of these?" she suggested. "And maybe Trishy's right. Maybe we should get back to talking about the gala. I hate to keep Savannah on the spot with something so sensitive and private. We can talk about it later if she wants."

"Maybe that's a good idea," Avery said, pulling

an egg white omelet toward her place setting. "By the way, Camryn, I meant to tell you before I forget—I spoke to the girls over at Shepherd Lovely and I suggested that we consolidate what's happening with Advent Ambassadors. Now that I'm here working with you on this party and the fundraiser, it seems silly for them to be spending all that money on both of us. I've been working closely with them for years, and they're just the best. Lara's going to get back to me, but I think they're going to pull back on Advent Ambassadors since the campaign has already been so successful. They're going to make a nice donation to ProtectUS instead. Isn't that amazing news?"

 Camryn should have been happy. She knew that. Cassidy looked thrilled. Avery did, too. With Avery's help, Cassidy and Kyle would get exactly what they wanted—more for ProtectUS. Not for themselves. Always more for others. Then again, Cam had been doing just fine before Avery Adams-Wallace's advice and influence had migrated from her phone screen to her real life. The woman was just as insufferable as she'd predicted based on her beige, fresh-chicken-egg-heavy feed. Camryn loved being right, even when it cost her. And Avery's presence in Cam's circle was about to cost her more than she could have guessed.

Alcohol hadn't carried the same sick flavor in Camryn's mouth since she was a freshman in college, back when she was trying to impress the older girls in the sorority with how cool and fun she could be. They'd wanted her to play the party girl and the well-mannered Southern belle at the same time when they had to know firsthand that doing both was impossible. Before she'd met Jeff and found her place within the church, so many people wanted her to somehow be two outrageously different people in the same size 2 body. Only God had given her permission to be exactly who she was.

"I can't afford to have Shepherd Lovely drop me," she said, only realizing once the words were out of her mouth the extent to which the mimosa—and the breakfast she'd made no time for as she ran out the door—had caught up with her.

"Is everything okay?" Savannah asked, leaning closer to Camryn and jumping into concerned teacher mode. Even with the secret she'd kept for far too long, she was Cam's only real friend in the room.

"Yes. I'm fine."

"Are you sure?" Savannah pressed.

"I got a little behind on a few bills," Cam said. Just because Savannah was concerned didn't mean she deserved to hear the whole story, especially since she'd been holding back herself. It was easy for her to embrace a plain house and a simple wardrobe, to be a "minimalist." She'd been raised with money and had chosen to walk away from it—and she had a husband who'd committed his life to her when he was too young to know or care that there were grown-up women in the world who had to fight the temptation to spend their paychecks on things like anti-aging serums and high-end purses. And then there were the even richer women at the table. Avery and Amber could never relate to what Cam was dealing with—and regardless of where her money had come from, Cassidy couldn't, either. "It's not a big deal. Too blessed to stress, right?" Cam's laugh felt staccato coming through her throat.

"You seem pretty stressed," Avery said. "I'm so sorry. I didn't mean to cause problems. I thought I was doing the right thing with Shepherd Lovely. The donation sounded like such a nice gesture for Christmas."

"You are doing the right thing," Cassidy said. "Camryn, can we talk about this another time? This money is really important for ProtectUS. This was very generous of Avery and her connections at Shepherd Lovely."

"I shouldn't have said anything. Not that it's anyone's business, but I'm trying to get ahead on things," Cam said, ignoring Cassidy. It was all about the bottom line for her. After what Kristin had said, could Cam even trust her? Never mind. Of course she could. She was the pastor's wife! Everyone should keep their nose out of their friends' finances. Out of everyone's finances! She'd always believed that. It wasn't anyone's concern how much Camryn owed anyone, either. What Kristin had done was gross. "I'm putting money away for a wedding and for me and Jeff."

"Did Jeff push you to take the Shepherd Lovely deal? For the money?" Savannah asked gently. Even through her frustration, Cam sensed genuine concern.

At the same time, Trishy said, "Wait. Did you get engaged?"

"Jeff and I don't talk about money," Cam said quickly. "That's tacky."

"Jeff is your boyfriend, yes?" Amber asked. "The tall one?"

Camryn nodded. "We'll be engaged soon."

"That's exciting," Avery said, betraying none of the awkwardness of the brunch so far, as if Camryn would give her the satisfaction of a chat about engagement ring styles and unity candles. "Marriage is such a gift."

"I don't mean to be rude, but I'm actually not feeling very well," Cam said. Remembering her manners, she folded the cloth napkin from her lap and set it on the pristine plate in front of her. Why was it taking so long for Kristin to get the message and slide out of the banquette so Camryn could disappear?

"Do you need someone to drive you home?" Avery asked.

"I'm fine," Cam said. She nudged Kristin hard with her knee. Finally, she got the message and began to move.

"I can drive you," Trishy said. "I don't mind. I haven't had much to drink."

"I'm fine," Cam said again, grateful to feel her feet on the ground as she rose from her seat—even more grateful that she'd decided to take her own car from Moving Word to the restaurant. "I need to get home. I'll see everyone at church tomorrow."

She gathered her things and walked toward the exit. No one came after her. At the very least, Camryn hoped they weren't letting the food go to waste. It looked delicious and expensive, and she'd wanted to taste it badly.

* * *

Camryn had never intended for the Mavens to have an official leader or governing body. The Mainframe was just supposed to be a committee of big sisters for the broader community. More than anything, it was a logistical necessity. Camryn already spent too much of her one precious life being a leader and making decisions. She hadn't been looking for that with the Mavens. Really, she hadn't. But now that the group seemed to have lost all control—looking to Avery Adams-Wallace as some kind of idol, cheering as Cam herself lost out on important opportunities that would also benefit the church, nodding along as allegations flew about the Welshes—she realized they'd needed her to be in charge all along. No one else could see it. They were too busy being dazzled by Avery and eating the waffles she'd ordered. As if they didn't have gala gowns to fit into in just a few days. Cam would have to take care of *this*, too.

All of it was infuriating. But there was a lesson in it somewhere. Cam just had to figure out what it was, and how she should respond to it and make it part of her testimony.

In the short term, though, she had to figure out how to respond to the email waiting for her when she arrived home after brunch. It was from Margo, her manager.

Cam,

You know I hate to reach out on the weekend, but something's come to my attention, and I wanted to address it with you ASAP. As you know, our corporate team has recently doubled down on its commitment to diversity and representation. In recent months, we've received feedback from employees and customers who are concerned about the restaurant's treatment of people of color, LGBTQIA+ folks, and other members of marginalized communities. Being a queer woman myself, I've made it my personal mission to support those efforts within our marketing group as much as I can.

Our customer service team has received a critical mass of complaints regarding a lack of compassion for othered identities among your Moral Mavens. They've cited, in particular, an abundance of homophobic comments on your feeds about which no action has been taken. 12th Pine is building deep roots in Charlotte, and as your profile in town grows, these matters do have consequences. I've tried to be supportive of your extracurricular social media activity thus far, but I can't be expected to defend this kind of behavior when it hits corporate's radar. They also have concerns about your public alignment with Kyle Welsh, who has given some questionable interviews over the years.

On a personal note, I'll take this opportunity to let you know that I've been hurt and offended by what seems to be brewing in your community. I've seen it for months now and had hoped that you would be proactive in reining it in. To see that you haven't makes me question some of the investment I've made in your career and in our relationship.

You'll be asked in for a meeting with HQ next week, and I think you should be prepared with a serious apology and to potentially exit the company. The powers that be are not at all interested in being associated with these situations, however tenuous the association might be.

Margo

The champagne taste was making its way into Camryn's mouth again. She couldn't move her legs. After making a concerted effort *not* to be the boss among the Mavens in the interest of sparing everyone's *feelings*, she was now held to account as though she *was* in charge. How could she be held responsible for what the rank-and-file Mavens chose to comment on the group's social media feeds, none of which were technically *hers*? Margo had to know that she couldn't be in control of all of it, that it didn't necessarily represent her perspective. She got none of the credit, but all of the blame.

Maybe she could have paid more attention to Kristin's concerns about the things being said in the comments, but was that really such a big deal? Plus, if Kristin didn't want people to think she was gay, maybe she should have worked harder on the way she presented herself. If Cam lost her job at 12th Pine, she'd be right back where she started—no, she'd be worse off—with a big pile of debt she didn't know how to tackle on her own and a boyfriend who couldn't find out about any of it. With the Shepherd Lovely deal now likely off the table as well, her heart was beating into her belly button. And what if Kristin *was* right about the Welshes, and her reputation was now at risk, too?

When Camryn Lee Cady felt moved to share her heart, there was no time to waste.

She situated herself in her familiar home studio on the bright yellow couch, quickly patting down the flyaways near her face. After brunch, her makeup could use fixing, but that wasn't important. Not right now.

"Good morning, y'all," she said, livestream running and follower count ticking up, up, up. "You probably weren't expecting to hear from me today, but I'm feeling convicted right now, and I had to talk to you. I'm having a tough day. Really, it's been a tough few weeks."

Red hearts bounced up from the top of the screen. They were worried about her.

"I appreciate your prayers more than you

know," she continued. "It's hard when you find yourself doubting the Lord's plans for you. Things are happening today that I didn't see coming. Things I don't think I deserve. My friends are making bad decisions. Have you ever watched your friends make bad decisions?"

Another parade of red hearts on-screen indicated that many Mavens could relate.

"I also just found out I might lose my job. And I'm scared for the future of our church. With the Mavens, we're doing such good work, which is great—but it also means we're under a microscope for the whole world to see, and that's really scary. Cancel culture is so real. Do you ever feel like you're being punished for your principles?"

She swallowed and tried not to think about what she'd already said. All Camryn could do was trust the words coming through her. They were bigger than she was, bigger than anything she was being forced to navigate in her earthly body.

"Maybe God's trying to teach me not to be so prideful. Maybe He's telling me my priorities aren't straight. Maybe He's pushing me to be accountable. Maybe He's still mad at me for wasting my purity on my high school boyfriend instead of saving it as a gift for my future husband. For Jeff."

Until now, the Mavens hadn't known anything about Bryce or the Christmas party. Neither had Jeff. Cam was the girl who preached chastity, who made it look cute and special with pretty outfits and much-photographed date nights. But now she had everyone's attention—and for an entirely different reason. Now they would really hear her preach.

"That's kind of a surprise, right?" She laughed. "I've never talked about it because I didn't want you to judge me. But maybe it's time for us to come out with our secrets. People might just find out, anyway. Everyone makes mistakes. Plus, I've been made new—and we all have that chance in the Lord. We're going to talk all about it during our Garnet Gals sessions in a couple of days, too. None of my mistakes matter, because I'm forgiven. And I forgive everyone who is hurting me right now, because God forgave me first. You're forgiven, too, and that means you also need to forgive. I hope you're willing to forgive me." She'd started sweating like she was in a hot yoga class. "Maybe this is all meant to be. Maybe I was always meant to leave my job. Maybe I'm supposed to be in ministry full-time with all of you, working to serve my church. The Lord's timing is always perfect. I'm always saying that. Maybe it's time for me to believe it."

The flow of comments and heart icons had slowed. Desperate, Cam looked down at her coffee table, hoping for guidance from her higher power. There on the table, open to the week of the gala and the online conference she'd planned and covered in doodles of holly and Christmas trees and music notes, was her favorite Shepherd Lovely planner.

"There's a lot of sweetness ahead for us, though. For all of us. We're going to sow some seeds of purity and rebirth and giving when we all come together for Garnet Gals. If you haven't bought your ticket yet, don't forget to grab it at the link in my bio."

The next comment that Cam saw at the bottom of her screen was an icon of a thumb pointing down.

"I appreciate y'all loving me through my mistakes," she said, working to steady the shaking in her voice. "This is always so fun."

26

Trishy

"We're absolutely sure this is the one we're going with, correct?" Trishy said to her phone, lifting the black dress in her right hand up a little higher by the rounded top of its hanger. "Like, one hundred percent, this is the one?"

A geyser of heart icons shot up from the bottom of the screen, confirming what Trishy already suspected: Her followers had picked the wrong gown for her to wear to the gala. She'd only chosen the plain black dress as the second option because she'd assumed the pink one she held in her other hand would win handily in a landslide. People *loved* pink—generally more than Trishy really understood, to be honest. The digital votes that had come in over the last few hours since she'd posted the choices had proven her trust misplaced. Had she taught these sixty-two thousand girls nothing? Why were they letting her down now?

With a few days left before the Gala for Goodness, Trishy had hoped that engaging her followers in a little pre-party glam preparation would distract her from how weird everything had been lately, especially since the brunch and Cam going totally underground after her live breakdown—but now they were making her *look* bad, and that wasn't helpful. The stylist friend she'd worked with on a vision for the event had given her the two dresses to choose from, but it had been obvious to both of them that the antique rosy-colored one was the better choice. It would beautifully complement Trishy's complexion and stand out among what she knew would be a sea of red, green, and black dresses. There was room for creativity, even at Christmas and even in black tie.

It was too late now. Trishy would need to find a way to style the black dress so it would make the statement she needed. There would be tons of photos from the event posted online—especially if Angela Maxwell and her family made good on their promise to show up and make what would likely be a scene—and her followers would be hurt to discover that she'd gone against their recommendation. Her success as a lifestyle brand relied on them being able to trust that she trusted them. It was one of the best ways she could forge friendships from her end of the parasocial relationship. Luckily, she still had a few days to figure out how to make the best of the unfortunate decision they'd made for her.

As usual, people had plenty to say in the comments, almost all of which had absolutely nothing to do with either dress.

> **xxheartofgracexx:** just donated to ProtectUS and bought my ticket for Garnet Gals! can't wait to hear your talk!

"Thank you so much, Grace!" Trishy replied with a wiggle of her fingers. "I know you'll be glad you made both of those investments."

In the several days since Kristin had aired her

concerns at the brunch, Trishy had started to feel significantly less confident in what the investments made to ProtectUS by way of the Gala for Goodness, the Moral Mavens, and Moving Word were actually accomplishing. At this point, though, she feared she was too far into the campaign to do anything about it. Even if Kristin was right (and that was still a big *if*), the Welshes had presumably already made off with the money they'd received so far. In that case, calling them out wouldn't make Trishy the hero—it would simply draw attention to her involvement with the whole situation and have her followers wondering why she'd been content to coast along supporting the fundraiser when the Welshes hadn't had her complete trust.

Still, Trishy hoped that Grace had exercised some restraint when deciding how much to donate.

Trishy knew only the basic details of what Camryn had arranged for Garnet Gals—only the information that had been necessary to create a basic landing page—but she wondered if throwing more of her support behind it could be the best next step, especially if it turned out that the Welshes were not operating in good faith. More than anything, Garnet Gals seemed like something that Cam felt she had to do to make a point—that the Mavens had always been poised to help the Welshes support the fundraiser more than they'd originally requested, and that she was glad to forge ahead with her own special event now that Cassidy was occupied with Avery and Amber and the imminence of the original party. Per Cam's request—and after that disastrous livestream—Trishy had agreed to put together an exclusive virtual session about modest and flirty (yet festive) fashion for the holiday season to present at Garnet Gals, which would be available live the week between the gala and Christmas and (obviously) recorded for playback later on, as well. Her plan had been to grab some outfits the morning of the event and make most of it up as she went along, but taking it more seriously could only pay off if Garnet Gals proved to be the Mavens' official entree into a post-Welshes world.

stillquestioning1_56: Sorry to be dramatic, but I'm new here and gotta tell you that Kyle Welsh has all the

RED FLAGS. We went to high school together and he's slimy af.

Trishy wanted to ask the commenter to enlighten her further. A red flag could be anything. The person might simply be one of Kyle's spurned homecoming dates or a youth group girlfriend from his middle school days—not someone who could produce damning evidence of the pastor's financial history or habits. Then again, they might also be someone with an anecdote in their back pocket that could fill in some of the gaps that Trishy was starting to admit were opening between what the Welshes wanted others to think of them and who they really were.

There was also a very small part of Trishy that would love to see Kristin get a win.

Before she could go to the trouble of figuring out an answer for stillquestioning1_56, Trishy heard a knock on her apartment door. Layla immediately let loose a snarly bark. The spaniel had a tendency to be judgmental, behavior that Trishy blamed entirely on breeding even as she considered her dog essentially a human child. "I'll talk to you all later," she said politely into her screen. "We're going to have such a fun week together with the festivities coming up."

When Trishy had finally contained Layla's outsized aggression and managed to open the door while clutching the wiggling dog under one armpit, she found a teary-eyed Camryn waiting for her on the Anthropologie welcome mat. They'd seen each other briefly at church on Sunday, but Trishy's prevailing recent memory of Cam was of a girl marching out of a brunch, coming off as a little self-righteous and silly—and certainly tipsy. Now, something about the contrast between Camryn's gorgeously waved hair and the mess that her eye makeup had become was especially disturbing.

"Jeff broke up with me," Cam said. She shoved past Trishy into the apartment. "I'm sorry. I know it's been a weird few days, but I didn't know where else to go. I feel like I can't talk to Savannah because of the whole IVF thing."

Trishy tried not to be offended about the implication that she was Cam's second choice. They were all close friends, but Savannah did tend to be the levelheaded, good-for-advice sort.

"You always know what to do," Cam added,

realizing, perhaps, that she'd offended Trishy in the heat of what looked a lot like heartbreak.

With the outsider now seated on the couch, Layla resumed growling.

"You need to get your dog under control," Camryn said before crumbling under sobs.

"Let me get you a drink," Trishy said. After Cam's performance at brunch, she wasn't sure alcohol was the best idea, but opening a bottle of wine had to be the go-to first step in situations of this nature. She set Layla down and walked to the kitchen.

By the time Trishy had finished pouring white wine into a pair of glasses—part of a set she'd received for free from a custom housewares company that had generously etched her initials along the rims—Layla had abandoned her former intensity and joined Camryn on the couch. Their guest accepted the glass and rubbed her finger against the rim. "I've seen these advertised before, but I didn't know anyone bought them." Weeping again, she took a sip. "Anyway. Yeah. Jeff broke up with me."

"What happened?" Trishy asked. She grabbed Layla and snuggled the dog close to her chest, grateful—for once in a great while—for her singlehood and the distance it afforded her from the pain unfolding in her living room.

Cam explained that Jeff had been a little distant in the days since what the blogs and snark forums were calling her "live meltdown." Cam's admissions had been a surprise, and Trishy would never have recommended that her friend stream such a thing, but secretly, she kind of respected it. Even with the resultant social media shade, it was a relief to discover that she wasn't the only member of the Mainframe with a less-than-perfect (by church standards, anyway) sexual history.

"He was being really weird about responding to texts and then he didn't show up to take me to church on Sunday," Cam said, sniffling. "He said he had to go to work. On a *Sunday*."

Trishy hadn't had a reason to clock Jeff's absence at the Sunday service, but she knew that, for Cam, their weekly ritual was almost as sacred as what went on within the sanctuary itself. Apparently, Jeff had continued to dodge her after the weekend, still blaming his behavior on commitments at the office. Earlier that night, Cam explained, Jeff had shown up at her apartment with a pizza and a sour look on his face.

"He said he'd been thinking about it and that it would be best for everyone if we ended things," she said, each word squeezed out of her phlegmy mouth like organic toothpaste from a tube. "He kept talking about our values and how our priorities aren't aligned anymore. What does that even mean? My priorities are the same as they've always been. Church and him and the Mavens and being with him and getting married."

Obviously, there had to be more to it than that. Trishy hoped that Jeff—who she'd never *loved* but who had always been largely inoffensive—had the decency to tell the truth. "And that's all he said?" she pressed.

"I asked him to tell me what was really going on." Cam rolled her eyes. The gesture made Trishy feel oddly relieved. "And then he started acting like such a wimp. He told me he can't handle what's been happening lately—everything with the Mavens and me losing my job and what I said—"

This was the first Trishy was hearing about Cam's job. "You got fired?"

Camryn nodded, wiping one eye with the back of her hand. "Yeah. It's whatever, though. I'll have more time to work on the Mavens this way. I was planning to quit soon. Well, eventually." She took a big drink of the wine. "Anyway. He also brought up what I said on my live."

"The sex thing."

"That's so crass, Trishy," Cam said. "But yes. I asked him if the intimacy thing scared him, and he told me that it was the fact that I *lied* that scared him. But I didn't lie!"

Leaning back into the couch cushions, Trishy kept her mouth shut.

"I *didn't*!" Cam insisted. "Technically, he never asked if I was a virgin. He was probably too scared. If he'd asked me outright—even one time—I would have told him everything."

"Okay."

"And then he laid into me about these unpaid bills that he found at my apartment a while back. So, yeah. Basically, he just broke up with me." Barely able to get out the final words, Camryn lost her composure completely, falling against Trishy's chest and (God forbid) startling Layla in the process. Trishy didn't have the heart to press her about the bills and how they might be related to the conversation they'd had at brunch. "We were supposed to be getting engaged for Christmas. If I knew it would end like this, I could have been married to someone else by now." Camryn wept.

Trishy didn't consider herself especially maternal, nor had she ever looked at Camryn Lee Cady and felt pity. But huddled together on her couch—clutching empty wineglasses in the emotional wreckage of a crummy dude who couldn't be bothered to respect a woman's sexual agency, still reeling from playing involuntary bystander to the invasive comments about Savannah's uterus—Trishy felt sure that she was the right person to take care of her friend in that moment and help her pick up the pieces once the tears had been dried. There was more to Camryn than the bubbly Bible lover she'd gotten to know over their years of friendship. A lot more. And maybe the missing information had been a direct result of Cam's dishonesty, but Trishy couldn't bring herself to be mad. Camryn had come to the right place and the right friend—and with so much still hanging in the balance for the gala and the fundraiser and the Mavens, Trishy couldn't wait to be the one to help her get revenge and get even and get to the bottom of whatever shady nonsense was happening in the church.

"Well," Trishy said, sighing. "Jeff clearly sucks. And you're not going to waste any more tears on him."

Camryn's voice was muffled. "That's what Mamaw said."

"We have way bigger things to get mad about, anyway."

"What are you talking about?"

"The Welshes."

"Oh, come on," Camryn said through a snotty exhale. "You believe that?"

"You don't?"

"I don't know." She paused before releasing another wave of tears.

"Have you heard anything from Cassidy since the brunch? Since your livestream?"

Cam shook her head, eyes fixed on the floor as they seemed to grow more swollen by the second. "I texted her a couple of times to say I was sorry. And I told her about Jeff."

"And nothing back?"

Camryn shook her head again.

"Fuck it," Trishy said. "That's really shitty. I know she's been shitty to Kristin, and she's been weird around Savannah lately, too. I'm not saying she's a criminal, but that's shitty. And she might *still* be a criminal. But you have the Mavens! We're here." She felt awkward reaching out to pat Camryn's shoulder, but she did it, anyway.

"You shouldn't talk like that," Cam said. She lowered her voice to a volume just above a whisper. "I just wanted to plan a wedding."

"Who needs a wedding?" Trishy said. "We have one hell of a party coming up."

Trishy: Hey... have you talked to Cam?

Savannah: Hi. Not really. She called to apologize for overreacting at brunch, but not much since the thing with Jeff. I've checked in with her a few times. She barely responds.

Trishy: Pretending like everything's totally fine and like she didn't just completely lose her cool in front of thousands of people on top of Jeff breaking up with her?

Trishy: (P.S. If you want to do IVF, you should do IVF and I think she probably feels bad for making you think you shouldn't.)

Savannah: Exactly...

Savannah: How bad do you think this actually is?

Savannah: The livestream, I mean.

Trishy: Scale of 1 to 10, I think we can safely call it a 7-8.

Trishy: 9.5 max

Trishy: And can we talk about the fact that Cassidy is ghosting her?

Savannah: Ugh...

Savannah: Poor Cam.

Trishy: I know.

Trishy: But I have an idea.

Savannah: ????

Trishy: Is your family still coming to the gala?

27

Savannah

Even before she'd heard anything about Kristin's suspicions regarding the Welshes and her family's intention to make an appearance, Savannah hadn't been excited for the party. She loved the way it felt to give back to an important cause, but she and Chad had made their donation almost immediately after the drive was announced at the fall carnival—and if Kristin and Trishy were right, that money wasn't even going where it belonged, adding another dimension to her nausea about the whole situation. Fraud aside, there were plenty of people, she'd learned, who would consider making a charitable contribution in exchange for an extravagantly good time, but that had never been Savannah's thing. In fact, she would have paid ProtectUS—that is, if the funds would end up at their promised destination, and there began another round of circular mental arguments—even more money to be allowed to stay home in her most comfortable clothes.

Sweatpants were certainly not an acceptable uniform for the role she was now set to play at the Gala for Goodness under Trishy's impassioned, slightly frantic direction. Savannah dressed in a simple blue gown she'd worn to a handful of campaign events with her in-laws years earlier, her progress through the party preparation process stalled as she stared for a little too long at her modest jewelry collection, most of which had been given to her as sentimental hand-me-downs from her mom. None of it was extravagant or expensive—her parents had only recently become big spenders—and that made her love the pieces more. Savannah wondered if she might see her mother that night. She wondered if, per her mother's suggestions when she'd gifted Savannah the earrings and bracelets, she'd have the chance to pass the tokens on to a daughter of her own.

"Don't you look gorgeous," Chad said, snapping her out of the staring contest she'd initiated with the faux velvet jewelry box she'd had since she was fourteen. Like Savannah, he'd dusted off formalwear that hadn't seen the light of day since they'd last agreed to make a public appearance on behalf of his father. She didn't miss those events, but perhaps she had missed seeing her husband dressed in a tuxedo. He looked incredibly handsome, as strong as she'd always known him to be. The hordes of people who marveled over Chad's fitness tips and physique on Instagram thought they knew how much weight he could carry, but they had no idea. Savannah was grateful to be the one who knew the whole truth.

"Thank you," she sighed, turning away from the patinated jewelry.

"You seem nervous," Chad replied. He knew all about Trishy's plan—the one Camryn was only reluctantly, passively allowing to unfold—and the giggle in the corner of his eyes was a reminder that Savannah had every right to her nerves. "Anything I can do?"

"I don't think so. Just don't leave me alone—especially with Cassidy," she said. Knowing she'd violated their agreement to keep their fertility struggles a secret, she'd been scared to bring her husband up to speed on her confession at brunch and the pastor's wife's response. Chad's indignation and protectiveness about the latter seemed to have dulled any anger he had toward his wife about the former. With that settled, facing Cassidy somehow felt scarier to Savannah than everything else the evening had to offer.

"I'd actually like to be the one to tell Cassidy about that appointment you made," Chad laughed. "Would you give me the honor?"

Savannah had made the call to the specialist the day after the devastating brunch with the other women. After so many months of developing a friendly rapport with the desk staff at Dr. Clark's office, it had been disorienting to find that she didn't recognize the voice on the other end of the phone, but the receptionist was kind enough. Begrudgingly, Savannah accepted the time slot the woman recommended—an all-too-distant three months away—and spelled out her full name slowly so that the office could get her set up in the system.

"Did you say you're Savannah Maxwell Truman?" the receptionist asked after a pause.

Savannah confirmed.

"Do you know what?" the voice went on. "I'm looking at the calendar again, and I think we might just be able to get you in a little sooner. We have a cancellation in two weeks. Would that Wednesday morning be too soon?"

Savannah had taken no time to question whether the receptionist was familiar with her name from *MAXimum Family* or from the Mavens before enthusiastically accepting the offer. If existing under an uncomfortable spotlight was going to make her life complicated, it might as well have some perks, too. She'd answered the rest of the woman's questions, shared her thanks again, and immediately forwarded the appointment details to Chad. Two weeks wasn't *so* soon that she wouldn't have time to squeeze in a little more prayer about the ethics of IVF, but it was also *soon*. She deserved for it to be soon.

"I thought we agreed that we still needed more information before we decided if we were going to do any treatments," Chad had said when he received the email invitation.

"The specialist would be a great place to get that," Savannah replied, the end of her response a period instead of a question mark.

"My parents are going to lose their minds over this. If this gets out, they might never speak to us again."

"Well, we know how that goes already," Savannah replied. "And it doesn't hurt anything for us to learn some more. Knowledge is power and all that, right?"

Chad had nodded, still distracted. "And I guess this means we're past caring about what the Mavens will think."

"After what happened yesterday, I don't think there's any reason for us to make big life decisions based on either of those things. I'd like to make things right with Camryn and the rest of the girls, but aside from that, I'm going to try not to stress over it. It's all just distracting from what's really important, don't you think?" she'd said, pointing her chin toward the Bible on the coffee table between them.

Chad nodded slowly. "Okay." He laughed quietly, obviously amused by something in his own head. "I assume you're not going to suddenly start posting about this online?"

"That would be a no." Savannah had laughed, stood up, kissed her husband, and departed the room to steam the dress now looking back at her in the mirror.

Chad was still standing there behind her in the safe little world they'd created together, unsure as he might be about the appointment and what it could mean. The evening would come to an end, and on the other end of it, there would be Chad and sweatpants and closure for at least a few things.

There would also be the appointment with the specialist. Savannah reminded herself of this as she shook out her hair, grabbed her simple silver clutch, straightened her posture, and grabbed Chad's hand to leave.

28

Kristin

Somehow, Trishy had managed to pull whatever influencer strings were necessary to land a handful of new gown options for Kristin. "You deserve the princess treatment," she'd explained when she dropped them off at Kristin's house the day before the gala. "You've been working so hard. Plus, I *live* to do things like this. But no pressure. If you hate them, don't worry about it."

Generosity aside, Kristin had been relieved to find that none of the dresses were covered in sparkles or cut so obviously with someone of a different body type than hers in mind, but still—none of them had actually looked right when she tried them on, either. On the night of the gala, she arrived at the ballroom dressed—just like she'd originally planned—in one of the prom gowns her mother had been wise enough to save in the cedar closet in the basement. For years, Kristin had been telling her mom to donate them, but Rae had been insistent.

"You're going to end up needing to look fancy again one of these days," she'd repeated a few years earlier, shortly after Kristin had—again—told her mother that she would never have another use for a full-length mermaid dress. "You don't give yourself enough credit. Those are nice dresses that cost good money, and you look beautiful in them."

Yet again, Kristin's mother had been right—and Kristin was appreciative. For the first time since getting involved with the Mavens, she felt worthy of standing alongside Camryn, Savannah, and Trishy. Maybe she could even hold her own in proximity to Amber and Avery. She couldn't be bothered trying to compare herself to Cassidy Welsh. She didn't want to.

Having spent the day setting up the space, Kristin didn't expect to be blown away by the completed decor when she arrived at the ballroom as a guest, but she had to admit that it looked magical. Her father dropped her off in the parking lot—thankfully, he was finished with sales calls for the year, but even with Kristin's connections, she couldn't secure tickets for her parents at a price point they could afford, which she knew was hard on her mom—and gave her a rare compliment on her appearance, lending her the final boost she needed to enter the building not as an assistant, but as a meaningful insider. Really, people had no idea just how *much* of an insider she'd become.

The first thing that struck Kristin as she entered was the stunning effect of the floor-to-ceiling snowflake lighting in the room. When she'd heard Kyle chatting about it with the production team that day at the office, she'd worried it might look tacky, especially when combined with the artificial snow scheduled to fall later in the evening. At some point along the way, the pastor had decided to start taking credit for the concept, and she hadn't fought him on it. Later on, when she saw the invoices arrive at the office, she'd been sure that it was too overpriced *not* to be tacky. Disturbing price tag or not, the effect of the lighting was far better than she could have predicted. Combined with the black-and-white checkerboard floors, the red velvet drapes on the windows, and the carefully curated table arrangements—the starring centerpieces of which were four-foot-tall evergreens trimmed with tiny crystal ornaments and white origami stars—the lights brought an unmistakable air of Christmas magic to what otherwise could have been the backdrop for any other upscale benefit. As she took in the scene, Kristin was happy to be a girl who had never taken much of an interest in a dance floor. The lights would look even more gorgeous appearing as falling snow on the bodies of the donors enjoying the musical stylings of the Luke Garfield Band. With no natural sense of rhythm, she would be able to stand back and watch them work their whimsy.

"You look *gorgeous*!" a voice said. Cam had sidled up to Kristin, dressed in a red velvet gown that hugged her slim figure and perfectly matched her lipstick. Her hair was parted down the center and set in old-fashioned waves, making her look like the star of a classic Christmas movie musical. Kristin knew that Cam and Jeff had broken up several days earlier, but she couldn't help looking for the tall man beside Camryn. It must have been hard to show up alone. Kristin respected that she had.

"Thank you," Kristin said, gladly accepting the hug Cam offered. "It's from my senior prom." She took a risk and gave a little spin, letting the black satin dance a bit under the snowy lights. "You look great. Are you holding up okay?"

"Of course!" Camryn said. No matter how tough the rest of the week had been, nothing would have stopped Cam from showing up looking flawless. There were photos to be taken and reputations to be upheld, regardless of Cam's new relationship status or what was happening with the Welshes. "Let's go," she added, grabbing Kristin by the arm and dragging her out of the room, which had started filling up rapidly with guests.

In the foyer, Trishy and Savannah lingered near the coat check. Kristin snuck a wave at Simon, the shy teenager manning the racks, who had introduced himself to her earlier during setup. Trishy, Savannah, and Camryn showered each other with their usual variety of compliments. As Kristin awkwardly received her share, she noticed Chad Truman lingering on the perimeter of the foyer like a security guard hired specifically for the jackets under Simon's care.

"Just so you know, a lot of shit could go down tonight. I'm sorry, in advance," Trishy told Kristin, reaching one arm out toward the ornate hall filled practically to bursting with lush greenery. She wore elbow-length emerald gloves studded with rhinestones of the same shade. The bold choice of accessories made her black dress and Kristin's black dress look like completely different garments. "We didn't want to put you in an uncomfortable position this week, since we know you've been doing so much for all of this. It looks amazing in here, but we're sort of just going to...see what all happens."

"I wish you wouldn't talk like that," Cam said, crossing her arms across her chest.

"I love you, but I wish *you* wouldn't insist on sitting back and doing nothing," Trishy said. She ran her fingers across the top of her head as if to double-check that her high, bouncy ponytail was still intact. "Kristin, you trust us, right?"

Kristin nodded.

Cam raised her hands in a gesture of innocence. "We've done all we can do," she said. "We blew the whistle. Our hands are clean."

"*Kristin* blew the whistle," Trishy said. Her tone sparked Kristin with pride, like she'd earned credit rather than blame. "And now Sav is our sacrificial lamb. She volunteered. Of course." She sighed and turned her eye contact back on Kristin, who wasn't sure she'd ever seen the normally poised woman looking so agitated. "We've been planning it all week. Anyway, we know the Maxwells are going to show up any minute now and that they're going to make a scene. We're going to let them."

If the other women had been so on board with Kristin's suspicions at the brunch—and even since—she would have lost a lot less sleep in the interim. "What changed?" she asked.

Trishy shrugged and smiled. "I just have a feeling about it. It's a God thing."

"Also," Savannah added, pausing from picking invisible lint from her navy strapless dress. "Amber called to check on me after the brunch. She has some friends who have been through IVF and she wanted to make sure I was okay. I figured she would ask me questions about the Welshes and the money situation, and she did. I got the impression that she was pretty concerned about it, especially with Bo being new to the team here and all that."

"Right. So *I* told Camryn that we should talk to Amber directly about confronting Cassidy, but that's not going to happen," Trishy said. "We'll handle it."

"I'm feeling very 'let go and let God' about all of this," Camryn said. "If the Lamberts want to bring the whole mess up tonight, let them. If they don't, maybe we can all talk to the Welshes after tonight. After Garnet Gals is behind us. Can't this wait?"

"That's so dumb," Trishy said. Kristin agreed. There was an intentionally ignorant character in every documentary she'd ever seen, and those people always looked silly in hindsight. "You're just going to let them take the money and win?"

"Is it so wrong that I want all of these efforts to be a success?" Camryn hissed. More familiar faces were arriving, and Kristin noticed each of the Mainframe girls glancing up and offering greetings even as they conducted their undercover conversation. "If Kyle and Cassidy *aren't* doing anything wrong and they *are* going to announce some big donation tonight, doesn't ProtectUS deserve to get all of that? And is it wrong for me to want to have *my* event, too? Avery has already messed things up for me enough. Is it so much to wish for some peace?"

"You're pissed about the Shepherd Lovely thing," Trishy said, nodding.

"Trishy, it's Christmas," Cam insisted, her eyes welling with tears. For a brief moment, she looked like any other girl who'd just been through a devastating breakup, who could use a few extra dollars to take the sting out of the nasty words from an ex who didn't know what he was missing.

"Stop," Savannah cautioned. She beamed angelically at an older couple entering the grand double doors to the main event space. "Since Cam wasn't comfortable getting involved—"

"Getting in the middle," Cam interrupted.

"Getting in the middle," Savannah repeated with a deep breath, "I offered to encourage my family to make a scene tonight and see what happens in the fallout. If nothing else, we'll get some bad publicity for the Welshes and make them look as silly as I've felt over the last few months."

"Not that we're *hoping* for anyone to feel bad," Camryn said.

Trishy ignored her. "Ideally, Amber will get

the message that we're on to them. Cam didn't want me to *ask* for Amber's help, but maybe the chaos will give her the opening she needs to pull them aside. *She* can blow Kyle and Cassidy's shit up while Angela and the other Maxwells are having a cow out here."

Camryn grimaced.

"And you're okay with all of this?" Kristin asked Savannah. With everything the Trumans were currently going through—on top of all of the drama she'd already weathered with her family—it seemed unfair that it should be Savannah of all people to take the brunt of this half-baked plan.

"I'm pretty good at being embarrassed by now," Savannah said. "Plus, let's get real—everyone's going to be pretty ruthless if they find out I'm doing IVF, anyway. I can afford to be the one to catch the heat now."

Clearly, some big decisions had been made between Savannah and Chad since the conversation at brunch. For that, at least, Kristin was glad.

"And through all of this," Cam said, "we keep our hands clean and let the chips fall where they may. We already exposed the truth to the

Lamberts. They're way more powerful than we are. If Amber chooses to take the opening tonight as an opportunity to talk to Kyle and Cassidy, so be it."

In the months since Camryn had recruited Kristin to help with the Mavens, it had become increasingly apparent that Cam loved the power that came with the Mavens and with a close association with church leadership. Kristin had observed it in the way she strutted into the office for unscheduled time with the pastors, in the way she conducted herself at fellowship hour after Sunday services, even in the way she now seemed capable of directing traffic among her core team while still claiming innocence in whatever was ahead that evening.

Suddenly, though, she was happy to cede her hard-earned power to Bo Lambert and his wife. It was a shame Camryn had never been into sports. The girl was a killer strategist, suited equally for offensive and defensive play.

"*Kristin* exposed the truth," Trishy said, looking pointedly at Kristin. Again, with the credit instead of the blame.

"Whatever," Camryn said. "Let's go work the room."

29

Savannah

Many times, Savannah had imagined what it would be like to see her extended family again. Even Chad didn't know how many hours she spent thinking of them, usually late at night when her brain gave her a rare break from worrying about their fertility issues or interrupting endlessly repetitive, numbing middle school choir practices. No matter how much she hated her parents and Angela and everything they'd taken from her, she wanted them back. She wanted Easters and Christmases and someday—hopefully—first and second and third birthday parties hosted in the comfort of home. She wanted to feel free to unpack the many framed family photos she'd hidden away in boxes in the attic. Depriving herself of this evidence of her past hadn't explicitly motivated her minimalism, but stashing her history as a form of decluttering had helped take the sting out of the Maxwell-shaped void left throughout the house.

To reunite with any combination of her family members at a formal gala would have been far from Savannah's first preference. Better still would have been the luxury of doing so without shouldering the possibility of and power to uncover a disgusting scam perpetrated by Moving Word's most adored pastor. Then again, did Carl and Angela and the rest *really* deserve something more authentic from her? Maybe finding her way back to her family of origin under kinder, gentler circumstances would have been a disservice to the months of pain they'd caused her. Maybe the bizarre, roundabout plan that her friends had devised was the best way to honor Savannah's righteous anger. The party, they'd said, was the only place where enough of the Moving Word community would be present that they could demand accountability from the Welshes. What a spiritual surprise it was, her friends continued, that the Maxwells were choosing to make their larger-than-life presence known at the precise moment that the right diversion might give the Lamberts a chance to approach the pastor and take them to task about the money.

"You don't have to do this," Chad said quietly as they leaned against the wall of the foyer—making a convincing impression, Savannah hoped, of a couple casually waiting to use the restroom. He'd been gripping her hand since the other girls excused themselves to the main event. "We don't even have to stay. We already gave our money. If the Welshes are running a scam, they know who's waiting to judge them at the end of all this. We can get out of here and you never have to talk to the Mavens girls ever again. There are plenty of other churches in town."

He was right. Since they'd decided to move forward with IVF, Savannah had been perusing information about their options. Even if the Mavens and Moving Word communities decided to be kinder to her than she predicted about fertility treatments, she imagined she would want a fresh start, somewhere that didn't bear the fingerprints of a period in her life that made her want to hide. Plus, she and Chad would need to choose a church with a Sunday school program they loved. Truthfully, she'd always thought the one at Moving Word was a little too big. Wherever they landed next would be the spiritual home for the family they would create.

First, though, she had to deal with the family that had created her. And while running away from the gala—high heels and all—was tempting, Savannah did owe Cam and the Mavens *something*. The group had embraced her when others hadn't, and Cam had set aside her original misgivings about a potential IVF attempt to call and check in earlier in the week.

Anyway, it would be kind of fun to go out with a little bit of a bang.

"I can handle it," Savannah said, squeezing Chad's hand. "They're not going to need a lot of convincing to make a production. This'll be easy."

There were benefits to coming from such a massive brood. Even on their best behavior and even if only a small fraction of the Maxwells decided to show up—and if Angela's threats were based in reality, it would be a larger fraction—they could never stay fully out of the spotlight.

For years, this fact had haunted Savannah. Now she embraced it.

After about ten minutes, the stream of gala arrivals—Kristin had said they were planning for about five hundred total guests—had started to thin. The line at the coat check station was short, and there was no longer a traffic jam of guests making their way into the ballroom. The sound from beyond the double doors had multiplied to reflect the many new arrivals, the drinks they were drinking, and the festive songs the band was playing to keep them happy. The Maxwells had to be nearby. They weren't above adultery, but they didn't like to be late.

"We can leave any time you want," Chad said.

Savannah nodded.

Her father's voice was one that *MAXimum Family* viewers across the world recognized from their screens, but one she knew intimately. It was the voice that had prayed with her every night before bed. The voice that had reminded her to stay calm in the final moments before their walk down the aisle at her wedding. The voice that laughed cheerfully along at family dinners as his small children—and later, grandchildren—attempted gamely to recite their assigned Bible verses each night. "Is that my Vannah?" the voice said now, echoing through the foyer.

Savannah was grateful that Chad knew to squeeze her hand again as she turned to face the small crowd of people entering the building, all of whom were related to her by birth or marriage. Dressed in a tuxedo that didn't quite fit his now larger frame, Carl Maxwell led the way, ever the fearless leader that his family claimed to need and that he claimed to be. He reached out his arms, and she let him hug her as the other Maxwells fell into step around them.

"We are so very happy that your church is putting on this event," Carl said, making a big show of looking around the room. "And so very happy that we were able to make a donation so we could be here with you tonight." He braced a hand on each of Savannah's shoulders and stepped back to look at her. "I never thought I'd have to pay this many thousands of dollars to see my beautiful girl, but I guess it's a good thing the Lord has blessed us materially."

For the first time in all the years they'd been together, Savannah wished Chad was the kind of person who might use a hand or fist to remove the smile from another man's face. He would never be that kind of man, but he was still faster to speak than his wife. "Good of you to come, Mr. Maxwell," he said. He reached out to shake a hand when Carl leaned in for a hug.

"I told you we would be here!" Angela chimed in, hustling her way to Carl's side. She wore the same houndstooth coat she'd been wearing when she'd crashed the gala planning session, and her hair was in its usual long braid. Savannah took some small pleasure in knowing that no amount of money or ill-won faith could equip someone with class or taste. While Savannah herself would never be one to criticize, she looked forward to listening in on Trishy and Cam's inevitable debrief of the look Angela Maxwell had selected for the Gala for Goodness. They would have plenty to say. "Oh, you know what?" Angela reached out behind her and wiggled her fingers, beckoning another Maxwell from the pack.

Savannah was surprised to find that she felt absolutely nothing when she saw that the woman stepping forward was her mother, looking as meek as she'd long instructed her daughters to be, standing alongside the only two people in the world who might have shaken her belief in a higher power.

"I told you we're all getting along," Angela went on, squeezing Joanne against her side. "See? We all rented a limo together. Abe set it up."

Abe—a Maxwell sibling who fell somewhere near the middle of the lineup—lifted a hand in a salute and smiled. Savannah wanted to smile back. Abe, the family's enthusiastic prankster, had always had the best sense of humor. He would have gleaned endless comedic material from Savannah's new life among Trishy, Camryn, and the others.

"It's nice to see you all," Savannah said. It was a lie, but one she couldn't control.

"I knew you would think so," Angela said, beaming. She turned to address the rest of the group. "Wasn't this such a good idea? Doing some good, celebrating the holidays, all being together? I assume Ruthie's inside?"

Savannah nodded. Having come through as a major sponsor of the event, Trishy's boss Claudia had purchased several tables and had been kind enough to let Savannah's sister and her fiancé take a place at one of them. Ruthie had offered to stake out the rest of the Maxwells in the foyer with the Trumans—she'd actually seemed excited about the prospect of a semi-public confrontation—but Savannah refused. If the Maxwells made it into the party, her little sister was welcome to reunite with them on her own terms. In the interim, there was no reason to make the encounter any bigger than necessary.

But everyone was being so frustratingly well-behaved.

As good Christians, Joanne and Carl Maxwell had raised their children to be obedient, abiding, demure, and polite. That was before they'd found themselves in the spotlight, acquired a little fame, and thrown their basic principles out the window. Savannah refused to believe that the horde of relatives assembled before her—a very small subset of which she would have enjoyed reconnecting with—had arrived at the gala for no other reason than to exchange some quiet words and enjoy a seated dinner.

"We did have a favor to ask," Angela said.

There it was.

"It's a teeny, tiny favor." She held up two little fingers with practically no space between them. "You won't even notice it." Angela signaled to someone standing out of Savannah's eyeline. A trio of tall men dressed in black approached the group. Two of them toted cameras, and the third was equipped with a boom mic. "You're not going to believe this, but there's been interest from some of the streamers in putting us back on the air. And they're *dying* to get everyone back on-camera together—plus the party, of course. I told them about this gorgeous event and how excited the family is to see each other. Plus, everyone knows that Moving Word is going to be the next Hillsong or Mosaic. It would be such a great opportunity for all of us—and also so glorifying to show how God can put the broken pieces back in place."

Again, Savannah was too stunned to speak.

"It really is a nice idea," her mom added quietly. "And I'm sure your church would be happy to have their good work out there in the public."

"Excellent points from both of you," Carl added, miming quiet applause. "Why don't we all take our coats off and head inside? Vannah, I assume we have a table set aside for us? Somewhere close to you?" He moved to gather coats from his family members. "The crew won't bother anyone."

"Don't you need release forms for that?" Chad asked, indicating the cameras.

"That can all be handled later," Angela told

him, shrugging out of her coat to reveal a calf-length gray dress that wasn't nearly formal enough to meet Cassidy's expectations. Again, Savannah took cruel comfort in how silly she would look. "We won't take it any further until after we talk to whoever's in charge and get the signatures we need."

At Carl's signal, the camera crew circumvented the Trumans and the Maxwells and reached the double doors to the event space first. Savannah imagined they'd been instructed to station themselves inside the entrance for the capture of some kind of grand arrival, ideally one that included her and her husband looking thrilled to be reunited with everyone else.

Chad took a step forward. "Shouldn't we—" he began.

"Nope," Savannah replied, blocking his movement with her hand. "This is perfect."

She watched the crew, then her family pass through the doors. Through them, she caught a glimpse of twinkling white lights that punched her somewhere in the gut in a way that didn't feel totally terrible, a reminder of the end of the holiday magic she knew but a promise that something better was on the other side. By next

Christmas, her life could be entirely different. Bigger in some ways. Smaller in others.

For all the misery her family had put her through over the last year, the uninvited camera crew they'd brought along for the evening was a gift. *And we know that all things work together for good to them that love God, to them who are called according to His purpose.* God had a funny way of showing His people that he was around. He also had a clear sense of justice. Savannah had never been surer that Kristin's suspicions about the Welshes were correct, and that they were about to be exposed for behavior heinous enough that only the Maxwells could compete. Perhaps her family would get their wish and be back on-screen after all, their hypocrisy and clownishness a bigger draw for viewers than their imagined wholesome conduct.

As she grabbed Chad's hand and pulled him into the gala space, Savannah thought of Proverbs 27:17. For years, it had been printed on a plaque in the hallway outside the powder room in the house where she'd grown up. *As iron sharpens iron, so one person sharpens another.* The women waiting inside—the women she'd chosen to surround herself with when much of the world seemed unfriendly—were made of sharp edges. They'd done plenty of damage to each other and to themselves, and Savannah was sure there was more fallout coming. But maybe—if only for the night—they'd be able to sharpen each other instead. Wasn't that why she'd agreed to get involved with the Mavens in the first place?

30

Trishy

"What are those cameras doing here?" Cassidy Welsh said, snapping out of the role of graceful hostess at the sight of the men with oversized equipment entering the ballroom. Trishy had been trying hard to keep the pastor's wife in constant sight and to work the room right alongside her. It was hard when there were plenty of good-looking—and presumably wealthy *and* generous *and* Christian—men in attendance, but she wasn't about to miss out on a big moment. While Camryn, Savannah, and Kristin had been the ones to bear the brunt of Kyle and Cassidy's manipulation, Trishy was nothing if not a fierce defender of her friends' honor. Plus, she'd lived in the world outside religion. She knew it wasn't the Sodom and Gomorrah that people in godly power could present it as, and there was something satisfying about helping to prove that sins could exist inside the church as much as outside. A buzz in the ballroom foretold a new normal where Trishy's past and present might coexist more naturally.

"Don't get worked up," Kyle told his wife. He wore a black brocade blazer over a T-shirt that read simply 3:16. "Didn't we hire our own videographers?"

"Yes," Cassidy said, pointing to a single camera operator making subtle rounds near the dance floor. "Over there."

A group of woefully underdressed people had followed the cameramen through the double doors to the event hall. Trishy vaguely recognized one woman wearing a horrible gray dress. Savannah and Chad crept in behind the rest, and everything fell into place.

The Maxwells had arrived.

"I *knew* they would turn this into a mockery," Cassidy said, suddenly unconcerned with the other church members she'd been chatting with before she'd spotted the intruders. She turned to Trishy. "I *knew* this would happen. Savannah shouldn't be here tonight. I've been backing you and Cam up with all of this ridiculous Mavens stuff and—"

"Ridiculous Mavens stuff?" Trishy said. For the first time since Cam's refusal to take real action against the Welshes, she was glad her friend had decided to be so passive, to morph into a wallflower now conspicuously absent from their post at the center of the party. Cam was far from perfect, but Trishy couldn't bear the thought of witnessing her reaction to Cassidy's tone, to the words dripping out of her mouth with such disdain and condescension. Establishing the Mavens had taken hours and hours of hard work and dedication, all of which Cam sincerely believed the Welshes appreciated. Because they'd told her they did. Over and over again. Trishy had been there to see and hear it happen.

"It is *ridiculous*," Cassidy said, throwing her arms up at her sides. Thankfully, her drink was empty. "It's tacky. Preaching about purity on social media? Cam's not qualified! She hasn't been to seminary. You know I love you, girl, but you really only got here because you like talking about clothes. You're not even all that pure. And you brought in Kristin, too? You couldn't find someone with some better family values? Kyle knows how I feel about this."

Trishy had seen Kristin with her parents. They were lovely. It wasn't *really* family values Cassidy was talking about.

"Why don't we all just take a deep breath?" Kyle suggested, reaching across his wife to grab the glass from her hand. "I can go talk to those camera guys and have this whole thing taken care of, and we'll forget it happened."

Trishy ignored the pastor. "Why have you been so nice to Cam about the Mavens?"

"Because we want the publicity!" Cassidy said, practically yelling. "A bunch of pretty girls talking about how much they love Moving Word on Instagram? Kyle loves that. He'd be an idiot to turn down that buzz. I've been telling him to keep Mavens stuff on the DL for this fundraiser, though, because it's too important—and we let you and this freaky former reality TV family stick around just to keep Camryn happy, and look what's happening. Our whole event is turning into a circus. It's disgusting."

Drawn, most likely, by Cassidy's steadily increasing volume, Amber Lambert and Avery Adams-Wallace had filled in the spaces in the circle left empty by the congregants who had been repelled by the discussion at hand. Trishy felt the stirrings of a small smile begin to bloom across her face as the sweeping brushstrokes of their vision for the evening sharpened into what they'd hoped.

"Is everything okay?" Avery asked. She was dressed in a gold jumpsuit so removed from her usual life among cattle and sourdough that it made even Trishy flare with a bit of envy. If her followers *had* chosen the right dress, she still couldn't have hoped to look as good as Avery.

"Nothing to worry about," Kyle said. "My lovely wife is just a little upset about some extra cameras, but I'm going to go ahead and get that taken care of before we make our big announcement." He excused himself from the group in pursuit of the Maxwells and the crew, all of whom were now taking the longest, slowest route possible to the tables reserved for them in the remotest corner of the ballroom.

"What's that about?" Amber asked.

"Just the embarrassing media frenzy I told

you was bound to come with Savannah's family." Cassidy sighed. "Everyone should have politely agreed when she offered not to come. Her family wouldn't have showed up here if she just stayed home."

"Savannah can handle herself," Trishy said.

"I think you should just enjoy the party, Cassidy," Avery said, taking a sip of her crimson beverage—a signature cocktail that Trishy had yet to sample. "More cameras can only help your cause. You've already raised all this money for ProtectUS. Getting upset is only going to turn it into a bigger scene. Don't give them that satisfaction. Let's dance!"

The band played an upbeat version of a Christmas carol that didn't sound like it was meant to be reinvented, not that anyone had asked for Trishy's opinion. Camryn, on the other hand, seemed to be enjoying their musical take. She'd identified the klatch of familiar women and was making her way across the dance floor in their direction, adding dance-adjacent movements to every step. Kristin walked beside her, walking too carefully in her heels to participate in Camryn's interpretation of the music. "How are things going, ladies?" Cam asked. "Or should I say, Garnet Gals?"

Trishy did her best to signal Cam to rein it in.

Avery put a hand on Camryn's arm. "Cassidy's a little concerned about the cameras that just walked in." She pointed them out to Cam. "But I told her she's overreacting and that we should join you on the dance floor. You had the right idea."

"I'm not overreacting," Cassidy said.

"I can go ask them what's going on," Kristin said, glancing at the crew behind her.

"Not you," Cassidy hissed through a grimace.

Amber finally opened her mouth. "What's the problem with more cameras?"

"I didn't say there was a problem," Cassidy said. "This is supposed to be an intimate evening. I don't want to make anyone uncomfortable."

"No one seems uncomfortable," Amber said, looking around. "They're having fun."

"It's disrespectful to show up with a camera crew."

"You could say that," Amber said. "But is it worth ruining the night over? Is there something you don't want people to see?"

"Nothing!" Cassidy said. "Amber, you, more than anyone, should know how dangerous publicity can be if it hasn't gone through the proper channels. After everything my husband and I have done for you and your family! I would be very careful about how close you get to all of this." She nudged her chin toward the center of the group.

"What is that supposed to mean?" Camryn said, her shoulders sagging.

"Are you threatening me?" Amber asked.

"Cassidy is apparently not a fan of the Mavens," Trishy said. It pained her to be the messenger, but Camryn deserved to know.

"What are you talking about?" Cam said, taking a step back.

Kristin stayed put, looking from one woman to the next.

"Yeah. She just told us." Trishy wished there was time to share a full recap, but things were moving at the rapid clip they needed. Slowing them down could stop it all before the Welshes were served the justice they deserved.

"I was only trying to be encouraging," Cassidy said, scrambling. Her expensive-looking false eyelashes fluttered only slightly. "Kyle thinks what you're doing is in the best interest of the church. You helped us raise a lot of money for this event. Whether I like it or not, it's getting the word out there, as long as you can stay in your lane. I just wish it wasn't so... What's the word?" She snapped her fingers a few times and looked up at the faux snowy ceiling. "Showy. I just wish it wasn't so showy."

"You and Kyle have a YouTube channel," Kristin said only a little cautiously. "You post on Instagram all the time. You're always promoting your speaking tours."

"Kyle's an actual *pastor*, though," Cassidy said, venom rushing back into her voice. "There's a big difference. He represents the church. And I'm here to support what he wants to do."

"We represent the church, too," Cam said, just as thin flakes of snowy whiteness began to settle on the shoulders of gala attendees. Partygoers gasped and squealed with glee, unaffected, apparently, by the plasticky smell of whatever chemical trick had been released from the ceiling in an imitation of a wintry storm.

Trishy felt a pang of satisfaction at how right her friend was—and at the delicious dramatic timing of fake snowfall during Cam's declaration.

Kyle and Cassidy had gained traction alongside the Mavens, thanks largely to the ability to connect with larger audiences through YouTube and the church's social media accounts. Who gave either of them the right to criticize what Cam was trying to accomplish—or worse still, to pretend to support it while laughing at her behind her back? Cam was tougher than she looked. She'd always had a strong enough vision for the Mavens to make it happen without the support of a fake friend.

"You know, I actually have some questions for you," Amber ventured, taking a step toward Cassidy. "As you know, Bo and I wrote quite a check for ProtectUS, and I'm a little concerned—"

Trishy wanted to applaud, but there wasn't time for Amber to finish her statement—the statement Trishy assumed might back Cassidy into precisely the corner in which she deserved to spend the rest of the night—because Kyle had taken his position behind the microphone and was clapping along with the music as the band's leader got the audience's attention. If he'd had any real intention of following his wife's demands and ridding the room of the Maxwell camera crew, he'd failed. Trishy could see them lingering near the family's table.

"Hello, hello, hello, Gala for Goodness!" Kyle shouted into the microphone with the same confidence and charm he brought to his sermons. "We are so thankful to have all of you here with us on this beautiful evening. Now, we've put together quite the event tonight, and I don't want to distract you from all of the eating and drinking and dancing and drinking." A few people laughed. "What? It *was* Jesus who turned water into wine."

Kyle got more laughs, as he'd surely calculated.

He went on to thank the gala's sponsors—Claudia and Twist got a well-earned shout-out, though Trishy worried her boss would regret it eventually—and pointed out a few of the items that had been donated by local businesses for the silent auction and swag bags. He introduced the band and performed some self-effacing dorky dance steps as they jammed on their instruments for a few moments. After inviting the other pastors in attendance to stand up for a brief acknowledgment, Kyle searched for Cassidy in the crowd and beckoned for her to join him at the front of the room. "Now, you all look just beautiful tonight, but I have to draw some special attention to my gorgeous wife," Kyle said. "Cassidy Welsh, will you join me up here so we can tell these fine people how much money they've raised for ProtectUS?"

Cassidy regained her shaken composure before removing herself from the group, straightening her posture and smoothing her hair behind her ears as she approached the microphone. Trishy's eyes frantically panned the ballroom for Kristin, who she found lurking in the shadows near the dance floor. More than anyone, she'd had to put aside her concerns about the Welshes and even the Mavens to stay loyal to the tasks she'd been assigned. She was probably the one responsible for ensuring that Kyle got up to speak at the correct time so that the catering team would know when to begin serving dinner. No one had given her the credit she was owed—not even the Mainframe, who'd made a habit of relegating her to grunt work and rarely looked to her for the meaningful contributions she'd been making all along.

As Cassidy took her place beside Kyle,

the room filled with another round of warm applause. She beamed like a pageant queen.

"I'm always happy to have my wife by my side, but I felt like it was extra important to have her here for this announcement," Kyle said, wrapping his arm around Cassidy's waist. "Bad news is always better coming from a beautiful woman, don't you think?"

An awkward silence coated the party like the fake snow, which was starting to make Trishy itchy. She could see Amber Lambert's fingers tapping nervously against the stem of her wineglass.

"Let's not get too down on ourselves, okay?" Kyle went in. "Unfortunately, I am here to tell you that we didn't meet our big five-hundred-thousand-dollar goal, but we have still done a lot of good for ProtectUS—and you know how Cassidy and I feel about those human-trafficking victims. With all of your generosity, we've managed to raise just short of a hundred thousand dollars. That's a Gala for Goodness if I've ever heard of one, don't you think?"

Timid applause grew more confident as Kyle left space for it. Against the tip-tap of polite fingers, Trishy's stomach sank down to her high heels. Would the congregation never know how generous they'd been, or how many people they'd be able to help? Even without the numeric evidence of Kristin's findings in the office, Trishy could clock a few dozen wealthy people in the room who she knew would have donated tens of thousands of dollars. Did everyone *really* believe they hadn't pulled it off? If so, they had a pretty flimsy version of faith.

"That's the right attitude. Maybe we dreamed a little too big, but it got us thinking about a larger mission, didn't it?" Kyle said, looking to a nodding Cassidy. "Before we eat, we have a video here that I think will help you understand your impact. Kristin, can you do the honors?" He signaled to Kristin, who pressed the button on a remote. The snow and fancy lighting stopped, and a giant screen descended slowly from the ceiling on the wall behind the band.

It would have been the perfect time for Amber to say what she had to say, to grab her sports star husband and make the Welshes look like the liars they were. Amber *knew* something funny was going on. She'd seemed concerned at brunch. She and Bo had reputations—real fame—to preserve! And she looked *great* in her champagne dress. Cam had been sure she would take the opportunity to reveal the truth. Having permission to make a scene seemed like a worthwhile enough reason to be recognizable to the general public.

But she hadn't moved from her spot.

Kristin, however, *was* moving—creeping, more aptly—away from Trishy and toward the camera crew that had arrived with the Maxwells, and whispering to one of its members. The trio shifted positions as she made her way back toward the band setup and to the projector screen, which seemed close to reaching its full size. From their new post, Trishy assumed they'd have a better view of the rest of Kyle's presentation.

The screen finally came to a halt, and Kyle stepped back as if to settle in to enjoy its upcoming broadcast. When nothing appeared, he looked toward Kristin, who shrugged.

"Sorry about this, folks," he said into the microphone. "Kristin, can you give us a hand? I'd hate for our family to miss out on the beautiful video ProtectUS put together as a thank-you."

Kristin shrugged again. The dress she'd chosen wasn't one Trishy would have selected, but she'd come a long way since joining the Mainframe. If she felt good, Trishy was happy.

Kyle wasn't used to discomfort. "No suggestions?" He laughed nervously.

Kristin shook her head, her fingers twitching. *I'm sorry*, she mouthed to her boss.

"Well, that's disappointing, folks," Kyle said. "I thought we had all of this under control. I guess our assistant isn't as smooth on logistics as I'm told she used to be in the college pool, you know?" There were a few laughs throughout the room, but thankfully, nowhere near as many as Kyle usually got.

From across the ballroom, Trishy saw something shift in Kristin's face as she approached the Welshes and whispered something quietly in Kyle's ear. He nodded, still looking discontent. As he listened to her words, Kristin reached down to grab the microphone from his hand.

"I'm so sorry about the delay, y'all," she said, her voice shaking. Kyle had taken a step back and looked too shocked to be mad. Not yet—but Cassidy looked livid. "I'm Kristin Rae Thatcher. I work in the church office, but I'm also on the Moral Mavens Mainframe. Yes, I used to be a pretty good swimmer. And I have something to say."

The room was as quiet as it had been all night.

Trishy wished someone would get the fake snow going again, a seasonal display to match the flurry of pride that was overtaking dread in her body. What was happening merited it. "I don't know how else to tell you this, so I guess I'll just come right out with it. And it's a good thing my parents aren't here tonight, because they would just about drop dead from embarrassment. But they're not here because they couldn't afford to attend, which I personally think is pretty messed up when we're talking about a charity and dedicated members of the church. Especially when Kyle and Cassidy have been hiding hundreds of thousands of dollars y'all raised and keeping it for themselves."

Fuck yes, Trishy thought. *Hell hath no fury like an office assistant scorned.*

The crowd murmured. Kyle moved to grab the microphone back from Kristin, but she was quick to dodge him.

"I know I'm just some kid who works in the office, and I don't pretend to be an expert or an accountant or anything like that, but I've seen proof of it, and I'm happy to point you in the right direction if you want to get to the bottom of this," Kristin said. "I don't know fashion and

I wouldn't know what to do with five hundred thousand dollars, but I *do* know about what Kyle Welsh calls a 'spirit of honesty.'"

Microphone still in hand, Kristin glared back at the Welshes and walked out of the room. Trishy couldn't be happier to note that her hair looked great as the double doors slammed behind her.

By the time Kristin made her exit, the rest of the room had started exchanging uncomfortable chatter across their tables. The audio system screeched in exasperation. A short, plain man—Cam had pointed him out earlier as Miles Mason, author of the financial information they would maybe one day share with the Mavens—stood up to his full but diminutive height, chest puffed out. "Is that why you turned down my offer to help with the books?" he called out in the direction of the stage.

Kyle and Cassidy exchanged frantic looks, and the pastor signaled to the band, who—after a few sloppy seconds—stumbled its way into a Lizzo song, having made what seemed like an executive decision to move past the planned soundtrack of holiday cheer. Cassidy's eyes were locked on her feet as Kyle held up a single finger to the audience, then grabbed his wife's hand to escort her off the stage. Their pace quickened as they neared the double doors to the foyer.

Bo Lambert, however, beat them to it, accompanied by a handful of other tall men who'd been sitting at his table. The Welshes could not penetrate the human wall of professional athletes that had assembled itself before them. It was unclear to Trishy what would happen next, but she was glad to take a drink and let some other authority—legal, spiritual, or otherwise—handle things for a moment. In the meantime, she nearly spit out her cocktail at the sight of Avery Adams-Wallace dragging Amber onto the dance floor, hips thrusting wildly.

Whether the embodiment of perfect Christian womanhood was buying Bo and the guys some time with a diversion or simply moving with the spirit of a Top 40 hit with a college friend, Trishy loved what she saw. She joined them on the dance floor.

r/SnarkyMoralMavens

Welcome!

CorduROY3141 (mod): Now that they've disrupted a massive megachurch fundraising event and unmasked their shady pastor, the MMM are officially getting their own sub!

Congrats, MMM (Moral Mavens Mainframe)!!! You've been promoted from the Minor Fundie tag on **r/FundieSnarkUncensored**. Can't wait to witness all of your future train wrecks and successes and to (loosely) moderate the chatter that follows.

Cam and Trishy, we know you're here. HI! We snark because we care (most of the time). Remember: racism is bad, queer people are real, and science is good for us.

Be kind, everyone! Unless you can't be. We'll be praying for you.

Ainttooproudtosnark47: FUCK yes. WE'VE ARRIVED!

brushwithlame314: good because i have a lot of thoughts

> **atheistnerddotnet:** How many of them are about how fierce Kristin is???
>
> **brushwithlame314:** at least like five
>
> **atheistnerddotnet:** BLESS 🙏

nostalgianellie__9: Is there anywhere on the internet where people are being nice to Savannah?

> **CorduROY3141 (mod) (OP):** Not sure. But this ain't it.
>
> **CJ___jean:** she's going to be off living her best life, anyway. she's back posting on her personal feed and said she's about to be done with the Mavens. i don't blame her
>
> **nostalgianellie__9:** I just want her to be happy!

LORDFARGOD: Sooooo did we ever figure out what happened to the money?

> **CorduROY3141 (mod) (OP):** It's in the hands of a higher power now (courts, not God lol)

Ainttooproudtosnark47: right because the legal system is SO fair

brushwithlame314: we gotta give the girlies credit where credit is due. they suck, but they DID unmask the assholes

Ainttooproudtosnark47: sure but where is all the cash they brought in from THEIR cult followers?????

CorduROY3141 (mod) (OP): STAY TUNED! I just popped the popcorn.

brushwithlame314: i don't think Camryn Lee Baby has that kind of money lying around

sparklebaby2009: The girls will definitely find out and tell us

Ainttooproudtosnark47: i see we already have a fan in the group

Ainttooproudtosnark47: Camryn Lee Baby is that you?

31

Camryn

TWO WEEKS LATER

"I almost forgot," Camryn said to her phone as she finished curling her hair. "If you're planning to join us for the Merry Mavens party tomorrow night, you won't be able to get in without a donation for the food bank. We're super excited to be partnering with an organization here in Charlotte, and we need all of your support so that these local families can have a blessed New Year. We can't welcome you in unless you have at least one canned good or nonperishable item with you—and I would hate to turn anyone away. Mavens like to have a good time, but they like doing good even better! You can grab tickets for the party until midnight tonight. That link is in my bio, too. If you're attending virtually, you can also make a donation to the food bank on Venmo there."

It had been Kristin's idea to coordinate an actual philanthropic event to go along with Garnet Gals, which she'd suggested postponing until the end of the month after the spectacular drama of the Gala for Goodness. Trishy had made arrangements with Claudia, who agreed to host the party as long as it benefited the food bank to which Twist donated a chunk of their December profits annually, anyway. She was happy to have some good publicity after being named a key sponsor for an event that ultimately served as the backdrop for the revelation of a pastor and his wife's mission to embezzle funds intended for charity. Thankfully, she wasn't mad at Trishy for getting her or the store involved—only relieved that there was a way forward.

After she'd left the party that night, Kristin had gone straight to Kyle's office, tearing it apart in search of the documentation he'd sloppily left on his desk weeks earlier. Luckily, the paperwork hadn't gone too far. By the next morning,

Bo Lambert had made calls to a series of lawyers, who had initiated the process of prosecuting the Welshes in civil court. While they awaited their trial in the new year, Kyle and Cassidy were—as far as everyone knew—hunkering down at home, their expensive security system keeping everyone out. At least they could enjoy the place's comforts and grandiosity for a while longer.

With so many new eyes on the Moral Mavens after the news from Moving Word had seeped out—first through niche corners of the internet, then via heavier media hitters—there were a lot of eyes on their content, and they'd seen ticket sales for Garnet Gals nearly double as a result. They'd added a casual in-person event for local Mavens and shuffled the slate of online events. The party would give the girls the opportunity to give back (even if the Welshes hadn't) and to meet and greet their followers. After Camryn had gone live to underscore the separation from the Welshes and to clarify that the Mavens hoped to rewrite itself as a more inclusive and affirming community going forward, Brandon Goddard had offered to create new branding and to overhaul their website in a hurry. The girls were loving all the bright colors in spite of Cam's initial concern that straying too far from the neutrals and pastels of the past might put followers even further off a group associated with the suddenly infamous Kyle and Cassidy.

"I'm worried this green eyeshadow is a little much, but I guess it's the right time of year for it," Camryn said, moving her face closer to her phone so her livestream audience could see her makeup. "If you see me in person, please come up and tell me it doesn't look crazy. I can't wait to see some of you there! I know the other Mainframe girls and I have been a little quiet over the last week or two, but it's only because we're all so excited about what's going to happen at the event."

It was one of the more honest things that Cam had said to her followers in a long time. She'd been mostly quiet on social media since the gala as she and the other Mainframe girls put their heads together to come up with a new strategy for the rest of the year. The tensions of the previous weeks hadn't disappeared altogether—Camryn supported Savannah privately but didn't like the fact that she had started openly talking about seeking IVF and leaving Moving Word, nor was she sure how to feel about the fool Kristin had made of herself at the gala or how to move forward with Trishy—but it hadn't gotten in the way of what they'd set out to do. Mostly, she felt silly for her blind devotion to Cassidy and disgusted by what she and Kyle had done to the good people of Moving Word. Through meaningful works, Cam hoped that she might redeem herself. It didn't hurt that planning Garnet Gals was fun. And all hers.

"If you want even more Garnet Gals, make sure you grabbed that premium subscription," Camryn said. "In addition to all the bonus content you'll get, you'll have access to a livestream of the Merry Mavens party."

The subscription had been Camryn's idea. It had made the other girls squirm at first, but in the end, they'd agreed to go along with it once the Lamberts announced their intention to donate the sum they'd already given the Welshes to ProtectUS via the Mavens. The proceeds from the subscription would help cover the massive financial losses Cam had sustained, especially since the dissolution of her relationship with Shepherd Lovely. When her lease was up in the spring, she would probably accept Trishy's invitation to sleep on her couch until she'd had time to sort things out. It would be good for their friendship after everything that had happened, and Trishy had a comfortable sofa and a closet's worth of high-end bedding, all of which she'd received in exchange for endorsing their manufacturers on her social platforms. With no job and no prospects, Cam was still committed to running the Moral Mavens full-time—but she'd need a financial runway to do so.

"I don't know about you, but this year has not turned out anything like I expected it to." She laughed, perfecting the curl of an errant piece of hair near her left ear. "If you'd asked me a few months ago, I would have told you I'd be engaged and planning a wedding by now. And I never would have seen all the changes coming for my work, my church, and my ministry. We won't get into all that drama right now. If you know, you know."

Things were awkward with the rest of the Mainframe team, but Camryn was trying to get over it. Too much had happened in the fall to come between them. If she'd underestimated anyone, it was Kristin.

Plus, she'd been having a nice time getting to know Micah Rivers, one of the more junior pastors at Moving Word. They were planning to have dinner together in a few days to celebrate the new year. Micah had invited her to join him at a trendy restaurant in town, where—according to Camryn's cursory perusal of the menu online—the cheapest entrée was twenty-nine dollars. She'd already ordered an outfit to wear for the occasion. With Kyle Welsh out of the picture, Micah was poised to become a bigger name within the congregation—and beyond, too. He'd been more than happy to let Camryn set him up with new branding for his social media feeds, a refresh that was already yielding benefits in terms of increased engagement from outside the Charlotte community. Moving Word needed all the help it could get to regain its standing.

Cam would always find people who backed her, especially with God on her side.

"This isn't from Scripture, but it's a saying I'm sure you've heard: *Man plans and God laughs*. We should keep this in mind any time we're looking ahead. Trust me when I tell you that I've tried my hardest to control everything in my life." She laughed and fluffed her hair. "But He's always known better than I do."

It was true.

But Camryn Lee Cady did know plenty.

Acknowledgments

Too Blessed to Stress is, in part, a social satire, but my goal in writing it was less to question my characters' actual faith systems and more to interrogate the ways in which the real-life overlap between megachurch culture and the influencer economy has changed the game for everyone involved. In that spirit, I'd first like to thank the many women who share their experiences with religion online (and now on reality TV, too!). I spent countless hours digesting their content as I researched this book, and while I may fundamentally disagree with many of their perspectives (and worry about the impact of those perspectives on our shared future), it's their commitment to a belief in something bigger than themselves that has always inspired me to write the story of Camryn, Kristyn, Savannah, and Trishy.

When you start seeking an agent to represent your work, all the writers you know talk about how grueling the process can be, but it's rarer to hear about the cosmic click that happens when you find the person who is exactly right. For me, that person is Claire Friedman, who recognized potential in a significantly more chaotic version of the book you now hold in your hands. Claire, thank you for getting it from day one and for always pushing me to be better. I promise I'm going to learn to outline one of these days. Having you and the InkWell Management team in my corner has been a #blessing.

Jacqui Young bought this book and made my biggest, oldest dream come true when I was in the thick of newborn parenthood, struggling to find my normal and desperate to connect with my old self. Her enthusiasm about the subject matter made for a fun, creative first call that was exactly what I needed after months of all baby, all the time—and her ongoing care with my work has affirmed over and over that she is the perfect person to bring *Too Blessed* to life.

Thanks to the rest of the wonderful team at

Acknowledgments

Grand Central: Lori Paximadis and Luria Rittenberg, for polishing the book into its best possible version; and the entire marketing and publicity family for supporting the big goal of getting it into the right hands (and as many of them as possible!).

I started pursuing my MFA at Temple University in the fall of 2020 in hopes of reminding myself of my love for creative writing and—to put it bluntly—to get my ass in gear. Many hours of Zoom class later, I couldn't be happier that I did. Thanks to Don Lee for making it all possible, reminding me of the basics, and teaching me that it doesn't all have to be so precious; to Liz Moore for reigniting my love for writing, bolstering my confidence, and remaining a supportive resource throughout the journey; and to Kiley Reid for understanding my fascination with this material, offering candid feedback, and generally being the best possible mentor throughout the semester we spent working on this project together. It was an honor to learn from all of you.

Any MFA community is a special one, and my little version is no exception. Chris Qualiano was kind enough to swap pages with me outside of workshop and Brighid Jackson hyped me up on our many commutes to class when we finally broke free from Zoom. Eli Raphael continues to field my unhinged voice notes about the publishing process, and I can't believe how fortunate I am to get to navigate it with her. After all of those walks around Chestnut Hill and all of our paralyzing insecurities, look at us—Grand Central debuts in the same year!

Above my desk on a series of Post-its, I've been keeping a list of the many other incredible people who read earlier drafts of *Too Blessed to Stress* and who offered their advice and guidance since it all began. I realize now that Post-its are a questionable place to do this, but I'm hopeful I've captured all of your major contributions! Thank you to Maura Finkelstein for the walks, kitchen table work sessions, and encouragement; to Rachel Broder for her *very* early read and thoughtful editorial input; and to Colleen McKeegan for paving the way and asking meaningful questions about my characters. Thank you to Joan DeMayo, Jo Piazza, Olivia Muenter, Megan Angelo, Jessica Goodman, Jennifer Close, Charlee Dyroff, Jaclyn Hamer, Angie Kim, Lina Patton, Becca Freeman, Alison Rose Greenberg, Caroline Frank, Genevieve Wheeler, Rachel Taff, and Morgan Pager for your pep talks and cheerleading. Abby Wolfe, your feedback came at a true turning point in this process and it made all the difference. Our friendship found me at the perfect moment, and it's been such a gift!

In 2018, I launched *The SSR Podcast* with essentially no idea what I was doing. It ran for seven years and gave me *so* much—and so much that proved invaluable to the journey of this book. Thank you to (literally) every single author guest who reminded me of what was possible when it was hard. My deepest thanks go to the community of SSR listeners and supporters who made sure that I never lost sight of what I love about books.

My therapist Meagan Faraone has remarkable professional boundaries and might therefore not pick this up, but she gets all the credit for holding me together while I finished this book and found a way for it in the world. I've long believed that everyone should be in therapy (including and especially the MMM), but our ongoing work together has confirmed it.

While we're talking about holding me together, a moment for my friends—everything that is kind and fiercely loyal and hilarious and creative and ambitious about the women in this book is inspired by you. I am a better person because you are in my life, and I'm humbled by your love and support.

I needed extra support in the last couple of years as I became a mom, and this book is also for Will, whose arrival to this planet is tied inextricably to *Too Blessed* in ways that might prove fodder for future therapy sessions (send me the bill!) but that remain so sweet to me. Thank you for being patient with me as I learned how to be a parent and how to be an author at the same time. Being *your* mom is a true gift—and I love knowing that the traces of our early days together can be found in the margins of this book.

I wrote almost every page of this novel with a floppy, fearful, perfect Golden Retriever close by (but always taking his own personal space). We don't deserve dogs, and I certainly don't deserve you, my Irv.

To my parents—Deb and Fred Stellato, Bill and Jane Hoff—thank you for the many blank notebooks, for trusting my instincts, for the endless encouragement, and for only very occasionally encouraging me to put down my book and engage with real people. Your belief in my ability to one day do this has been one of the luckiest things of my life. That day is here! My big, blended family could not be more special to me. I love you all.

Matt, the life we've built together is better than anything I could have imagined. Writing and publishing this book is a dream, but it means infinitely more because I get to do it with you as my partner. Thank you for the laughter, the endless confidence, and the infinite coziness. You are my rock, always.

 Visit **GCPClubCar.com** to sign up for the GCP Club Car newsletter, featuring exclusive promotions, info on other Club Car titles, and more.

  @GrandCentralPub

Discussion Questions

1. After Camryn, Trishy, Savannah, and Kristin were first introduced, what initial judgments did you have about them? Which of the women did you identify with most at the beginning of the book? How did your feelings change over the course of the novel?

2. For the women in the Moral Mavens Mainframe, how does faith impact their relationship with social media? How does social

media impact their faith? Which has a stronger influence on the other—and what are the implications of that?

3. How would you describe the journey that each of the main characters takes to religion and Moving Word? Is there one path that feels more authentic to you than the others? Is there one that feels the least authentic?

4. What is each of the main characters getting from church? What is church costing them?

5. *Too Blessed to Stress* explores the differences and overlap between faith and church (or organized religion, more broadly). Based on this fictional world, how would you describe that distinction?

6. How are each of the Moral Mavens Mainframe members complicit in Kyle and Cassidy's behavior? Who is most complicit? Who is least complicit?

7. Describe what Camryn, Savannah, Trishy, and Kristin each want the most. Is the

thing they *think* they want what they *actually* want? How do you see these distinctions play out in your own circle?

8. Which of the Moral Mavens leaders would be most likely to convince you to explore religion in a new way, whether online or IRL? What is it about their approach that you consider persuasive or effective?

9. Had it not been for Cam's "meltdown," do you think she and Jeff would have gotten engaged? Do you think their long-term relationship would have been a happy one? Are they actually well-suited for each other?

10. In its best version, what do you think the Moral Mavens community is capable of?

11. Amber Lambert and Avery Adams-Wallace operate in fame niche circles of their own. How is their respective fame—and the parasocial relationships and cultural capital that come with it—different than that of the Mavens? How do these nuances in the book characters mirror patterns of celebrity IRL?

Discussion Questions

12. We talk a lot about the loss of "third places" in contemporary American culture. How do you feel that loss in your own life? How do you think *Too Blessed to Stress* contributes to that conversation?

VISIT **GCPClubCar.com** to sign up for the **GCP Club Car** newsletter, featuring exclusive promotions, info on other **Club Car** titles, and more.

@grandcentralpub 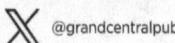 @grandcentralpub @grandcentralpub

About the Author

Alli Hoff Kosik is a full-time writer and editor. For seven years, she independently produced and hosted *The SSR Podcast*. Alli holds an MFA from Temple University and lives in Philadelphia with her family, where she enjoys crossword puzzles and reality TV. *Too Blessed to Stress* is her first novel.

www.ingramcontent.com/pod-product-compliance
Lightning Source LLC
LaVergne TN
LVHW031534060526
838200LV00056B/4495